I FOLLOW YOU

Peter James is a UK number one bestselling author, best known for writing crime and thriller novels, and the creator of the much-loved Detective Superintendent Roy Grace. Globally, his books have been translated into thirty-seven languages.

Synonymous with plot-twisting page-turners, Peter has garnered an army of loyal fans throughout his storytelling career – which also included stints writing for TV and producing films. He has won over forty awards for his work, including the WHSmith Best Crime Author of All Time Award, the Crime Writers' Association Diamond Dagger and a BAFTA nomination for *The Merchant of Venice* starring Al Pacino and Jeremy Irons, for which he was an executive producer. Many of Peter's novels have been adapted for film, TV and stage.

By Peter James

The Detective Superintendent Roy Grace Series

DEAD SIMPLE   LOOKING GOOD DEAD

NOT DEAD ENOUGH   DEAD MAN'S FOOTSTEPS

DEAD TOMORROW   DEAD LIKE YOU   DEAD MAN'S GRIP

NOT DEAD YET   DEAD MAN'S TIME   WANT YOU DEAD

YOU ARE DEAD   LOVE YOU DEAD   NEED YOU DEAD

DEAD IF YOU DON'T   DEAD AT FIRST SIGHT

FIND THEM DEAD

Other Novels

DEAD LETTER DROP   ATOM BOMB ANGEL   BILLIONAIRE

POSSESSION   DREAMER   SWEET HEART   TWILIGHT

PROPHECY   ALCHEMIST   HOST   THE TRUTH

DENIAL   FAITH   PERFECT PEOPLE

THE HOUSE ON COLD HILL   ABSOLUTE PROOF

THE SECRET OF COLD HILL   I FOLLOW YOU

Short Story Collection

A TWIST OF THE KNIFE

Children's Novel

GETTING WIRED!

Novella

THE PERFECT MURDER

Non-Fiction

DEATH COMES KNOCKING: POLICING ROY GRACE'S
BRIGHTON *(with Graham Bartlett)*

BABES IN THE WOOD *(with Graham Bartlett)*

I FOLLOW YOU

PETER JAMES

MACMILLAN

First published 2020 by Macmillan
an imprint of Pan Macmillan
The Smithson, 6 Briset Street, London EC1M 5NR
Associated companies throughout the world
www.panmacmillan.com

ISBN 978-1-5098-1628-6

3 5 7 9 8 6 4 2

A CIP catalogue record for this book is available from the British Library.

Typeset by Palimpsest Book Production Ltd, Falkirk, Stirlingshire
Printed and bound by CPI Group (UK) Ltd, Croydon, CR0 4YY

MIX
Paper from
responsible sources
FSC
www.fsc.org
FSC® C116313

Visit www.panmacmillan.com to read more about all our books
and to buy them. You will also find features, author interviews and
news of any author events, and you can sign up for e-newsletters
so that you're always first to hear about our new releases.

TO MY BELOVED WIFE LARA – YOU GAVE ME THE IDEA
AND THE INSPIRATION FOR THIS BOOK.

1

Friday 7 December

Timing is everything.

Marcus Valentine lived by those words. They were his mantra. He was always scrupulously punctual and, equally, punctilious in all that he did, starting with his attire. It was important to him to be appropriately dressed for every occasion, with each item of his clothing immaculately clean and pressed, whether the business suits he wore to work, his golfing kit, or the cardigan, polo shirts and chinos he favoured when at home.

With his greying hair groomed immaculately, straight but prominent nose and piercing grey eyes, his perfect upright posture making his corpulent figure look closer to six foot than he actually was, he had the demeanour at times of a bird of prey, studying everything and everyone a little too sharply. Legions of his patients adored him, although a few of the hospital staff found him a tad arrogant. But they put up with it because he was good – in truth, more than just good, brilliant. Regardless of his particular field of expertise, he was the consultant many medics in the hospital would go to as first port of call for advice on any issue with a patient that concerned them.

In his mid-forties, he was at the top of his game. He had to admit he lapped up the attention, but he'd worked hard to get there, sacrificing much of his social and family life for years. So now was the time to enjoy it.

Today, though, had started badly. He was late. So late. He had overslept. He knew it shouldn't stress him out, but it did.

He glanced at his watch, then at the car clock, checking their times. Late. So late. All his timings for the day now out of sync.

His wife, Claire, had told him mockingly more than once that the words *Timing is Everything* would be carved on his gravestone. Marcus knew he was a little obsessive, but to him timing was a matter of life and death. It was crucial, in his profession, in the calculation of due dates of the babies of expectant mothers, and equally so during those critical moments of delivery. It mattered in pretty much every aspect of his life. Of everyone's life.

Claire's job, as an executive coach, was much more flexible, and she worked it around her schedule – something he could never do. He always wanted to be early for a train, a flight, even for his golf. He'd be at a concert for doors opening and at the cinema for the trailers, whereas Claire constantly drove him nuts by leaving everything to the very last minute. But then again, she'd arrived into this world three weeks overdue so maybe that had something to do with it.

And this morning, at 8.40 a.m., squinting against the low, bright sun and reaching out with his left hand for his Ray-Bans, speeding in the rush-hour traffic along Victoria Avenue on his daily commute to the Jersey General Hospital, timing was about to matter more than he could have imagined.

As he pulled on his glasses, he didn't know it but the next sixty seconds were about to change his life forever.

Well, forty-seven seconds, actually, if he had checked.

2

Friday 7 December

Timing wasn't happening.

Georgie Maclean's sports watch had frozen. The lights at the pedestrian crossing she took most mornings over the busy road to the seafront were red, against her, as they usually were. But for some moments she was fixated on her watch. She'd been running fast, on course for a personal best – and then the damned watch crashed.

No, don't do this to me!

These lights were the slowest in the world. They took forever to change. They messed up her times for her run when she missed them, forcing her to wait, jogging on the spot to keep warm in the freezing early-morning air, with traffic streaming past too fast to risk a dash between the vehicles, almost all of them way exceeding the speed limit.

She stared at her fancy new running watch, silently pleading with it, the all-singing, all-dancing, top-of-the-range model that seemed to do everything but tell the time, and which wasn't doing any of those other things either. Right now, it was a useless big shiny red-and-black bracelet on her wrist.

All she had wanted was something to replace her trusted old sports watch that had died, something that had a heart-rate function and GPS that would connect her to the app RunMaster. The salesman in the sports shop had assured her this one had more computing power in it than NASA when they put the first man on the moon. 'Seriously, do I need that just for a running watch?' she'd asked him. 'Seriously, you do,' he'd assured her, solemnly.

Now she was seriously pissed off. As she finally got a green and ran out into the road, she noticed too late the black Porsche. The driver hadn't seen the lights were now red, against the traffic. The driver with fancy sunglasses who wasn't even looking at the road.

She froze. Flung her arms, protectively, around the tiny bump growing inside her.

3

Marcus Valentine was irritated by what part of *I have to go, I have an emergency operation,* Claire didn't understand.

He'd been besotted with her the very first time he'd seen her. It was when he'd attended management development training she'd delivered at the hospital, the year after he'd moved to this island to start his new life as a consultant gynae-oncologist. She was tall, willowy, beautiful and always smiling. Although blonde, she'd reminded him so much of the girl he'd been infatuated with as a teenager – Lynette.

He would always remember the first time he'd seen Lynette on that perfect mid-summer Saturday afternoon. He was sixteen, lying in long grass behind a bush, out of sight of teachers, smoking illicitly with a bunch of schoolmates, all of them skiving off from cricket. Jason Donovan had been playing on a radio one of them had brought along. 'Sealed With a Kiss'.

When an apparition had appeared across the field.

Impossibly long legs, flowing red hair, dark glasses, in a tantalizingly short white dress that clung to the contours of her body. She'd walked over, introduced herself, bummed a cigarette, then sat and flirted with them all, asking their names. Each had done their best to chat her up, before she'd left, striding away and blowing a kiss, then giving a coy wave of her hand.

At him, he was certain.

'You're in there, Marcus!' one of his friends had said. 'She liked you – dunno why she'd like a spotty fatso like you.'

5

'She was probably blind – that's why she wore those glasses!' said another.

Ignoring the comments and jeers, Marcus stood up and hurried after her. She gave him an inviting sideways glance and stopped. And right there, in full sight of his now incredulous – and incredibly jealous – friends, had snogged him, long and hard.

They'd met three times over the next few days, very briefly, just a short conversation then a deep French kiss each time. Nothing else as she always had to rush off. Marcus was becoming crazy for her.

'When can I see you again?' he'd blurted on the third meeting, barely able to believe his luck.

'Same time, same place, tomorrow?' she'd replied. 'Without your mates?'

Marcus had barely slept all night, thinking about her. At 3 p.m. the following afternoon, half an hour before she was due, having ducked out of a cross-country run, he'd positioned himself behind the bushes. She'd arrived on the dot and he signalled her over, standing up to meet her.

This time they'd kissed instantly, before they'd spoken a word. To his astonishment she'd slid her hand down inside the front of his shorts and gripped his penis.

Smiling into his eyes, and working her hand up and down, she'd said, 'Wow, you're big, do you think it would fit me?'

He was gasping, unable to speak, and seconds later he came.

'Nice?' she asked, still gripping him.

'Oh my God!'

She looked into his eyes again. 'Let's do it properly. Next Saturday, same time?'

'Next Saturday.' He couldn't wait to tell all his friends. But equally he didn't want them spying on him. 'Next Saturday, yes, definitely!'

'Bring some rubbers.'

'Rubbers?'

'Protection.'

It had taken him most of the rest of the week, during which again he'd barely slept, to pluck up the courage to go along to the local town, which was little more than a large village, enter the chemist and ask for a packet of Durex. He'd been served, his face burning, by a girl only a few years older than himself, while he looked furtively around in case there were any teachers from his school in there.

To his dismay, it had pelted with rain through the Saturday morning. And he realized he didn't know Lynette's number – nor even her last name. Lynette was all he had. By 3 p.m. the rain had eased to a light summer drizzle. With the condoms safely in his blazer pocket, trembling with excitement, reeking of aftershave and his teeth freshly brushed, he walked out across the field towards the bushes. He held his parka folded under his arm to keep it dry. They could lie on it, he planned.

3.30 p.m. passed, then 4 p.m., then 4.30. His heart steadily sank. At 5 p.m. he traipsed, sodden and forlorn, back to his school house. Maybe she'd come tomorrow if the weather was better, he hoped, desperately, his heart all twisted up.

Sunday was a glorious sunny day. He again waited all afternoon, but she never appeared. Nor the following weekend.

It had been three agonizingly long weeks before Marcus saw Lynette again. Three weeks in which he'd fantasized over her, constantly. Three weeks in which she was never out of his thoughts or his dreams, distracting him hopelessly from his studies. On the Saturday morning, after class, he'd changed into shorts and a T-shirt and mooched down into the town, hoping against hope that he might find her there shopping.

Then to his excitement he saw her! At last! Outside a biker's cafe. She'd dismounted, right in front of him, from the rear of a motorcycle pillion. The guy she was with was a bearded, tattooed hulk, in brass-studded leathers.

Marcus stopped dead and stared as she removed her helmet

and shook out the long strands of her hair, tossing her head like a wild, beautiful free spirit.

'Hi, Lynette!' he said.

She didn't even look at him as she put her arm around her hulk and kissed him. Holding their helmets, they strode towards the cafe.

'Lynette!' he called out. 'Hi, Lynette!'

As he hurried towards her, she shot him a disdainful, withering glance and strutted on.

The biker stopped and blocked him. 'You got a problem, fatty?' He held up a tattooed fist glinting with big rings. 'Want a smack in the mouth?'

'I – I just wanted to say hello to Lynette!'

She had stopped and stared at him, then turned away, dismissively.

Marcus had watched as, arm in arm, they'd entered the cafe.

But he had never really stopped thinking about her. Sure, she wasn't part of his everyday thoughts, but at milestones – like both his wedding days – he had to admit to himself she did come into his mind. Wondering. Wondering what if it had been Lynette he was marrying? After he'd graduated from Guy's Hospital medical school he'd taken a post at the Bristol Royal Infirmary where he'd met and married his first wife, Elaine. The marriage had been a disaster. Within months, as he was working round the clock to build his career, Elaine, to his dismay, had fallen pregnant. But she'd had a miscarriage. In the aftermath, with Elaine in emotional turmoil and him working even harder, the marriage had disintegrated into an acrimonious divorce.

It was while the proceedings were going on that he'd seen the post in Jersey advertised and had successfully applied for it.

Then, working at the General Hospital in Jersey, he'd met Claire, and all the memories of that blissful summer's day with the Jason Donovan song playing had come flooding back.

Marrying Claire had made him feel whole. Those first two years in their beautiful hilltop home in St Brelade, with its striking sea view, they'd been so close. So very comfortable with each other that there had been moments – when he'd had perhaps a drink too many – when he'd been tempted to share with her a dark secret from his childhood that he'd harboured for years. But, always, he'd held back.

Then the twins had come along, and their relationship had inevitably changed. Even more so when their next baby had arrived. Unlike in his previous marriage, he had now been ready for children. They completed him as a family man, but he didn't like the feeling of being relegated to fourth place in Claire's affections, behind the children.

Claire kept her humour even though she was stuck in the house for much of the time with needy three-year-old twins, Rhys and Amelia, and an even needier nine-month-old baby boy, Cormac – the 'Vomit Comet'. In hindsight, three children under five was hugely stressful and had taken a toll on their relationship. He could only hope it would improve as the kids got older. But despite his misgivings, to the outside world he was the proud, happy father.

He'd seen so many friends grow apart when their children came along, and, Christ, his own parents had hardly been a shining example. He'd come to realize over the years that, far from being the glue that held relationships together, children could easily become the catalyst for their disintegration. Yet, though parents blamed the children, he knew the truth, that it was the other way around. Just like the words of that poem about your parents fucking you up.

Would he and Claire break the mould?

Not if this morning was anything to go by. She'd been so distracted by the twins fighting, she'd given Cormac milk that was far too hot. On top of that she'd begun firing questions at Marcus, blocking him from leaving the front door. A human barrier, as tall as him, long fair hair a wild tangle around her face.

When are we putting up the Christmas tree?

Who's coming?

What outside lights shall we put up?

When are you going to give me a list of what you want for Christmas? And shall we get the twins the same presents or different? We've got to get them soon or they'll all be gone.

'I've got to go – later, please, Claire. OK? Friday's my morning in theatre – and I have an emergency ectopic – everyone will be gowned up and waiting, they know that I'm never late for knife to skin.'

'Come on, you always have an emergency something. Later isn't a time! Later is *never*! Is that what you tell your patients when they ask you when their baby is due? *Later?*' She shook her head. 'No, you say June 11th or July 16th. Or, knowing you, you probably say at 3.34 p.m. precisely.'

When he had finally left the house, he was eleven minutes behind schedule. Time he was never going to make up on an eighteen-minute journey.

The joy of kids! All those pregnant women he would be seeing in his consulting room this afternoon. Smearing on the gel and moving the ultrasound scanner around their expectant bellies. Showing them the shadowy silhouette of the little lives inside them, on the screen.

Watching their happy faces. Their own worlds about to change.

Do you know what's ahead? Months of sleepless nights. And for some of you, the end of your life as you know it. All the sacrifices you'll both make over the years to come? Will you produce geniuses who'll change the world for the better or ungrateful little bastards who'll turn you into an anxious mess? The gamble of life. A good kid . . . or a waste of space? Nature, nurture; good parents, crap parents. You needed a licence to keep certain animals, but any irresponsible idiot could have kids.

He knew he should be more positive, change his mindset. But he couldn't help it, that was how he felt. Increasingly. Day by day. Working all hours in the hospital. Frequently on call, working weekends. He'd kept in touch with a few of his old friends from his time at boarding school. One had gone on to become an insanely rich hedge-fund manager, and was now a tanned, relaxed hedonist with his super-rich hedge-fund manager wife and retinue of white-suited acolytes. They proudly called themselves the TWATs – only working Tuesdays, Wednesdays and Thursdays. What a life!

Another old buddy seemed equally relaxed working as a sailing instructor. Marcus admired his choice to live modestly and still, at forty-five, to go on backpacking adventure holidays with his wife.

It seemed, some days, that he envied everyone else's life.

Sure, he made a good living, and he loved the kudos he got for his role at the hospital, but at times he couldn't help feeling he'd made the wrong life choices – including the wrong career. And possibly the wrong discipline within it. Sometimes he made people happy, but not this morning. His first operation was to remove the remaining fallopian tube of a thirty-nine-year-old woman who'd endured nine tough years of in vitro fertilization and whose final chance of a natural pregnancy was now gone. Her symptoms had been confirmed just over an hour and a half ago and he had little time to lose.

Cursing for being so late, he was now driving faster than the 40 mph speed limit along Victoria Avenue, his baseball cap pulled low over his forehead against the low, dazzlingly bright sunlight in his eyes. Over to his right, the tide in St Aubin's Bay was a long way out. Full moon. His own tide felt just as far out.

Snapping himself out of this mood, he hit the speed-dial button on his phone to call his assistant, Eileen, to give her his ETA.

Then he looked up and saw the red light.

Bearing down on it at speed.

A young woman, with Titian-red hair, in running kit, had stopped right in front of him. Staring at him in horror.

Frozen in her tracks.

Hands clamped over her midriff.

Shit, shit, shit.

He stamped the brake pedal to the floor.

The wheels locked. The car slithered. Yawed left, then right, then left again, the tyres scrubbing and smoking.

Oh Jesus.

Heading straight towards her. No longer driving his car, just a helpless passenger.

4

The Porsche stopped inches from Georgie. Like, *inches.* Another foot and it would have wiped her out.

She stood still, staring, momentarily rooted to the spot in shock. Through the windscreen the driver, in a baseball cap pulled low and sunglasses, also looked shocked. She shook her head and opened up her arms, mouthing an exasperated, *What?*

He put his window down and leaned out a fraction. Then froze as he saw her properly.

Lynette.

Was this Lynette, after all these years?

No, it couldn't be. Couldn't. Could it?

'It's a red light,' she said, tartly. 'Or are you colour blind?'

'I'm sorry,' he said. 'I'm—'

She shook her head and ran on.

Marcus sat staring after her, stunned. His mind flooded with emotions from the past.

She was exactly how he imagined Lynette might look now – some thirty years on. Handsomely beautiful, alluring, and in great shape.

God, how ironic if it really was Lynette and he'd run her over!

Could it be possible that it actually was her? A million-to-one coincidence?

Destiny?

He'd never made any attempt to find Lynette – he'd never even known her surname. And in any case, he was well aware it had

13

only been a teenage obsession at best. But suddenly the sight of this woman had reminded him of that summer. That girl. Those fumbling, tantalizing moments when she had touched him, that he had replayed in his mind countless times. And still occasionally did when he was making love to Claire. All that Lynette had promised. And never delivered.

A horn blared behind him. A large white van.

The lights were now green.

He raised an apologetic hand and, as he drove on, shot the woman another quick glance.

Followed by a longer one.

Could it possibly be her?

He felt stirring in his groin. He was aroused.

5

Georgie Maclean finally got the watch restarted, although to her annoyance it had frozen again and not recorded all the details of the past two miles of her daily morning run. And, incredibly, given her current condition, just when she was sure she had smashed her previous five-mile time.

Whatever.

She was still shaking. Shit. That idiot in the Porsche. She patted her midriff again, where tiny life was just beginning, a few millimetres in size but growing daily.

At forty-one, she was only too aware her biological clock was ticking away crazily fast now, like it was on speed. Which was why it felt so very good to be pregnant, after years of yearning for a baby. She'd left it late, and hadn't even started trying until she was thirty-three, after she'd finally found Mr Right, the man she wanted to have a child with, back in London. Mike Chandler, a teacher at a tough comprehensive. She'd been working as a PE teacher back then. After years of no success, her gynaecologist discovered she had a tilted – retroverted – uterus but did not operate as he did not feel that should stop her falling pregnant. But still nothing had happened. Then Mike had been diagnosed as having a low sperm count. When that had been sorted, it was discovered she had hostile mucus.

She recalled going to see a sweet, elderly specialist up in Hampstead, who had helped a close friend with her fertility issues. As she'd lain in his reclining chair, feet up in stirrups, while he inspected her with a vaginal speculum, tut-tutting, she'd exclaimed in anger that she couldn't see how the hell anyone ever got pregnant. And always remembered his words, in his strong Scottish burr: 'What you have to understand, Mrs Chandler, there is an awful lot of copulation that goes on in the world.'

Several years of infertility treatment had followed. Her menstrual cycle logged into her laptop and phone. Making love according to a date stipulated by an ovulation kit and an app. Followed by expensive and painful attempts at IVF. It sure had been a romance-buster. Finally, they'd separated, sadly and very painfully. Mike had quickly got together with a fellow teacher, who was now pregnant by him, and Georgie had gone back to her maiden name.

After a sudden bout of acid reflux, something that was occurring constantly at the moment, she ran down the side of the Old Station Cafe, crossed the cycle lane and turned left, following the curve of the bay towards St Helier. To her right, below on the beach, people were walking their dogs, some of which were bounding, free of their leads, across the vast expanse of wet sand left by the retreating sea. Further over, the rock outcrop to the east of the harbour, topped by Elizabeth Castle and separated from the mainland by a causeway, was now walkable with the far-receded tide.

To get away from the trauma of her marriage split, she'd come to Jersey for the summer at the invitation of an old girlfriend, Lucy, who she'd known since primary school. Lucy had moved to the island a while back with her sister, and Lucy herself was training to become a nutritionist. Georgie loved her passion for this and for going back to study. They'd both made a big leap to change career well into their thirties and were a huge support to each other. In fact, whenever they met up, which was often, they were normally in tears of laughter within minutes. 'The Gigglers', as they had been known back when they were five years old. That had stuck, and they loved and cherished it.

Soon after Georgie's arrival on the island she'd had a short relationship with an estate agent, which hadn't worked out. She hadn't been ready to return to London and had really grown to love everything about Jersey – the calmer pace of life, the rugged land-scapes and the beaches, and the feeling of safety that the island community offered. She'd decided she wanted to stay. She managed to get accepted as a Jersey resident and was making a life here, building a new career as a personal trainer. She called her company Fit For Purpose.

Although this island she now called home was small, just nine miles by five, it felt much larger. One of her clients, who had spent all her life in Jersey, had told her that it increased its land mass by one third when the tide was out. Not hard to believe, from the vast amount of beach she could see.

There were also hundreds of miles of lanes and roads, with stunning coastal views around almost every corner. Its only town, St Helier, which she was now heading towards, with its port, network of pedestrianized streets and vast array of shops and stores, felt substantial, almost a bonsai version of an English city.

The one oddity was St Helier's principal landmark, an inciner-ator chimney, and she always wondered why, with its inhabitants so keen on preserving the island's natural beauty, nothing had ever been done to somehow mask it. But it hadn't spoiled her love of the place. And the one thing she loved more than anything was how safe she felt. The crime levels were so low that she felt completely secure running here, even at night, and she never bothered to lock her car.

As she ran on towards the Esplanade, where many of the banks were sited, passing a closed ice-cream kiosk, shading her eyes against the low winter sun, she didn't notice the Porsche which had now made a U-turn and was cruising back past her. Slowly. But not so slow that it was obvious.

6

Friday 7 December

Inside his car, Marcus was unsettled. And hard.

Lynette?

The slender woman on his left in the pink top, bright-blue shorts and compression socks, who he'd almost run over, was now heading in the opposite direction, grim determination on her face.

As he drove, he discreetly held up his phone and took a photograph of her. Then he did a quick mental calculation, wondering how Lynette would really look today – assuming she was still alive? Was she still beautiful like this running lady? Or was the Lynette of his dreams now fat, tattooed and living miserably with her bolshy biker husband? Her likeness was uncanny, although he knew that in reality it almost certainly wasn't her.

And yet?

The clock in the round white dial above the dash said 8.42. It was running sixteen seconds fast against the dial of his wristwatch and the imprecision angered him. The watch that received, each night, a radio signal from the US atomic clock in Colorado. It was accurate, every day, to within nanoseconds.

He was really late now, but at this moment did not care. He turned round at the first opportunity, catching one more glimpse of her from the other side of the dual carriageway, then drove on. He wanted to see her again. With a small population of around 107,000 on this island, you were constantly bumping into people you knew, or at least recognized. For sure, he would see her again.

Finally, he pulled into an underground parking space at the

rear of the tired old granite buildings of Jersey General Hospital and hurried from his car. Still thinking about the woman.

Running.

He'd taken up the sport at medical school and after losing a lot of weight had become a useful runner himself, often winning cross-country races at county standard. He'd always loved the buzz, the competitive high. How long had it been since he'd stopped running seriously because of a ligament injury and just did the odd jog here and there? Three years? God, no, four. He felt his stomach. *I'm turning into a paunchy bastard. Just like I was once mocked for being a teenage fatty.*

Got to get back on it on a regular basis. Get a training regime set out. And maybe see her again?

With three young kids and a demanding career, where would he find the time – or the energy? But he needed to. His lack of exercise was already taking a toll on his health. At his last check-up, his GP had prescribed him statins, telling him he was overweight, his blood pressure wasn't great and that he was drinking too much – and he'd lied about his weekly alcohol units, which were double at least what he had told the quack. Oh, and he'd conveniently forgotten to tell him that he'd taken up smoking again. Not much, but enough for disapproval.

He knew he wasn't a great example to his patients, if they were to find out, as he told all of them to cut down their drinking and quit smoking.

Maybe he could try a longer jog over the weekend, see if he could stretch it to a run? For his birthday, a few months back, Claire had bought him a sports watch, which he'd only used a handful of times. Was it a hint, he wondered, that his changed physique and his increasing belly were turning her off? Did he care?

And hey, he knew his looks and charm were still there, even with those few extra pounds on him; some of his patients clearly fancied him – and, he thought, at least two of the staff members at the hospital – well, three actually.

He strode towards the main entrance. Twenty-two minutes late. Normally this would have stressed him, but not now that a plan was forming in his mind.

Start running again properly. Yes.

And maybe he'd see the redhead sometime, out on the promenade.

Although he did not know it, he *was* going to see her again. Very much sooner than he thought.

7

Friday 7 December

After Georgie and the estate agent had split, she had briefly considered leaving Jersey and returning to London, but two things had happened in rapid succession. The first was that her father, her only close relative in England, died suddenly from a heart attack, aged just sixty-five. It was a massive shock to her, but equally, she was sadly aware, he'd never done any exercise in his life and was extremely unfit.

She liked the island and, after the funeral and sorting out her father's affairs, decided to stay. Spurred on by his death, she used her share of the small inheritance, along with her savings, to set herself up as a personal trainer, helping people – particularly those at risk from previously sedentary lifestyles – to get fit. Occasionally, she saw some of her clients at their homes, but mostly she used one of the island's gyms. She was fond of chiding them with a saying she'd once heard: *So many people sacrifice their health to gain wealth and later in life they spend their wealth trying to fix their health.*

Within a few weeks one of her new clients introduced her to Roger Richardson, a debonair, divorced, former RAF test pilot, at a party. They hit it off and Roger, who now worked as a flying instructor, had invited her out for a drink.

Followed by dinner.

Followed, the next day, by a flight in a little single-engine Piper he part-owned with six others. They flew over all the other islands, circled the Cherbourg Peninsula and the Plogoff nuclear power station, and landed in Dinard for lunch.

Followed, two weeks later, by the best weekend of her life. Followed by countless more.

Followed by a missed period.

Then, last Tuesday, a home pregnancy test from a kit she had bought in a chemist showed positive! Confirmed yesterday by her doctor who, to her surprise, only used a similar kit to the one she had purchased. He'd carried out some basic health tests on her and scheduled an appointment with a midwife at his medical centre for a week on Monday.

It was almost impossible to believe it, after all those years of treatment, but to her utter delight she'd finally become pregnant. It was even more miraculous as she'd had a brief cancer scare the year before. Even though it had turned out to be nothing to worry about, it had made her even more doubtful that she would ever have a baby.

Now Georgie was living with Roger in a small, cosy flat, with an ocean view, in St Aubin. Lucy, who was currently single after kissing too many frogs, lived only a few roads away, and she had made many other solid friends. Roger had asked her, two days ago, to marry him, and she'd accepted. It had been a long while since she'd felt so excited about the future.

Reaching the start of the harbour basin, she turned and began heading back home against a strong, westerly headwind. She glanced at her watch, relieved it was back up, but annoyed that it would not be recording her PB due to crashing earlier.

8.57.

Just time to get home, shower, grab some breakfast and then head to the gym for her morning session with the first of her clients.

Fortuitously, one of her regular clients was Tom Vautier, the owner of the large Bel Royal Hotel in St Lawrence, which was closed for the winter from the end of September to the beginning of April. He'd kindly suggested she might like to make use of the gym, in exchange for helping to keep an eye on the hotel during those months. She wouldn't have to do much because there was a caretaker there in the week, doing some cleaning and a bit of maintenance. But even empty, it was too much of an undertaking for just one person – and Tom was off-island quite a bit, going backwards and forwards to visit his elderly mother in Madeira, and also running his ski hotel in Méribel. Georgie could have the whole gym at her and her clients' disposal for six months, free, no rent. It would save her a packet, and all she had to do was help the caretaker by making a quick check of all the rooms, for leaks or any other problems, every week.

So now she could offer her clients the extensive range of the gym's equipment, and her business was growing. At times, though, especially late afternoon when it was dark, she found the silent hotel just a bit creepy, and the oddball caretaker added to her unease. The place reminded her of the Overlook Hotel in the Stephen King novel *The Shining*.

Roger had come to do the check-round with her a few times, and they'd laughed about it together while he'd teased her about her 'overactive imagination'. 'You'll get used to it,' he'd said. And she had. Besides, Jersey was a really safe place. And she didn't believe in ghosts, not in real life.

There was enough to worry about in real life anyway, without ghosts. As she ran, she patted her tummy again. 'How are you doing, Bump?' she asked.

Bump was a tad too small to respond. But she smiled, thinking of Bump moving with her.

From her PT training she was aware she could continue running right up to term, if she was careful. She'd also trawled the internet for any differing opinions and, of course, there were loads.

Fine. OK. She'd learn more when she saw the midwife.

And it was the weekend tomorrow. She'd been looking forward to a quiet time with Roger, catching up on a couple of box sets everyone was talking about, but they'd had a last-minute invite to a dinner party from a doctor Roger flew occasionally on business and had become friendly with. It was something Roger did, although it wasn't strictly legal without a full air-operations certificate, to supplement his income and to help people out when the island was fog-bound – as it sometimes was in the winter months – preventing commercial airliners getting in. With his experience, he could take off in most conditions. And his background, as a former RAF test pilot, gave his clients confidence.

Roger had harboured an ambition to become a commercial pilot, but at fifty-two the only employment he'd been able to secure, other than a position as first officer with a low-grade turbo prop airline he did not rate, was as a flying instructor in Jersey. Still ambitious, he was now trying to build up a local clientele, particularly in the medical profession, many of whom made regular trips to Southampton, with a view to eventually starting his own air taxi business.

A few years before he and Georgie had got together, Roger had been through a heart-wrenching divorce after trying for years, just like she had, for a baby. Georgie adored him and, despite knowing just how good a pilot he was, she couldn't help feeling nervous every time he left to fly his little plane, whether it was to take a student up for 'touch and goes', or to ferry people to mainland England or France.

Normally, Georgie enjoyed meeting new people, but now she was pregnant and couldn't have alcohol any more, she wasn't happy about the idea of spending an evening with a bunch of people, most of whom were strangers, stone-cold sober. But, hey, she thought, a tad gloomily, she was going to have to get used to not drinking for many months to come.

And there was at least one small positive – they'd save money on taxis, as she could drive them home. With Roger no doubt well-oiled as he wasn't flying again for three days.

8

The twins raced around the kitchen table, amusing and annoying Claire Valentine in equal measures. Then they ran into the living-room area, perilously close to the Christmas tree that she and her husband had spent the previous evening decorating, in preparation for tonight.

'Rhys! Amelia! Stop it! Mummy's trying to do something. OK?'

'Yaaaaaaa!' shouted Rhys.

'Yaaaaaaa!' shouted Amelia, snatching several of the white place cards Claire had carefully laid out, and throwing them in the air as if this was a huge joke.

'NO!' Claire shouted, turning towards her husband in desperation.

Dressed in a tracksuit and trainers, Marcus was standing by the island unit, a partially eaten banana beside him. He was staring up at one of the antique clocks on the wall, a round, wooden, nineteenth-century Shoolbred of London, which was running two minutes slow.

Annoyed by its inaccuracy, he pulled up a chair, climbed onto it, opened the glass face and, checking against his watch, moved the minute hand.

'Marcus, can you give me some help? We need to do the seating plan.' She knelt and scooped up the cards from the floor, glancing at the names. 'Tonight we have a vegan, a peanut allergy, someone lactose intolerant and another I'm pretty sure is a pescatarian, so I've got some salmon en croûte as backup. Whatever happened to

25

the days when you could just have a dinner party and everyone ate everything?'

'They all died!'

She grinned. Marcus looked around in disapproval at the floor of the large kitchen–living room littered with toys, along with Cormac's play mat, playpen and the mobiles suspended above it. Cormac was feeding plastic food discs into the mouth of a roaring green dinosaur with a red flashing light on its head.

Marcus climbed back down. Then he saw to his alarm that Rhys was about to topple an antique wooden stand. 'Rhys, no!' he yelled, running over and just rescuing the situation in time. He went through into the dining room, joining Claire at the table, and looked down at the place tags.

'Who do you want to sit next to?' she asked.

He studied the names on the white rectangles. 'Not Lizzy Lawrence – all she can ever talk about is how awful everything is – I feel like I want to go and hang myself after half an hour listening to her.' He looked at the other names. 'I like Matt and Aron – I honestly don't mind. Oh, but please not that woman – the one I got stuck with at the Aldridges' drinks party last week – she nailed me in a corner and spent an hour telling me the entire plot, chapter by chapter, of the dreary novel about a doctor she's been writing for the past five years.'

He glanced over the rest of the names. 'Did we really invite all these others?'

'You were the one who said we should ask some of the people who've had us to dinner in the last year, to be polite. Stop being a sourpuss. You like the Pedleys, too.'

He nodded.

'Why are you in such a grumpy mood?'

He shot a glance up at the wall. At the clocks. 'Why can't they keep proper time?'

'For God's sake!'

'You just don't understand, do you?'

'No,' she said. 'Actually, I don't.'

He shook his head. 'So who do you want to sit next to?'

'Any of them!' she said defiantly. 'I'm actually looking forward to tonight, even if you're not. Someone to have a conversation with – you don't have any idea, do you, what it's like being stuck home all day making baby talk? I'm looking forward to having a proper conversation, with adults.'

'What do you mean? You're on the phone to your clients every day. And you should be bloody grateful for the time you have at home with our kids. You know damned well that when I was a child my mother was a drunk and my father had sodded off. You'll look back at this time with affection one day. Seeing the kids grow up much more closely than I do – and you're still able to work as well. My mother—'

'I know about your mother,' she said, stopping him in his tracks. 'I've heard it all before so many times and I've told you repeatedly: you can't let that dictate your whole life.' Changing the subject, she asked, 'Have you sorted the wines?'

'All done.' He huffed, pointing at a row of flute glasses. 'Champagne cocktails when they arrive – get everyone in a festive mood. I could do with one now.'

'What's Roger's new lady called?' she asked.

'Dunno,' he replied. 'Oh, I forgot to tell you. He emailed to say she doesn't eat shellfish.'

'Shit. We're doing prawn cocktails as starters.'

'There's some mackerel pâté in the fridge, I bought it last week – she could have that, perhaps?' he said. He shot a glance at the television, at a cookery programme, the sound muted. Then peered into a large carrier bag on the island unit. 'What's this?'

'Party poppers! Must remember to put those out.'

He looked at her as if she was mental. 'You're not serious?'

'What do you mean?'

'Poppers? We're not having a children's tea party, Claire.'

'It's Christmas, in case you've forgotten. I've got these and a cracker for everyone – really classy crackers. What's your problem? You wear your Christmas hat in theatre.'

'Sterile cap,' he corrected her. 'That's different.'

'So, you're Father Christmas when you deliver babies, but turn into Scrooge when you come home?'

'Ha bloody ha.'

'I know why you don't like the idea: it's because you don't like mess. But we have Debs coming Monday so anything we've not cleaned up she can do then. Chill, relax, enjoy. Anyway, I need your help – can you nip to Waitrose and get some French bread or Melba toast for the pâté? And there's some other bits and pieces we need – those olives are out of date, we need some more, and some vegetable crisps.'

'I was planning to go for a run – I'll go straight after.'

'A run? I thought you were taking the kids to Aqua Splash?'

'I will,' he said. 'Later.' He patted his belly. 'I need to get rid of some of this.'

'Are you sure it's sensible to go running after your medical report? You've only been jogging a few times lately – and even then you had to power walk most of it.'

'What do you mean? He told me to start exercising more.'

Claire tossed hair from her face. 'From the way his report read, he's suggesting a gentle jog – not a run.'

'Yeah, yeah. Don't worry, I'm not quite ready for a Zimmer frame or a mobility scooter. I thought that was why you gave me the sports watch, to encourage me to start running more again.'

'That was before your check-up.'

'Meaning what?'

Claire looked at their daughter, who was about to snatch another place card. 'Amelia, NO!!!' Then she grinned at her husband. 'Meaning that the man I love and the father of our children is not in great shape. Meaning that he is in the prime early heart-attack band. You need to be careful if you want to get back into running seriously. Build up to it. Maybe a brisk walk first would be more sensible.'

Ten minutes later, Marcus left the house and stopped at the bottom of their steep driveway to do some dynamic stretches. As he swung his leg, he was thinking about what presents to get his wife for Christmas. He had hardly any time to go around the shops, so he'd have to order stuff online. Claire had been wanting a tennis bracelet for some time and had hinted at one she'd seen in a jeweller's window in town. But it was a ridiculous price. He also needed to get her a few other, smaller gifts, and a card, as well as some stocking fillers for the kids.

After power walking down the road towards St Brelade's Bay, Marcus stopped by the church to do some more warm-up exercises. The tide was even further out than yesterday. He began jogging down to the promenade and turned left. A bearded man in running shorts, at least his age if not older, loped past him at an easy gait, at probably twice his speed.

He upped his pace, determinedly, but almost immediately was aware of a slight pain in his right calf muscle. The other man was way in front of him now and for a short while disappeared as he headed along the old railway track to St Aubin. Marcus managed a few hundred yards more before stopping and limping for some yards, getting his breath back.

Jesus, I'm unfit.

As he began a slow jog again, two men, running and talking, passed him. Then a woman running with a baby in a pushchair shot past.

Overtaken by a sodding pram. No way, José!

As he approached St Aubin, ignoring the twinge in his calf, he began to run fast again, and despite his body telling him to stop and walk, he forced himself to keep going. And keep going. No way was he going to let other runners see him flagging.

Especially not the gorgeous Lynette! The island was so small, and from where he'd seen her before, it was likely this was one of her routes.

His pace was slowing, but he kept on. Doggedly. Kept on. More runners raced past him, as well as intermittent cyclists. His heart was bursting. *Keep going!* He kept on until he had nothing left in the tank. Lame-spirited, he walked again. Glanced at his watch. His heart rate was over 180. His head was light. Giddy. He needed to sit down.

But that would be defeat.

He continued, past the turn-off to the harbour, around the yacht basin, with dozens of boats lying on their sides on the mud.

Finally, he stopped, panting, getting his breath back. He turned around and ran again for a short while before stopping and then walking, his heart rate now up in the 180s again.

Arriving back home at last, he entered the front door, removed his trainers and tucked his laces, tidily, in the shoes. He saw Claire, across the open-plan area, giving the twins their breakfast, Cormac in his high chair, food spilled on the floor around him. A cartoon was playing on the television on the wall.

'How was it, darling?' she asked.

He nodded, almost too tired to speak, and boiling hot. Holding the banister rail, he hauled himself up the stairs and into their bedroom. He flopped down on the bed, closed his eyes and lay there, gratefully, for several minutes. *I really am out of shape*, he thought.

When he had recovered enough, he limped through to his den and plugged his watch into his laptop to download his stats.

The RunMaster app, which he didn't fully understand yet, appeared. It gave him his overall time and then a section-by-section time for parts of the area he had covered, together with a comparison to others in each section.

He was dismayed – although not surprised – to see he was the bottom of each recorded segment for his age group and then for all age groups. Out of interest, he tapped on the number one for the St Aubin to St Helier section.

And stared as a photograph of the current record holder appeared. Thirteen minutes and twenty-five seconds faster than him.

It looked very much like the jogger he had nearly mown down yesterday.

And it gave her running name: *Rocket Girl*.

Plus the timings of her run.

He checked her other recorded runs. Many of them started and finished at the same point – and time.

Could it be her? Could it?

Was that start-and-finish point her home?

Almost certainly.

9

'What do you think?' Georgie said, walking into the living room in a slinky black dress, giving a twirl, then provocatively raising part of it above her right thigh.

'I want to take it off.'

'You don't like it?'

'I like it too much,' Roger said with a grin. He was tall, fit and ruggedly good-looking, with short, salt and pepper hair, the kind of person who inspired confidence, who looked like he could take care of any situation. Tonight, he was dressed in a black jacket over a sharp white shirt, dark chinos and loafers.

'Too much?' she frowned.

'You know what they say about dresses?' he said, going to the drinks cabinet.

'No, what?'

She watched, enviously, as he poured a large slug of whisky into a tumbler.

'That the dress a man really likes to see his lady wearing is the one he'd like to take off the most.'

He carried the tumbler to the fridge and dropped several ice cubes into it.

Georgie grinned. 'Really? Well, you are just going to have to wait. And perhaps stay sober enough to appreciate your bride-to-be later!'

'I'm up for that!' He took a step towards her and said, jokily, 'We could just have a quickie now!'

'Hands off! I'm all made up. But I like your thinking!' She smiled.

'I think it was Henry Miller who said something like, a dirty mind is a perpetual feast!'

'He must have been writing about you! You are full of quotes tonight – have you been boning up to impress all the posh guests we're going to meet?'

He laughed. 'Marcus and his wife are lovely – he's a hugely respected medic, I've flown him many times and we've played golf together a couple of times. Enough about them, you look absolutely stunning. Though as I've said before, you'd look stunning in a bin liner!'

'I don't feel stunning, I'm a bag of nerves. I spoke to Lucy earlier and she said to get some champagne down me and it'll be fine. I can't wait to tell her about the baby. Champagne would be nice right now. Do you really think we'll get on with the other guests?'

'Darling, they wouldn't have invited us if they didn't think so – and at least you'll have Kath there.'

'Really? So why didn't they invite us weeks ago, when they invited all their other guests, rather than late yesterday evening?'

Roger had been phoned by their host, saying they'd had a last-minute cancellation from a couple down with flu, and were they free tomorrow evening by any chance?

Their host and a number of the guests attending were medics, some of whom Roger flew regularly to England. It was a chance, he had convinced her, to network and help build up his client list for his air taxi business. And, of course, he had told her, a chance for her to meet some possible new clients herself.

'My hair up – is it OK like this?'

He cocked his head one way then the other in mock appraisal, and with pursed, smiling lips, gave her his approval. 'More than OK.'

'Are you still going to love me when I'm all swollen up like a barrage balloon?'

He walked over to her. 'Sure, I'll get you a Certificate of Airworthiness.'

'Bastard!' She kissed him.

He glanced at his watch, downing a large gulp of his drink. 'We should leave.'

'Promise we won't stay late?'

'With you wearing that dress? I solemnly promise. I'm already looking forward to getting home and removing it.' He kissed the back of her neck, then took another gulp of his whisky.

'Yeah, yeah, darling! I'm serious. An evening of meeting all these posh strangers without drinking any booze isn't going to be easy, you do understand, don't you?'

'I've been to parties where I can't drink because of my job for years. I've got used to it, it's fine.'

'Which is why you're downing a seriously large whisky?'

He shrugged. 'If it would make you happy, I won't drink any more tonight, either. OK?'

She shook her head. 'No, I want you to enjoy yourself.'

'And you'll be the martyr?'

Georgie smiled. 'No, not the martyr, I'll be the chauffeur, for now. But just don't forget it – I'm building up credits for the future. Deal?'

'Deal.'

They high-fived.

Then Georgie said, 'It's too early to tell people I'm pregnant – in case – you know?'

The unspoken word hung in the air. The ever-present fear she had of a miscarriage.

'I won't say anything.'

'So, what's our story about why I'm not drinking?'

'Easy. You're the designated driver.'

'Almost genius!'

He dug his hand into a packet of nuts and pulled out several. Shovelling them into his mouth, he said, 'Mediocrity recognizes nothing higher than itself. It takes talent to appreciate genius.'

Smiling, she said, 'So I'm just the *talent*?'

Putting down his glass, he swept her into his arms and stared at her face. 'You are the love of my life. You are the reason I want to wake up in the morning. You are my life, I love you to bits. I will love you to the ends of the earth and beyond. OK?'

She looked into his eyes, grinning. 'OK, I'll take that.' They stared at each other for several seconds then Georgie said, 'And right back at you. I love you more than I can ever say. I can't wait to be married to you.'

He looked into her eyes. 'I can't wait either.'

He downed the rest of his whisky, then they picked up their gifts for the hosts, went out and along the corridor, through the rear door and down the two flights of steps into the parking area. They climbed into her elderly VW Golf.

As she started the engine, Georgie felt a deep sense of foreboding that she could not rationalize. She knew just one thing. However *lovely* these people might be tonight, as Roger insisted they were, she was pretty sure they would seem a lot more lovely with a few glasses of wine inside her. And that was so not going to happen.

10

Saturday 8 December

At 7.30 p.m. on the kitchen clock, which was – give or take a few nanoseconds – 7.30 p.m. precisely, Claire, still wearing her apron, saw lights suddenly come on through the kitchen window. The driveway courtesy lights. Which meant someone was arriving.

'I can't believe it,' Marcus said, panic in his voice as he put the finishing touches to the prawn cocktail starters, not daring to hurry and make a mistake. He was a stickler for detail at all their dinner parties, and they would almost come to blows sometimes over his perfectionism. Claire often wondered, since they stressed him so much, why he was so keen to have them.

But she knew the answer as she watched him sprinkle exactly the right amount of Sevruga caviar – six eggs each – alongside the precisely measured lemon slice that lay on top. He enjoyed the feeling of status that grand dinner parties gave him, and she actually found his meticulousness endearing – most of the time.

Marcus had gone through the archway into the dining room, where he was now adjusting each of the place mats and name tags into perfect alignment. He selected his carefully curated classical music playlist on the Sonos. So vulgar, he thought, when people had pop music at a dinner party.

'Why can't they be late, like any normal people?' she called out.

'Or perhaps on time, like any normal people?' he muttered under his breath, holding up a wine glass to the light and wiping away a tiny smear with a napkin, which, after replacing the glass, he then carefully refolded – and then refolded again. He was dressed

36

in his flamboyant smoking jacket, quilted with embroidered gold fleur-de-lis scattered across it. 'Is *on time* really too much to ask?' he murmured, again to himself. Then he checked each of the champagne flutes, which had a drop of Armagnac and a sugar cube in the bottom, for his cocktails.

Claire glared at him. 'Oi, I heard that, misery-guts.' She held up a prawn cocktail. 'Want one of these tipped over your head?'

'Calm down, relax, I'll go and open the door, take the coats, hold the fort.' *As always*, he thought.

Their first guests, prosecution attorney Richard Pedley and his actress wife, Alex, gratefully accepted the champagne cocktails Marcus offered. The moment he had poured their drinks the doorbell rang again.

Marcus rushed back through the hall. As he passed the row of labelled coat hooks, he noticed Amelia's hoody was on Claire's. He moved it to the correct one before opening the door. Matt Stephenson, a consultant breast surgeon, and his husband, Aron, stood there. Just as he had escorted them through into the drawing room and introduced them to Richard and Alex, the doorbell rang again.

Claire had still not appeared.

Excusing himself, he ducked his head into the kitchen.

'The bloody Aga's playing up, nothing's cooking! Can you get it?' she pleaded.

Marcus strode through the hall, holding a magnum of champagne, and opened the front door.

And froze.

The bottle nearly fell from his hand.

Standing on the doorstep, wrapped up in overcoats against the cold, was his pilot friend, Roger Richardson, with a bottle in a sparkly gift bag. His lady clutched a large bouquet of cut flowers in one hand and a box of chocolates in the other.

She was the spitting image of the woman he had nearly run over.

The one who had thrashed his running time on his RunMaster app.

Was it her?

Roger said, 'It might be a bit early, Marcus, but Happy Christmas!'

'And you too!'

'This is my fiancée, Georgie!'

He stared at her for some moments, absorbing this, before responding.

Georgie.

It was her. It was definitely her.

So that was her name. She bore such an incredible resemblance to Lynette.

'Great to meet you – ah – Georgie,' he said, kissing her lightly on each cheek and inhaling her scent. She smelled just – incredibly – sexy.

'And you, too, Marcus, I've heard so much about you from Rog!' she said.

He liked her voice. And her perfume. And most of all her smile. He was shaken but tingling all over. Had she recognized him? He didn't think so, and she wouldn't have seen the Porsche, it was in the garage.

Claire appeared, minus apron now, and more kisses and introductions followed.

'What beautiful flowers!' she said, the charming hostess as ever. 'So lovely to meet you, Georgie! I'll go and put these into water right away. And my absolutely favourite chocolates! Thank you so much.'

Marcus hung up their coats, then, taking Georgie's hand, led them through to meet the Pedleys and the Stephensons.

'Beautiful house you have,' she said, looking around, admiringly.

And you, Georgie, are incredibly beautiful!

As soon as he had made the introductions and given them each a glass – champagne cocktail for Roger and a sparkling water for Georgie – he went into the dining room, checked himself in the mirror and hastily made a couple of changes to the seating plan. He placed Georgie next to himself.

11

Saturday 8 December

Claire and Marcus had originally planned that they would sit down to eat at 8.30 p.m. but it was gone 9 p.m. before she was finally confident that the lamb casserole was cooked enough. By which time Marcus had lost count of the number of champagne cocktails he'd replenished – and drunk himself to calm down. There was a hefty stack of empty bottles of Pol Roger lying on the floor by the kitchen bin, along with a spent bottle of Armagnac. All their guests seemed to be getting along famously. Georgie was deep in conversation with a lady called Kath Clow.

He was a little unsteady on his feet, he realized, as he ushered everyone through into the dining room, telling them to find their name tags and to help themselves to water. He picked up a magnum of Meursault.

'Darling, can you give me a hand putting out the starters?' Claire asked, coming out of the kitchen with a tray of prawn cocktails in crystal goblets.

'On my way, *darling*, I'm just trying to make sure our guests don't dehydrate!' he said, rather more loudly and acerbically than he had intended. It created a momentary awkward silence among their guests.

Kath Clow, whose husband was away, went through into the kitchen. 'I'll help you, Claire,' she said. Kath was a work colleague of Marcus at the hospital and the two couples had been good friends since he'd arrived on the island. They'd hit it off from the start, so much so that they were godparents to each other's children.

40

The guests congregated in the dining room, found their name tags and sat down, Marcus guiding Georgie to her place himself.

After completing his task of filling all the glasses with wine, except for Georgie, who was only on water, Marcus picked up his phone and asked everyone to raise their glasses for a group photo. He had Alex Pedley to his left, but his whole focus was on his guest to his right.

'Have we met before?' Marcus asked Georgie.

'No, I don't think so.'

Good, he thought, relieved. *She doesn't remember the incident at the traffic lights!*

'So, have you and Roger set a date yet? Soon as you do let us know so we can book a babysitter!' he said, cheekily. 'And my wife will need to buy a hat!'

'That's if you make our list!' she replied with a smile.

Alex engaged in conversation with Matt Stephenson, seated beside her. On the other side of Georgie was a lively but pompous dermatologist sporting a pink waistcoat, busy pontificating to the unfortunate Aron, who was looking a little bored by him.

'Not drinking, Georgie?' Marcus said.

'I'm afraid I'm the designated driver.'

'A pity, we've some really fabulous wines tonight. You could always leave the car here and cab it home – or take that service where they come and drive you back in your car. I have their card.'

'Thank you,' she said, 'but I'm fine with water.' Then, lowering her voice, she said, 'I'm also on antibiotics.'

'That's too bad.' He raised his glass. 'Cheers!'

'Cheers!' she responded. 'It's great to get to finally meet you, Roger has been talking about you for months.' Their eyes met and Marcus felt a strange, deep connection to her. There was something about this woman.

'He's not been giving away my secrets, I hope,' he said.

'And what might they be?' she quizzed, smiling.

He stared at her intently. 'Now that would be telling.'

She gave him a look that made him feel like he was the only man in the room.

God, she was beautiful.

A raucous male voice from the far end of the table said, 'Don't you think, Marcus?'

'I'm sorry,' he replied. 'I didn't hear what you said.'

'Childbirth – it's magic, isn't it?'

'Really? Come and watch a C-section sometime and then tell me where the magic is,' Marcus retorted. 'The magic would be if a stork brought them. There's nothing magical about a bunch of people in green gowns and blood-soaked gloves pulling away at a woman's insides like mechanics with monkey wrenches.'

'Marcus, we're eating!' Claire chided, rolling her eyes at the guests next to her.

Ignoring her, he went on, 'Robbie Williams, or whoever it was, had it right, he said that watching your wife giving birth was like watching your favourite pub burn down.'

There was a burst of laughter from a few of the guests around the table.

Marcus turned to Georgie and said, quietly, 'You remind me of someone I once knew. A girl I was crazy about when I was at school. I was just a fat little spotty teenager and she was going out with a biker.'

'What was her name?' Georgie asked.

'Lynette. You really remind me of her so much.'

'I do?'

'Yes, you really do. Guess it was my first experience of unrequited love – isn't that what the old romantic poets called it?'

The way she was looking at him – was she aware of it, that allure? She must be. As she must be aware of his response to how gorgeous she was. She was looking at him the same way Lynette had that very first time. That same, incredibly sexy mouth. The curve of her lips. Was he imagining it or was she coming on to him?

'You're an obstetrician, Roger tells me. What made you choose to go into that?'

She definitely had a sparkle in her eyes. *What exactly is she thinking about?* he wondered. There was no way he could tell her what was on *his* mind. He was seriously lusting after her.

'Well, I practise obstetrics, yes. But my main work is with gynae-oncology.'

'Which is?'

'I specialize in gynaecological-related cancer.' He leaned closer. 'Ovarian and cervical cancers mostly.'

'Is that tough?' she said. 'I mean, when you have to deliver bad news to people?'

'Yes, that's the hard part. But when I bring new life into the world, that's the joy. Life and death in my hands. A bit like God, really.'

She grinned and put a hand on his arm for an instant, leaning in. 'Really, you think so?'

Down the far end of the table, Roger, as usual, was holding court, while several of the guests, mostly women, listened with rapt attention to one of his stories.

Marcus smiled, enjoying this moment of closeness. 'Tell me, Georgie, you look like someone who does a lot of sport.'

'I'm a personal trainer,' she replied, sitting back.

'Ah. Right. I'm just getting back into running myself.'

'Really?'

'I was pretty useful when I was at uni and I'd lost my puppy fat and shaped up – cross-country was my thing. But work sort of got in the way. How often do you run?'

'Every day, if I can,' she said. 'I did the Jersey Marathon back in October.'

'Wow, that's impressive. So, where do you run?'

'I have a circuit from where we live in Beaumont, along Victoria Avenue.'

'Beautiful route,' he said, thinking to himself, *And I know your exact route from home and back!*

'It is – apart from the traffic along Victoria Avenue. It gets very busy.' She smiled at him.

Including idiots in Porsches not looking at the road? he nearly said through his increasing drunkenness.

She had looked fit in her running kit, but now, in her revealing, slinky black dress, she looked even more so. Fit enough to—

'If you ever feel the need of a personal trainer,' she posited, 'I'd be very happy to give you some sessions.'

He stared back at her, aroused. 'Really?'

'Sure.'

'I'd like that very much. I was diagnosed a couple of years ago with type 2 diabetes. Exercise is the best thing for coping with it, apparently.'

'So I've heard. Do you manage it well?'

He smiled, happy she seemed so concerned. 'When I first got the diagnosis, I thought that was it, my life was over. But now it's like I don't have it at all. I'm actually in the process of writing an article for *The Lancet*, on why having type 2 diabetes can be good for you.'

'Really? Good for you?'

'Yes, because if you take care of yourself it's just like not having it. So, it forces you, unless you are totally stupid, to take more care of yourself than ever before. I do need to lose a bit of this weight though.'

His mind was racing. Booze-addled, he knew. Saying too much. Needed to rein it in.

Suddenly he heard Claire from down the far end of the table. Her voice was raised. 'Marcus,' she said, very pointedly. 'Lana completely agrees with me. You are exactly the wrong age and weight to suddenly start madly running again. You need to build up gradually.'

Lana Nela, seated diagonally across from Claire, was a cardi-ologist.

Marcus raised a glass. 'Thank you, my darling. Cheers for that. I'll try not to drop dead before the end of this dinner!'

There was an awkward moment, guests unsure whether or not to smile, before the buzz of conversation resumed again.

He turned to Georgie and said, quietly, 'Perhaps my dear wife is right. You're a trainer – do I seem unfit to you?'

'Do you want me to answer as a polite guest or as a professional?'

'The latter.'

'Well, I'd say that you could lose a little weight as you mention yourself. If you wanted, I could help you. I do private sessions in my gym.'

'You have a gym?'

'At the Bel Royal Hotel.'

'Is that open in the winter?'

'The hotel is closed, but they let me use the gym, in exchange for helping the caretaker keep an eye on the place. I just have to check the rooms and I'm the principal key-holder in case of an alarm, which there never has been.'

'Sounds perfect.' He smiled at her. *Oh yes!*

'I'll give you my phone number,' she said, smiling, and suddenly leaned forward, startling him. For an instant he thought she was going to kiss him, but instead she flicked a crumb off his jacket lapel. 'On weekday evenings I usually have an open session from 6.30 to 7.30 p.m. at the gym – you can just turn up and join in, unless I've got a client. On Thursdays I do a specialized running drills training session – if you think that could be helpful?'

'I might just do that.'

As they exchanged mobile numbers, Marcus watched Roger, still holding court at the other end of the table. The pilot had the attention of all the guests around him.

He's just a fucking pilot, for God's sake! he thought to himself. *He's just a taxi driver that drives a cab with wings.*

Continuing to completely ignore Alex to his left, Marcus carried on talking to Georgie. He got up only to offer his guests more white, then red, then vintage port along with his *pièce de résistance*, his dazzling cheese platter.

Georgie studied the assortment he held in front of her.

'The Brie is sensational,' he said. 'And so is the Camembert – we get it from a specialist who really knows his stuff.'

'No Brie, thank you, I'm—' She stopped, sliced herself a tiny sliver of Cheddar and took a couple of sticks of celery.

As the platter moved on to Alex Pedley on his left, he turned back to Georgie with a knowing grin. 'No shellfish, no alcohol and no soft cheese? And on *antibiotics*?' He waggled a finger in the air. 'Could there be something you're not telling me?'

She blushed.

'Don't worry, your secret is safe with me.' He winked and patted his tummy, looking at her quizzically again.

Relishing the fact that he knew.

After the cheese, Claire served coffee and Marcus went around the table with a decanter of brandy, helping himself to a hefty quantity in a large balloon glass. He sat back down, engaging Georgie again, putting his hand on her arm. She withdrew it a little abruptly, stood up and yawned. 'I'm sorry to be a party pooper, but we're going to have to go.'

Georgie walked around the table and up to Claire. 'Thank you both so much,' she said. 'It's been a wonderful evening, just flown by – I can't believe the time! You've both been such charming hosts and your husband is great fun.'

Claire smiled at her. 'You certainly seemed to be getting along well. Perhaps we could all go for a drink or a bite after Christmas is over. It would be lovely to get to know you guys better.'

Marcus let Georgie and Roger out of the front door. He watched Georgie as she climbed into their car, noticing Roger's hand on her back.

You don't deserve her, mate, he thought. *She's much too good for you.*

12

After their last guests had departed, Claire said to Marcus, with only the merest hint of jealousy, 'You and Georgie seemed to be getting on rather well.'

'She's a nice lady, and I need to be sweet to her – she's a possible future patient. She's pregnant.' Marcus, aware his voice sounded a little forced, topped up his brandy glass and sat down on a sofa more heavily than he had intended; some of the drink slopped over the rim, onto his hand, and he spilled the ash off the end of his Cohiba.

Often, Claire wondered just what her husband was really thinking. There was a part of him that she didn't know at all. Was that the same with all people – did we all keep part of ourselves private, concealed from the world, even from those closest to us? Yes, he was obsessive about things, especially about *time* – possibly, he was even on the spectrum – but he was a good father. She knew what a terrible start in life he'd had with his parents. His father had been a brutal womanizer who loathed him and abandoned him at a young age. His alcoholic mother was a constant source of embarrassment and frustration to him. She was obsessed with turning him into a concert pianist, despite his lack of interest or aptitude, and regularly dragged him out of bed at night to come downstairs and play the baby grand for one or another of the stream of men she brought home for sex. It was no wonder he behaved oddly at times.

Once, early in their marriage, after a dinner party she tried hard to forget, they'd had a row and he'd disappeared for two days. All these years on, she still did not know where he had gone. But, to her relief, it had been a one-off, and for the sake of harmony she never spoke of it again. And if she was honest with herself, she knew she wasn't a complete angel – she'd had plenty of opportunities at conferences with guys she'd enjoyed flirting with, but she'd never let it go further. She'd been determined to make their marriage work and had always resisted the temptation to stray, so far. Because she loved him.

She sat down next to Marcus, with a glass of Baileys. 'Wow, I think we managed to pull that off, somehow!'

He yawned and checked his watch. 'Oh my God, it's nearly two. We're going to be knackered tomorrow.'

She put an arm around him. 'Chill, Mr Valentine, I love it after everyone has gone home and we can just relax. Life's no dress rehearsal, isn't that what they say? Enjoy each moment.'

He gulped some brandy, then picked up the soggy stump of his cigar which, like the rest of him at this hour, was past its peak. As he relit it and blew out smoke, he said, 'I'll remind you of that when Rhys and Amelia wake us up in a few hours, all bright and demanding.' He yawned again. 'God, I'm desperate for sleep.'

'It would be nice to have a lie-in tomorrow,' she said, suggestively. 'Like we used to before the children came along.'

'Those days are long gone.' He drank some more. 'Oh God, I'm just so tired, I need to sort my life out.'

'What do you mean by that?' Claire said, unsettled.

'How did we get ourselves into such a bloody rut?'

'We're not in a rut, Marcus. I love our life, don't you?'

'Sometimes I don't know what I really feel. I'm probably too fat to feel anything. Thanks for telling all our guests that, by the way. Calling me fat and that I was daft to go jogging. That made me feel really good.'

'I didn't say that, I said you were the wrong age to suddenly start going mad with the running and that you need to build up gently. I don't want you injuring yourself and I simply thought, as we had one of the top cardiologists in Jersey in the room, and you don't listen to me, it would be good to get her opinion,' Claire retorted.

'Really?' He poured himself another large brandy. 'Well, I tell you what I'm going to do about Lana Nela's opinion. I'm going to go for another run in the morning. Just watch me. She can shove that opinion up her jacksie.'

13

'You and Marcus seemed to be hitting it off,' Roger said, slurring his words, as he climbed out of the Golf.

'Hitting it off? Not exactly. We had a few laughs – he's quite a flirt.'

'Really? Marcus? Pot and kettle?' He laughed.

'What do you mean?'

'Come on, my darling, you know how flirty you are!'

'I so am not!'

'Really?' He grinned, giving her a look.

'The guy on my right didn't speak to me for ages – when we did talk all he did was tell me about himself, but he seemed a lot more interested in some of the other guests. The woman next to Marcus was really nice – Alex, I think – she's an actress. But Marcus – well, I thought he was quite entertaining at first, but he was getting a bit lechy as the evening went on.'

Roger grinned again and said nothing for a moment.

'What?' she asked.

'Nothing.'

'Tell me!'

He shrugged as they walked up the stairs to their second-floor flat. 'You seem to have that effect on men, look what happened to me!'

She punched him playfully on the arm. 'But you don't just have looks, you have the seductive charm to go with it.'

Roger flopped down on a sofa in the living room and yawned.

'And look what happened – bun in the oven straight away and now you're stuck with me!'

In daylight, the huge window had a magnificent view across St Aubin's Fort and the whole bay. Now they could see just the twinkling lights of the road and promenade, and the inky black of the sea beyond.

'Stuck with you? Aren't I just!' She blew him a kiss. Then she frowned. 'You know, Marcus asked me some really some odd questions. Oh and he guessed I was pregnant, probably his medic mind.'

'Well, you are!'

'Yes, I know! But how would he know?'

'He's smart. You weren't drinking, for starters.'

She nodded. 'I told him I was on antibiotics – but when he really twigged was when I wouldn't eat any soft cheese.'

'Bit of a clue there,' he said.

'I guess.'

'So, what questions were odd?'

'Well, he asked me if I'd ever hated someone – like, hated them enough to kill them.'

Roger shook his head, curious. 'What did you reply?'

'I asked him if he had and he gave me a very, very strange look. I actually thought for a moment he was going to confess to some terrible crime. Then he told me he'd hated his mother.' She fell silent.

'And?'

'He changed the subject, quite abruptly. Later, he kept on and on about him knowing I was pregnant. I mean, he's not odd in an Edouardo way.'

'Edouardo – the caretaker at the hotel?'

'Yeah, not like that. Marcus is more quirky than weird. I think he was pretty smashed to be honest. Claire suggested we all meet up for dinner, us four. We're going to need friends with young children soon!'

'Yeah, he's definitely quirky but he's a good man with a big heart, he'd do anything for his friends, and he's very highly respected at the hospital – he's probably the obstetrician you should have.'

'Oh my God, no – I'm having Kath Clow – but I might take him on as a client. He told me he's got back into his running recently and was asking all about how fast I do the parkrun – I've a feeling he's going to try and beat it!'

'I think that's just him, he's very competitive and a stickler for punctuality. Not that you'd know it tonight with the time we all ate, I was starving.'

'Me too! Oh, and he also wanted to know how you and I met, and what was my favourite song.'

'And what is your favourite song, my sweet bride?'

'As I told him, Van Morrison, "Queen of the Slipstream", the song we're going to have for our first dance.'

Roger looked at her lovingly. 'Gets me every time I hear it. The first song we ever danced to. The song that was playing when I proposed to you. If I'm driving somewhere and it pops on the radio it makes me feel happy.' He put his arm around her. Then with his free hand he lightly patted her tummy. 'Look, darling, I hear what you're saying but especially with your previous cancer scare, Marcus would be the best person on the island to go and see about checking out our Bump.'

'No thanks,' she said flatly, 'I'm having Kath.'

She nearly added, but didn't, something about Marcus making her feel uncomfortable. She couldn't put a finger on it. But it was a bit like looking at a flat, calm, enticing ocean then noticing the red flags along the beach.

14

After the impeccable tidy-up before their guests arrived last night, it had only taken a few hours for the kids to turn the living room back into a tip again today, with toys strewn everywhere. Rhys was pedalling around on a big, yellow tractor and Amelia had arranged a highly messy dolls tea party on the floor, alongside Cormac who was on his play mat, hammering away at the keys of the toy marked with animal symbols.

Marcus normally played golf on a Sunday morning with his regular partner, Nick Robinson, but today he had blown him out with the excuse that he'd ricked his back. But in truth he wanted to go for a run – to try to shake off his hangover, he'd told Claire, but that wasn't the whole reason.

Now he lounged back on a sofa, soaking his left foot, which had a painful blister on the big toe from his exertions this morning, in a bowl of warm, salted water. By his side was a large dish of peanuts, which he was steadily munching through. On his lap was a medical paper by a surgeon at Sloan Kettering in New York on a new early surgery procedure for cervical cancer, which the man had pioneered and had a good success rate.

But Marcus kept putting it down and looking at his phone. Looking at the photographs he had taken of his guests last night. Although only one interested him.

Georgie.

He zoomed in on her. Stared at her, fixated. God, she reminded him so much of Lynette.

Claire, curled up on the sofa opposite him, was reading a Sunday supplement. A rugby match was playing on the television, but Marcus only glanced at it intermittently, his focus was on his phone. He clicked on various posts related to his new obsession, the online running community.

His right calf was hurting badly – poetic justice, he wondered? He'd strained a muscle attempting to better his 3-mile run of yesterday – more accurately, his 3.1-mile run. Things had changed a lot since his own athletic days. This new running community he had discovered referred to distances in kilometres – and 5K was the equivalent of 3.1 miles. He'd limped most of the way home, slinking in through the back door so that Claire didn't see him, not wanting more earache from her about his fitness. But she'd noticed him in pain later on and had just given him a rather sad, knowing look.

'Rhys! Be careful!' she shouted, as the boy crashed into a marble plinth on which sat a bust of John Harrison, the man who'd built the first marine chronometer. Claire had bought it for Marcus as a Christmas present last year, from a vintage fair. She leaped out of her chair and just saved it from toppling.

'I really don't think we should have it in here, Marcus,' she said. 'It would be a lot safer in your study.'

'I'll move it,' he said, barely looking up from his phone as she sat back down.

'What are you looking at so studiously?'

'Weight-loss sites,' he fibbed.

'This would make a good photo,' she said with a grin. 'You trying to lose weight with your foot in a bowl of saltwater while you stuff your face!'

'Huh,' he grunted and chucked another handful of peanuts into his mouth. He focused back on his phone, now opening RunMaster and entering 'Rocket Girl' into the search.

She had 534 followers. He didn't understand all the social media apps well enough to know whether someone could tell if they were being looked at, but his real name and position as a consultant was disguised from his patients – his identity on RunMaster was Dr Runboy. There was an option to follow her. He hovered his finger over it but decided against. Just in case she noticed. He didn't want Georgie to think he was stalking her.

Instead, he looked up her activity. And saw that she, too, had done a run today. An hour earlier than him, and once more she was the fastest of today's runners. Part of their route again coincided. And, when he'd checked his stats, he'd been last or close to the bottom of each segment, as before. He brought up the times for the St Aubin to St Helier section, and was listed as one from bottom for today. But the runner below him was so slow it didn't exactly motivate him.

He logged out and began a trawl for her name on social media. He found Georgie on Instagram. She had 2,300 followers, and seemed, from the photographs, to be posting a daily image of pre- and post-running exercises with short written tips beneath. She had 1,553 followers on Twitter and 4,784 on Facebook. All the same kind of stuff, with occasional pictures of herself and Roger on their travels. Clearly laid out in her bio were her up-and-coming races and her personal best running times.

So, you're really consistent here, Georgie. Same time, same days. Very similar routes. It's not that hard to find out a whole lot of info on you. Like today, out at 8.30, over to town, round St Aubin's Bay, back up the old railway line. Like the same day last week, and the week before, and like the day I first saw you. I don't think it's going to take much for me to find you again on one of your runs. You've got the same Instagram name as you have on your RunMaster and your Twitter, and no doubt countless other social media profiles. You overshare! How do I know all this? I don't need to be a detective, do I? I know where you are racing next, what your best times are, your kit all laid out flat and your running number. Nice pics, good times, happy families.

He tried to focus back on the rugby. Normally it was a game

that gripped him, but right now his mind drifted as he watched it, not caring which team won. He was feeling in need of a drink. Glancing at his watch, he saw it was only 4.20 p.m. There was over half a magnum of a superb Chambertin left over from last night. It was unlikely to remain in prime condition for another day.

He stood up, carefully removing his foot from the bowl, hobbled over to the kitchen area and removed a glass from the drying rack. Filling it almost to the brim with wine, he went back to the living room, put the glass on the coffee table in front of him and sat back down, placing his foot, gratefully, back in the bowl.

'That's about two hundred calories,' Claire said, glancing up, cheekily.

'Yep, well I burned off some of them walking to get it.' He focused back on his phone. On Georgie Maclean. But he wasn't looking at her times, he was looking at her photograph. He expanded the image.

Then enlarged it some more.

He stared at her face for a long time, drinking repeatedly from his glass, then hovered his finger over the 'follow' button. Wondering. Should he? Would she work out it was him? And thinking . . .

You might be number one now, Georgie, but I know you're pregnant. And in a few months' time you won't be running so fast, whilst I'll be a lot slimmer and a lot fitter!

The wine had gone straight to his head. Making him feel confident. Invincible. Competitive.

He looked across at Claire; she was engrossed on her laptop. He hit the button.

Dr Runboy is now following Rocket Girl.

15

Sunday 9 December

Roger hadn't moved from the couch for most of the day, which was unusual for him, Georgie thought. When his schedule gave him a weekend at home, he normally went off for a two or three-hour bike ride. But today, nursing the Hangover from Hell, he lay there, barefoot and unshaven, surrounded by the newspapers, in his tattiest old jumper and tracksuit bottoms.

A pint glass of water sat on the coffee table in front of him, along with a tepid mug of tea and a partially popped blister-pack of paracetamol. His eyes were shut most of the time, with just the occasional glance at the rugby on the television. He'd only got off the couch, some hours earlier, to dutifully make his signature dish brunch of scrambled eggs and smoked salmon, as he did every Sunday – the best scrambled eggs in the world, Georgie always said. Today, the food made him feel a bit queasy.

Seated in an armchair opposite him, reading a book on the week-by-week stages of pregnancy, she suddenly laughed.

'What?' he said. 'What's so funny?'

'You!' She picked up her phone and took a photograph of him. 'Imagine if your students or your passengers on your next flight could see you now! Think how confident they'd feel!' She giggled again and took another photograph.

'I'm glad you're enjoying my hangover, because I'm not!'

'You did rather hit the booze last night, darling.'

'They served some dangerously good wines.'

'And port – oh, and Cognac, too,' she reminded him. 'A rather special vintage one, wasn't it?'

He grimaced. 'What is that thing inside your head that tells you if you have one more glass of brandy, you'll feel better the next morning than not having had it?'

She grinned again. 'Hopefully it will all be out of your system by Tuesday morning when you're next flying.'

He glanced at his watch, then reached for the paracetamol, popped two more out and downed them with some water. 'This is the worst I can ever remember.'

'Look on the bright side – at least it made your evening a lot better than mine!'

'Hmmmmn.' He looked at her ruefully.

'You're not getting any sympathy!'

'Not even the tiniest bit?'

She put down the phone and the book, walked over to him and curled up beside him, putting an arm around him and kissing him on the cheek. 'My poor brave soldier's got a hurty head. Let me make it better.' She kissed him, then again. 'Is that helping?'

'It is.'

She kissed him once more and returned to her chair. It was already dark outside, the ocean no longer visible, and spats of rain were striking the huge windows. 'What do you fancy for supper?'

'You,' he said.

'In your state?'

'Maybe comfort food. How about a baked potato and tuna – or beans on toast? I can make it.'

She shook her head. 'You rest your pretty little head – I'll sort something in a while.'

Settling back down, she picked up her phone and read a text that had come in from her first client tomorrow, asking if she could change the time of her session. She replied that was fine. There were several emails she hadn't looked at and she scanned through them, but there was nothing important, other than a cancellation from one of her regulars for her 11 a.m. group session on Tuesday.

She returned to her book, then after some minutes announced, 'Did you know that my body is busy preparing for the months ahead?'

'What?'

'It says so here.' She glanced down at her midriff. 'Hello, busy body!'

'Aren't you meant to have symptoms?'

She tapped the open page. 'Morning sickness, sore breasts and cramping.'

'You have those?'

'And acid reflux.'

'Sounds nasty.'

'It is, I keep getting it.'

'What about cravings? Shouldn't you be having those, too?'

She nodded, looking a little guilty. 'Uh-huh. You know those pickled onions your aunt gave us – the ones she said would be ready to eat by Christmas?'

He nodded. 'I'm really looking forward to having those with a fine Cheddar – making a ploughman's.'

'Well, there's a slight problem with that plan – will you forgive me?'

'Forgive you what?'

'I – er – ate the whole jar earlier today.'

It was his turn to burst out laughing. 'Probably best I am flying on Tuesday and away for the rest of the week, with your onion breath.'

'You should love me all the more for it!'

On the screen, the right wing, clutching the ball, was racing to the touchline, but Roger had totally lost track of the game. 'I couldn't love you any more than I do,' he said. 'Not possible.'

'You sweet-talker, you!' She blew him a kiss.

'I mean it.'

I. Love. You, she mouthed.

And. Me. Loves. You, he mouthed back.

She blew him a kiss then glanced at her phone again. There was a new email.

You have new followers on RunMaster.

She swiped across to the app and tapped on it. There were twenty-three new follower requests, which really pleased her. More people she might be able to convert to YouTube followers in her ambition to turn that into a commercial enterprise – *Keeping fit while pregnant and afterwards! Fit For Purpose!*

'Hey, darling, I've got another twenty-three RunMaster followers,' she said. 'Isn't that great?'

But there was no response from Roger. He'd fallen asleep again. And was snoring.

Five hundred and fifty-seven followers, she noted. *Brilliant!*

She put the phone down and sat, looking at Roger, feeling a sudden deep sense of contentment.

She picked up her phone again and scanned down the list of names, not really fussed about who any of them were, clocking a running coach, a chiropractor – and a doctor.

It was great, she thought, that these professionals were following her – brilliant for her credibility with her clients.

16

Monday 17 December

Time is the enemy.

Marcus Valentine's mother was late, always late. She was forever leaving him standing outside the school gates, freezing in the cold or soaking in the rain, as he watched all the other pupils walk or drive off with one or the other of their parents.

'The enemy beat me!' she'd say matter-of-factly, when she finally drove up. 'Get in the car, you'll catch your death.'

In the mornings, when he was ready for school, breakfasted, his coat on, rucksack packed with his homework and lunchbox, he'd stand in the hallway, close to the front door, all knotted up inside because of the ticking-off he would be getting for being late – again – listening for the sound of the bathroom door opening upstairs.

His wristwatch, day after day, would be telling him it was just fifteen minutes to the start of morning assembly and he knew that, with the best will in the world, even breaking the speed limit and catching all the lights, it was going to take his mother an absolute minimum of twenty minutes to get there.

Finally, the click of the door and his mother's voice calling down. 'How's the enemy?'

'Twelve minutes, Mum, we're really late. Like, *really* late.'

Like, *every* day.

The irritation of the teachers. The excuses he'd long run out of. Puncture. Dog eaten rat poison. Sister half severing her finger cutting an apple. Grandmother rushed to hospital. And, of course, *My dad's left home.*

It was the unsaid part that stung most of all. *My dad chose my sister to take with him.*

And not me.

That was a year after the big fuss of his younger sister Claudine's disappearance. Age six, last seen by a passer-by standing outside the school gates with her rucksack, after their mother had totally forgotten to pick her up.

What a shitstorm her disappearance had caused until she was found again – only a day later! Marcus had lured his sister into being lowered down a dry well in local woods, telling her it was a prank. He had then pulled the rope up and, ignoring her screams of terror, had left her there overnight – to teach his mother a lesson not to be late. But it had really backfired. The police and dozens of volunteers had searched through the night, and his sister, after he had finally revealed where she was, had been deeply traumatized. He'd had a severe lecture from the police, a thrashing from his father, and his sister was scared to be anywhere near him – which was no great loss to him.

His erratic and always heavy-drinking mother, Angela, from both his childhood memories and the photographs he was left with, had once been a beautiful and glamorous woman, until his father, failure and the booze had destroyed her. In her teens she had dreamed of becoming a famous actress. Too busy preparing for her roles in the amateur dramatics productions at Brighton's Little Theatre to do a full-time job, she made ends meet by giving piano lessons in whatever free time she had.

She'd met Marcus's father, Robert, after he'd seen her in a stage production of *Who's Afraid of Virginia Woolf?* and become infatuated with her, turning into a regular stage-door Johnny, she had joked, greeting her nightly with a huge bunch of flowers. But as soon as they had married, he became increasingly jealous, wanting her to quit acting and be at home for him.

He got his wish. She managed to secure a respected London theatrical agent, but had then blown the two chances he'd provided her with – her two breakthrough opportunities to turn professional. The first was when her agent had got her the title role of Lady Windermere in a touring production of *Lady Windermere's Fan*, and she'd been fired for continually being late and missing her stage calls. The second was when he'd got her a decent part in a multi-million-pound John Schlesinger movie and she'd overslept, then misread her call sheet and drove to the wrong location. Twice.

Her agent had fired her.

After that, hugely bored being stuck at home, with her husband away a lot having affairs that she knew about, and resentful that the world had been deprived of her talents, she'd gone back to am-dram. Until the company at the Brighton Little Theatre had tired of her unreliability, too, and voted her out. Marcus was born soon after and Claudine three years later. From his earliest days, all he could really remember about the occasional times his father was actually at home with them was arguments. Mostly he was absent. His mother became obsessed with transferring the abject failure of her own career into Marcus becoming a child prodigy and eventually a famous concert pianist. Although he had some ability, he'd had little interest in playing the piano, preferring to be up in his room, but he was too scared of his mother's drink-fuelled rages to disobey. She forced him to practise for hours on end whilst standing over him, metronome ticking, ready to rap his knuckles with a ruler if he made a mistake, and shouting at him, 'Timing, Marcus, timing, timing, timing!'

His father became increasingly absent, spending weeks away at their London flat or abroad on his property interests, and – if Marcus's mother was to be believed – womanizing.

He had barely known his father throughout the first decade of his life, other than as a man who seemed permanently angry at his mother or him, or both. Whatever Marcus did was either wrong or not good enough in his father's eyes. There was never any praise if he scored a goal or a try on the school playing fields or got good marks in an exam. It was quite different for Claudine, of course, clearly the apple of her father's eye, who could do no wrong. And on the rare occasions she was mischievous, it was always somehow Marcus who copped the blame from their father.

If he had one abiding memory of his father, it was an almost constant look of disgust and hatred in his eyes, as if he had nothing but utter contempt for his son – when all he had craved was for some recognition from him.

It was shortly before Marcus's tenth birthday that his father left home, taking Claudine with him. He'd overheard his father say to his mother that he was taking his 'little princess' and leaving the idiot boy, who would never amount to anything, to her useless care.

After they'd left, Marcus's mother drunkenly told him it was good riddance to both of them. It was from then on that her drinking, barely controlled to that point, finally fell off a cliff. And for a while seemed to turn her man-crazy.

Marcus frequently found himself being dragged out of bed at all hours by his drunk mother to play the piano to her succession of men friends and chastised afterwards for missing notes. One time he'd walked in on her to see her lying back on a sofa with a guy with his head under her skirt.

As he had retreated, embarrassed, he'd heard his mother saying loudly, laughing, 'Don't have kids, they fuck up your life, they fuck up all your fun.'

In his twelfth year, he increasingly turned into his mother's carer as she became more dysfunctional, leaving burning cigarettes in ashtrays, pans on the lit hob, and passing out on the floor. Then he came home one day and saw a note from her, in her exaggerated handwriting, warning him not to go upstairs, but to call 999 and ask for an ambulance.

She had swallowed an entire bottle of bleach. It took her three days of agony to die.

Marcus, who had not spoken to his father in the two and a half years since he had left, had been taken into the temporary care of his mother's elderly, dull parents. At his mother's funeral, his father and Claudine, to whom he also had not spoken since she had left, barely even acknowledged him, keeping their distance. Marcus had tried hard to reconnect with them there, but both coldly rejected him, neither uttering a single word.

To prevent him being a burden on his in-laws, his father had paid for him to go to boarding school. Marcus stayed on throughout most of the holidays, burying himself in his studies rather than be with his grandparents. But he had been on another mission, too. He was utterly determined to get high grades and win a place at a top medical school, and perhaps then his father, from whom he never heard a word, would finally be proud of him. As soon as he'd got into Guy's, he'd moved into digs. One of his tutors had admired his long fingers. 'You have surgeon's hands,' she'd said.

He'd preferred that a lot to his mother telling him he had 'pianist's fingers'.

Marcus wrote to his father, proudly telling him that he had started at medical school. Three weeks later he got a terse reply from a solicitor telling him that his father had died of a heart attack on a tennis court in Marbella, two months previously.

This Monday morning, Marcus was earlier than usual, 7.15 a.m., because he had a full day ahead. He'd be able to catch up on emails and paperwork in his office before attending a meeting at 8.30 a.m. The car radio was tuned to Radio Jersey, as it always was on his commute, enabling him to catch up on the local news. Today a presenter whose voice he particularly liked, Ashlea Tracey, was on.

But Marcus was barely listening. He was peering to his left and right. He knew from looking in detail at her historical activity pattern on RunMaster, going back many months, when and where she most likely went out for her regular runs. But he hadn't seen Georgie Maclean all week or over the weekend, and this was bothering him more than he wanted it to. He'd been out running trying to coincide with her regular runs but so far hadn't had any success.

He repeatedly looked at his running times and the running community posts. It was the first thing he did in the morning and the last thing before he went to sleep. He constantly checked Georgie's photographs on his phone, and he'd had a close call a couple of nights ago when Claire had almost seen what he was looking at, when he'd enlarged one of her photos.

And increasingly he was questioning why he was so bothered about her – and trying to put her to the back of his mind. But nothing seemed to shift her from his seemingly every waking thought. He kept telling himself to stop. He was aware it was becoming dangerously preoccupying. But he couldn't stop.

He was excited by Georgie. There was no excitement with Claire. Sex had become a rare occurrence, and when it did happen it was quick, perfunctory, servicing a need.

When did we last have any fun? When did we last do anything spontaneous? Are we ever going to feel the same way we felt about each other before we had children? When did we last have sex? When did I last actually want to have sex – with Claire?

He couldn't remember when a woman had last aroused him like this. He'd drunk too much at the dinner party, but he and Georgie'd had a lot of fun – and she wanted to train him!

An affair with Georgie Maclean? Do I dare?

Would she dare?

I know I shouldn't do it, should I?

But I have to.

The thrill of the chase!

But. Big but. She's pregnant.

Get over it, Marcus Valentine. Get back to your boring old safe life. Suck it up. This is ridiculous. You know you're always flirting with your female colleagues and friends, with no intention of taking it further – what's so different this time?

He felt a sudden charge of energy. For months he'd been exhausted. Mentally tired. Overworked. All his friends seemed to be having a nice life. He and Claire had been having a nice life, too.

So why was he now being stupid enough to even think about another woman? What had changed?

Perhaps everything had changed the day their twins, Rhys and Amelia, had been born. That was the day he ceased to be the love of Claire's life and was replaced by their children. The arrival of Cormac three years later just compounded the situation. Rejection, the story of his fucking life. It was all he'd ever had from anyone, all his life. And probably when they grew up, they'd reject him, too.

As he approached the lights where he had nearly run Georgie down, he slowed, looking around even more carefully, oblivious to the angry horn blast from a car behind him.

No sign of her.

Then he was jolted by Ashlea Tracey's voice. 'It's Monday! Let's have some Van the Man to get us all back into work in a good mood. One of the great tracks of all time!'

The music began playing.

You're the queen of the slipstream . . .

The song caught Marcus. As he drove on, he was nodding his head in time to the music. *Oh yes.* My *Queen of the Slipstream.*

Georgie had told him on that Saturday night that this was her and Roger's song. The song they had fallen in love to. The song that was going to be their first dance at their wedding.

How bizarre this should come on just as I was thinking about you, Georgie. Although I'm thinking about you a lot of the time.

Minutes after the song had ended, he took a diversion away from the clogged rush-hour traffic, passing the pet-food store and around past the north entrance to the hospital, with the wide green to the left where the town's homeless drunks hung out, as he kept on singing the words aloud.

He was still singing them as he drove into the car park.

Will you breathe not a word of this secrecy?
Will you still be my special rose?

He switched the engine off. Smiling.

He glanced at his watch.

Later than he'd intended.

But he didn't care. He was smiling.

My Queen of the Slipstream.

And she had accepted him as a follower on RunMaster!

Does she know it's me? he wondered. *Is it a further sign of her interest? Along with giving me her mobile number and wanting me to join her class?*

Before getting out of the car he looked at the app on his phone. But to his disappointment she had not recorded any new activity today. No morning run.

Why not?

Hey, the day was still young.

He strode into the Gwyneth Huelin wing entrance with a spring in his step that he'd not felt in a long while, and smiled at a young ICU nurse, Theresa Adams, getting a coffee at the cafeteria counter.

'Hi, Theresa! Let me know when you're going to dump your husband, won't you!'

She patted her swollen midriff. 'Marcus, can't you see? It will be a while, so dream on! Any case, I'm not sure you could handle me!'

'Oh, such a waste . . .'

'I thought you liked babies.'

'Yes, but not when they get in the way of you and me!'

'Yeah, yeah, keep dreaming – laters.'

'You know where I am.'

'You are incorrigible!'

'And you are bloody gorgeous. Make sure Mr Adams cherishes you!'

I FOLLOW YOU

Smiling as he climbed the stairs, he was humming the tune again.

You may not know it yet, Georgie Maclean. But you are going to be my Queen.

Oh yes you are!

17

Monday 17 December

A few minutes later Marcus entered his small, immaculate office and looked around, disapprovingly. The cleaners had, as usual, moved stuff about.

He was sure they did it just to show they'd been. And it really pissed him off.

Sitting at his desk, he carefully adjusted the position of his computer screen, keyboard, phone, mouse mat and pens, stood up and straightened some crooked files on a shelf, then looked at the round, utilitarian wall clock. It was running a minute fast. He adjusted it then sat back down and checked everything else in the room, noticing a tin of furniture polish spray and cloth that the cleaner had left on a bookshelf.

He dropped both items in his bin.

Finally satisfied, he tapped his keyboard to wake his computer, entered the new password he'd created – Georgie4Me – and began to deal with the emails that had come in over the weekend. Referrals from doctors. Requests for him to talk at various conferences. Notification of the Obs and Gynae department Christmas drinks party. Another notification for the Friday afternoon consultants' meeting – this week to focus on abnormality and morbidity.

He looked at his schedule for the day. Meetings all morning, then theatre in the afternoon. A couple of caesareans, followed by a relatively simple early-stage cervical cancer op, which would be shifted in case of any complications with either of the C-sections

– which there sometimes were. Followed by one he was not looking forward to at all.

A nice lady in her early thirties on whom he'd performed an operation a few months back for borderline ovarian cancer. Now the cancer had returned, a very aggressive tumour that was metastasizing. And, sadly, she was pregnant. He was going to have to abort the foetus, and in a couple of weeks he would have to perform major surgery on her. Even then, her prognosis was not going to be good. Life was so random, so damned cruel and unfair at times.

He was the on-call obstetrician today, which meant he would have to stay at the hospital until 9 p.m. and be prepared to come out at any time of the night until 8 a.m. tomorrow. But as he looked down his list, his mind was drifting. To Georgie. To running.

He needed to be fully kitted out to become a competitive runner again. He opened Google and typed in 'best running shoes for speed', thinking that, just like cars needed good tyres for optimum performance on the road, he needed good running shoes to help him perform. Next, he trawled a couple of running websites to upgrade his kit. He ordered a basket load. Then he googled 'personal trainers in Jersey'. Near the top appeared 'Georgie Maclean, Jersey, trainer'.

She just kept popping up into his life.

He googled some more, and a row of images appeared. He saw Georgie halfway along them and clicked to enlarge it. An instant later she appeared full screen. In a slim-fitting tracksuit. Red hair pinned up. Challenging smile on her face.

Beneath was the legend:

BE FIT FOR PURPOSE! BEL ROYAL HOTEL GYM – FREE ASSESSMENT SESSION – ONE-TO-ONE OR GROUP CLASSES, CALL OR EMAIL FOR DETAILS.

And suddenly his day felt a whole lot better. He felt *fit for purpose*!

As he waltzed into the meeting room, one floor down, he had a smile on his face, despite the seriousness of the meeting. In a conference call with a cytopathologist from the Cervical Cancer Screening Centre in Sheffield, they would be discussing the management of three Jersey women with cervical pre-cancer or cancer.

Two fellow obstetrician/gynaecologists were attending, two pathologists and a medical student.

'You're looking very sunny this morning, Marcus,' fellow obstetrician Kath Clow said. 'What was that delicious white wine you served us up last week?'

'It was a white Burgundy – Meursault. I get it from that rather splendid wine cellar over in Gorey. How was your weekend?'

'Good, thanks. Saturday was mostly taken up by Charlie – he was playing in a rugby match, so I had to be the dutiful cheering parent on the touchline. Then Sunday I was the taxi service to take him to his best friend's house for a party and fetch him later – typical that they live on the furthest point of the island from us!'

Marcus was aware she doted on the boy, her only child, and his godson. 'The joys of parenthood, right?' He raised his eyebrows.

Kath grinned back. 'Yep.'

'I can't believe my little blue-eyed godson is nine now!' Marcus said.

'Ten in February.'

The meeting started and for the next half-hour Marcus barely absorbed a single word spoken. He was elsewhere. Thinking about his running. How he could get fit quick.

Thinking about Georgie Maclean.

Looking surreptitiously again at his phone, below the tabletop. At her photos. He'd cropped and saved his favourite from the dinner party, in which she was smiling at him.

He was looking at that now. The way she was smiling at him excited him. He knew it was wrong, but he was increasingly craving her. She was under his skin. God, how he wished he was under her skin – no, not under – inside. He felt his cock growing at the thought.

He had a choice, he knew that. He could stop. He should stop.

These things rarely had happy endings. And there were so many obstacles on the way. Claire, their kids, Roger, Georgie's pregnancy. Why couldn't he just knock this on the head?

But Georgie wanted it too. He could tell from the looks she'd given him that she was up for it. Tired of her pilot? Craving excitement? He felt it. The electricity she had radiated.

However hard he tried to put her out of his mind, she came back into it even more strongly. And with even fewer clothes on.

18

Monday 17 December

Two thirty on Monday afternoon, the time Roger always joked – cheesily, but it made Georgie smile – was 'dentist time'. *Toof hurty. Geddit?* Georgie perched, nervously and awkwardly, on a hard chair in the waiting room of the Little Grove Medical Centre, along with a mother with a crying child and several other, mostly elderly, patients who sat in rigid silence, reading magazines or watching *Countdown* on the television screen on the wall in front of them, waiting for their names to be called.

It felt like they were all actors in a stage set, seated motionless as the curtain rose, waiting for their cues.

She tried to focus on an article in a fancy publication called *Lux* she had picked up from the table, on lifestyle and interior design, but all she could think about was what the midwife was going to tell her. She was too anxious to focus, reflecting on the warning her GP, Dr Doyle, had given her last week about pregnancy at her age. She faced, he had told her, what seemed to be a whole minefield of risks. But he had reassured her, too, not to worry.

How could she not worry?

Her dream had finally come true, but at her age she knew there was so much that could go wrong.

After an eternity she heard her name on the tannoy.

'Georgina Maclean for Midwife Fletcher.'

Midwife Fletcher? Wasn't Fletcher the name of the actress who played the terrifying Nurse Ratched in the movie *One Flew Over the Cuckoo's Nest?*

She closed the magazine, jumped up and walked along the corridor, passing several closed doors before she reached the one labelled with the name LOUISE FLETCHER.

The same first name, too!

She knocked and heard a woman's voice. 'Come in!'

The short, plump, dark-haired woman in her early thirties was as far from Nurse Ratched as could be. She greeted Georgie with a warm smile, instantly putting her at ease, and ushered her to a chair in the tiny room. Georgie noticed the notepad on the clipboard on her desk, with her own name typed in large letters at the top and a whole page of handwriting beneath.

'So – Georgina – is it OK if I call you that?'

'Georgie's fine.'

'Georgie, good! I'm Louise. So, how are you feeling?'

'I don't know. Nervous, I guess. Worried.'

Louise Fletcher smiled. 'Don't be, this is a very exciting time in your life, embrace it!'

'Well, I'd like to – but—'

'Tell me your concerns?'

'I guess, my age.'

'There are plenty of women considerably older than you who have given birth to bonny, healthy babies. Of course, there are risks, but there are risks at every age, so let's take the positives, shall we?'

Georgie smiled. 'Thank you.'

The midwife looked at her notes for some seconds, then back at her. 'You're forty-one?'

She nodded. 'Guess I'm in the last-chance saloon.'

'I wouldn't put it quite like that, you've a few more years yet, but yes, forty-one is approaching the upper age for conceiving. I don't want to worry you, but I'd be wrong not to warn you that statistically the risk of pregnancy complications does rise exponentially after the age of thirty-five.'

'What kinds of complications?'

'Well, I don't want to give you a rose garden. You need to be aware that you do risk one or more problems: miscarriage, hypertension, pre-eclampsia and gestational diabetes. And the odds of genetic problems also hike up because of your maternal age.'

'Great!' Georgie said with a bitter twinge in her voice that she couldn't help. 'I feel like – I don't know . . .'

'Most people at your age have completely healthy babies, but I wouldn't be doing my job if I didn't point out the risks,' Louise Fletcher said.

'There are tests that can be done, right?'

'Indeed, but none are completely one hundred per cent. There's a basic twelve-week series of tests they do at the hospital, which include a dating scan and blood test. The blood test will look for chromosome 21, which is Down's syndrome, as well as chromosome 18 – Edwards syndrome – and chromosome 13, Patau syndrome, which causes abnormal morphology mainly incompatible with life. These tests are about 85 per cent accurate. But if you wanted to spend the money, you could go private and have a Harmony test that costs £350. In that there is 99 per cent accuracy in the risk assessment of those three chromosomes.'

'I'll go for the Harmony,' she said.

Fletcher nodded, approvingly. 'I think that's sensible.' She handed Georgie a green-and-white A4-sized booklet headed 'Pregnancy Notes'. 'This is your pregnancy planner. We'll just fill in some details, then you'll need to take this with you to every appointment.'

Georgie flipped through a few pages. It appeared pretty thorough.

'Have you given any thought to where you might like the birth to take place?'

She shook her head. 'No, none. I'm still kind of – in – sort of shock that it's actually real. I mean – like – wonderful shock. I'd almost given up all hope of ever having a child.'

For the next twenty minutes, the midwife noted down a detailed medical history of Georgie, as well as taking blood and urine samples and her blood pressure.

When those were done, she asked Georgie about her current mental state. She assured the nurse she was fine. Her biggest concern was about her business – how long could she go on running, training clients and exercising with them?

Right through to the last few weeks of pregnancy, the woman assured her, so long as she had no other obstetric problems and felt up to it. She questioned Georgie about the date of the start of her last period, in order to calculate the due date, then said, 'I estimate that you are currently eleven weeks into your first trimester. For someone of your age, we like to closely monitor your baby's growth and your blood pressure. If there are no other problems, I hope you will go into spontaneous labour around your due date.'

The midwife consulted a chart. 'So, the due date is Monday, July 22nd.' She smiled. 'What a perfect day – remember that poem, "Monday's child is fair of face"?'

'I'll take that!'

The midwife looked serious again. 'So, given your age and your medical history, I think it would be sensible to refer you to an obstetrician, in addition to the normal regular antenatal clinics, to do your first trimester scan. I'd be present for that, also.'

'Sure, I'll be completely guided by you,' Georgie replied.

'The consultant I advise is the top man on the island. He's very thorough. He delivered both of our children, which tells you what I think of him!'

'That's a pretty good recommendation.'

'His name's Mr Valentine, I'll—'

'*Marcus Valentine?*' Georgie interrupted.

'Yes.' The midwife hesitated, looking at her strangely. 'Is there a problem?'

'Well, yes.' She hesitated, wondering if she was being silly. 'I've actually met him socially – and it just feels a bit weird to have him as my obstetrician.'

The midwife absorbed this for some moments. 'Well, he is a

very fine consultant and his patients worship him. To be honest, you'll get to know any obstetrician pretty well!' She smiled.

Georgie laughed. 'Funny, my fiancé said the same thing!'

'Ha! It's no problem, Georgie, if you want someone different. There's a lovely lady consultant obstetrician who I think you'd get on with very well. She's a keen runner, as you are. She does triathlons – I think you two will really hit it off. She's called Kath Clow – how does she sound?'

'Oh yes, I know, I know, Kath and I are friends, and I was going to suggest her. That's great! I feel very safe in her hands.'

19

Twins!

Two new little mites to bring into the world. To add to all the others in the Postnatal ward, with their exhausted mothers and fretting fathers. New life. In his hands – what an amazing thing, what a gift! Brand-new parents as yet unable to comprehend how these little bundles of joy would change their lives forever. Beautiful!

He remembered one young mother lying in bed holding her baby, just a few days after a traumatic birth, looking up at him and saying, 'Strange to think this tiny thing will one day be pushing me around in a wheelchair.'

Everyone reacted differently to their first experience of parenthood, Marcus Valentine thought, as he stood in the small locker room with his registrar, a short-arse in his late twenties called Barnaby Cardigan, who always rubbed him up the wrong way, and a Romanian medical student, Robert Resmes, a lightly bearded, intense young man, who was currently shadowing him before moving on to Kath Clow. Marcus felt Resmes would one day make a fine doctor.

'Don't you think a caesarean makes it too easy for a pregnant woman?' Cardigan asked him, suddenly. He was constantly asking questions, but half of them made Marcus feel the man was interrogating him in the hope of tripping him up.

'Not when there's a breech birth, no. Back in the old days that could be fatal.'

'But surely that's the point?' Cardigan pressed. 'Natural selection? Eventually that mother will be edited out of the gene pool.'

Pulling on blue sterile trousers, wriggling into a smock and shoving his feet into his white clogs, Marcus gave him a withering look. 'Barnaby, I didn't take the Hippocratic Oath out of allegiance to the sodding gene pool. I went into medicine to help people. If you don't get that, then you're in the wrong bloody profession.'

He popped a mint into his mouth and donned his sterile cap, festively printed with snowy scenes and Santa Claus with his reindeer – one of a bunch of identical ones he wore every December to add a festive touch, to put a smile on his patients' faces. They all seemed to notice, and it was a good icebreaker.

Resmes had told Marcus earlier that he was minded to specialize in obstetrics because he liked the idea of dealing with mostly happy, excited patients. 'Is that what you feel too, Mr Valentine?' Resmes had asked him.

'Babies, yeah, I love 'em!'

As he made his way to the operating theatre, followed by the two men, he was thinking, as he did so often, *Why indeed am I an obstetrician?*

In the past, he'd always known the answer – before he'd had children of his own. The excitement of seeing new life full of hope and expectation. He loved the parents treating him like a god. He loved that feeling most of all. Playing God. But it was more than that, wasn't it? If he dared to be truly honest with himself, wasn't it about those feelings of intimacy with women? Being allowed to see what in his mind was the holy grail of femininity; to experience the touch, the smell. The smell of . . .

Power.

But sometimes he struggled with his conscience when he saw happy couples, the wife pregnant to bursting. Was tempted to warn them, to tell them about the changes his own children had inflicted on his life. *Do you really want to know what lies ahead for you?*

He entered the busy theatre to join the team similarly gowned to himself, with plain blue or green gauze caps, as well as the nervous, gowned-up father in the far corner. His patient, a very nice Irish woman, was seated upright on a white cloth spread over the operating table, her long dark hair hanging loose. The anaesthetist was giving her a spinal block, holding a hypodermic through a large area marked out within a sterile clear plastic sheet covering part of her back.

Marcus glanced up at the four clocks on the wall. The first, on the left, an analogue clock, was running slow, which irritated him. Alongside it were two digital clocks showing zero and an analogue timer, also showing zero. He went over to a trainee paediatric nurse, a young Scottish girl who was chatting to a colleague, and said to her, 'Please could you get a technician here quickly, to adjust that clock before we start.'

She looked up at the wall. 'It's only a couple of minutes out, sir, I think,' she replied. 'That's pretty much the right time.'

The change in his demeanour startled her. 'It's a couple of minutes out but I'd really prefer it on time,' he snapped and guided her towards the deserted scrub area.

He peered at her name tag. 'Annie, right?'

She nodded.

'You're at nursing college?'

'Southampton University.'

'You want to be a paediatric nurse?'

'Yes, yes I do.'

He smiled and she lightened up, for an instant, hopeful the moment was over.

He said, calmly, 'You want to go into one of the most critical areas of nursing, yet you don't mind that a clock is running nearly three minutes slow? Young lady, in an operating theatre, ten seconds can be the difference between life and death.' He leaned forward. 'If you want to be in my operating theatre, in my Obstetrics department, in my hospital, *timing is everything*. Do you understand, have we got this?'

She nodded.

'Now can you go and get a technician? Knife to skin will happen as soon as the time on that clock is correct and not one second before.'

As she hurried out of the room, he looked at the list on the wallchart, doing the calculations for each stage. Forty-five minutes start to finish. Across the room sat the nervous father-to-be. Marcus gave him a friendly nod, secretly thinking, *Good luck, mate.*

Then he looked back at the chart.

ITT – *into theatre*

KTS – *knife to skin*

KTU – *knife to uterus*

TOB – *TW1* – *time of birth of twin number one*

TOB – *TW2* – *time of birth of twin number two*

SEX – *TW1*

SEX – *TW2*

PLACENTA

He went through into the sink annex, where he rigorously washed and dried his hands, before a scrub nurse helped him into his gloves.

Back in the main area of the theatre his patient was now on her back, her legs encased in white stockings, the rest of her body, apart from her naked, swollen belly, covered in white sheets. A nurse was talking to her, reassuring her, while a technician, who had just corrected the clock, was now adjusting the overhead lamps. A blue plastic sheet was raised in front of her face, enabling her husband, seated behind her, to see and talk to her, but blocking out his view of her body and the brutal invasion of it that was shortly to take place.

A nurse swabbed the distended belly with antiseptic, then green drapes with a window were laid across. Music suddenly boomed through the speakers. The Eagles, 'Peaceful Easy Feeling'.

Marcus, who always had music playing during his operations, turned to his registrar in anger. 'Barnaby, who chose this?'

Cardigan pointed a discreet gloved finger at the patient's husband. 'He did, the father.'

Lowering his voice to a whisper, Marcus said, 'I need the right music, are you with me? Is there any Van Morrison?'

'But the Eagles is what he specifically requested, Marcus. What do you want me to tell the father? He's been very particular about their playlist for the birth.'

'Tell him that the moment I pull those little brats out of her womb, the music will have gone out of his life forever!'

Seeing Cardigan's shocked face, Marcus said, 'That's the truth, you'll understand one day. Get over it.' Then he smiled. 'But the poor sod wants the Eagles so, hey, the Eagles it is. Let's go!'

20

George Ezra's 'Shotgun' boomed through the ceiling speakers in the gym. This was currently Georgie's favourite feel-good track on her playlist for when she was training clients, and for a few seconds the lyrics distracted her from her work.

There's a mountain top . . .

The mountain she was now climbing with her baby inside her.

The festive lights she'd put up around the gym, and the small artificial Christmas tree she'd bought, took away a little of the sterile and lonely atmosphere of the place. State-of-the-art Life Fitness and Octane equipment sat all around silently. Treadmills, cross-trainers, multigyms, mats, kettlebells, weights, leg presses.

She was feeling light-headed, as the midwife had warned her she might. And she was craving more pickled onions – she'd bought several jars earlier today from a farm shop. Roger had texted her to say he was cooking a Moroccan dish for their evening meal. She hadn't the heart to tell him that, actually, all she wanted tonight was a cheese and pickle sandwich. All her tastes in food had changed, quite suddenly.

She focused back on her client, her last of the evening. The clock on the wall was showing 7.20 p.m. Ten minutes to go. 'How's your heart rate?'

Michael Longcrane was a banker in his mid-sixties and was determined to defy his age. Married to his third or perhaps fourth wife, he regularly dropped unsubtle hints to Georgie that fidelity wasn't his thing. He worked every set of exercises with an enthusiasm she seldom saw in someone twenty years his junior. She sensed in him a desperation and that worried her – she was scared he might drop dead on her at any moment. Among the gym's First Aid equipment was a defibrillator, which fortunately she'd never had to use – so far.

Glancing at his Fitbit he announced with pride, 'One hundred and sixty-three.'

That heart rate was high for his age bracket, she worried. 'Do you want to rest for a few moments?'

'No way. Go for it!'

'OK, final set for the last ten minutes of our session, but we'll go gently.' She zeroed the middle of the three large glass egg timers with green sand that she had fixed to the wall. The first timer was one minute, the second three minutes and the third, five. 'Three minutes rowing, three minutes cycling and finish with three minutes on the cross-trainer to cool down. OK?'

'Rock and roll!'

She set him an easy target, which he ignored, totally going for it. He heaved himself backwards and forwards on the rower, grunting and sweating, his face contorted into a mask of grim determination. Georgie's eyes moved from his face to the last few grains of green sand falling down the egg timer, her back to the row of dark windows overlooking the car park, and she took a bite of an energy bar.

'Good!' she said. 'Well done! A big improvement!'

'You think so?' he gasped, his face puce.

'I really do! Now on to the next!'

She waited for him to settle on the static bike, then flipped the egg timer to the start position. 'OK, three minutes, your target is fifteen miles an hour!'

He began pedalling furiously and she watched the display, anxiously, as it passed 15 mph to 20, then peaked at 23 before dropping back to 19.

Other than this gym, the rest of the two-storey building, with rooms spread along the hilltop, was in complete darkness and would remain so, apart from the caretaker's office, and visits from various maintenance people, until next April. The caretaker, Edouardo Goncalves, a Portuguese national from Madeira, was a quiet man, about forty years old, who glided around the property in what appeared to be his only pair of trousers, dirty, and frayed at the bottom as they were too long for him. He seemed to pop up whenever she least expected him to. Tom Vautier, the owner of the hotel, had given Georgie a master key, and in exchange for the deal on the gym had appointed her manager de facto for this period – her only duty being to work with Edouardo to make a periodic check of the place to ensure there were no leaks from burst pipes or damage from vandals.

She found it creepy enough in daylight, when she carried out an occasional check on each of the rooms. And she didn't have the inclination to check any part of the building at night, although sometimes she had to.

She intended to switch off the lights, lock the door and hightail it out of the place once Longcrane had left.

As he started on his final set of exercises she picked up her phone and saw she had a text from Roger.

In Co-op, foraging. Anything you need? Love you. xx

Keeping an eye on her client, she replied.

Pickled onions, mature cheddar and you! xx

She put the phone back down, smiling.

21

Tuesday 18 December

Marcus Valentine, in a tracksuit, gloves and beanie, had decided to run over to take a look at the open gym sessions Georgie Maclean had told him about, and perhaps join in. He stood in the blustery wind outside the brightly lit gym, peering through a window, invisible in the darkness to anyone looking out. Hesitant about interrupting the session in progress but wondering how it would look to her if she spotted him.

He could feel the chill of the wind and his sweat, from his exertion, was cold against his skin, but he didn't care. He was fascinated by the egg timers, wondering why she used such a primitive device rather than her phone's stopwatch. Maybe so her clients could race against something visual?

The man moved on to the cross-trainer, his exertion slower now as the sand trickled through the glass. Finally, after some stretches, he was done. He nodded his thanks, gulped down a glass of water and pulled on a fleece top. They appeared for a moment to be checking their phones, then the man disappeared through a door at the rear of the gym.

Georgie, her outfit showing every inch of her very fit body, walked around, kneeling and switching off the Christmas lights. Marcus liked her hair clipped up the way she had it, with a short bob of a ponytail at the back.

A door was opening. Her client was coming out.

This was his opportunity to go in and say hello. But something held him back. The time wasn't right, he was all sweaty, this wasn't the moment. When he next saw her, he wanted to impress her. He scurried into the shrubbery at the rear of the car park, concealing himself behind a mature leylandii. Ridiculous, he knew, he just prayed no one saw him. How could he explain this away if anyone did, he wondered? The man, stooping slightly, walked a short distance across the car park, past a row of wheelie bins and a skip full of rubble, got into his car and started it, but then just sat there for an age, exhaust rumbling, farting around with his phone before driving away.

Georgie, this place is really creepy at night, you're pretty brave being here all alone. You deserve better than this, your fiancé shouldn't be making you work so hard in your condition. I'll have to mention it to him next time I see him.

As he stood there looking at her, he couldn't help thinking again how much she reminded him of Lynette. He couldn't help but stare.

And think.

What might have been.

What might be.

You and me and your little foetus, just a few centimetres of it now.

22

'About three centimetres, I'm estimating this little Jersey bean,' Kath Clow said brightly in her Yorkshire accent, as Georgie Maclean reclined on the couch in the hospital consulting room. The obstetrician, a slim, energetic and highly positive lady in her early forties, moved the Doppler sensor around the gelled area of her friend's exposed tummy. There was a steady roaring sound through the speaker, with the fast *wuff-wuff-wuff-wuff-wuff* of the heartbeat and a sudden scratching noise.

'This is so exciting, Georgie. I couldn't be happier for you both, and you have a very lively baby!'

'We do?'

'Yep, you won't feel it yet but there's quite a bit of movement.'

The midwife, also seated in the room, gave Georgie a reassuring smile. Roger sat on the chair beside Kath's desk, looking happy and worried in equal amounts.

'Good heartbeat – about a hundred and fifty,' Dr Clow announced.

The midwife handed Georgie a printout of the scan. She and Roger looked at it excitedly.

'Amazing such a tiny creature can already be making such a noise!' Georgie said.

Kath smiled at her again, then switched off the equipment. 'OK, you can sit back down now.'

Kath returned to her desk and, for the second time, went carefully through Georgie's pregnancy notes booklet. 'When did you last have your blood pressure taken?'

'On Monday, in my room,' the midwife answered, '125 over 74.'

Kath nodded. 'Let's take it again.'

This time it was 141 over 86.

Georgie knew blood pressure measures, and 141 was heading into the high range. Hypertension. 'Is that a concern?' she asked and noticed Roger's worried expression.

Kath did not seem too fussed and answered reassuringly. 'Sometimes just being in a doctor's room raises people's blood pressure and even though we know each other well enough it can still have an impact just being in here.' She turned to the midwife. 'If you could take it again in a week's time, we'll monitor it closely.'

'I will do.'

Clow peered at Georgie's notes on her screen. 'So just over eighteen months ago you had a routine Pap cervical smear which indicated abnormalities. It was followed by a colposcopy and biopsy which just showed high-risk HPV change and stage-1 pre-cancer and was to be repeated in a year. Was that done?'

'Yes, and it showed the same as previously,' Georgie said.

The obstetrician nodded. 'I can see that. Good. But, I have to say this, and I don't want it to feel awkward between us as friends, if you get any signs of vaginal bleeding – after intercourse or at any other time – I want you to come and see me straight away.'

'I will. But you're not worried?'

She shook her head and smiled. 'No, you know I'd be the first to tell you if I was. I'm sure you are absolutely fine! And don't panic if you do have any bleeding, there are plenty of possible causes should that happen.'

Georgie pulled up her jeans, buckled the belt and sat back down next to her fiancé. Roger took her hand and squeezed it, reassuringly. 'Amazing to hear the baby's heartbeat!' she said.

'Incredible!' Roger agreed.

'So, a few more questions to run through and although I think I may know some of the answers let's just make sure we've covered everything. Any nausea or vomiting in this first trimester?'

'Some nausea, but no vomiting.' Georgie glanced at Roger. 'Apparently I've started snoring a bit.'

'A bit?' Roger said, good-naturedly. 'Like someone trying to play a trumpet, I'd say.'

'Yes, well, I'm afraid pregnancy can affect mucus levels in the nasal passages. That will pass. Are you eating regularly?'

'Yes, I'm grazing a lot – every hour or two – although my taste in food has changed.'

'That's normal. It will revert. And good you're grazing, much better than loading up with big meals as you might have done previously. You don't smoke. Unless you've suddenly taken it up?'

'No.'

'And you are taking vitamin supplements?'

'Yes.'

'I know you're exercising and taking care of that side of things and there's really no harm in continuing with that level of exercise until it becomes uncomfortable. I know you've told me that you are wanting a vaginal birth. I'd recommend some antenatal hypno-therapy classes, to help you relax when the time comes.'

'OK.'

The obstetrician turned to her screen and tapped her keyboard, making some more notes for a brief while, before turning back to look at both Georgie and Roger. 'Right, we are making a plan. I'd like to see you back here again towards the end of your second trimester, at twenty-eight weeks. At that appointment I'll check your cervix with a colposcopy to ensure it's still only stage-1 pre-cancerous changes. Meanwhile you'll be seeing the midwife on a regular basis. And we'll be catching up soon anyhow!' She smiled at Georgie.

'Now you don't want to know the sex of your baby and that is absolutely fine. You didn't elect to know from the Harmony test, but it's possible we may be able to tell you during your second trimester, at around twenty weeks, if you change your minds. Sometimes it's very obvious on the scan but we can never tell one hundred per cent. If you want to reconsider at any time, just let me know.'

Georgie looked at Roger then back at Kath. 'What do you recommend in your experience?'

'Well, it's such a personal choice, Georgie. Knowing helps you plan, for instance the colour of your baby's room, clothes, things like that. And, of course, the name.'

'We'll have a chat and let you know.'

'What we can do is put it in a sealed envelope and give it to you. Did you know this? Then if you change your minds at any time, you can open it and find out, with reasonable certainty. Also, Roger, I think you might find it helpful to attend our Expectant Fathers programme. I'll grab you a brochure on it. There are also a number of websites you can both take a look at – one's called What To Expect. And ask me anything whenever you want, guys – you know I'm here on a professional basis but I'm always on the end of the phone for you.'

A few minutes later, hugging Kath Clow and thanking the midwife profusely, Roger held the door and Georgie walked out into the corridor.

As the two of them headed towards the exit, Marcus Valentine, in blue scrubs, happened to see them from the far end of the corridor. Unable to stop himself, he followed them, at a safe distance, past a hand sanitizer, a noticeboard and then the antenatal nursing station, where a row of thank-you cards hung on a rail outside.

The happy couple stopped at the lift. He watched from a distance as they looked lovingly into each other's eyes. Holding hands. Georgie whispered something to him, and Roger kissed her.

They looked so excited. It reminded him of when he and Claire were first expecting. Happy times. Georgie was really – as they say – blooming. Pregnancy suited her. Roger was such a lucky man.

The thought was eating Marcus up inside.

23

Wednesday 19 December

As the lift doors closed, Marcus Valentine chided himself.

Got to stop this. Now.

Ridiculous!

Snap out of it!

He'd seen what affairs had done to his parents' marriage and remembered the vow he'd made long ago not to be like them.

Don't let history repeat itself. Appreciate what you have. A wife and three young children who all need you. Now is not the time for having thoughts about straying. Just think of the grief if it happened. This could fuck up your whole career. He reminded himself of the mantra, *Success is not getting what you want – it is wanting what you have.*

Putting Georgie Maclean out of his mind, he focused on his busy day ahead in theatre. First up was a very charming Jersey lady, the mother of a three-year-old boy he'd delivered by C-section. It had been her first child and she was planning to have a large family, she'd told him. But the unfortunate woman had been suffering ever since from constant vaginal bleeding due to severe endometriosis, and a hysterectomy was the only real solution. He felt for her.

Life's a bitch.

After Marina was an induction for another lady suffering acute symptoms of pre-eclampsia. And waiting in the wings was a woman in her early thirties with a potential breech birth. He would try to turn the foetus to head-first by external cephalic version if still showing breech on scan. But if that did not work, she would also require a caesarean.

It was a short list. If there were no complications.

Which might see him getting home in daylight. In time to go for a run. A nice early run, maybe swinging by the gym and catching a glimpse of Georgie again, and finally going in this time.

Or perhaps just look up her activity on RunMaster? And check out the results of the race he missed last night on the running club page.

The thought put him in such a good mood that he didn't challenge the operating theatre team's choice of heavy metal for today – music he normally avoided.

Riding on razor's edge . . .

Holding out his hands for the scrub nurse he thought about Georgie again. *You and me? Riding on a razor's edge?*

24

Three hours later, after he had finished in theatre and changed back into his consultant's uniform of suit, shirt and tie, ID card hung from a red cord around his neck, Marcus was ravenous. It was 3 p.m. He bought a cheese and ham sandwich, a Twix and a bottle of water from the cafeteria counter and carried them up to his office. There was a pile of letters on his desk which his assistant, Eileen, had put there for him to sign.

Carefully placing his jacket on a hanger behind the door, he moved the pile out of his way, then began working on the plastic wrapping of his sandwich. He put the sandwich on a plate and cut it into quarters. As he did so he was interrupted by his registrar wanting advice on a patient, a woman who was presenting with problems. She and her partner had been trying to conceive through IVF for five years, and she was now twenty-one weeks pregnant with triplets. Marcus looked at her notes then agreed to come and see her in half an hour in the Antenatal ward.

'I hope you don't mind me bothering you while you're having your lunch,' Cardigan went on, irritating Marcus, who just wanted to get on with his sandwich. 'Isn't that Resmes a bit intense with his patients? He's always got his head in his books and he hardly speaks to me, do you find that, too? I'm starting to get a complex!'

'He's fine with me, and that's the second time you've mentioned it. What have you got against him?' Marcus asked.

'Oh, nothing, but he always listens to you, yet it's like he doesn't hear or respect me. Perhaps it's just a clash of personality. And he doesn't find my chart funny.'

They both walked over to the other side of the office. Fixed to one wall, high up, was a rack of shelves containing a neatly stacked row of folders and essential medical reference books. On another wall was a whiteboard on which several notices were attached by coloured magnets. Below these were fixed a collection of thank-you cards from happy patients.

To their right was a graph that Cardigan had obtained from a New York psychiatrist who had given a paper on parenthood at a conference he'd attended a few years ago. It charted the moment a couple first met, rising in steep increments as they fell in love, peaking the day they got married. The line remained at the top of the happiness level right through that first period of their married life, until their first child was born.

Whereupon it plunged down to the very bottom. And remained there before eventually rising sharply again at the twenty-year mark.

The psychiatrist had gaily said that happiness went out of couples' lives the moment their first child was born and didn't return until the day that child – and any subsequent children – left home. There would of course be spikes in the interim, every time the child looked into its mother's or father's eyes and said, *I love you, Mummy/Daddy*. At which moment the parents would forget all the shit their lives had become and go completely gooey-eyed. Cynical, he knew, but Cardigan loved the irony of it. And, just occasionally, he took pleasure in pointing it out to expectant parents. He'd pinned this copy up on Marcus's wall as a gift. And Marcus did actually find it quite funny.

Cardigan left and Marcus finished his lunch. He wheeled his chair back up to his desk and placed his long fingers – his 'pianist's fingers' as his mother had often told him, through a haze of alcohol – on his keyboard, logging on to his computer. There were several emails which needed immediate responses. He dealt with them.

Then he hesitated.

Pondering. Hesitating again.

Should I be doing this?

The boss inside his head said, *Yes, you should! You have to, they are your friends.*

The boss that sometimes took control, whether he liked it or not.

But he was thinking, wary of leaving an audit trail. Some while ago, he'd seen Kath Clow entering her password and he'd chided her for using her date of birth instead of something more secure. He wondered if she had changed it – with luck, she would have forgotten.

She had.

He entered it and was in. It took him only a matter of seconds to find her file on Georgina Maclean. He read Georgie's estimated due date. Her blood pressures. The supplements she was on. And all the rest of her notes.

Just looking after your welfare, guys. Two heads are better than one!

Thoughts went through his mind. All kinds of thoughts.

He told himself to stop. Enough. Log out. Forget it. Let it go.

But the boss chided him. Taunted him.

You can't, Marcus, can you?

25

After leaving the hospital, Roger hurried off to the airport for a flying lesson that had been booked with him for the last hour of full daylight. Georgie headed to the gym, where she had wall-to-wall clients for the next four hours. She felt so excited, she wanted to share the news with all of them.

So far, she and Roger had only told their close family and friends, in case . . .

In case of the unspoken word. *Miscarriage.*

Kath Clow had told them today that many couples tended to keep it a secret until that first scan, but now if they wanted to shout about it from the rooftops, why not? There were still risks, of course, but those would diminish with every week of the second trimester.

And they would need to decide whether they wanted to know if it was a boy or girl. Maybe Kath was right, knowing it would enable them to make the right choices about the baby's room. As well as giving them time to focus on the name.

She liked the idea of the envelope and made a mental note to ask Kath for it.

Turning off the main road, she wound up the steep, narrow drive of the hotel. It was lined with tall shrubbery on either side and even on a bright day it felt dark and gloomy, more like the approach to a creepy cottage than to one of the island's popular tourist hotels.

Cresting the rise, there was a magnificent vista across the bay of St Aubin towards St Helier. And an unimpressive view of the rear car park of the hotel, with the wheelie bin storage shelter and a skip overflowing with building debris, which had sat there all winter so far, as if someone had forgotten it. But right now, she didn't care, she was in such a great mood. And hey, they would shortly be past 21 December, the shortest day, and it would begin, very gradually, getting lighter again in the evenings. Which would make this place feel slightly less desolate.

She let herself into the freezing gym, switched on the lights and heater, and then the music. Eminem's 'Till I Collapse' began pounding out of the ceiling speakers. Playfully, she flipped all three egg timers over – one minute, three and five – and went into the back room to change into her tracksuit and trainers. Then, with half an hour before her first client, she dutifully started her check of the guest rooms on that floor.

Opening door after door onto the rooms and suites, all with dreary maroon carpets, washed-out candlewick bedspreads and trouser presses awaiting their pensions, she tried to imagine under what circumstances she and Roger would stay here. And couldn't. It felt like such an old-fashioned seaside resort hotel, compared to so many really great ones the island offered. As she opened Room 211, she heard a cough and it startled her. She'd thought she was here on her own. She looked across in the gloom and saw the stick-thin figure of Edouardo standing in the doorway of the en-suite, staring at her.

'I didn't realize you were still here, Edouardo.'

'I leave now, Miss Georgina. You join me this weekend on jog round the island?' he asked, jokily, in his thick Portuguese accent.

'Same answer as always, Edouardo, big N-O, but thanks for the offer.'

'You fast! You know? You really fast last few runs. I see your times.'

'You've seen my times? How do you know my times?'

'I follow you.'

'You do?'

He held up his phone and tapped it. 'I follow your routes! You do always short, you should do long, like me. Ultramarathon!'

She gave him a slight forced smile. 'Great. But I'll stick to my shorter runs. What on earth do you think of for all those miles out there on your own? Over twenty miles some days, right?'

'I like be with nature, close to God. It give me time to sort the shit in my head.'

'Do you have a running partner to keep you company? Does your wife like running?'

'No partner, no wife, marriage doesn't work. Women change.'

'Well, that's quite a statement!'

Then, tapping his head, 'They tell me things.'

'Who tells you things?'

He gave a strange smile. 'They.'

Edouardo was weirding her out again, as he often did.

'OK, right, I better get on, maybe see you tomorrow,' she said. 'I've ten more rooms to check tonight.'

He was quite sweet, but Christ, he made her feel uneasy, she thought. As if being here in the dark wasn't eerie enough.

In the immediate post-war period of the 1950s, as life on Jersey had returned to normal after the harsh years of the German occupation, it had become again the UK's favourite – and classiest – beach holiday and honeymoon resort. Package holidays and cheap flights to the Costa Brava and elsewhere on continental Europe had changed all that in the 1960s, and Jersey had changed with it, becoming a major financial centre, its hotels forced to sharpen up to the standards expected by the international business community.

But it seemed to Georgie that this hotel was still locked back in a time warp. At least the gym had been modernized, and over this winter all the rooms were going to be updated – although there was little sign of it so far.

She was three-quarters of the way done before she saw through a rear window that her first client, a banker, was arriving, a few minutes late, at 5.05 p.m. Georgie had been intending to share the news of her pregnancy with her, as normally they got on really well and because, in honesty, she wanted to tell the world. But the woman was in a neurotic mood, launching into a monologue about the precociousness of one of her three young – and clearly spoiled – children, and a tirade about a teacher at her school who had totally confused her nine-year-old by trying to explain gender neutrality to her. She was going to kick open the headmaster's door tomorrow, she threatened darkly, and render the weedy little prat gender neutral himself.

Her next client, an architect who had been going through IVF with his wife for the past two years, arrived at a few minutes to six. Not the moment to share her news with him, either. Then she got an apologetic text from her regular 7 p.m., a woman who worked in financial services, who was stuck in a meeting and wasn't going to make it.

After the architect had left, the cancellation gave her the time to continue her dutiful weekly inspection of the remaining rooms. It was dark outside now, and despite having a powerful torch as back-up, and switching on every light, she found the long, dimly lit corridors and silent doors unnerving. Especially – ridiculously – the door of Room 237, the same number of the Overlook Hotel room in which, in *The Shining*, the slime-covered dead woman had climbed out of the bathtub. Here, it was one of the honeymoon suites.

She opened the door with her key card and heard a steady, echoing *plop . . . plop . . . plop . . .*

Like the dripping-wet woman in the film.

She hesitated, scared suddenly. Should she get Edouardo? But it was well past seven, he would have gone home by now. She snapped on the light and looked around the room, heart in her mouth.

God, I'm a bag of nerves!

She'd read in one of the books on motherhood that pregnancy caused heightened awareness – all part of your genetic programming to help protect your baby. Was that why she was so tense recently?

PLOP . . . PLOP . . . PLOP . . .

The sound was much louder now in the complete silence. Coming from the en-suite bathroom. She walked across, then stopped by the door, which was ajar.

PLOP . . . PLOP . . . PLOP . . .

Louder still. Definitely coming from in here. Plucking up courage, she pulled the door wide open, turned on the light and walked in. And immediately saw the problem. Large droplets of water falling onto the tiled floor from a bulge in the ceiling. A leak or a burst pipe in the roof space above.

She hurried along to Edouardo's office. The cluttered little room was in darkness – he'd gone for the day, as she had suspected. Pinned to a cork noticeboard on the wall was a list of numbers for tradespeople as well as after-hours emergency services. She dialled the one for plumbing and the woman who answered said she would have someone there within the hour.

She emailed Tom Vautier to alert him, then headed back down to the gym.

As she approached it, she could hear the Black Eyed Peas were playing, 'I Gotta Feeling'.

She had a feeling. But not a good one. Something was wrong.

The gym was in darkness. She had left the lights on. All of them.

She stopped. How could the lights be off? Had a fuse blown? But music was still on? Frowning, she switched on her torch and stepped forward, flashing the beam around the gym, at the bank of treadmills, the cross-trainers, the racks of weights.

Something moved. Out of the corner of her eye. A figure stepping forward from the darkness.

26

In the jigging light of her torch she saw a circus clown moving towards her, smiling through thick lipstick. He wore a pointed hat, polka-dot pantaloons and a painted face, and held a small dumb-bell in each hand.

She took a step back, trying to scream, but her voice came out in a muted yammer of terror.

Another step back.

'Miss Georgina, don't be afraid. Smile! I make you laugh!'

It sounded like Edouardo's voice.

She aimed the beam at his face, and he put his arms up to shield his eyes. 'Edouardo?'

'Yes, Miss Georgina, it's me, Edouardo!'

She lowered the beam a little. 'Jesus, you scared the hell out of me.'

Edouardo had a sideline as a children's entertainer for which he normally wore this clown outfit, although personally she had always found clowns sinister.

He raised his arms up and down, as if weightlifting. 'I clown in gym!' he said. 'I keep-fit clown! I try to make you happy!'

'By scaring me to death?'

'I want surprise you! I do runs for charity, in this suit. People love it! I want to surprise you tonight!'

'You did that, all right.'

She swung the beam to the wall, found the switches and turned all the lights back on.

'You not looking happy this week,' he said. 'I wanted to make you happy, to smile.' He sounded hurt, disappointed, the clumsy clown lips turning down in genuine dismay. 'I sorry if I scare you.'

She stared at him, at the slightly dishevelled (and, to be honest, smelly) clown suit, the white paste on his face, the big red smear of lipstick, and felt very sorry for this strange, lonely man. 'You did all this to make me smile?'

'I like to see people happy,' he replied, simply. Then made a big clown-looking-sad face.

A toilet flushed behind her, momentarily startling her.

'OK, thanks, Edouardo, that was a nice thought. But I think I have my client here.'

'Man in Mercedes? Five minutes ago, he in changing room.'

'Right. Well, you make a good clown.'

'Another time, I make you laugh, yes?'

'That would be nicer than frightening me! By the way, we have a leak in 237. I've called the plumber out but you might want to put some towels on the floor.'

Edouardo put the dumbbells down, bowed as if he were in the circus ring with a wave of the hand, and hurried out of the room. As she politely clapped, her client, Michael Longcrane, who was on his second weekly session, strode out of the changing-room door in yet another of the fancy designer tracksuits he wore. He gave her an odd look, as if questioning why she was applauding.

'The caretaker,' she said by way of explanation.

'You always applaud him?'

'You didn't see him when you came in? Dressed as a clown?'

'Nope.' He shook his head. 'But I've been dealing with clowns all day. Ready to rock and roll?'

'Yep! We'll start with a five-minute warm-up on the cross-trainer.'

Obediently, he clambered aboard the machine, carefully planting his feet, while Georgie zeroed the five-minute egg timer.

As he began striding and pushing with his hands, Georgie adjusted the level.

Longcrane was panting and grunting away. From where she stood, several feet away, she could smell alcohol on the man.

'Nice lunch today?' she asked.

'Yes. Green Island. Been there?'

'Roger and I love it.'

Continuing on the machine, he puffed his cheeks and exhaled. 'Oysters and grilled lobbies. Very nice.'

'Unless you were one of the oysters or lobsters,' she teased.

'I'm sure they all died happy in the knowledge they were appreciated,' he said.

'As did all the grapes in the wine you drank with them?'

'Totally.'

'Do you really think you're going to get fit arriving here after a boozy lunch?' She grinned to soften the critique, though wasn't sure she'd kept the irritation out of her voice. *And should you have driven here?* she nearly added.

He looked at her apologetically. 'I'm afraid I had clients over from England. Had to entertain them. They always insist on going there. And having a jar or two. I only had a small glass myself.'

'Right. We're going to do the ski machine, leg presses and then rowing. One-minute sessions each. And were they? Entertained?'

'They were, I think,' he puffed and walked gloomily across to the ski machine like a condemned man.

Georgie showed him the right grip, told him to flex his knees and start. She turned the first egg timer over. But he hesitated, then said, 'Nice outfit you're wearing, Georgie.'

'Thank you,' she replied, politely, watching the sand trickle down.

'Fancy a drink one night, after our session?'

'That would be very nice, I'm sure my fiancé would love to join us.'

Before he could reply, her phone rang. She grabbed it and looked at the display. It was Marcus Valentine. She was curious as to what he wanted but it was her rule not to answer any calls when she had clients, so she diverted it to voicemail.

27

Wednesday 19 December

Marcus Valentine, standing in his tracksuit in the darkness outside the gym, holding his phone in his hand, looked at Georgie through the window. He felt the stab of rejection in his belly. He started listening to her recorded message then killed the call.

Georgie, I was being polite, I wanted to ask if I could join in your session – as you invited me to at our dinner party. I didn't want to interrupt if it was a private one. That's why I called you.

Why did you just reject my call?

Rejection. He knew how it felt. He saw the disdain in her face, he was a nobody to her. A bitter taste in his mouth, he turned away and started to jog slowly back down to the promenade, heading to St Brelade's Bay and home. Thinking, thinking about Georgie. And then, an idea forming. Yes. He stopped in his tracks, turned swiftly on his heels and headed back up to the gym. Now was his moment. He paused to catch his breath a little, then rapped on the gym door and walked confidently in.

Georgie looked up, surprised, but a little relieved that she was no longer alone with her client. 'Oh hey, Marcus! You look ready for action!'

'Oh, I'm sorry, I can see you're busy. I did just try to call you.'

Looking innocent, she said, 'Oh, did you? Sorry, I'll be another ten minutes with my client, if you want to wait—'

Annoyed at her fib, he answered, holding her gaze. 'It's OK, I'll get my exercise on my run back home. I'll call you.'

She smiled back. 'Sure.'

After an awkward pause in which he seemed about to say something else then changed his mind, he left, fumbling clumsily with the door handle and nearly tripping over the step.

Longcrane gave her a knowing look. 'Sorry to be the gooseberry!'

'What?'

'With you and Mr Tubby.'

'Gooseberry?' she quizzed.

Gym Class Heroes' 'Cookie Jar' was booming out of the speakers. Longcrane mouthed the suggestive *'can't keep my hands out the cookie jar'* lyrics. He gave her a knowing stare.

'What?' she demanded.

'He has the hots for you.'

'No way.'

He raised his eyebrows.

28

'Marmalade?' Roger said, snuggled up beside Georgie on the sofa. 'Seriously? You've always hated marmalade!'

'I know, it's strange – it's like my taste buds have reversed – or become totally confused. Or my brain!'

'Obviously it's a boy!'

She gave him a sideways look. 'A boy? What makes you say that?'

He tapped his chest, grinning broadly. 'He's carrying my genetic memory and saying to you, "Mummy, gimme marmalade please".'

'Rubbish!' She punched him, playfully. 'And, smarty-pants, if our baby is lucky enough to have inherited all your clever genes and none of mine, how come he – or *she* – has turned me off your absolute favourite food?'

Something she and Roger loved doing was to have a takeaway Thai curry and watch something on Netflix. It had been their plan for tonight, but the idea of a Thai now revolted her.

'Touché! So that's what you want for supper tonight? Just marmalade?'

'On toast.'

'You had it for breakfast!'

And lunch, and tea, before my evening gym sessions, Georgie thought, but did not say.

'So you've gone off pickled onions?'

'Yechhh!'

'We've got six jars to eat that I bought you a few days ago. You asked me to get them.'

The thought of them made her feel ill. 'No way!'

'OK,' he said, handing her the remote. 'Find us something to watch and I'll go and make you marmalade on toast.'

'Really thick,' she said. 'The marmalade. You don't have to eat it too, my darling.'

'I'm not planning to. Nothing personal against marmalade. I'll find something in the freezer.'

She gripped his hand. 'You don't mind?'

He kissed her. 'My angel, our baby's telling you he – or she – wants marmalade on toast. You'll both have it!'

'Do you want to know?' she asked suddenly, holding on to his hand tightly.

'Know?'

'The gender. Sex. Of our baby.'

Roger shrugged. 'How do you feel about knowing? All we have to do is open the envelope Kath Clow's mailing us.'

Georgie stared through the huge curtainless window at the light of cars travelling along the road and the bitumen blackness of the sea in the bay beyond. How did she feel about it, she wondered? She wasn't sure, was the honest answer. She really wasn't sure.

The only thing she was sure of at this moment was how grateful she was to be pregnant. After all the years of desperation, it was finally happening, even though she was still very anxious and would be until they passed the twenty-week mark. She had looked up a few websites, as Kath had suggested. The one she'd found easiest to navigate, What To Expect, had told her that her hormones would settle down then.

'Kath said knowing the sex is helpful, in planning. We'll need to start thinking about names.'

'Maybe,' Georgie said. 'But it seems like tempting fate – to start coming up with names – you know – in case it goes . . . wrong.'

'At twenty weeks you'll be through the danger period.'

She nodded. 'I guess – I'm scared.'

'Scared?'

'All the years I've been trying for a baby. And now, suddenly, it's happening, it's real. But twelve weeks is very early, there's a lot that can still go wrong. I – I'm scared as hell.'

He hugged her and kissed her on the end of her nose. 'Nothing's going to go wrong. We're going to have the healthiest, most amazing baby ever in the whole world.'

She gave him a hug back. 'I think my hormones are all over the place. Yes, I want to believe that too, but – I don't know – I keep feeling some dark shadow lurking out there.'

'Shadow? What do you mean?'

She thought for a while before replying. 'I suppose because it just feels too good to be true, to be real. It may sound silly, but I used to have a terrible fear throughout my childhood every time something good happened, or was about to happen, that I would be stricken with a terrible disease and die.'

'Because of what happened to your sister?'

She closed her eyes. Thinking back to that terrible day her sister died. A week before her tenth birthday when her parents were going to take her and Liv to Disney World for her birthday treat. Liv was one year younger than her, and they were so close, best friends. Liv had gone to run an errand for their mother, cycling from their cottage to the local farm shop to get some eggs. A van driver, dazzled by the sun in his eyes, hadn't seen her and had killed her outright, hitting the rear of her bike, sending her hurtling, head-first, into a tree.

'Yes, I suppose. After that I always felt scared of looking forward to anything too much.'

Roger kissed her lightly on the cheek. 'You poor darling. I can't even begin to imagine how you felt afterwards. And then to lose your dad so suddenly, you're bound to feel like this.'

'It made me think that when anything good comes into my life, something will take it away. I know it sounds silly, but—' She fell silent. Feeling very vulnerable. More vulnerable than she could ever remember.

'Our baby is going to be fine. Nothing bad's going to happen. I'm going to make sure of that, OK?'

She nestled her head against his chest, feeling his warmth, his strength. 'You make me feel safe,' she murmured.

He caressed her hair, then her cheek. 'And you, me. You're a strong woman,' he replied. 'I'm right behind you and we'll do this together. I love you to bits.'

'I love you, too. I'm sorry this isn't normal me. I know it sounds irrational, but ever since I found out I'm pregnant I worry about you flying. I worry every time you go up in that fragile little machine.'

'Don't, it's a great aircraft with a terrific safety record. It has hooks in the sky!'

'It's not you, I know you are a great and careful pilot. It's the thought of – I don't know – one of your pupils doing something stupid.'

'I've got dual controls. If any of them did anything I wasn't happy with I'd take over immediately. You honestly don't need to worry.'

'I know I don't.' She gave him a pursed smile. 'But I can't help it.'

Lowering his hand to her tummy, he pulled up her jumper and T-shirt beneath, exposing the bare flesh of her belly, then he leaned forward and kissed it. 'Hi, Bump!' he said. 'Hi, marmalade-loving Bump!'

He sat back up, leaving her belly exposed, about to kiss her on the lips, then suddenly, stiffened.

'What?' Georgie said, sensing something wrong.

'Look!'

'At what?'

'Your tummy.'

She peered down. 'Am I getting fat?'

He shook his head, frowning. 'I just saw a green dot on your tummy.'

'A what?'

'A green dot. It was dancing around your belly.'

Assuming he was joking, she said, 'Oh, right, a green dot? So now we're not having a boy, we're having a Martian?'

He gave her an uneasy smile.

'Lucy always says that if we think Martians are little green men, what do the people on Mars call us? Oh, by the way, did I tell you she was totally blown away when I told her about our baby. She's already got a list of names!'

'I'm serious, darling. There was a green dot on your tummy.'

She turned to look at him and, for a fleeting second, saw a green dot on his forehead before it vanished. 'It's—'

'What?'

A shiver rippled through her.

She pulled herself free, jumped up and ran across to the window. Staring out into the night, she could see only the darkness of the sea out in the bay. The street lamps. Lights of cars.

Was someone out there with a laser pen? Some stupid kids pranking around?

Or someone with a proper laser, attacking them? Attacking her baby? A nutter?

She barely slept that night. Thinking. Wondering. Nightmare following nightmare.

In one dream she saw Liv pedalling away from the cottage on her sit-up-and-beg bicycle with a shopping basket in front of the handlebars. As she turned to wave goodbye, Georgie saw a green dot on Liv's forehead.

29

Wednesday 9 January

A green dot danced around the black-and-white image of a cervix, which was projected onto the large screen behind the speaker at the podium. In the lecture theatre of Southampton Hospital, the hospital's General Manager addressed the group of thirty-five consultant obstetricians from around the Channel Islands, as well as Southampton and local area medical centres, at their bi-monthly symposium.

The image of the cervix was replaced by another slide showing the name MARCUS VALENTINE, FRCOG.

'We are very fortunate today to have one of the most respected surgeons in his field, Jersey-based consultant gynae-oncologist, Mr Marcus Valentine, who is going to give us a talk on the latest advances in cervical cancer detection and surgical intervention.'

Following a ripple of applause, Valentine walked onto the stage, notes in hand. He shook the General Manager's hand, thanked him and stepped up to the podium. He checked the time on his watch and on the clock on the wall, laid his notes out in front of him on the wooden lectern and clicked the PowerPoint remote, bringing back the image of the cervix.

'Ladies and gentlemen, I'm going to talk to you about the prevention of cervical cancer by cervical screening for human papillomavirus – and also by not smoking, which can promote the development of cervical cancer. What you are seeing on the screen behind me is the tragic result of failure of early diagnosis. I'm able to show this photograph thanks to the kind permission of the lady's husband. Sadly, she died just seven months after this picture was taken. Her death was completely unnecessary and entirely preventable had there been earlier intervention following this scan in her first trimester.'

He pulled a laser pen from his breast pocket, switched it on and aimed it at the screen. An instant later a green dot jigged around the base of the cervix.

'This tiny shadow, barely visible to the naked eye, was the tumour in its early stage – and it was, understandably, missed by her consultant. By the time of her second trimester scan, the tumour had metastasized and spread to her lymph nodes, and pretty much everywhere in her body. Had it been diagnosed sooner, the foetus could have been aborted and preventative treatment commenced, which would almost certainly have saved her life.'

He took a sip of water and peered around the audience. Looking for one face in particular to see if she'd been able to get here despite all her hospital commitments. And saw her. Kath. She was looking attentive, of course. Good.

30

Thursday 10 January

Georgie awoke with a start, feeling a deep sense of dread. Panic. Her pillow was sodden. She was drenched in perspiration. The Christmas break with Roger's elderly parents, away from the island and her work, had had its stresses but she'd forgotten about her other anxieties. She'd forgotten too about the strange experience with the green light, but now it had surfaced again in her dream, darting about frenetically, making her feel dizzy with fear. She couldn't quite remember any of the details of her receding dream, but clearly she had been subconsciously fretting about her baby. This tiny creature growing inside her, totally oblivious of the world beyond. Utterly dependent on her. Was it OK? What was it doing – moving, sleeping, or just lying still, staring? Were babies' eyes shut or open in the womb?

She wished so much she could feel it move now, to be sure it was alive.

Roger was sound asleep beside her and she envied him that. The sleep of the innocent. From the moment he hit the pillow, he was out. Whereas since being pregnant she woke repeatedly through the night. Having to get up to pee. Worrying. Carrying the weight of the world on her shoulders.

The clock showed 2.15 a.m.

Slipping out of bed as quietly as she could, she tiptoed to the loo. When she returned, she felt wide awake.

And afraid.

Thinking back to that dark December night. Thinking more clearly.

116

Someone had been outside their home, in the darkness, with a laser pen.

Why on earth would someone be pointing a laser at her and Roger?

Someone trying to give her a message? A sign?

Who and why?

Someone trying to harm her baby?

Was it someone who knew where she worked? And lived? One of her clients? She just couldn't imagine any of them standing outside in the freezing cold and wind pointing a laser through their living-room window.

Was she overreacting? Perhaps it was just kids messing around, as she had thought at the time. Must have been.

She closed her eyes and tried to sleep. But she felt wired. The clock showed 2.45 a.m.; 3.05 a.m.; 3.17 a.m.; 3.22 a.m.

Sod it. She eased quietly out of bed again, picked up her phone and switched on the torch app, then unhooked her dressing gown from the door, pulled it on and slipped out of the room. She closed the door quietly behind her, went through into the living room, switched on the table lamps and sat on the sofa.

Staring at her phone.

She went through each of the social media apps where she had a presence. Twitter, Facebook, Instagram. Looking at all her followers and everyone who had engaged with her in the past few weeks, back before Christmas. There were a few strange ones, but nothing to indicate someone messing with a laser.

Craving marmalade again, she walked over to the open-plan kitchen, toying with making a piece of toast. But she was concerned that the smell might disturb Roger, and he had an early-morning flying lesson. Instead she buttered a piece of bread and slathered on a generous coating of her current favourite thick-cut marmalade and ate it ravenously at the breakfast bar.

When she had finished, she went back to the sofa, sat down and wondered whether she had overlooked an app. What had she missed?

She checked carefully through her apps – many of which she never opened and should delete, she knew. Then she opened RunMaster and began scrolling through her followers.

The app offered each follower the option to have their activities public or private. The majority of them opted for public, which meant she could compare her times over segments with theirs, according to male and female and age groups.

It worked better than counting sheep.

Roger found her sound asleep on the sofa, phone on the floor, when he came in to make himself breakfast a couple of hours later.

31

Friday 11 January

Marcus left the operating theatre shortly after 4.30 p.m., having carried out a complicated caesarean section. He was exhausted. And concerned. He had a feeling that the woman might have some ongoing internal bleeding.

He entered the changing room with Barnaby Cardigan and Robert Resmes. He told them both his worries, then wiggled out of his scrubs and dumped them into the bin. Resmes, as ever, fired question after question at them both. Marcus respected the Romanian medical student's thirst for knowledge, but he seemed to be irritating Cardigan again today with his persistence. Marcus was surprised how easily Cardigan was riled by Resmes's curiosity. He needed to keep an eye on them both to make sure this didn't escalate. Out of nowhere, the two young men suddenly started pushing at each other, shouting.

'Whoooa, whoa, what's going on? Leave it out, guys.' He stepped in between them, arms raised. 'You're not bloody children!'

The pair changed in sullen silence and departed, leaving Marcus alone. He stood in front of the mirror working at his tie until he had both the knot and the length of each end exactly right. Then, as he was tucking the short end inside the label, something occurred to him. He had not thought about Georgie Maclean for an hour at least. Maybe longer.

As soon as he was back in his office, he logged on to his computer and checked the Jersey Hospital Forum page on Facebook as he did most days. He saw that one of the ICU nurses was moaning

119

about the hospital canteen mayonnaise again. This made him smile. First-world problems. While he was on Facebook, he couldn't help having a sneaky peak at Georgie's page. There was a new post from her, along with a photograph.

Doing parkrun tomorrow. Here's my kit. 'All the gear and no idea!' Hey, only jesting! I'm going for a PB. Have you always fancied running a 5K? Why not challenge yourself? If you're looking for a running coach, even if you've never run, I can help you get there! PM me or visit my 'Fit For Purpose' website (link in bio).

The picture was a flat lay of her kit artistically laid out on bare wooden floorboards. Her trademark bright-pink and blue kit.

Marcus grinned. The parkrun! Of course. Saturday mornings. A big thing these days.

See you there!

32

She must be here somewhere. But where?

Marcus stood, freezing, in the driving rain and ferocious wind among the huge, noisy crowd of runners gathered, waiting, outside the Quennevais Sports Centre. He was looking around for Georgie in her kit. He ought to be able to spot her, except, he fretted, she may have decided to put some different gear on to cope with the elements. The weather was pretty much as bad as Jersey winter weather got.

Someone was calling out instructions through a loudspeaker, saying it was five minutes to the start. People were jogging on the spot to keep warm, chatting about races they had coming up; a woman on her phone was talking loudly above the hubbub to a friend, asking her where she was. Spectators were standing at the side, marshalled by volunteers in high-vis jackets.

Where are you, Georgie? Are you here or did you decide the weather was too shit to come today? I so hope not!

He bullied his way through the hundreds of people, all ages, past one woman with a barking labradoodle, then a man with two weird-looking mutts on leads. Looking. Looking.

Georgie?

Then, suddenly, she was right in front of him, facing away. He almost collided with her.

She was fiddling with her sports watch.

Before she saw him, he took a furtive photo of her on his phone. Then he stepped forward. 'Hi!' he said.

She didn't seem to hear him in all the surrounding noise.

He touched her shoulder. 'Georgie!' he said, louder. 'What a coincidence!'

She turned and looked at him, seeming to not recognize him for a moment.

He lifted his baseball cap. 'Marcus,' he said. 'Marcus Valentine!'

'Oh, hi. How are you? I thought you were going to call me,' she said, very matter-of-factly.

'I'm afraid I've been really busy,' he said. Petty, he knew, but he felt he'd scored a point.

'No worries, I'm pretty booked up at the moment anyhow.'

Marcus was hoping she'd be more enthusiastic than this.

'Great.' Then he said, 'Are you doing the parkrun too?' And instantly realized how dumb it must have sounded.

'No, I just love standing in the pissing rain and howling wind, ogling men's legs.' She gave him a smile and made a show of admiring his legs.

At least, Marcus thought, his knobbly knees were concealed inside his smart jogging bottoms.

'Don't tell me you're doing it too?' she asked, with feigned surprise.

He smiled back, holding eye contact with her for a lingering moment. Feeling his excitement rising. His chance! 'Do you fancy a coffee afterwards?'

Her face clouded, the moment gone as fast as it had come. Breaking eye contact and looking at the ground, she said, 'I've actually got a pretty busy morning. I suppose I could have a really quick one.'

'That would be great!'

She added, hesitantly, 'The only thing is, no disrespect, in case I come in quicker than you, I don't want to have to hang around, freezing, for long.'

Marcus felt a little slighted. 'Sure, of course. How's Roger? I haven't heard from him this week.'

'He's great! Really great! Busy as ever. He's got loads of work on at the moment, a lot of people seem to be wanting to learn to fly all of a sudden. But yes, he's well, thanks.'

He saw in her eyes that she really was smitten by her fiancé.

'Good,' he said. 'Terrific – so – tell him to get in touch, we need to fix up that meal together.'

'I will,' she said, looking distracted, staring around as if looking for someone. 'I'll wait for ten minutes after I finish, OK? I'll hang around the finish line.'

'I'll be there!'

She suddenly turned away from him and called out to a tall, muscular iron man in his early thirties, kitted like a pro. 'Hi, Chris!'

'Hey, Georgie!'

Marcus watched them kiss. Old buddies. They looked very happy to see each other.

'What time are you going for?' Iron Man asked.

'If I break twenty-four in these conditions, I'll be happy. You?'

'Well, I got my PB last week – nineteen forty-seven.'

'Pretty good! Wow!'

'Thanks. I didn't see you.'

'I had a client with an injury who was going away, so I had to see him.'

Marcus stood still, watching and listening as they chatted, all touchy-feely with each other, Georgie putting a hand on his arm, then playfully stabbing his chest in response to something he said that Marcus could not hear.

He stared at the two of them, anger rising inside him. Georgie seemed to have totally forgotten him. Or was deliberately ignoring him.

He did some half-hearted warm-up stretches.

Over the loudspeaker an echoey female voice boomed out, 'Welcome, parkrunners! Do we have any visitors?'

Several people put up their hands.

'Welcome!' the commentator said.

There were a few claps.

'Do we have any Jersey parkrun first-timers?'

Marcus didn't bother raising his arm.

There were several cries of 'Yay!' followed by more claps.

She explained the route, then she said, 'Dave Woodsford is on his hundredth parkrun and it's Chris Dorey's birthday!'

There were several desultory cheers and more clapping.

'Don't forget about all the brilliant volunteers that make this happen. You can do your bit by volunteering in the future!' Then she called out, 'Timekeepers ready? Three . . . Two . . . One . . . PARKRUN!'

They were off.

Iron Man sprinted ahead with Georgie close behind, weaving through slower runners, whilst Marcus followed, barging his way past people, determined to keep pace with her. But within minutes she was way ahead of him and he was losing sight of her pink cap through the bobbing heads. He stepped up his speed and immediately felt a stitch developing. He kept going, faster, faster. The jabbing pain was worsening.

Shit.

They were going up a hill.

He did his best, but he was running out of breath and the stitch was almost unbearable now. And then the agonizing pain started once more in his calf muscle. He needed to stop. But he couldn't allow himself that luxury. Georgie said she could only wait ten minutes. He glanced at his watch. He'd heard her tell Iron Man that she was hoping to get in under twenty-four minutes. He tried to calculate how far behind he was at this moment. No way could he stop. Had to keep on, run through the pain.

A motivational expression popped from a dark recess of his memory banks. *If you're going through hell, keep going.*

Trying to think who it was who said that, he stumbled on. Driven by the thoughts of a coffee with Georgie. Everything was becoming a blur. People were passing him, bashing his arms, some calling out apologies.

'Hey!' he shouted out to one lanky man in loose fluorescent shorts and wearing ear buds, who almost knocked him over.

After a few more paces, murmuring to himself, 'Going through hell, keep going, keep going,' he stopped and attempted to touch his toes, to relieve the stitch. But a few seconds later someone ran straight into him, sending him sprawling, face first, into the muddy grass. The man stopped to help him. 'So sorry! My mistake, I was going a bit enthusiastic there. You OK, mate?'

People were pounding past him on either side as he hauled himself, miserably, to his feet and carried on, trudging up the hill, head bowed against the stinging, blinding rain. He didn't start running again until he had crested the hill, by which time almost all the pack was ahead of him, except for a couple of old men who were power walking and a woman determinedly striding with a pushchair and gaining on him fast. The baby inside, protected by a crinkly see-through rain cover, looked like a ready meal from the chill section of a supermarket, he thought. *Microwave five minutes!*

It was over thirty-eight minutes before he limped across the finish line, barely aware of the applause from the cheerful volunteers and spectators, and hit the stop button on his running watch. It was a good time, but he had been hoping to have done faster, closer to Georgie's time.

Soaking wet from the rain and perspiration, his hands almost numb with cold, he looked around for Georgie. For her pink cap. Was she still here? She'd said she could only wait ten minutes but surely she could have had the decency to hang on. She'd have waited for Iron Man, wouldn't she?

Maybe she'd gone to the loo. He decided to hang around and see. Five minutes passed, ten minutes. The rain was still teeming down, and the few remaining people were rapidly thinning out.

After a quarter of an hour it was clear she had definitely gone.
Has she gone off with Iron Man?
Leaving me here in the rain?
Thanks, Georgie.

33

Saturday 12 January

Georgie stood in the shower, grateful for the needles of hot water pelting down on her as she gradually warmed up. She was pleased with her time today. Twenty-three minutes and three seconds, her PB. Eight seconds off last week and in such rubbish conditions – and carrying a passenger!

She was pleased also, and not a little relieved, that Roger had cancelled his scheduled flying lessons because of the weather and lousy visibility, which meant they'd spend the day together. He'd suggested lunch at El Tico by the sand dunes of St Ouen. And she had already decided what she was going to have to eat there – Yankee pancakes with vanilla mascarpone cream and warm maple syrup.

After that they were going to catch a movie at Cineworld, and this evening she would make a salmon and avocado salad with the bits Roger had gone to buy whilst she was doing her run.

But minus the wine she normally enjoyed with him at the weekend.

Hey, that abstinence wouldn't be forever.

Would it, Mr Bump?

Or Miss Bump.

Your dad and I don't mind. We will love you forever whichever you turn out to be.

Mike Uniform Mike to Bravo Uniform Mike Papa. Are you hearing me? Over.

34

Saturday 12 January

'Did you fall?' Claire asked, concerned.

Marcus, dripping and still cold, limped into the kitchen. 'Fall?'

'You've got mud on your face.'

And egg all over it, too.

'How was it, how did it go?'

'Let's just say OK for a first effort.' He looked around. 'Now where are the little darlings?'

The twins were bunched up together on a sofa, absorbed in a cartoon they were watching. Cormac was crawling around on his play mat, with the determination of an explorer on a mission. Marcus sat down next to the twins and tickled each of them in turn, sending them into a frenzy of giggles. But his focus was on Claire. She looked worn out. And she was wearing the rubber Crocs, which she insisted were the most comfortable shoes ever and he insisted were the least sexy creations. Ever.

She had always taken great care in her appearance, but much less so since the children came along. There used to be times when they were home alone and not even going out anywhere, when she wouldn't answer the door without lipstick on. Now, he supposed, it wasn't such a high priority – or was it that he wasn't such a high priority? In his mind he kept contrasting her with Georgie, who even looked good in her gym kit at the Bel Royal.

His phone pinged with an incoming email. It was an automated message from noreply@parkrun.com.

Hello Marcus.

Jersey parkrun results for event #174. Your time was 00:38:20.

He stared at the email, angry and ashamed of his performance in equal measures.

Thirty-eight minutes and twenty seconds. He should be faster.

Shit. Georgie wouldn't even bother looking that far down the list when she checked her time against others, as many parkrunners did.

He hoped.

'Nick called while you were out,' Claire said. Nick Robinson, his golfing partner. 'To remind you it's the monthly medal tomorrow.'

'I thought I told him, I'm taking a break from golf to get fit.'

She peered at his soaking tracksuit, matted hair and cheeks purple from his exertion, and grinned. 'I'd go back to golf, it suits you better.'

He felt the sarcasm in her voice. 'Very funny.'

'So, let's make a plan for today,' she said.

'I have to go to the hospital.'

'But you said you had the weekend off,' she protested. Lowering her voice, she added, 'We promised Rhys and Amelia we'd take them to the zoo.'

'Something's come up. I'm needed – an emergency op, just got a call.' He pulled his phone out of his pocket and held it up, as if in evidence.

'Great,' she said, dispirited.

He ignored her tone; he really didn't have time for a row now. 'When will you be back?'

'I don't know. You think I really *want* to spend my Saturday in theatre?'

She looked a tad more understanding and put her arms around his neck. She smelled of face cream and onions. 'Of course not, it's just they're going to be so disappointed.'

Isn't childhood all about feeling disappointed when your parents let you down? Doesn't every child have parents who let them down?

he thought. 'Why don't you take them yourself and I'll try to join you as soon as I'm finished?'

'OK,' she said. 'Sure. It's just it would have been nice to do something all together. But it never happens, does it? It's difficult, but we've both got to try harder to find quality family time.'

'Well, hopefully I'll be able to get away.' He went upstairs to strip off and shower. And standing on the scales, he was annoyed to see that instead of having lost any weight from his exertions these past weeks, he'd gained two pounds.

When he came back down thirty minutes later, changed and refreshed, the television was still on, now with a cookery show, but there was no sign of anyone. Just a note on the island unit.

See you at the zoo, if you can make it! X

He made himself some porridge and ate it whilst reading the island's paper, the *Jersey Evening Post*, noting with particular interest the ongoing controversy over the location of the new hospital, and wondering if it would ever actually get resolved. Then he flipped through the first few pages of *The Times*.

Half an hour later, Marcus drove to the hospital. Although ailments and injuries did not adhere to a Monday-to-Friday schedule, this place was always quieter at weekends. Which meant less risk of being disturbed. Good.

After first checking Kath Clow wasn't in and on call today, he entered his office and closed the door, then sat at his desk and logged on. Without a glance at the emails that had poured in since yesterday, he went to the parkrun website and looked up Georgie Maclean's time.

And grimaced when it came up.

Twenty-three minutes and three seconds. She'd done the course fifteen minutes faster than his time.

At the start he'd heard her say she was going for under twenty-four minutes.

Maybe she'd never had any intention of waiting to have coffee with him. Or was he just overthinking all of this?

I will get faster, just you watch, Georgie! I will get closer to your time.

He pulled up the images on his phone that he'd started to group into an album called 'Running'. Screenshots of running drills and exercises, stretches and routines. He smiled to himself, realizing that nearly all the images were of super-fit young women. Perhaps he needed to redress that balance. Then, more recently, the photos of Georgie running along the promenade which he had taken the first time he'd seen her. Followed by the pictures he'd taken of her earlier today, at the parkrun. Added to them was a screenshot of the photograph Georgie had posted of her flat lay.

He stared at the neatly laid-out, brightly coloured kit, and for some minutes luxuriated in the mental image of Georgie naked before she put it on. And afterwards, of her drenched and sweaty, peeling it off. She had a great body, for sure, the kind of tight, slender body that had always turned him on.

He was so absorbed in his thoughts he didn't hear the sound of his door opening. Then, suddenly, he became aware of a shadow.

He spun round and saw his medical student, Robert Resmes, standing right behind him.

He jumped up, startled, slamming the phone face-down on his desk and obstructing the Romanian's view of his screen. 'Haven't you heard of knocking, Robert?'

'I did knock,' Robert said, giving him a strange look.

'What are you doing here?'

'I didn't realize you were coming in today,' he said. 'I had a free day and Dr Noon invited me to spend it with him in the Emergency department. One of the nurses said she'd seen you entering the building, so I thought I'd come up and see if you were dealing with an emergency or something.'

'I came in to get some filing done, all right?'

'Yes, of course.' Resmes stood, giving him an odd, knowing smile.

'You can go back to Adrian Noon, OK?'

'Yes, right, good. I'll see you Monday, then?'

Resmes continued to stand for some seconds. Then, taking his time, he went out calmly, closing the door behind him.

Marcus again entered Kath Clow's username and password and pulled up her files on Georgie Maclean. He wanted to make sure everything was going well, taking care to note anything significant so he could impress her next time they met.

Georgie had had her twelve-week scan before Christmas. She was now in her second trimester. She had recently received the Harmony test results and it was good news. The 99 per cent risk assessment chances of the baby having any of the three chromosomes they were most concerned about – thirteen, eighteen and twenty-one, or Patau, Edwards and Down's syndromes – were less than one in ten thousand.

He studied her notes and her entire medical history once again, with great care.

35

Saturday 12 January

El Tico was rammed with couples and families seated at the long wooden tables, and Georgie and Roger had to stand in a queue, the tantalizing smell of hot food and the near-deafening babble of conversation all around them, before being told they could be seated in half an hour. Roger laid his keys and his phone on the bar counter while they waited.

'Don't you forget those, they've got my hotel keys on there.'

'They're quite safe, don't worry.'

They didn't worry, as they stood watching, through the rain-spattered windows, a few brave surfers out on the grey, roiling waves, Roger with a Bloody Mary, Georgie with a Virgin one. The fingers of Georgie's free hand were entwined with Roger's.

'Cheers!' he said.

'Isn't it bad luck to clink glasses without alcohol in both?'

He shook his head. 'Do you know why people touch glasses?'

'I suspect I'm about to find out!' she grinned.

'Goes back to the Middle Ages, when no one trusted anyone. If you went to someone else's castle and were offered a drink, your glass would be filled to the brim as would be your host's. As you touched glasses, you'd make sure some of your wine, or ale, slopped into your host's – that way if you were being given poison, he'd drink it too.'

'I like it, but what's that got to do with alcohol?'

He shrugged. 'Maybe the alcohol killed whatever poison might be in your drink.'

'Any other superstitions you can diss?'

At that moment, much sooner than they had expected, a server came over to them. 'Mr and Mrs Richardson – your table is ready.'

They took their seats at the window end of a long table, next to a glum-looking elderly couple who were sitting in silence, and picked up the menus. For a short while they studied them. 'I'm having the pancakes,' Georgie said. 'I've been craving them! And I'm ravenous.'

'With marmalade?'

'With mascarpone cream and warm maple syrup – and I'm going to ask if I could have some marmalade as a side order.'

'Go for it! I've got an expectant father craving too!'

'What for?'

'A burger, mustard, pickle, fries, ketchup!'

'You go for it, you've earned it, all that hard work!'

'Hard work?'

She leaned across the table, whispering so the elderly couple next to them couldn't hear. 'All that sacrificial sex!'

He gave her an impish smile. 'Wasn't totally hard work – not all of it.'

'No? Wasn't tooooo tough for me, either. Not all of it, anyhow.'

They locked smiling eyes.

The waiter arrived just then and they gave their orders – luckily, marmalade was no problem – with a glass of red wine for Roger and a Diet Coke for Georgie. They sat in contented silence for a couple of moments, then to their relief the couple next to them departed and no one took their place.

'I quite liked her calling us *Mr and Mrs Richardson*,' Georgie said. 'I think I'll be able to get used to that!'

'Me too, *Mrs Richardson*. Has a nice ring to it! So, have you had any thoughts about that envelope? About finding out whether our bump is a boy or a girl?'

'Have you? What names would you favour?'

'I've been thinking. I did like George but that would be too confusing. I really like Robert, too. For a girl, I quite like Edith – I know it's old-fashioned, but it seems to be coming back,' he said.

'What about Archie or Kit?'

He nodded. 'I like those too, especially Kit.'

'For a girl I like Laura or Rebecca. Edith is cute though.'

'Well, you're the one doing the heavy lifting!'

'When you and Roxanne were trying for a baby, did you think up names?' she said.

'Yes, but it was the same way we always used to decide on everything. She said what she wanted and I'd go along with it.'

'I never took you for a doormat or a pushover.'

'Yup, well, you never met Roxanne. She was a control freak – if she didn't get her way she'd go into a sulk for days.' He shrugged. 'In the end it just became easier to say yes.'

'Which is what you said when she told you she'd fallen in love with someone else?'

He smiled. 'I've never owned a boat, but an old mucker of mine, Paul Templeman – who was my best man first time round – you'll meet him one day – made a shitload of money in a property development and bought a yacht – which turned out to be a money pit. He said you have two moments of happiness when you own a boat. The first is the day you buy it and the second is the day you sell it.'

She gave him a quizzical stare. 'Meaning in your case?'

'The day Roxanne and I married. And the day we were divorced.'

'I hope you never say that about me.'

He stared at her. 'Never, ever, ever.'

Georgie leaned across the table and kissed him. As she sat back, their food arrived.

Both of them tucked in, ravenously. She stole one of his chips, dunked it in the bowl of ketchup and ate it. 'Know what I fancy, when we've finished?'

'Tell me?'

I FOLLOW YOU

'Going straight home and taking you to bed.'

'Funny you should say that,' he replied, raising his wine glass. 'I was just thinking the same thing.'

36

Ignoring his nagging calf muscle, Marcus let himself out of his front door. The low winter sun shone from a clear steel-blue sky on a chilly, but glorious, morning, the kind where the island looked its very best. Perhaps he'd see Georgie again today, out in this good weather.

He'd been frustrated that aside from yesterday he'd not spoken to her for several weeks, not since before Christmas. He'd noticed she'd done several runs in and around York over the festive season and, checking her social media, he'd found pictures of her and Roger with her in-laws-to-be. He hated all those smug, smiling faces – except Georgie's, of course, and did she even want to be there? – and the ridiculous photo of them all around the Christmas dinner table wearing party hats.

He began his warm-up, stopping periodically to do his stretches as he headed down toward St Brelade's church.

During the evening, whilst Claire had been drooling over Richard Madden in *Bodyguard* on catch-up television, he'd been thinking about Georgie Maclean's latest activity, wondering whether her pregnancy was affecting her performance. He so desperately wanted to beat her!

Aside from the York trip, she was a creature of habit with her routes, and since returning from her travels she had slipped straight back into them. But the times of her weekday runs varied a little, presumably to fit around her work. She seemed to prefer early morning, but a few were quite late in the evening, he noticed. On

Saturdays she either did a long run on her own or the parkrun, and Sundays she began pretty much on the dot of 8.00 a.m.

For one of her regular runs she would head west from her home in Beaumont over to the Corbière Lighthouse, from which she looped back. Either continuing past Beaumont towards St Helier or, on her longer run days, carrying on some distance past the port of St Helier. His watch showed 8.32 a.m. If he headed west, towards Corbière, on the track she always looped back on, there was every chance he would see her.

Forget it, stop being stupid. Take a different route. Stop torturing yourself over her. Why are you obsessing so much over this one woman? She is just rejecting you like all the rest. Move on.

But he couldn't.

He stretched once more, then broke into a run, almost immediately stopping as his right calf muscle tightened. Cursing, he knelt down and began massaging it. A male jogger pounded past him, from the Corbière direction. He began running again, and although feeling tight, close to protest, the muscle held. For several minutes. Then spasmed again.

It felt like someone had dug a knife into the lower half of his leg and was twisting it.

Gasping in pain, he knelt and massaged his calf, hard. He heard footsteps pounding towards him and turned, peering up from beneath the peak of his baseball cap. A young man with a tiny rucksack on his back, sucking on a water tube, ran full-tilt past him.

He returned to his calf. The massage was working, it was starting to feel better. Then more footsteps approached, but before he could turn, a woman shot past him. In a pink baseball cap.

Too late, he realized it was Georgie.

She ran on, in her pale-blue top and shorts. Running belt. Ray-Bans. Ear buds. Easy strides taking her towards a blue horizon.

What are you listening to through those ear buds? Van the Man?

Such gorgeous, sexy legs inside her compression socks.

He changed direction and began running after her. Getting ten yards before his calf muscle griped again.

No.

He knelt and massaged it once more. By the time he stood up again, Georgie was way in the distance. No chance of catching her up.

But he knew her likely route – if he could head over to where she would be looping back, he might be able to see her then. Perhaps catch her for a chat right at the end of her run?

He began running once more, but his calf muscle felt like an elastic band about to snap. He slowed to a power walk and it felt better. He carried on, as fast as he could, continually looking at his watch, calculating. How far was she going today? When would she be coming back?

He had to stop and massage his leg again.

A group of four guys, all chatting, raced past him. Cyclists. Joggers with pushchairs. And more headed towards him. Then he saw the pink cap.

Georgie! Bearing down fast. Her face set in grim resolve. It was definitely her.

He stood up, all smiles, and raised a hand in recognition. 'Hi, Georgie!' he said.

She half raised a hand back, barely glancing at him, before looking straight ahead again. 'Hi, Marcus!'

As if he was just another meaningless stranger in a crowd.

37

Monday 14 January

The stage of tuition before student pilots made their first solo was known as 'touch and goes', also known as 'circuits and bumps'. With the instructor alongside them in the cockpit they would complete circuit after circuit of the airfield, landing, slowing but not stopping, then opening the throttle and taking off again and repeating the process.

Roger Richardson usually loved seeing his pupils at this stage, where they rapidly gained in confidence. His best ones had what he liked to call 'kind hands' – it meant they were gentle and smooth with the controls. But not this idiot. The man in the hot seat to his left, gripping the control column as if he was steering a Grand Prix race car, was a contender for the title of his least favourite student pilot. Ever.

Byron Wilding was fifty-seven, overweight and held the misguided belief that he was immortal. American born and raised, he had relocated many years earlier to England and subsequently, some years later, had moved to Jersey.

Wilding's life had been punctuated by a couple of incredibly lucky escapes. In 1995 he'd been the sole survivor in a private charter jet that had crashed in Portugal, killing the pilot and three of his board members. On 11 September 2001, he had overslept – due to a booze-fuelled night spent with his mistress in a Manhattan hotel, as he'd bragged to Roger. It had meant him failing to turn up for an early-morning meeting in the South Tower of the World Trade Centre.

When Roger had asked him to what he attributed his luck, he'd replied with his catchphrase, 'I guess someone up there likes me.'

Why on earth *anyone up there* should have liked this conceited tub of lard, in Roger's view, beggared belief.

Byron Wilding had amassed a fortune through building one of the largest groups of outlet malls in the world, proudly telling Roger that he'd done it all himself from humble roots. His father, back in Baton Rouge, had been a hospital janitor and his mother a school dinner lady. He had survived three heart attacks yet had somehow sailed through his medical, being signed off fit to fly.

'I guess someone up there likes me,' he'd replied again when Roger had quizzed him about this.

As further evidence of his belief in his invincibility – and clearly in his immortality too – Wilding had bought an expensive twin-engine executive plane which had been delivered to Jersey some months earlier and was parked in a hangar. Obtaining his basic Private Pilot's Licence was his first step towards getting his ticket to fly his aircraft himself.

God help his future passengers, Roger thought. However much Wilding thought he had the Almighty on his side, he simply wasn't pilot material. To be a safe flier, in Roger's opinion, you needed to be both cautious and extremely methodical. The best private pilots, other than those who'd come from an RAF or commercial pilot background, tended to be engineers or doctors or those with similar precision backgrounds where attention to detail was enshrined in their DNA. However much 'someone up there' might like you, there was an immutable law of physics called *gravity*, and that was never going to be a bad pilot's best friend.

And boy, this guy was bad. He didn't always listen and was slapdash in his approach, the kind of person who might take risks. Roger could just imagine him, at some future point, jumping into his plane despite a weather warning, and taking off, reliant only on his pal 'up there' who liked him. One day, for sure, his pal was going to be away from his desk, having a coffee break.

There were many levels of licence for a private pilot. The elementary one, which Byron Wilding was currently going for, was single-engine VFR – daylight visual flying – which required a minimum of forty hours of tuition. A further level was multi-engine rating. Another was night flying. Followed by instrument rating, which took as long again as getting a licence in the first place. That could be followed by several more levels and even more stringent medicals to gain a commercial pilot's licence.

'Touch and goes' were a key part of the first level. Could the student pilot take off and land safely? Once the instructor was confident his – or her – pupil was up to it, after safely taxiing the plane to a halt and without giving the pupil time to think, they would jump out of the cockpit and tell the pupil to go for it. Solo!

It was the big moment for anyone learning to fly. They would have to take off, return to the airfield and land, all on their own, without an instructor to their right at the dual controls. Reliant now completely on their newly learned skills.

Or more likely in Byron's case, his buddy 'up there'.

Roger squinted as the plane banked steeply, turning south into the dazzling morning sun, then stiffened as they banked again, turning towards the runway. They were approaching too fast. Far too fast.

With a sharp intake of breath, he spoke into his mic, informing his pupil he was taking control. Opening the throttle, engine roaring, he pulled back on the control column, lifting the nose sharply in the air and adjusting the trim wheel.

'What did you do that for?' came his pupil's voice through the headphones.

'To save both our lives,' he answered, calmly. 'You forgot to lower the flaps and slow the aircraft right down. We'd have hit the runway at around 120 mph instead of the landing speed of 60 mph for this aircraft. If we didn't break the undercarriage and flip over, we'd have ploughed off the end of the runway and ended up in the sand dunes.'

'Bollocks, I had it under control. I was going to do all that.'

'Let's go around again,' Roger said, not rising to the challenge of the man's indignation.

They flew out over the Corbière Lighthouse, banked right further out over the sea, and then right again.

Roger radioed the tower. 'Mike Whisky Seven Four Zulu to Jersey Tower, request another approach to runway 26 for a touch and go.'

'Golf Uniform Zulu maintain 1,300 feet on reaching QNH 1020 and fly heading 180 degrees Golf Uniform Zulu.'

'Understood, maintain 1,300 feet on reaching QNH 1020 and fly heading 180 degrees Golf Uniform Zulu.'

'Golf Uniform Zulu, correct.'

Roger continued flying the aircraft himself as they climbed, heading well away from the airport. Two minutes later the controller came back on the radio.

'Golf Uniform Zulu you are cleared touch and go runway 26 into a left-hand VFR circuit.'

'You have control again,' Roger instructed Wilding, routinely running his eye across the instruments.

'I have control,' Wilding replied.

As his student banked the plane too steeply, forcing Roger to make a small correction on the rudder and control column, his mind drifted momentarily to Georgie and the baby. Should they find out the sex? It had been the luckiest day of his life when he had met her. After all the crap he'd been through with the break-up of his marriage, and the joy Georgie had brought to him, maybe he should be the one saying that someone up there liked him.

He longed, as he did every workday, for the evening. To be home with her. With this amazing, beautiful, lovely woman. Who was now carrying their child.

Life right now was as good as he could ever imagine it getting.

He always felt happy up in the sky. Perhaps it would have been marginally better if he didn't have a total dickhead at the controls.

Roger's phone began vibrating.

He looked down. The display read GEORGIE.

Much though he would have loved to answer, he let the call go to voicemail.

Looking down at the airport as they turned onto their final approach, he saw a twin-engine private plane, a Beechcraft, moving slowly along the taxiway. Over his headphones he heard the tower giving it instructions to continue taxiing to holding point G and hold position.

Wilding reduced the throttle and this time remembered to lower the flaps. The Piper slowed sharply.

A text from Georgie pinged in.

Was just calling to say I love yooooooou xx

Roger watched the altimeter descending – 700 . . . 600 . . . 500 . . . 400 . . .

And the airspeed dropping – 90 . . . 80 . . . 70 . . .

The tarmac strip of runway was looming ahead.

100 on the altimeter . . . 90 . . . 80 . . .

The dickhead was actually doing it right! A couple more of these, like this, and he *might*, at some point in the next lesson, be confident enough to jump out and let Wilding do a take-off and landing solo.

60 mph.

Any minute the wheels would bump down.

Then something hurtled towards the windscreen, like a mad bird.

A drone.

Wilding shouted, 'Holy shit!' He swung the joystick as if it was the steering wheel of a car, so hard it jerked out of his instructor's hands, at the same time kicking the rudder pedals so hard that Roger's feet momentarily lost contact with them. With no time for Roger to react, the plane veered sharply left. There was a massive bang.

Wilding screamed in terror.

Splinters shot past the windscreen.

The plane was sideways, at a sharp angle, its left wing tip inches from the runway.

Roger pulled the joystick back, as hard as he could, at the same time ramming open the throttle.

The plane levelled out, but the stall warning alarm began. A dumb sound, like a foghorn. They were veering sharply left, away from the runway.

Barp . . . barp . . . barp . . .

Wilding shot a terrified glance at him.

They were losing control.

There was no resistance from the joystick. It came right back to his chest.

Shit. Shit. Shit.

Then, to his horror, through the cracked windscreen, he saw the Beechcraft, right in front of them.

Someone in the Beechcraft's co-pilot's seat looked at them in total, frozen shock.

The gap was closing.

A screech as their wheels hit the grass, between the runway and the taxiway.

Followed by an instant of total silence as they bounced up in the air. Rolling right then left. Then bounced on.

Reeling the Beechcraft in towards them, like it was a big fish.

Again, Roger desperately pulled the joystick back as far as it would go.

Nothing happened.

The gap was narrowing.

Closing.

They hit the grass again.

Stayed down. Bouncing. Bouncing.

Hurtling towards the Beechcraft.

Closing on it.

'Jesus!' Wilding shouted.

Roger pressed down on the right-turn pedal as hard as he could, as Wilding, in his panic, was stamping on the left. They continued heading straight on.

Roger braced himself. 'Shit,' he said.

38

On Saturdays Marcus liked to do the cooking, leaving the Sunday roast to Claire. That suited him as he used to play golf on a Sunday morning, although running now gave him more time back with the kids. Sunday lunch was normally the time of the week he looked forward to the most. A few glasses of red wine, a snooze in his armchair in front of the television, then taking the twins out for a walk around the quay, with Cormac in a buggy.

But yesterday, after his morning run, everything had irritated him. Claire was annoyed that her pork crackling wasn't crisp enough, which she blamed on the Aga being too low, and that the roast potatoes – her absolute speciality – weren't cooked enough. Cormac, teething, hadn't stopped screaming all morning. And the twins were playing up as well – something that was supposed to improve after they'd passed through the stage of the 'terrible twos', wasn't it?

As a result he'd actually – and unusually – been looking forward to Monday morning and escaping to the relative calm and sanity of work. First up had been a number of private patients he'd seen in his consulting rooms in the Bon Sante suite, a couple of miles from the hospital. Then, shortly before midday, he'd headed across to the hospital for a brief meeting, followed by a busy operating list in theatre which would take him well into late afternoon.

He was in his office reading the *Jersey Evening Post*, whilst eating an early lunch of a cheese-and-tomato sandwich, catching up on the minutiae of island life.

I FOLLOW YOU

The headline on page five said:

NEW YEAR GOOD NEWS FOR FLYING INSTRUCTOR!

Beneath was a photograph of his loved-up mate Roger Richardson with his arms around Georgie Maclean.

The story, by staff reporter David Edbrooke, read:

Popular Jersey flying instructor, Roger Richardson, has double reason to be celebrating the start of the year. His application to launch an air taxi business is expected to be approved by Jersey States at a States sitting this coming Thursday. And his fiancée, personal trainer Georgie Maclean, is expecting their baby later this year.

Marcus didn't bother reading the rest of the story. He'd already read it twice before.

How wonderful for the happy couple – not. So why are you such a flirt, Georgie? Why did you touch my lapel at dinner? Why have you given me your phone number? Why did you want me to turn up to your class? Why are you playing games with me?

You and I both know we're meant to be together.

He stared at Richardson's face, all smiles. At Georgie, looking so in love.

And thought, *Really?*

39

Monday 14 January

'OK,' Georgie said to her group of six women who were coming to the end of their fifty-minute, mid-morning spinning session. 'Three minutes' cool down!' She liked this group, they were all fun, and earlier in the warm-up, when they weren't too breathless to speak, had showered her with congratulations over the news of her baby, which they'd read about in the newspaper that morning.

She was in a great mood and looking forward to her next client, who was utterly charming. Bless him, although in his late eighties, he was determined to get his fitness level up. He was due at midday – in ten minutes. She glanced at her phone, to double-check the time, and saw a Sky newsflash. Breaking news. But her mind at the moment was on another leak that had appeared, this time in the empty hotel's dining-room ceiling. She'd noticed it on Friday and had called the hotel owner. He'd asked her to check with Edouardo about it to see if it was spreading at all and get the plumber to come back and sort it.

As she left the gym and walked along the long, slightly musty-smelling corridor past the kitchens and staff toilets, she dialled Roger. They normally spoke and texted each other several times a day and she particularly liked speaking to him when she was doing her round of inspection of the hotel. Even though it was now broad daylight the place still spooked her.

The phone went to his voicemail again. He was probably instructing, she thought, he had three or four lessons booked for today. She left him a message.

'Hi darling, just wondering what you fancy for dinner tonight?

I'm suddenly feeling like a really old-fashioned steak and kidney pie – I know it's strange, I've not eaten meat in a while, but I'd like that with some baked beans – and some very creamy coleslaw! If you want anything different, just let me know in the next couple of hours – I've got a free afternoon and I'll be going out foraging. Call me when you can. I love you.'

Like her, Roger rarely ate meat and he wasn't a big fan of pies. But too bad if he didn't call back before she went shopping, he'd have to lump it. Hell, if she was doing all the heavy lifting, as he put it, he could make a few small sacrifices with his diet.

As she ended the call, a streak of red and white on the screen caught her eye. A newsflash again.

This time she looked at it.

Major incident declared at St Helier Airport,
Jersey, following collision between two aircraft.
Multiple casualties reported.

As she read the words it was as if a bright light inside her had been switched off, plunging her into darkness.

Roger was instructing there all today.

Roger had told her over breakfast that one of his students today was an over-confident nutter who scared him.

Oh God, Roger, please be OK. Please don't be involved in this.

He hadn't responded to her text of an hour or so ago, which was unlike him – unless she'd missed it during this last session. Normally, he replied within minutes.

She checked her messages. Saw the last one she had sent.

Was just calling to say I love yoooooou xx

There was no reply.

She dialled his number. It rang six times, then went to voicemail.

Hi, this is Roger, I can't take your call right now, I may be flying. Please leave a message and I'll call you back as soon as I'm back down on terra firma.

It was followed by a beep.

She left him a message.

'Hey, it's me, I've just seen on the news about an accident. Please call me as soon as you get this to let me know you're safe. I love you.'

She closed her eyes and took a deep breath. *Please be OK.*

40

Monday 14 January

There were two hotline phones in the Emergency Assessment Unit of Jersey General Hospital. They were mounted prominently on a column in the open-plan admin station, directly above the duty staff nurse's desk. The top one was on a red base marked AMBULANCE, the bottom one on a blue base marked POLICE.

Dan Bathurst, an exhausted A&E registrar, who had been in the hospital all night covering for a colleague who'd gone home sick, was also at this moment covering for the staff nurse who'd gone to get an early lunch. Stethoscope hung around his neck, he sipped a tepid coffee and yawned, struggling to keep his eyes open. He checked the time – 12.09 p.m. Someone would be relieving him at 1 p.m. – not a minute too soon.

The red phone rang, startling him.

He had to stand to reach the receiver. Lifting it from its cradle, he presumed it was going to be a routine call from an incoming ambulance, informing the hospital of the status of the patient. Mostly it was cardiac arrests or suspected strokes, mothers going into labour, work-place accidents, road-traffic collisions and, without fail on Friday and Saturday nights, at least one pub or nightclub fight victim.

But not today.

As Bathurst answered, ready to brief one of the two on-call Emergency department consultants who would make the decision on whichever medics would be required, an authoritative female voice said, 'This is Jersey Ambulance Service. Two light aircraft have collided at the airport and we have multiple casualties, including reports of fatalities. We're declaring a Major Incident. Police and the Airport Fire Crew are attending and we're setting up triaging. One ambulance is now at the scene, with all the others arriving imminently.'

'Do you have an estimate of the number of casualties?' Bathurst asked.

'I believe seven, possibly eight at this stage, but we're getting constant updates.'

Whilst she was speaking the Major Incident METHANE report appeared on the screen on his desk. It gave the exact location; the type of incident; hazards – one plane on fire; access and egress routes; number of casualties – it was showing now as ten; emergency services now present – Ambulance, Fire crew, Police and Coastguard.

The hospital had a clear procedure laid out for the instances – few and far between – when such an incident was declared. Blinking nervously through his glasses, the registrar looked around the large room for any sign of either of the two duty consultants. Not able to see them, he paged them with the simple message:

MAJOR INCIDENT

Within moments both doctors appeared from different directions. Nick Greene, a tall, former military doctor who'd had battlefield experience in Afghanistan and was unfazed by anything, loped towards the registrar. He was dressed in the pink scrubs worn by all the team in this department. He was followed, seconds later, by the suited figure of Adrian Noon, a calm, highly experienced man, who had started his career as a GP, before becoming Medical Director of the Essex Ambulance Service and then moving to Jersey as an A&E consultant.

As soon as Bathurst had brought them up to speed, Noon and Greene made a quick decision. Greene left to go to the airport to supervise the triaging of the casualties at the scene there. He grabbed a wedge of Triage Sieve Diagram leaflets, which would be handed out to non-medical emergency workers at the scene to assist in grading the injured into three levels of priority: Immediate, Urgent and Delayed.

Adrian Noon began implementing the hospital Major Incident Plan. First, he put out the call to evacuate all patients from the Emergency department. Those needing beds were to be found temporary ones in other wards. Next, he asked the switchboard to cancel all scheduled operations in the hospital's five theatres, except for any life-threatening situations, and to request all consultants, anaesthetists, doctors, nurses, students and porters to assemble immediately in the Education Centre. He needed to know what resources were currently available to him. And if there were ten casualties all needing surgery, he would have to organize a rota of surgeons – sending some home to get some rest and come back in later to relieve others who would be starting in theatre right away. From past experience he knew the dangers of an exhausted surgeon. It was all too easy for a tired surgeon to do the major part of the surgery and miss the one tiny bit of damage that would end up killing the patient – hours, days or even weeks later.

Noon checked the time. It would take a good five minutes before everyone was assembled, and it would be fifteen to twenty minutes at the very earliest before the first ambulances arrived. He hurried into the changing room, undressed and donned his pink scrubs. He had a feeling it was going to be a very long day.

41

Marcus Valentine was going through his list of operations scheduled for the afternoon, with his student, Robert Resmes – his registrar, Barnaby Cardigan, was away at a funeral – when his pager beeped. He glanced down. The message read:

MAJOR INCIDENT DECLARED. ALL MEDICAL STAFF GO TO THE EDUCATION CENTRE IMMEDIATELY. ALL NON-EMERGENCY SURGERY CANCELLED.

Holding up the message for Resmes to read, he hit the fast-dial button for the hospital manager, asking him what had happened.

'Marcus, we have a report of a major incident at the airport, with multiple casualties. The information is sketchy, but it sounds like there's been a collision between two small aircraft. At present we have four confirmed dead and up to ten seriously injured. Every ambulance we have is at the scene. Can you step in and join the emergency team?'

'Oh Jesus, yes, of course,' he said. 'I can cancel my whole list for today – there's nothing too time critical.'

In addition to his roles as consultant obstetrician and gynae-oncology surgeon, like all the surgeons here, he was also able to perform most general surgery procedures. With this being a relatively small hospital, all the hospital staff were regularly rehearsed in dealing with an emergency such as this, when all hands were needed at the pump.

'Thanks. The first ambulances will be here in ten minutes. If you can go to the Education Centre right away for a briefing, please.'

'I'm on my way.'

Aside from the slight unease about what he was going to be facing, he was excited at the prospect of doing something different to his routine obstetrics surgery. Doing what he had originally signed up for when he had made the decision to go into medicine. Saving lives.

He turned to his student. 'Looks like the big one! You're going to be thrown in the deep end, Robert. Now, some things you may see today could be quite distressing. But this is a learning curve, an opportunity to develop your skills. Don't forget I'll be alongside you, just keep talking.'

Then the two of them ran through the list of scheduled operations, agreeing there was nothing that couldn't wait until later today, at the earliest. Resmes was already dressed in blue scrubs, as he was all the time they were at work. Marcus changed rapidly, then they hurried down to the large room of the Education Centre, which was packed. Adrian Noon, in his pink scrubs, stood on the podium, in command.

'How many surgeons do we have present?' Noon asked. 'Please raise your hands.'

There were seven in the room, including three orthopaedics. Two general surgeons were off on leave, one was down with flu, and another two were currently in their private consulting rooms in the Bon Sante medical centre some distance away in the Hotel de France building.

Noon formed the assembled company into three teams, each headed by an anaesthetist, orthopaedic and general surgeon. Identification bibs were distributed for each team member to wear, labelling them Team Red, Team Green and Team Blue – one for each of the bays in the Emergency department. Marcus and Resmes formed part of Team Green.

Two minutes later, Adrian Noon stood outside the emergency receiving bay in light drizzle, as the first ambulance arrived, siren wailing. It contained a badly burnt woman. He did a quick triage, deciding in moments that she was in a critical condition, categorized her as grade 1 and assigned her to the Blue Team in Bay 1, headed by the surgeon Matt Stephenson, assisted by Kath Clow.

The second ambulance reversed in and the stretcher was unloaded. On it was the lean figure of a man in his late forties or early fifties, with short salt-and-pepper hair. He was conscious but confused, with several facial lacerations. All his clothes apart from his boxer shorts had been removed. There was a wide area of bruising across his abdomen.

The man's initial triage report from the airport, delivered verbally by the paramedic, was a ruptured spleen and suspected fractured skull. Noon carried out a capillary test, squeezing his index fingernail hard and then releasing it. In a normal, healthy person the blood would have returned under the nail instantly. He timed this man's – it was taking dangerously longer. Next, he felt for the radial pulse. A normal systolic pulse should be above 90, but this was way below, he could tell within seconds.

Noon escorted the porter wheeling the trolley along to Bay 2, where the Green Team were waiting, and shouted out an urgent request for an ultrasound machine. It was brought in rapidly. As he applied gel to the man's abdomen, then placed the ultrasound nozzle just below the left side of his ribcage, Noon announced to the team, 'The ultrasound is showing a lot of free fluid in his upper abdomen.' He moved the nozzle across the bruised area. 'He has a capillary refill of four seconds and an absent radial pulse. This is almost certainly indicative of a ruptured spleen. He also has a possible fractured skull and broken left tibia and fibula. But more concerning at this stage is his blood loss. I need a general surgeon to take this patient to theatre right away.'

Marcus Valentine was staring down at the barely conscious man. Although his face was camouflaged with streaks of drying blood, he recognized him instantly and went cold.

He stepped forward. 'Jeez, this poor chap, I know him, Adrian,

156

I've flown with him a few times. And I did that surgery as part of my general medical training. I can take him.'

Noon thought for a moment. Under normal circumstances an obstetrician would not operate on a male. But these were not normal circumstances. He could already hear the wail of another approaching siren. He had ten possible critical casualties and maybe more. There were three emergency bays down in this department and just five operating theatres upstairs. Some of the patients might be in theatre for hours. Removal of a spleen was a relatively simple procedure. Better to keep some of the more experienced general surgeons fresh for potentially complicated operations.

'OK,' he nodded. 'Thank you, Marcus. He's yours.'

42

Monday 14 January

Georgie hurried into the caretaker's office and switched on the radio to BBC Jersey, just in time to catch the start of the 1 p.m. news and the solemn voice of the anchor. Half a mile away, from Victoria Avenue, came a constant din of sirens.

'A major emergency has been declared at Jersey Airport following a collision between two aircraft. First reports indicate a number of casualties, with several dead. We will bring you further updates throughout the day. The airport authorities say that all outgoing and incoming flights are cancelled, and the airport is likely to remain closed for some time.'

Georgie felt every fibre of her body tightening. Her next appointment sauntered in through the door, an elderly, retired English dentist, Steve Cowling, who had recently moved to Jersey with his wife and was determined to keep fighting fit after a liver transplant a few years back. He gave her a cheery wave and hurried through to the changing room.

She had the number of the flying club programmed into her phone, found it in her contacts list and dialled it.

Engaged.

She dialled again.

Still engaged.

She dialled the main airport switchboard and that was engaged, too. Finally, she tried Gama Aviation, the private commercial aviation hub, and also got the busy signal.

Oh God, please be OK.

Roger was probably helping out with the situation, she thought.

Hoped.

Fervently hoped.

Please God.

Sirens continued wailing.

Her first instinct was to apologize to Cowling, jump in her car and head over to the airport. To make sure Roger was OK.

But he would be all right. He was highly experienced. He couldn't possibly have let his plane collide with another. It was almost certainly a couple of the amateur, recreational pilots, and Roger would be there, doing whatever he could. He didn't need the distraction of her turning up. She ran through all the sensible, calming thoughts in her head, trying not to revert to the panic she'd felt so often since her sister's childhood accident, making her fear the worst, but gradually learning to control the irrational anxieties.

She left messages with Lucy and Kath to contact her if they had heard anything, then, hoping that Roger would call her back or text her as soon as he was able, she decided to carry on. She pulled up Cowling's training programme on her phone. She'd get this session over as quickly as she could.

His first activity was to be five minutes' warm-up on the cross-trainer, at Level 2. She swivelled the five-minute egg timer and released it. As soon as he had started, she hurried back into the office and listened to the radio again.

'*What we understand so far is that an incoming Piper plane veered off the runway and collided with a taxiing Beechcraft.*'

Roger gave his lessons in a Piper. Goosebumps ran down her back and along her arms.

She returned to her client and watched the last grains of sand in the egg timer. Then she installed him in the leg press and set the one-minute timer, her mind elsewhere.

Glancing at her phone again.

No more updates.

She got Cowling to lie back on an exercise mat and gave him a weighted ball to lift repeatedly in the air.

While he was doing that, she checked her phone.

Still no message from Roger.

Feeling sick with dread, she dialled the airport again. Still busy.

She rang Roger again.

Voicemail again.

'Right,' she said to Cowling, as enthusiastically as she could muster. 'Assault bike next!'

'Welcome to the Georgina Maclean torture chamber,' he said with a smile, as she helped him to his feet, for once not smiling back. This time, she was the one enduring torture, and she felt an immense flood of relief when the session was over and she could usher him out.

By then, Georgie was shaking. Unable to stand not knowing any longer, she jumped in her car and drove, faster than she should, towards the flying club. As she came off the roundabout, turning towards the airport, a short distance ahead of her the traffic was backed up. Some cars were turning round.

As she crawled in the slow-moving queue of traffic past St Peter's Garden Centre on her right and the display of cars outside the swanky car showrooms of Jacksons to her left, she saw blue lights in the distance. All the vehicles ahead were now making U-turns and heading past her in the opposite direction. Drawing nearer, she saw a police car parked across the road, with two officers, a male and female, standing beside it, blue-and-white tape stretched across the road behind them. A sign read:

POLICE – ACCIDENT – ROAD CLOSED

In the distance she heard the wail of yet another siren.

She pulled over, jumped out of her car and hurried towards them, her heart in her mouth. 'My fiancé's an instructor at the flying club – is there any way you could let me through?'

'I'm sorry, madam,' the female officer said. 'Emergency vehicles only, the airport's closed.'

'Can you tell me what's happened?'

'I'm afraid not,' she said, friendly and apologetic. 'There's an incident at the airport but we have no more information at this stage.'

'If you tune in to Radio Jersey, I'm sure there will be bulletins,' the male officer suggested.

Georgie went back to her car and turned up the volume on the radio. A Tom Odell song was playing and normally she liked him, but all she wanted now was for it to end and to hear some news. She turned the car round, and when she reached the garden centre pulled in and drove into a parking bay. The song was still playing. She googled Jersey General Hospital on her phone, then dialled the number, turning down the radio.

When the switchboard operator answered, Georgie said, 'Hi, could you tell me if a Mr Roger Richardson has been admitted?'

'One moment please.' Then he asked, 'Are you a relative?'

'I'm his fiancée.'

'And your name is?'

'Georgina Maclean.'

'Can you hold please, madam?'

After an age, he came back on the line. 'Yes, Mr Roger Richardson has just been admitted.'

'Is he all right? Is he OK?'

'I'm afraid I cannot give you any information.'

'Oh God. Oh God.'

Tears welling in her eyes, she started the engine, reversed out and drove, as fast as the heavy traffic allowed, towards St Helier and the hospital.

43

Monday 14 January

In the scrub area of Theatre 3, Marcus Valentine washed his hands twice, dried them and held them out. A nurse helped him into his gloves. Behind him, Roger Richardson lay on the operating table, swathed in sterile green cloth. Heart-rate patches were stuck to his chest, trailing with wires to monitors with digital readouts; a grey pulse oximeter was clipped to his index finger. Veins were cannulated with drip lines into the back of his hand and there was a plastic ID tag around his wrist. Next to Richardson was an anaesthetic machine and trolley, with the anaesthetist standing beside him, studying the readouts in deep concentration.

Out of respect, there was no music today, and Marcus had donned a plain blue cap.

All the theatre team were fully gowned up. The anaesthetist informed the surgeon that his patient was ready. Marcus, followed by Robert Resmes, went across to the table. He stared down at the unconscious man. Thinking about how he had held court at the table in his house last month, captivating all the ladies.

What a difference a few weeks make.

He was handed a scalpel from a tray of sterile instruments by a scrub nurse and hovered it over the flying instructor's abdomen.

He stood in silence, holding the scalpel, aware of all the eyes on him.

Waiting and thinking. Then he started.

Knife to skin.

He began making a steady, long incision midline from the

xiphisternum straight down to the pubic bone. As he cut, a ribbon of yellow, fatty flesh followed the path of the blade, filled seconds later by bright-red blood.

Assisted by his student, and a theatre nurse who was suctioning away the blood, he clamped back the folded tissue and began to prod around, pushing down the top of the bowel to expose the spleen.

'I can see the immediate cause of the internal bleeding,' Marcus announced. He liked to keep his team well informed during all emergency surgery procedures. At this moment, here in this microcosm of the universe, this crucible, he was the master.

'A badly ruptured spleen. There is no possibility of repairing it, so our safest chance to stop the haemorrhaging is to remove it.'

For the benefit of Resmes and any of the juniors attending, he continued. 'The spleen's not that important an organ. It will leave him more open to infections, so he will need pneumococcal vaccinations and antibiotics for the rest of his life, but hey, that's better than the alternative.'

'Bleeding out until death?' Resmes queried.

'Exactly,' he said.

Marcus Valentine was feeling extremely happy he'd made the incision so long, because it had exposed something very interesting. Something no one in the theatre team could have spotted without peering in as closely as he did. And even then, they almost certainly would not have noticed what he could see.

The tiny perforation in Roger's bowel.

Just a faint nick.

He remembered from his medical training that such holes in the bowel could be caused by a number of reasons. Appendicitis; bowel disease; cancer; or, in this case, trauma.

Richardson had been through a pretty big accident. Perfectly credible that among his injuries would be a perforated bowel.

And perfectly credible that his surgeon might not spot it. Especially such a tiny hole as this.

It would be a simple procedure to repair it. Two, maybe three sutures. Self-dissolving ones. In three or four days, assuming no brain damage from his fractured skull, Roger would likely be well on the road to recovery.

But we don't want that, do we? You'll recover when I decide you recover. If, of course, I decide that at all.

He could easily ignore it. Simply remove the man's catastrophically damaged spleen, and under normal circumstances that operation would save his life.

But, of course, these were not normal circumstances.

They're not, are they, Roger? he nearly whispered, excitedly.

He held the power of life or death over this man. Literally. In his two hands. All the team around him assumed he was doing his very best to save Roger Richardson. And what possible reason could he have not to? It was the perfect opportunity!

All he had to do now was what everyone was expecting him to do. Remove the spleen.

And nothing else.

Over the next few days, bile from the leaking bowel would start to enter his system. Blood poisoning would set in. Sepsis would attack all his internal organs, causing gradual failure. When Roger Richardson began to regain consciousness, his speech would be slurred – which the hospital team would put down to concussion from his skull injury. He might shiver, stop passing urine, perhaps become breathless. His skin would eventually start to become mottled, at which point an alert medic would diagnose possible sepsis.

And it was then he could make a decision. Save him or let him die.

If he did nothing, within days any treatment would be far too late. Because that good old, trusty perforated bowel would keep on poisoning him from within. Roger would be beyond antibiotics at that stage.

Of course, much later, if he did not intervene, the pathologist performing the postmortem would find the tear in the bowel. In his report, the pathologist would write that it was almost microscopic in size and would have been virtually impossible to spot during the emergency operation, in which Dr Marcus Valentine carried out an exemplary removal of the spleen, doing all he could to save Mr Richardson.

No question of any blame on him, Marcus thought. This was a gift, fallen into his hands. Such good fortune he had a non-emergency list today and had been able to attend to the injured man. So lucky, being in the right place at the right time . . .

Timing is everything!

44

Monday 14 January

After her long, anxious wait in the Relatives' Waiting Room of the Intensive Care Unit, a nurse came in to see Georgie. A slim lady with long dark hair, she wore black trousers and a charcoal short-sleeved top embroidered in white with the words CRITICAL CARE UNIT. Her plastic name tag, clipped to a pocket, read STATES OF JERSEY. KIERA DALE. CRITICAL CARE MANAGER.

'Georgina Maclean?'

Georgie stood hastily. 'Yes.'

'Shall we sit down and have a quick chat?'

Her heart plunged. *Please God, tell me Roger's alive.*

The nurse perched on a chair next to her. Georgie noticed she was holding the form she had completed earlier on her arrival at the hospital.

'Roger Richardson is your fiancé, is that right?'

Georgie nodded.

'OK, don't be worried! He's just on his way from the Recovery ward to ICU, you'll be able to go in and see him in a few minutes. You may be a little shocked by his appearance, but he's doing really well.'

'Yes? He is?'

'The doctors were concerned about his head injuries, that he might have a fractured skull, but he's had a CT scan which has indicated some bruising from the accident, and possible concussion, but his skull is intact and his brain functions are normal, which is a good sign. But what the surgeon has had to do is perform a splenectomy.'

166

'*Splenectomy?* What does that mean, exactly?'

'Do you have any medical knowledge, Georgina?'

'A little – I'm a personal trainer, so I have some, and I'm First Aid trained.'

'Roger suffered a ruptured spleen, causing severe internal bleeding. It's a common injury in a major trauma. His spleen had to be taken out in order to remove any risk to his life from internal haemorrhaging.'

'Jesus,' Georgie said. 'What – what does that mean for him? Will he be able to keep his pilot's licence? He's a flying instructor – that's his livelihood – and he's just launching a new air taxi business.'

'I'm pretty sure he can retain his licence. We had a patient here only a few weeks ago who had a ruptured spleen from a motorcycle accident. He was a commercial pilot, very panicked about his career. I looked into the situation for him and spoke to the island's Aeromedical Examiner, Dr James Mair. The doctor told me that the CAA would temporarily suspend his licence, but there was no reason why he wouldn't be signed off as fit to fly after his recovery. The liver takes over most of the spleen's functions if it's removed. Healthy people can live quite normal lives without their spleen – but it will mean that your fiancé has to take penicillin, daily, for the rest of his life.'

'Why's that?' she asked.

'It's an important organ but not a vital one. The spleen provides antibodies – what it means for your fiancé is a slight decrease in his immune system. The penicillin will counteract that. The important thing is that he's strong – he seems a pretty fit man.'

'He is – he likes to exercise.'

The nurse smiled. 'Good. There's absolutely no reason why he won't make a full recovery and be able to continue with his career.'

'Thank God!' She dabbed her eyes. 'I still don't know what happened. Do you know? No one's given me any information. He left home this morning for a busy day of instructing. Then I heard on the news there'd been an accident at the airport. I tried to get hold of him and couldn't. I panicked and phoned the hospital and they said he'd been admitted. So I came straight here.'

'I'm sorry, Georgina, I don't know any more than you do at this time.'

Georgie sat for some moments, twisting her hands nervously. The clock on the wall said 4.43 p.m.

'As I said, don't be worried by his appearance, Georgina. You're OK with me calling you that?'

'Everyone knows me as Georgie,' she replied, quietly.

'OK, Georgie. When we go in, you'll see Roger surrounded by a lot of apparatus, which may look a little alarming, but it's all to help him in the critical next few days. He'll be wearing an oxygen mask, but that's just to assist with his breathing during the recovery process. We'll be assessing his post-op pain and delivering morphine intravenously. He's connected to monitors for his heart rate and blood pressure, and to take his ABG – his arterial blood gas readings – every one to two hours and he's cannulated with intravenous fluids to keep him stabilized. There's also a wound drain in his abdomen. You might find him a little confused and talking a bit of nonsense, but don't worry, he'll soon be getting back to normal conversation. In a day or two the physiotherapist will get him sitting up and walking around. We have one-on-one nursing care in the unit, which means Roger will have a rota of nurses dedicated solely to him, twenty-four-seven. He's going to be fine, trust me!' She gave a reassuring smile.

Georgie nodded, trying to absorb it all. 'How long before he can come home?'

'That will depend on how well he responds, but normally a splenectomy patient would be in hospital for a week, with a further four weeks convalescing at home.'

'Can I stay with him? Overnight?'

'If you want to, of course you can. We don't restrict visiting hours – but our advice is always to get some rest. He has the best possible care here. Stay with him this afternoon but go home tonight and get some sleep. Come back refreshed. It won't only make you feel better, but psychologically it'll make him feel better too.' She smiled again. 'OK?'

Georgie shrugged. 'OK,' she said, meekly. 'Thank you.'

As the nurse left, Georgie was scared rigid. Her insides in turmoil. She wondered if any of Roger's family in England had been informed of the situation. With trembling hands, she dialled the number of his parents in York.

45

Monday 14 January

Nurse Dale returned twenty minutes later to take Georgie into the ICU. She followed the nurse into the ward, a warm, bright, modern-feeling room painted in soothing tones of fresh mint green and soft white. There were five bays containing beds, each separated by a column, with the nursing station directly opposite.

Male and female medics were attending every bed, and more nurses were occupied behind the rack of monitors at their station. The room was filled with apparatus, wheeled cabinets and numerous yellow sharps bins, as well as red and white garbage containers side by side. There was a constant beeping.

Georgie walked past a thin, middle-aged man propped up in bed, with a large blue pad taped to his chest, and past a skeletal elderly woman the colour of chalk, her eyes closed and an oxygen mask over her face.

Then she saw Roger in the next bed along, lying semi-upright, his eyes open, hair awry, some strands sticking up.

She hurried over, so relieved to see him. 'Darling! Darling, hi!'

He looked around, confused, as if wondering where her voice had come from.

She stooped and kissed his cheek, which felt cold and moist. 'My darling, you're OK, you are!'

Kiera Dale had warned her not to be shocked. But it was hard. Hard to believe, for an instant, that this was the man she loved so much. It was like looking at a bad facsimile of him. A faded photo-copy.

His face was translucent, almost colourless, with two strips of gauzed plaster on his forehead and another one on his right cheek. He was plumbed into a stack of monitoring apparatus. A rail went around the whole bay, from which hung a green curtain, at this moment wide open. A metal table on wheels, with a number of drawers, stood at the end of the bed, with a chart on top of it.

Roger was dressed in gauze underpants and a cotton gown which was untied, exposing his bare, muscular chest and six-pack midriff, to which were taped a number of pads. He was hooked up via a cannula on the back of his left hand to a bunch of drip lines, and a meter was clipped to his index finger. What Georgie presumed was the wound drain was inserted in his abdomen.

Monitors on either side of him beeped steadily. Georgie took a moment to study the digital readouts, trying to work out what each represented. Blood pressure, currently 115 over 68. Heart rate 64. Another monitor, Kiera told her, was the blood-oxygen level, but Georgie wasn't sure what it should read to be normal.

She took his free hand and held it. 'I'm here, darling. How are you feeling?'

Suddenly, to her joy, he gripped her back, very faintly. 'They want me to retake geometry,' he mumbled.

'Geometry, my love? Who wants you to retake *geometry*?' She ran a hand gently through his moist hair, smoothing it down, trying to smarten him up a little.

He replied, his voice slurred. 'Thing is.' Then he lapsed back into silence.

Georgie waited. 'Yes? The *thing* is what?' she asked gently, encouraging him to talk more. To come back to her.

'I was like – fishing. My dad said it was too small. We should throw it back.'

'Where were you fishing? And what do you mean about geometry?'

'The blasted mower never worked. Was always conking out.'

'Mower? Lawn mower?'

He lapsed into silence again. Georgie turned to the nurse and smiled. She grinned back, then she leaned and whispered to Georgie, 'It's the anaesthetics and concussion. A splenectomy is a pretty big operation. Give him a bit of time and he'll start to talk more sense.'

'Thing is,' Roger said. 'The thing—'

'What *thing*, darling?' Georgie asked.

He gave her a dumb, vacant smile as if his brain had become a vast, empty cavern.

She held his hand, then stroked his hair again. One strand defiantly popped up, sticking in the air. His lips moved but no sound came out. It looked to her as if he was trying to say, *I love you.*

'I love you so much, my darling.' She wiped away tears with a tissue from the box on the tray beside him. 'You're going to be fine. You'll pull through. Fight!'

Kiera Dale had said, earlier, he was going to be fine.

Of course he would be.

She just wished she could totally believe that in her heart. But instead there was something telling her that maybe he wouldn't. And he looked terrible. Worse than the nurse had prepared her for.

Hell, of course he looked bad. He'd just been in some kind of major accident. Hopefully it was just her messed-up hormones that made her so afraid of everything.

She sat, stroking his head and feeling hot. Too hot. She'd wrapped up warmly against the cold day outside but was now sweltering in here. She'd already removed her coat when she'd first come in and she was about to take off her pullover when, suddenly, a whole team in scrubs descended on the bay.

Kiera led Georgie away into the middle of the room, explaining it was a ward round, and telling her who they all were. One of the hospital's top general surgeons, the duty consultant anaesthetist, the nurse in charge and the pharmacist, to check on Roger's medication and ensure he was being given sufficient morphine. At the rear was the physiotherapist who would be assessing how soon he could get Roger out of bed and sitting up.

Green curtains swished around Roger, sealing him from sight.

The nurse suggested, very kindly, that Georgie took a break, perhaps either sitting in the Relatives' Room or popping down to the snack bar to get a cup of tea and coming back in a short while.

But Georgie did not want to leave this room. She took a few paces back and stood beside a yellow triangle warning of a slippery floor, feeling utterly helpless and lost. Behind her was an old man, hooked up to a ventilator, who looked like he had been carved from alabaster. In the furthest bed was someone swathed in bandages, head to foot, moaning in what sounded like terrible pain.

Maybe she should get some fresh air, she decided. Take a walk around the block.

Very reluctantly, she left the ward, walked down the corridor, past the Relatives' Room, and turned a corner, passing a hand sanitizer, an empty trolley and a plethora of signs and arrows.

SECOND FLOOR. ROBIN WARD. LE QUESNE UNIT. HAEMATOLOGY/ONCOLOGY UNIT. INTENSIVE CARE UNIT. MAIN HOSPITAL AND CHAPEL.

Chapel?

For bereaved relatives?

She walked past the open doors and glanced uncomfortably at the interior of the large chapel.

Shit. What kind of message was that giving off? The chapel just along from the Intensive Care Unit?

A nurse hurried past her.

Georgie stood still. In another life, as a child, with her deeply religious mother, she might have gone and sat in that chapel and prayed for Roger to be OK. But her father had died from a sudden heart attack. No amount of praying had saved him. And prayer hadn't saved her mother from dying of cancer.

She walked on and saw the lift and a sign to the stairs just to her right.

She changed her mind. She didn't want to leave this floor, did not want to be too far away from Roger. Ahead of her she saw a blue pedal bin with a red bucket on top. On either side was a row of collapsed wheelchairs, and beyond them several stacked plastic chairs.

She removed the top one, sat down on it and put her head in her hands. Moments later she felt her tears trickling through her fingers. *Please make Roger well again. Please.*

Suddenly, she was aware of someone standing over her. She heard a familiar, well-spoken male voice she could not immediately place.

'Georgie, hello!'

She looked up at the man in blue scrubs, who was staring down at her with a deeply sympathetic smile.

Marcus Valentine.

46

Monday 14 January

After checking on Roger Richardson, Marcus had helped out in theatre on two more of the casualties from the airport. One was a man in his late fifties, suffering from massive internal injuries. He hadn't made it. Someone mentioned he was a student pilot who had been under instruction from Richardson at the time of the accident.

There was always an air of gloom and despondency in the theatre when a patient died – not to mention, he thought, irreverently, as he drove home in the darkness shortly after 7 p.m., the ensuing paperwork, including the report that would have to be written for the coroner about Byron Wilding. But tonight, as he accelerated along Victoria Avenue, enjoying the music of the engine behind him and the responsiveness of the Porsche, he wasn't feeling any of that. He was feeling pensive.

He'd seen Georgie Maclean sitting, downcast, in the corridor outside the ICU and, being the kind, caring man he was, had taken the time and trouble to sit down beside her and talk her through all they were doing to save her beloved's life. Omitting, of course, one small and rather vital detail.

His little secret.

How much he'd wanted to hold Georgie's hand. Put his arm around her and pull her close, breathe in her scents. But, of course, he'd played it straight and proper. The good news, he had been able to tell her, was the successful removal of Roger's spleen and, honestly, so long as he took penicillin daily, it was barely more relevant than an appendix – and hey, did you ever hear of anyone that had a problem because they had no appendix? It was just a useless remnant from our evolutionary past – one day humans would be born with no appendix, just like hundreds of thousands of years ago they'd begun to be born without gills. One day they'd be born without spleens, too. Good old Darwin, eh!

That had made her smile. Albeit thinly.

He'd qualified it by explaining to her something she might like to know about her developing foetus. That at the early stages of a baby's development there is a structure known as the pharyngeal arches, which later become the jaw and neck. These, he told her, bear more than just a passing resemblance to the gills of fish.

He could see his chat was taking her mind off things, and when he finally left, she thanked him and gave him a sad little smile.

Ten minutes later he was home. He drove up the driveway, clicked the app on his phone to open the garage door, parked next to Claire's Evoque and killed the engine.

Then he sat in his car for a while, reflecting. Enjoying this moment of calm. Luxuriating in the comfort of the Porsche's cabin, the elegant ergonomics and the surroundings of his nice, orderly garage. Keeping the stereo on, he selected some music, the 'Soldier's Chorus' from Gounod's *Faust*. Claire wasn't such a fan of classical music, preferring mindless pop. He turned the sound up loud, almost deafeningly loud. There were moments like this when music lifted him so high he felt he could almost touch the heavens.

And here in Heaven, he pictured the smile he had brought to Georgie's face. Despite all her fear and worries, he'd created that smile, and that was enough. The sign he needed. He was the one who could lift her beyond the sadness of this turgid relationship she was in – and be her saviour. *Oh Georgie, do trust me!*

He loved this garage; here, everything was in its place. Each of his tools on the wall rack, perfectly aligned – by him. Screwdrivers; chisels; hammers; saws; the perfectly matched rubber tyres hung at the far end, in front of both Claire's car and his own, at exactly equal heights, to prevent them from ever hitting the end wall. The identical shrimping nets for the twins. The shelf on which sat a row of cans of oil, WD40, 3-In-One and de-icer spray arranged in order of height. Everything where you could see it, find it. Just like the instruments on a surgical tray.

A few minutes later he walked out of the garage, tapping his phone to close the doors behind him, and climbed the short path and then the steps to the front door. As he let himself in through the outer door to the porch, he heard the sound of a child screaming, and Claire's raised voice.

Oh joy!

This was becoming normal, as were the tiny, discarded wellies strewn across the porch floor, along with a bunch of trainers. He shook his head. These should have been put away in the racks of carefully labelled shelves he had made for them, painstakingly, over many weekends in his garage.

Adding to his exasperation, he saw that Claire's Barbour coat was hung on the wrong peg. *His* peg.

Jesus! He moved it, then hung his velvet-collared Crombie in its place. Its rightful place. *His* peg.

He looked down at the trainers. The tiny ones belonged to the twins and the much larger pair was Claire's. All with their laces sprawling untidily from them.

He tut-tutted and knelt down. No self-respecting surgeon would ever tolerate such untidiness. He coiled and then tucked each pair of laces inside the shoes, before placing them in their correctly labelled cubby holes. When he had finished, he stood up and entered the hallway.

To be greeted by an exhausted-looking Claire cradling a sleeping Cormac in her arms. She gave him a smile.

'How was your day, darling?' she asked.

'Interesting and knackering,' he replied, as he kissed her on the cheek. 'I've been dealing with the crash victims.'

'Crash?'

'Haven't you seen the news?'

She shook her head. 'I've been a bit busy with work, with the Vomit Comet and our darling terrorists, trying to keep our home intact.'

He peered at her. 'You've got puke all over your top.'

'It's my new look! Like it?'

'Very fetching!' he responded, forcing a smile.

'You look like you could do with a stiff drink – or are you going for a run?'

No, Georgie's not running at the moment, she's sitting in the hospital by Roger's bed, he nearly replied. Instead he said, 'Yes please to the drink. A very large Martini.'

'Funny you should say that – I have one all ready for you. I just need to put it into the shaker with some ice.'

'I never knew I married a mind-reader.'

'Ain't life full of surprises?'

47

Wednesday 16 January

Life was full of surprises, and many of them totally shit, Georgie thought, seated at the breakfast bar in her tracksuit. And they didn't come much more shit than this. She'd spent the whole of yesterday at the hospital with Roger and was exhausted.

Late yesterday afternoon, to her delight, he had started to become more lucid and they'd been able to have a conversation – in between bouts of him drifting off to sleep – when he'd started to tell her about what had happened. How some flying object came out of nowhere, and his panicking student pilot jammed the pedals.

'Isn't that why planes have dual controls?' she'd asked. 'So you can take over from someone who's acting irrationally?'

Roger gave her a slow, wry smile. 'An engineer I knew, back in my RAF days, once told me something that's very true. He said the problem with making anything idiot-proof is that idiots have a great deal of ingenuity.'

They'd both laughed and Georgie was happy to see some of his normal, positive and jokey self. He *would* be fine. It was all going to be fine. He'd be coming home in just a few days' time. And in just a few months' time, his only after-effect would be that he'd become a penicillin junkie. There could have been a lot worse outcomes, she thought with a shudder. Half the people in the accident were now dead. It could so easily have been him.

So very easily.

Those poor families.

She thought back to the conversation she'd had with Marcus

in the corridor. He'd been really positive, but she would have preferred less humour and more reassurance. There was something about him that made her more unsettled than comforted, something she could not put a finger on. He came across all superior, but Roger had said that was 'just him'. At the end of the day he'd saved Roger's life so she would forever be grateful to him for that.

Kiera Dale had gone off shift late in the afternoon. The equally friendly and attentive ICU nurse who had taken over from her, Theresa Adams, who was also pregnant, had suggested to Georgie, sometime after 10 p.m., with Roger sound asleep and breathing normally and unaided now, that she should go home and get some rest. It was the same advice Kiera had given her the day before. That she would feel a lot more refreshed after a decent night's sleep and a change of clothes. And besides, she wouldn't be able to come into the ICU again until after 11 a.m. when the morning ward round would be finished. The nurse assured Georgie that she, or someone from the team who took over from her in the night, would call if there was any change in Roger's condition, although all looked positive.

But she'd not slept a wink all night. Again. She'd just lain there in the empty bed, tossing and turning, fretting about Roger and about the baby inside her. Wondering, fearfully, if it was still alive. Finally, shortly after 6 a.m., she'd had enough and got up, walking over to the window and opening the curtains onto the pre-dawn darkness. She stared at the lights of St Helier in the far distance and the occasional flicker of light from a fishing boat out in the bay. Roger was improving, wasn't he? That's what Kiera had told her, and Nurse Adams too.

That he was fine, doing well, heart rate good, blood pressure pretty much back to normal. The team seemed happy with the arterial blood gas readings which they took every couple of hours – although she didn't fully understand what they were.

She was desperate to speak to someone at the hospital now.

To make sure Roger was OK. She'd been given a direct number to the ICU. She could just pick up her phone and dial. But she didn't want to sound needy, and besides, what could they tell her? He was obviously OK, otherwise someone would have called.

Wouldn't they?

She pulled on a tracksuit, gloves and a bobble hat and let herself out into the darkness. Then she set off, at a quickening pace, on a short run along the promenade. As soon as she had returned home, she switched on the television to Channel TV. On her iPad, she downloaded the online version of the *Jersey Evening Post*. And stared at the front-page splash:

WAS DRONE CAUSE OF MONDAY'S AIRPORT CRASH KILLING FIVE?

The picture beneath showed the tail section of the Beechcraft aeroplane sheared off and lying at an angle, in the foreground, with the wrecked Piper close by. Further away was the burning fuselage, with firefighters playing hoses on it.

Beneath the splash was a smaller headline:

Miracle Escape by Mother and Baby

The story went on to say how a Piper, with a trainee pilot under instruction, had apparently veered off the runway on landing and collided with a taxiing Beechcraft awaiting clearance for take-off. The woman carrying her baby had stepped out of the rear of the tail section with only minor injuries. Four people, including the pilot and co-pilot of the Beechcraft, had died instantly when the privately owned aircraft had burst into flames. One person in the Piper, the trainee pilot, had also died subsequently from his injuries, but there were four survivors from the accident who had been taken to the Jersey General Hospital, two with life-threatening injuries, the other two being kept in overnight for observation.

Life-threatening injuries.

The words chilled Georgie's bones. Roger was one of those with *life-threatening* injuries.

If he hadn't had his spleen removed, he would have bled out and died. Would never have lived to see his child born. And their baby would have grown up never knowing his – or her – father.

There was no doubt Marcus Valentine had saved his life.

It was ironic, she thought. They were all at dinner in Marcus's house, just over a month ago, little knowing what lay ahead. All the times that Roger had flown Marcus, holding his life in his capable pilot's hands. The consultant relying on Roger to take him up into the sky and land him safely at his destinations.

Now Roger owed his own survival to Marcus's surgical skills.

Strange how life worked out.

When Roger was safely out of hospital and back home, they should sort out that catch-up with Marcus and Claire.

She made a note on her phone to do just that.

The story came up again, on the 8 a.m. news on television. She watched, clinging to every word the presenter said. As if by doing that, she could somehow influence the situation. Somehow make Roger whole and completely OK again.

At least there was still no call from the hospital. Hopefully, the physiotherapist, as Kiera Dale had told her, would get him sitting up and out of bed this morning.

She took a bite of toast, on which she had spread a thick layer of marmalade, and instantly felt queasy.

She ran to the toilet and threw up.

Afterwards she felt marginally better. She returned to the kitchen and sat back at the breakfast bar. On the television screen she saw the front facade of the hospital. A presenter stood outside, speaking into a large microphone. Alongside her, to Georgie's surprise at seeing a recognizable face, stood Marcus Valentine.

The presenter said, in a voice that seemed a little too upbeat, Georgie thought, 'The survivors of Monday's accident at Jersey

Airport were ferried by ambulance here to Jersey General Hospital, which has long been prepared, through regular Major Incident scenario rehearsals, for such an emergency. I have with me one of the hospital's senior consultant surgeons, Marcus Valentine. Mr Valentine, can you tell us how the hospital has been dealing with this horrific situation?' She thrust the microphone at him.

The face of the obstetrician filled the screen. 'As you rightly said, my colleagues and I have regular worst-case-scenario drills. I believe that, despite our small team here, we coped with the emergency extremely well. The loss of life in this terrible accident is tragic, but all the injured have been given the best medical care possible.'

Georgie watched, avidly. She wondered if he'd had press training for this sort of occasion.

When the item was finished, she went along to the bathroom, turned on the shower and stripped off her running kit whilst waiting for the water to run hot. Then she stepped in and stood there for a long while, pounded by the soothing water. She felt, momentarily, shielded from the world. Maybe as safe as her baby was feeling inside her womb. Her baby, as yet happily unaware of all the shit that lay waiting out there. Waiting to screw you up. Waiting to get you no matter how much your guard was up.

You'll beat it, little one, my very special Bump. You're going to be one of life's winners. Your daddy and I will make sure of that. OK?

The running water of the shower made her want to pee. She stepped out, dried off, then sat down on the loo. Before flushing, she followed Kath Clow's advice, as she did every time she peed now, and peered down to inspect what she had done before flushing.

To her dismay, she saw a small trace of blood.

She stared at it for some moments. It was tiny. But it worried her deeply. Oh God, was it the start of a miscarriage?

She quickly dried her hair and, as soon as she had finished, she hurried back down the corridor into the small entrance hall. Just inside the front door was a Victorian coat rack, hung with several of her and Roger's hats and caps, one of which was an antique leather flying helmet she'd bought him in the St Aubin's Vintage Fair as a Christmas present last year.

Below the rack were their wellingtons, hiking boots and her trainers. As she looked down at them, she was puzzled.

All the laces of their boots and her trainers had been folded neatly and tucked inside the shoes.

48

Wednesday 16 January

Had Roger done that before he'd left the flat, Georgie wondered? And she hadn't noticed?

He could at times be almost irritatingly precise, which she put down to his pilot training. But he'd never before left his shoes – or hers – that neatly.

At this moment, wanting to get back to the hospital as soon as possible, even though she knew she would not be able to see him until 11 a.m., she had no time to dwell on it.

She gave their close friends a round-robin-type text update on Roger's condition then spent more time than usual deciding what to wear. Something comfortable and not too warm, as she would be having a long day at the hospital and it was damned hot there. She changed from jeans and a blue sweater to a skirt and top, then back to jeans.

Shortly after 9.15 a.m., having finally decided on a thin roll-neck, suede ankle boots, the black-and-white patterned overcoat and a flat red cap, she drove her Golf up towards the entrance to the Patriotic Street multistorey car park.

She reversed into a bay in the hospital visitors' section, paid on her phone for twelve hours and hurried across the road to the Gwyneth Huelin wing. Entering, she almost bowled over an elderly man on a stick. She murmured an apology, strode past a row of wheelchairs and the snack bar counter, checking the signs on the wall for the ICU, still not used to the warren this place was. Then she set off, as fast as she could, desperate to get to Roger's bedside.

Ignoring the lift, she sprinted up the two flights of stairs, and then walked quickly along the zig-zagging corridors until she reached the entrance to the ICU, and the sign to the right, above a bell, instructing all visitors to press the button. She looked at her watch and hesitated. It was only 9.30 a.m. and she'd been clearly told she wouldn't be able to go into the unit until after 11 a.m. But at least she could speak to someone and get an update on Roger. She pressed and heard a rasping sound. And read the sign that said visitors sometimes might have to wait for a response if they were busy.

Georgie waited for what seemed an eternity. Finally, a male voice in broken English asked her name.

After a further short wait, Kiera came through the door, closing it behind her. She was all smiles, to Georgie's relief. That had to mean good news, didn't it?

'You're back bright and early, Georgie! Did you manage to get some sleep?'

'Not really. I've been worried sick all night. How – how's Roger?'

A shadow flitted across the nurse's face. Just the tiniest hesitation, a barely perceptible twitch of a muscle, then all smiles again. 'He's doing fine, he's had some breakfast and he's quite chatty.' She paused. 'But—'

Georgie felt the hesitation as heavily as if a sack of lead weights had been dropped inside her stomach. 'But?' she echoed.

'He's perhaps not doing quite as well as we would have expected. He is OK, but I would have liked to have seen a little more improvement at this stage. There could be a number of reasons for this – it's most likely that we haven't quite got his medications right yet. But there's no cause for concern.'

Georgie could see from Kiera's expression that there was, very definitely, cause for concern.

Trembling, she asked, 'Am I able to go in? I know you said that I'd have to wait till after 11 a.m., but—'

'You can go in as soon as the ward round is over, Georgie. We'll know a lot more after the doctors have seen him, but really try not to worry too much. Roger's a strong, fit man, and everyone reacts to major surgery in a different way. As I say, it's probably just a question of adjusting his meds and that will all be sorted during the ward round.'

Georgie nodded, bleakly.

'Really don't worry,' the nurse reassured her.

A tear trickled down Georgie's cheek and she wiped it away with a finger. 'I'm sorry,' she said, crushing more tears with her eyelids. 'I – hoped I'd come and find he was well on the mend.' She smiled and sniffed. 'I thought – you know – that you were going to tell me he was out running a marathon or something.'

Kiera smiled. 'I think that would have been slightly optimistic, don't you? Hey, you know, we're doing everything we possibly can.'

49

Wednesday 16 January

For the next hour and a half, Georgie sat alone on a chair in the Relatives' Room, her coat and cap on the chair beside her. She distracted herself by contacting by phone and a few emails Roger's frail parents and lots of friends who were keen to know how he was doing. His dear old mum and dad wouldn't be able to travel to Jersey as they were not fit enough, but they were desperate to hear regular news. That in itself was quite draining just keeping everyone up to date. Trying to stay on the positive side of things. She hoped she hadn't missed out anyone. No one else came into the room and she was glad about that, she didn't want to have to make small talk to anyone. Did not want anyone to see her tears.

She liked Kiera but, equally, she knew her job was a tough one. Trying always to be positive. Comforting. Trying to break bad news as gently as possible to relatives – as Georgie could clearly see in her face that she was trying to break it to her.

She stared at the speckled floor. At the recently painted wall. Checked the news constantly for any further information on what had happened on Monday. The online version of the *Jersey Evening Post* and the *Bailiwick Express*. Something was plaguing her – something she was meant to be doing. She'd called all her clients booked in for today, cancelling their sessions, so she couldn't think what it was.

Trying not to dwell on the trace of blood in her urine, she sat, cradling her phone in her hand, occasionally staring at it, as if waiting for a message from Roger, a text or a WhatsApp or an email.

Stupid, she knew, there wasn't going to be anything coming from him because he didn't have his phone with him. She googled 'spleen removed recovery' to kill time but as so often with internet searching on medical issues, she wished she hadn't. She'd asked a nurse last night where the clothes that he'd been wearing had been put. They were all in a plastic crate, ruined. The Emergency team, she'd explained, had cut them off him, to avoid the risks in lifting him to undress him in case he had any spinal injuries. His wallet had been removed to confirm his identity, she'd told Georgie, and had now been placed in the hospital safe along with all the belongings he'd had with him.

She'd gone down to have a rummage through his clothes, checking all the pockets, but there was no sign of his phone or keys.

When she'd finally got through to someone at the Flying Club, the helpful and sympathetic man had informed her that Roger's phone, and that of his student pilot, had both been found in the wreckage of the Piper, but had been impounded by the Air Crash Investigation team and would form part of their enquiries. To establish, she presumed, whether either of them had been using their phone at the time of the crash. He also said he would enquire if a set of keys had been found.

Roger wasn't going to be happy, she thought, when he learned that his beloved vintage leather flying jacket, with its cosy fleece lining, had been cut to ribbons. She decided to start looking online for another one for him as a gift.

If he lived.

Of course he would live. All Kiera had said was that his recovery was a little slower than they expected. Nothing more, nothing sinister.

Except her expression.

Fear shimmied through Georgie.

Please be OK, Roger. For me. For our Bump.

You will be OK! Of course you will!

50

Wednesday 16 January

After a long wait, during which Georgie had found the perfect jacket in Roger's size on eBay and placed a high bid, she heard footsteps approaching. The clock on the wall read 11.11. The critical care nurse came into the Relatives' Room with a smile.

'All right, Georgie, we can go in now!' Kiera Dale said, brightly.

She stood immediately, picking up her things. 'How is he?'

She nodded. 'Yes, he's doing a little better now and looking forward to seeing you.'

Georgie held her hands under the sanitizer, rubbing the gel in, then they walked across the ward. Passing the middle-aged man she'd seen before with a blue pad taped to his chest, Georgie noticed that the bed at the far end that had yesterday contained the woman swathed head to foot in bandages was now empty.

'Where's she?' she asked, barely above a whisper. 'She was one of the air-crash survivors, wasn't she?'

'I'm afraid we weren't able to save her,' the nurse said. 'Did you know her?'

Georgie shook her head, her throat tight. Then, ahead to her right, she saw Roger, propped up against pillows. His face was paler, chalkier than yesterday. The drain was still in his abdomen, there were pads still fixed to his chest and his left hand was still cannulated.

He looked at her and smiled.

'Darling!' she said, bending down and kissing him on the lips. They were cold and dry. 'So good to see you. So good!'

'And you,' he replied, quietly. 'How are you?'

'So much better for seeing you. God, I've been so worried.'

The nurse slipped discreetly away.

Georgie sat on the chair beside him and took his right hand. It felt cold. 'How are you feeling? Did you sleep OK?'

An alarm somewhere near beeped increasingly loudly.

He shook his head. 'I had a bloody awful night. Constant noise, constant racket. Beeping of sodding monitors, like that one now – just non-stop.'

'My poor love.'

'I felt so lonely – although the nurses are all lovely, and very attentive.' He gave her a faint smile as she squeezed his hand. 'Someone died in the night. There was frantic activity. I saw a man and a teenage girl crying – I think they're relatives.'

'Was that the woman wrapped in bandages in the bed at the far end?'

'I don't know.'

'She'd been in the other plane – the one that collided with you?'

'Yes, I think she was.'

'That's terrible. So sad. The whole thing is just so—' She fell silent for a moment. 'Thank God you're OK. How do you feel?'

'Muzzy. Like my brain has been in a blender.' He grinned.

She smiled back. 'I'm not surprised. You've been through a pretty horrible experience, but you're on the mend.'

He nodded. 'Yep.'

His eyes closed, momentarily, before opening again. 'Sorry, it's so good to see you, but I'm so tired.'

'Do you want me to leave you and let you sleep?'

'No. Don't. Don't leave me. I – I – I'm just happy you're here.'

She blinked away tears. 'I was so scared. When I heard the news. I thought I'd lost you.'

'I'm a fighter.' He closed his eyes again, then opened them and looked straight into hers. 'I'm a tiger!'

'You are! You're my tiger!'

Drifting into sleep, he said again, slurring his words, 'I'm your tiger. I love you, Georgie. Babes. I love you so much.'

A different monitor alarm began beeping. Somewhere else in the ward.

'See what I mean?' Roger said, waking. 'It's just constant.'

'Isn't that a good thing? Better to be here where you have really good medical care available, surely?'

Roger gave a blank look.

'So, tell me, what happened? I still don't really know anything about the accident. What can you remember?'

'I – we were coming in to land – doing touch and goes. Something small suddenly hurtled towards us and hit us. Byron panicked and seized the controls like someone possessed. I was – trying – to correct him. He was – just – just in total panic. Jammed the rudder – jammed the pedals – fighting me. I—'

He lapsed into silence and his eyes closed again.

Georgie looked at his monitors. His blood pressure had dropped a little since last night, from 92/60 to 80/50, with a heart rate of 82.

She leaned over and whispered into his ear, 'You're going to be fine! A couple of days in here and you'll be right as rain again!' She kissed his cheek.

The alarm, a couple of bays away, was beeping more urgently. A team of medics hurried into the room, passing them, and Georgie heard the swish of curtains closing. But she barely noticed. She was totally focused on Roger. She held his hand, gently. 'I know I imagined it, but I was sure Bump was moving in the night,' she said. 'He – she – *whatever* – was missing its daddy. I said you'd be home very soon. You will be.'

There was no reaction.

From inside her handbag, her phone vibrated with a text. Without letting go of his hand, she extricated it and looked at the display.

Hi Georgie, we are all at the gym waiting. Did we get the time or day wrong?

Shit, she thought, dismayed. Her over-70s ladies spinning group which was at 11 a.m. on Wednesdays. She'd totally forgotten to cancel them. *Shit, shit, shit.*

Letting go of Roger's hand, she tapped an apologetic reply, explaining she had a family emergency. Just as she sent the text, her phone rang.

She saw on the display it was a friend of hers, Margot Aldridge. She sent the call to voicemail.

Then she took his hand again. And almost instantly felt a squeeze.

'I'm back,' she whispered. 'I'm staying with you.' She looked at the monitors again. His blood pressure was now 64/48. Was it her imagination or had it dropped further? His heart rate was now 100. Hadn't it been 82 a few minutes ago?

A text pinged, from Margot.

Georgie darling. I heard the terrible news about the air crash. Is Roger OK? Call me when you can. Thinking of you guys. Big love and hugs from us both. M xxx

She texted back a thanks, then sat with him for the next hour, repeatedly squeezing his hand and getting a faint response, watching the monitors like a hawk while he slept. No change.

That had to be good.

51

Two nurses, one of them Kiera Dale, approached, saying they were going to wash Roger and make him comfortable. As they began pulling the curtains around him, Kiera suggested Georgie might prefer to go back to the Relatives' Room or down to the snack bar to get a cup of tea or coffee.

Nodding like an automaton, she stood up, left the ward. She entered the Relatives' Room and saw a tearful young woman, holding hands with a distraught-looking man. Unable to face sitting in there, she carried on out into the corridor, deciding to go to the snack bar and get a coffee. She needed some air.

As she went down the stairs and reached the first floor, a familiar figure, elegantly dressed in a checked tweed suit and smart shoes, was striding up from below.

Kath Clow.

'Georgie!' her friend said. 'I apologize I haven't got back to you yet, we've been frantic here. I'm so sorry to hear about Roger.'

Unable to help herself, tears rolled down Georgie's cheeks.

'Oh no!' Kath took her arm. 'Come with me, let's have a quick chat. I've got a few minutes.'

The obstetrician led her along past the Paediatrics ward nursing station and in through a door above which were the signs COLPOSCOPY and CONSULTING ROOM 5.

Georgie followed her into a small, cluttered office. There was a desk with a computer screen, keyboard and phone, racks of shelving loaded with files, and a noticeboard to which were pinned

194

a photograph of Kath's beautiful white house together with several views of the Lake District. Next to it was a timetable.

'Cup of tea?' Kath asked her.

'I'd rather some coffee, Kath. Is that OK please? Weak with some milk. Or green tea if not?'

'I've got both.'

'Actually,' Georgie said, reflecting on her lack of sleep, 'maybe coffee, please. And not so weak after all.'

Clow grinned. 'You look like you need a strong one, my love.'

She did. And a few minutes later, the coffee hit the spot, perking her up a little.

'So, how are you coping with all this?' Kath asked, sitting down next to Georgie with a hand on hers.

Tearfully, she told her.

'Don't worry, Georgie, I'm sure Roger will be fine. The whole ICU team are brilliant. Roger is in the best possible care.'

'That's good to hear,' she said, flatly.

'Believe me, he is.'

Georgie managed a weak smile.

Kath stole a glance at her watch. 'I'm going to have to shoot in a couple of minutes. So, tell me, is everything else OK? We haven't really spoken since your last appointment, what with Christmas and everything. How've you been?'

Georgie blushed. 'Actually, I was going to make an appointment with you.'

'Oh?'

'I've been checking the loo – as you suggested – each time I go. I had a wee this morning and saw a trace of blood. A very small amount.' She shrugged. 'Just a trace.'

Kath frowned. 'Blood in your urine?'

'A little, yes – just a tiny bit. I'm so scared I'm having a miscarriage. Stress can cause that to happen, can't it?'

'What colour was it?' asked Clow.

'Bright red – it seemed fresh, Kath,' Georgie replied.

'Well, it can be a sign of miscarriage, but if it was just a small amount it's probably nothing to worry about. There could be a number of reasons, but in view of your past history we'd better check it out. If there is anything there, we can deal with it. Far better than ignoring it and taking the risk, however tiny – and it *is* tiny – of something nasty developing. Better to rule it out and have peace of mind.'

The words sent a chill spiralling through her. 'Nasty? Do you mean cancer?'

Clow put an arm around her, reassuringly. 'Georgie, really, there's almost certainly nothing to worry about, as I said, that blood could be present for all kinds of reasons, but let's just make sure. I'd like to do another colposcopy on you, just as a precaution.' She pulled out a business card from a drawer and scribbled on it. 'This is the mobile number of my secretary, Gwynne – it will save you going through the switchboard, and it's better than calling my mobile for this type of appointment. Tell Gwynne that I've told you I want to see you this week for a colposcopy examination, and she'll squeeze you in. OK? I will also refer you to Urology just to cover all bases.'

Georgie thanked her and hugged her goodbye.

But as soon as she had left her office, the obstetrician pulled up her notes on her screen and pored through them. Despite the assurances she had given her friend, Georgie Maclean, she did not like the sound of blood in her urine.

Had she missed something significant?

Something potentially life-threatening?

52

Wednesday 16 January

Marcus Valentine yawned, feeling tired because he'd been up since 5 a.m. Far earlier than normal. Out on *black ops*, he grinned to himself. Georgie might not even have noticed. But surely, with her fiancé incapacitated, she would have appreciated a helping hand keeping her house tidy, and it was exciting seeing where she lived, how they lived. Boy, they were messy!

It was handy having the keys. Marcus had taken them from the box containing Roger's clothes before they were locked in the hospital safe. It was the impulse of a moment, but as he did it he'd felt a rush of excitement. A surge really. A sense of power.

Accompanied by his registrar and his student, he completed his ward round, laying on the charm and apologizing profusely to a number of his patients who had been awaiting C-sections and other procedures, explaining the emergency that had arisen, although all of them were aware of it. Next up was to visit Roger Richardson and see how he was doing. But first, he needed a shot of coffee. Telling Barnaby and Robert he would catch up with them later, he made his way along to the staff kitchen and turned a corner. Then abruptly slowed his pace.

Georgie Maclean was just ahead of him, dressed in jeans, a chic coat and red cap, walking along while talking on her phone, in the same direction as himself. He knew where she was heading. To her beloved's bedside.

Of course that's where you are going! How lovely, kind and caring you are, Georgie. I'll catch you in a few mins!

Georgie Maclean was just so alluring. She looked sensuous, receptive, vulnerable. And at this moment he was feeling a huge power over her life.

He entered the tiny kitchen, checked there was water in the kettle and switched it on. He lifted a mug from the drying rack and spooned two large heaps of coffee into it. Then added a third. Hey, why stint himself?

Opening the fridge door, he took out a carton of milk and tipped some into the mug. One of the few valuable things he had learned from his mother was always to put the milk in first, to prevent the water from scalding the coffee. It made it taste much better.

A few minutes later, he took his steaming mug, sat down on a stool and ripped open a packet of digestive biscuits someone had left on the table. He ate two of them. Then, greedily, and knowing they weren't great for his waistline – but what the hell, he was back into running now – a third. He blew on his coffee, trying to cool it. After several minutes, anxious to see Georgie in case she left, he ran some cold water into his coffee until it was cool enough for him to gulp straight down. The thought of seeing her again gave him butterflies in his stomach.

Behind him he heard the sound of a door opening. Robert Resmes came in. 'Ah, you are here,' he said, with a strange expression. 'Sir, I understand from the ICU team that Roger Richardson is not recovering as well as expected.'

'Really?' he said.

'I just wanted to mention something, Mr Valentine. I did not think it was appropriate at the time – in theatre – during the operation. But it looked to me that there might have been a tiny tear in Mr Richardson's bowel.'

'It did?' Valentine did his best to look surprised.

'I could be wrong, of course – you have all the experience, but—' He hesitated. 'I just wonder if – possibly – maybe you did not notice, in the heat of the moment.'

'In the heat of the moment, Robert? What do you mean?'

His face reddened. 'Well, I'm just trying to be helpful,' Resmes said.

'You are? Have I missed something?'

'No – no – not at all. I—' The young man was stammering, his face turning the colour of beetroot. 'I – I—'

'That mark that you thought was a tear is actually old scar tissue.'

'It is? Ah, I'm sorry, I did not realize.'

'All right?'

'Of course, if you say so, of course.'

It was Valentine's turn to redden. 'If I *say so*? Let me tell you something, I know you are keen to learn but I've been a surgeon for twenty years. I know what I'm doing. I know what a tear in a bowel looks like and I know what scar tissue looks like.' He leaned over, his face inches from Resmes. 'If you want to remain in this hospital you could do well to remember that. Do you understand?'

Nodding and blushing furiously, Robert Resmes said, 'Yes. Yes, I am sorry, I apologize, I was only trying to be helpful.'

'If that's your idea of being helpful, God help the medical profession.'

53

Wednesday 16 January

With a chastened Robert Resmes in tow, Marcus strode along to the ICU.

Georgie was seated by Roger's bedside. He was asleep, and she was texting.

Not another man, I hope, Valentine wondered, with a sudden pang of jealousy. He approached quietly until he was standing almost behind her, looking down, trying to read her phone. The text was too small, but he could make out the name *Margot* at the top. Relieved, he glanced at each of the monitors, reading the digital displays.

And was unhappy with what he saw.

Roger's condition should have started to deteriorate a lot more by now, but instead all the indications were that he was fairly stable. Blood pressure wasn't great, nor was his heart rate. But neither of them was in any danger zone.

Resmes was looking at them, too.

'He's stable,' Marcus said, pointedly, to his student.

The Romanian nodded, staring at the displays, looking thoughtful.

Marcus comforted himself that this stability would not last. It could not. Roger was like a ship that had an undetected leak deep in its bowels, and eventually the weight of water would cause it to start listing, he thought. He smiled approvingly, liking the analogy that had just popped into his head.

Bowels!

He nearly turned to his student to share the joke with him. Before remembering that it wasn't appropriate, particularly bearing in mind Resmes's concerns.

Stuff was popping into Marcus's head all the time since he had met Georgie. She was attached to every thought he had, like protons attached to a nucleus; she had become part of the fabric of his DNA. Another analogy. He liked that one, too.

He liked the way she smelled, also. Very much. A faint musky tang of scent rising from her skin. It aroused him.

'Hello, Georgie!' he said quietly, laying on the deepest sympathy in his tone.

She turned around, looking startled. 'Oh, hi! You gave me a fright!'

'Am I that frightening?' he smiled, locking eyes, connecting, until she glanced away, looking embarrassed. 'No,' she said. 'Not at all. I – I just didn't hear you. How – how is he doing?'

Without introducing his student, he stared down at Roger for some while, in silence. She waited for him to say something. But he continued to just stare at him. Studying the monitors, she thought. Checking all was OK, she assumed gratefully.

But he was only glancing at them cursorily. What he was really doing was thinking about time. And dates.

And breathing in her intoxicating scent.

One month – almost – to Valentine's Day.

My special day!

Are you going to be my Valentine, Georgie?

Perhaps an anonymous card. Something neutral and tasteful. From a secret admirer letting her know there was life beyond Roger – regardless of whether he survived or died.

S.W.A.L.K!

This was a bum deal for Roger, wasn't it? His friend, Roger. Do it, don't do it. Those decisions constantly rattling through his head. It was getting out of his control, and Roger really was getting in the way of *his* Georgie now. This was his lucky chance and he wasn't going to let it pass him by.

He turned to her. 'I think he's recovering well, Georgie. I'm happy with how he's doing.'

'They seem worried that he's not progressing as fast as they'd hoped,' she replied, anxiously.

Of course they are, they're not stupid in here!

'Everyone responds differently to major surgery, Georgie.' He turned to Resmes, expecting a nod of affirmation. But the Romanian, studying all the displays intently, appeared not to have heard him.

'How soon do you think he'll be coming home?' Georgie asked.

Depends how you define 'coming home', my gorgeous. If you are thinking about bringing home an urn containing his cremated ashes, then two or three weeks, I would hope. At the very most.

It was such an opportunity that had fallen into his lap! Such a big prize if he played it right. He chose his words carefully. 'Difficult to say, Georgie, but if he progresses well, in less than a week.'

'Thank you for all you are doing,' she said. 'I really appreciate it.' She gave him a weak smile.

'That's what we are here for. To save life.' He returned the smile. Thinking.

Primum non nocere.

First, do no harm.

People attributed that, mistakenly, to the Hippocratic Oath, the ethical principles to which all medics adhered. But, actually, the maxim had appeared centuries after that old Greek doctor's death. Hey, no matter. In removing Roger's spleen he'd adhered to the principle, totally. He had a clear conscience.

He'd done no harm. He'd always be able to look Georgie in the eye with a clear conscience in their future life together. He had it all mapped out in his mind. Just a few more obstacles in the way: one he was dealing with now, the others he had plans for. And then the issue of Claire and the children, but that was further down the line and wouldn't be a problem. Deal with the pressing one first, hey-ho!

'How does Roger look to you?' he asked. Sounding kind and genuinely concerned.

'I don't know. Maybe a little better than yesterday,' she said, hopefully. 'But his blood pressure and heart rate don't look that good to me.'

Valentine made a show of studying first Roger and then the readouts again. He wasn't acting when he assured her, 'All the signs are good.'

Too damned good. But that would change. It must!

'He's going to be OK, isn't he, Marcus? Do you think he's out of danger?'

'Well, that's too early to say for sure, Georgie. He's been through a big trauma and had major surgery, in addition to concussion.' He patted her on the shoulder, reassuringly. 'But I would say his prognosis is encouraging. As I told you before, most people go on to make a complete recovery after a splenectomy.'

Most.

She looked up at him. 'I didn't sleep a wink last night – I was so scared – you know – I – love him so much.'

He gave her a sickly smile. *Of course you do.*

The young student doctor in scrubs with him was looking at her intently through black-rimmed glasses. His expression was stern.

'I lay there praying,' she said. 'It may sound silly, I've never really believed in God, but last night I prayed.'

It was tempting, so very tempting, Marcus thought, to quote Shakespeare back at her. *King Lear*, Act Four, Scene One. And so appropriate!

'*The worst is not, so long as we can say this is the worst.*'

But maybe not a good idea, she wouldn't be amused.

But he was. Very amused. It really was turning into quite an interesting day. He shook his head. Thinking. Doing his best to study his patient with a solemn expression, to give the impression of how much he cared.

You've no idea what's in store. He's not been through the worst yet. He's not even been through the beginning of the worst. But don't you worry, I'll be here to hold your hand through that. Sure, he's had a bounce today, all that blood removed from his abdomen. That cheeky ruptured spleen, causing all those problems, is now lying in a toxic waste bin.

No one knows yet about the stuff that is slowly, steadily, seeping into his blood system from that tear in his bowel. Poisoning him from within. A doomed ship!

With a bit of luck – bad luck for him, good luck for me – you'll be weeping and putting flowers onto his coffin in a week or two. Three at the most. Sepsis is a terrible thing. A horrible death.

And, of course, I can intervene at any point I deem suitable. Take him back into theatre and open him up again, discover that tiny tear in his bowel and heroically save his life.

Ensuring your eternal gratitude!

But what then? How would you show that gratitude? By marrying him and rejecting me yet again?

On the other hand, if he died, I would be here to comfort you, my lovely.

So many options going through his mind, he thought. Such power!

Georgie, you prayed last night to a god you've never believed in. Poor, sweet girl, you prayed to the wrong god, really you did.

You should have prayed to me.

He led her away out of sight and earshot of his student, dug his hand in his pocket and pulled out a small glass vial of tiny pills. 'Georgie, I knew you might have trouble sleeping. I shouldn't be doing this, but I want to because we are friends.' He handed her the vial, discreetly. 'Take one tonight half an hour before bed. Everything will seem much better in the morning after a good night's rest.'

'That's very kind of you, thank you. I will, I've got to get some decent sleep.'

She slipped them into her handbag.

'All I want is the very best for all of you, including our Bump here.' Marcus smiled.

'I appreciate that.'

He smiled again, then, followed by his silent student, he walked off.

54

Georgie felt in turmoil after she watched Valentine and Resmes stop to use the hand sanitizer and then exit through the door. Marcus had now not given her any reassurance about Roger's condition. If anything, the reverse. And she hadn't liked Kath's reaction when she'd told her about the blood in her urine.

The risk, however tiny – and it is tiny – of something nasty developing.

How tiny?

Clearly not tiny enough to dismiss. If it was really that tiny, would Kath have been so keen to fit her in for a colposcopy this week?

She rummaged anxiously in her handbag for the card Kath had given her, retrieved it and stepped away from Roger's bedside, not wanting to wake him. She dialled and Kath Clow's secretary answered keenly, clearly expecting her call. She made an appointment.

Then she sat back down beside Roger, stroking his forehead, staring at his face, watching his fluttering eyelids. This gorgeous, funny, caring man she loved so much – and had so nearly lost. When he was better, would she worry even more every time he went off to the airfield?

It was gone half past one. Lunchtime, but she wasn't hungry. A cold, wintry draught swirled inside her. Marcus came across as a little arrogant, but thinking back, she realized that some of the consultants she'd seen in the past, on her long journey to become pregnant, had been similarly arrogant.

Roger stirred. For a moment, Georgie was hopeful he was waking. But he continued to sleep.

Valentine's voice echoed in her head. *But I would say his prognosis is encouraging. As I told you before, most people go on to make a complete recovery after a splenectomy.*

Most.

Leaving unsaid the words, *but some do not.*

Kiera had told her Roger was not making as good progress as they had expected. So why hadn't Marcus Valentine commented on that?

The optimist in her said that was because he'd seen no need for concern. The pessimist said he hadn't wanted to worry her.

She looked around the ward. Two women at the nursing station were chatting. Another monitor alarm beeped. A medic hurried past. She felt so helpless. Afraid. Everyone spoke highly of Valentine, but he was an obstetrician, not a general surgeon. Might Roger be recovering more quickly if a specialist in spleens had done the operation?

No, stop these negative thoughts. Roger needs positivity now.

She studied all the monitors again, her insides knotted with worry. Worry which increased as the afternoon wore on, with nurses carrying out regular checks on Roger. She felt she could read the increasing concern in their demeanour. Twice during this time a doctor had been summoned, and the curtains had been closed around Roger.

Something was not right. She was becoming more and more certain of that. And the nurses were being evasive, brushing her off with smiles and platitudes.

To distract herself, she logged on to eBay to check the status on her bid for the flying jacket. She was pleased she was still the highest, with six hours to go. Fingers crossed, she'd get it. It would make a great coming home gift for Roger.

When he came home.

If he came home.

There was a whole ton of messages on her phone – texts, WhatsApps and emails from concerned friends and family who had seen the news. She did her best to respond to each, updating them with everything she knew.

Late afternoon, the ward round team reappeared, and Nurse Dale, about to go off shift, asked Georgie to step away whilst they drew curtains once more around Roger.

'What – what's going on?' she asked, her voice trembling. 'No one's telling me anything. Roger's not right, is he?'

Kiera's face confirmed her fears.

'I don't want you to be worried, Georgie, we are monitoring him very closely and he's in the best possible hands here. But there's something going on that we need to get to the bottom of.'

'What do you mean? Like *what* going on?'

'Well, his heart rate is a little high and his blood pressure lower than we would like to see at this period of time after his operation. And his lactate level is elevated.'

'Elevated?'

'To be honest with you, it's just not quite the improvement in his condition we'd expect. But there's really nothing to worry about.'

'Really? I'm not an idiot. Tell me the truth. You don't have to dress anything up for me.'

'I am telling you everything, Georgie, honestly. There's a little abnormal swelling in his tummy, which indicates something's not quite right. But this could simply still be a reaction to the operation. He is also showing symptoms of pain. We're going to give him intravenous fluids to try to bring his blood pressure up, and we'll give him supplementary oxygen, which we'll be monitoring through the night.'

'If that doesn't work?' Georgie asked, fearfully.

'Let's be positive and hope it does!' she said. 'There's a possibility – very remote – that he's picked up an infection, which we'll be able to knock out very quickly with antibiotics.'

Georgie looked at her, dubiously.

'If it's any comfort to you, I've been an ICU nurse for nine years. In all this time I've worked on countless splenectomy patients, every single one of whom has gone on to make a complete recovery. Does that reassure you?'

'I'd like to say yes. But—'

Kiera smiled, expectantly.

'This is going to sound silly.'

'Try me!'

'Well, I used to be terrified of flying. At one point, I would only fly to airports where there had been a major air disaster, on the basis that it was highly unlikely there would be another at the same place.'

Kiera frowned. 'Are you saying you'd feel happier if we'd recently had a patient who'd died following a splenectomy?'

Georgie gave a nervous smile. 'I'm sorry, I realize how stupid that sounds – stupid and selfish.'

The nurse smiled. 'I like your logic. I just hope that none of our patients here ever needs to become a statistic that helps you prove it!'

So do I, Georgie thought, looking at the closed curtains around Roger's bed.

55

Wednesday 16 January

Marcus Valentine arrived home shortly after 8 p.m. He needed just time and patience for now. Sure, Georgie was worried sick about her man. He could understand that. It was only natural. But what he could not understand was why Roger was still so stable. He wasn't recovering as well as the ICU team expected, but neither was he going downhill as fast as he had hoped. Was it possible the tear in his bowel had healed? That could happen, although it was extremely unlikely.

So what the hell was going on?

He stopped in the porch and stared at the mess of his children's shoes – and Claire's – littering the place. Why couldn't his family ever clear up after themselves?

He knelt and put the shoes in their correct cubby holes. Then he went into the hall, where there was a tantalizing smell of food, and called out, 'Hi, I'm home.'

'I'm upstairs!' Claire called back.

Claire was lying on their bed, holding a Jojo Moyes paperback, the television on with a bunch of half-dressed hunks on a beach on the screen. She was wearing a short, floral dressing gown which she had bought a couple of years back, on a holiday blessedly without the kids in Portofino. It was just covering the top of her thighs, showing her long, bare, white legs. He used to fancy her in it, and the reading glasses made her even more alluring. 'That sexy librarian look,' he called it.

But it wasn't working like it used to.

'Hi, what are you watching?'

'Catching up with *Shipwrecked*.'

He could never understand how she could read and watch TV at the same time. 'You all right?'

'Dreadful, since you asked. Cormac's been a bloody nightmare and I'm exhausted. The twins are fine though. You? How was your day?'

He tried to remember the last time they'd had sex. Two weeks ago, or was it three? Four? He should be raring to go, but . . .

'There's a beef casserole in the Aga, top left, with a baked potato, and salad in the fridge. And there's half a bottle of a nice Rioja on the table. I thought we might have an early night.' She gave him a smile.

An invitation.

He hesitated, wondering whether to go through the motions, make her happy, play the attentive husband. But could he, really, when he had other things on his mind? A plan that had been forming on his drive home. Just a little way to feel closer to Georgie.

'Thanks, but I'm on call, I can't drink.'

'You were on call last week,' she said, looking genuinely disappointed. She moved, stretching out a bare leg, revealing even more of her thigh, and for a moment he was tempted, so tempted.

But he had an even stronger urge, pulling him in a different direction. The plan that had been hatching in his mind during the past hour. One he liked more and more.

'Yep, I'm having to cover for someone who's away,' he replied. He began to strip off.

'Mmmmnnn!' Claire said. 'I'm liking what I'm seeing. So you are coming to bed after all?'

'No, I'm going for a run.'

56

After Marcus had departed for the day, Resmes stayed on in the hospital, with an hour or so to kill before—

His date!

Tilly Roberts. A young nurse in the Maternity ward he'd been sweet on for weeks, ever since he'd first noticed her. But being awkwardly shy with women he fancied, it had taken him time to strike up a conversation with her. Then, a few days later, he'd plucked up the courage to ask her out for a date tonight, after work. She came off shift at 10 p.m.

His stomach churned with excitement and he couldn't sit still. He paced around the hospital corridors, aimless, for a while, constantly looking at his watch and at every clock that he passed. Time was passing slowly, agonizingly slowly. He couldn't remember when he had last felt like this. Not since he'd been at medical school in Bucharest and had the hots for Alina, who'd been giving him sly glances for some while. It had taken him weeks before he finally asked her out. But he'd left it too late. Quite apologetically, she'd told him she now had a boyfriend.

He'd been determined, with Tilly, not to make the same mistake again. He was taking her to an Italian restaurant he liked in town, which stayed open late. And after then, who knew?

He only had a couple more days of being with Mr Valentine. Then, after the weekend, he would be moving on for the next month, to shadow Dr Clow, who seemed a nice lady.

He looked at his watch again. Still an hour to go to Tilly! But time to start getting ready. He went into the changing room, undressed and dumped his scrubs in a laundry bin, then washed, sprayed himself with aftershave and dressed in the fresh white shirt he had brought along especially for this evening. But as he checked his appearance in the mirror, he felt a sudden hollow sense of panic in the pit of his stomach.

No. Shit. No!

His jacket wasn't in here. Quite apart from needing its warmth, his wallet was in it. He remembered now, earlier today, before he'd changed into scrubs, sitting in Mr Valentine's office, while the obstetrician showed him different images of ovarian, cervical and vaginal cancers. It had been hot in the room and he'd removed his jacket, hooking it behind the door.

He hurried along the network of corridors, passing a yellow warning triangle placed by the cleaners, and arrived at Valentine's door. It was locked. Of course. He always locked it.

A short distance away, Resmes heard the *whirr* and *bang-bang-bang* of a hoover. Rushing up to the cleaning lady, whom he'd always greeted with a smile and a hello, he explained his predicament. Without questioning him, she used her swipe card to unlock the door.

As he switched on the light and entered the freshly tidied room, he saw to his relief that his jacket was hanging where he'd left it. Unhooking it, he put it on.

A ping startled him. The alert of an incoming text, from somewhere in the room. Frowning, he looked all around. The desk was neat and tidy. No sign of a phone. He saw a photograph of a tall, fair-haired woman pinned to a noticeboard, along with photos of two small children and a baby. He saw a copy of the 'Happiness' graph that Cardigan seemed to have taken great pleasure in showing him pinned beside the family photos.

He peered up at the file folders and reference books, neatly arranged in height order on the shelves. At the whiteboard with its several notices attached by coloured magnets. All arranged with mathematical neatness and precision.

Ping.

The sound came from right behind him.

He turned. Stared at a metal filing cabinet. Was it from in there? Had Mr Valentine inadvertently left his phone there? But why – how – could he have put it in there? He was such a meticulous man, surely he wouldn't have left the hospital without his phone – especially as he was on call this week? How odd, how puzzling.

There was so much that was puzzling about Mr Valentine. And worrying.

When the surgeon had opened up Roger Richardson, Resmes had been absolutely certain he'd noticed a tear in the bowel. Yet subsequently, when he'd ventured to mention it, Mr Valentine had been aggressively defensive.

Why? Especially when now the man's recovery was not going as well as had been expected. Wasn't that a sign something might be wrong? That maybe in all the heat of the moment, Mr Valentine might have missed something? Sure, he had a great reputation as a brilliant surgeon and Resmes had already learned much from observing him across many differing procedures, but he wasn't a trauma surgeon. All of the surgery Resmes had witnessed him doing, to date, had been carried out in Valentine's own time and at his measured pace. Splenectomies were not his specialty – might it be possible, even for a surgeon of his experience, to have missed something because his focus was elsewhere?

He closed the office door behind him and stared around for a moment, then decided to ring Marcus's number to see if it was his phone and to put to bed these thoughts. The number was on his speed-dial on his own mobile.

It began to ring, but there was no sound from the filing cabinet. The obstetrician answered, curtly, on the second ring. 'Yes, Robert? What's up?'

Flustered, he blurted, 'Oh, I'm sorry, Mr Valentine, sorry to disturb you. I – I just wanted to check what time and where I should meet you tomorrow?'

'I'll be at my consulting room in the Bon Sante clinic at the Hotel de France until 11 a.m., Robert. I've got some paperwork to catch up on, so rock up at the hospital about 11.15, unless there is any emergency, OK?'

'Yes, thank you, I'll be there then.'

Valentine ended the call.

Resmes stared at the cabinet. So he had another phone, inside it? Why? What was this all about?

His concerns about Marcus Valentine had been deepening throughout the day. He still did not buy the consultant's explanation that what he'd seen in Roger Richardson's bowel was scar tissue. It was a tear, he'd been sure of it. And yet, before he told anyone else and began making very serious accusations, he had to be absolutely certain of his ground.

He went over to the cabinet where the phone ping was coming from, and tugged the handle, but as he had anticipated, the file drawer was locked. Would Marcus have the key with him or would he have concealed it in the office somewhere?

He stared nervously at the door, terrified that Marcus might come in at any moment. Taking a deep breath, he began opening and carefully rummaging through each of the drawers in the desk. In the bottom left-hand one, under a pile of documents, he found two small, thin keys attached to a metal ring. He lifted them out and tried the first one in the lock at the top of the cabinet, turned it, and bingo!

The first two drawers, stacked with orderly hanging files, each of which he checked through, revealed nothing. But halfway along the files in the third drawer down he noticed a bulge. And there, nestling between the green sleeves, was a phone, a few years old but, as the display showed, almost 96 per cent charged.

Which meant it had been handled recently.

The message that had pinged was an alert from Jersey Telecom, but he could also see part of a message on the home screen which made him deeply worried.

Almost certain that the phone would be password-protected, and well aware it was none of his business to be touching it, he was curious to know what it was that Mr Valentine wanted to keep locked away – from his colleagues and perhaps from his wife. He swiped up and saw:

Enter Passcode

He had no idea what that might be. He did know the surgeon's date of birth and tried a couple of combinations of that, without success. Then he had another idea. On a street below the Snow Hill car park he'd passed a mobile phone repair shop that offered in its window display to repair or unlock any phone. He googled it and saw its opening time was 8.30 a.m.

Marcus Valentine would be going straight to his private clinic first thing. That gave him almost three hours in the morning to get the phone unlocked, take a look at it and return it to the filing cabinet. He felt this was easily doable, and a low-risk strategy – he'd be back in no time.

He closed and locked the cabinet, replacing the keys where he had found them, slipped the phone into his pocket and left the office, jamming the door lock with a strip of cardboard, excited about his date and very curious about what the morning would reveal.

57

Wednesday 16 January

Georgie remained at Roger's bedside until 8 p.m. Throughout the evening, he had barely opened his eyes. Finally, the nurse who had taken over from Kiera Dale suggested she went home and got some rest. It was like they were all trained to say this, she thought. He had been stable for some while, which was a good sign, and she promised to let her know if there was any change in his condition.

She drove back to their flat on autopilot, parched, having drunk nothing for hours, she realized, and shaky from lack of food. And worried as hell. They had expected her beloved to have been sitting up this morning, starting physiotherapy.

OK, he was stable now. But what did that really mean?

As she entered the flat and switched on all the lights, she was trying to take comfort from Kiera's words, earlier. Gulping down a large glass of water, she peered inside the fridge. There was some bread, a lump of Cheddar, some coleslaw, coconut yoghurt and a bottle of white wine. She opened the freezer and rummaged through the contents: fish pies; curries; a vegetarian Wellington containing beetroot and cheese which they'd bought as an experiment; and lamb moussaka.

Nothing appealed.

She made herself a bland cheese sandwich and ate it in front of the news, which did nothing to lift her from the deep gloom she felt.

Roger should have been improving throughout the day. Instead he was deteriorating, slowly, as if his life was steadily trickling away.

217

Why? What was going on? The medics were concerned, she could see it in their eyes. Kiera had done her best to reassure her, but she needed more than reassurances. She wanted to see his blood pressure rising and his heart rate lowering.

She glanced at her watch. It was almost 9 p.m. She should have an early night and try to sleep, but she felt wired. Maybe she could have a bit more cheese.

As she stood up to go to the fridge, her phone rang, startling her.

Shit. Was it the hospital?

She answered.

'Miss Maclean?' asked a male voice she did not recognize.

'Yes?'

'This is the control room of G4 Security. We have you listed as the principal key-holder for the Bel Royal Hotel.'

'Yes, correct.'

'There's an intruder alert showing. Are you able to attend please?'

That bloody hotel. This was all she needed, but she had an obligation to Mr Vautier, having taken advantage of his generous offer of the gym all these months. With Roger unwell and perhaps not able to fly for a while, she needed the goodwill and the income more than ever, while she could still work. 'Yes,' she replied. 'Yes, I can be there in about a quarter of an hour.'

'Thank you. When you get there, let us know if there is anything you are uncomfortable about and we'll ask the police to attend.'

'I will,' she said. 'Thank you.'

It was probably just another false alarm; she'd drive there and check it out. The hotel was fitted with motion-sensors, and one had gone off in the night on a couple of previous occasions. The first time it had turned out to be an infestation of ladybirds around a sensor – gathered there, the pest control man had later told her, because it was warm. On another occasion a cat had got in somehow and then not been able to find its way out. Perhaps it was another animal trapped.

I FOLLOW YOU

Leaving everything on the island work surface, she texted Lucy so at least someone knew where she was, grabbed a torch and the hotel keys, pulled on her warm fleece jacket and hurried out to her car.

58

Wednesday 16 January

Fifteen minutes later, the headlights of Georgie's Golf picked out the blue-and-white Bel Royal Hotel sign with its three gold stars. As she turned in through the pillared entrance and wound her way up the steep, twisting driveway, she was feeling increasingly apprehensive. It was bad enough coming here alone in the daytime, let alone late at night after an intruder alert had gone off.

Hopefully and almost certainly it would turn out to be another false alarm. But she wasn't going to take any chances, and as one precaution she'd already locked her car doors. She had decided that if she saw a vehicle parked anywhere on the premises, or any sign of a broken window or open door, she would stay put and dial 999.

The wind had risen and the leaves of the dense shrubbery on either side were shaking and rustling. Shadows jumped all around her. A rabbit darted across in front of her. Cresting the rise, she could see the lights of St Helier way in the distance, which increased her sense of isolation. Creeping the car down the ramp towards the rear of the hotel, her eyes tracked the darkness either side as she approached the entrance to the staff and gym car parks. She was debating whether to stop here or go round to the front first. But then, as she saw the row of wheelie bins and the builders' over-flowing skip in her headlights, two ruby-red dots glowed in the darkness to her right. Then they vanished. A rat?

Yech.

She decided to check the front first. But she would have to come back to the rear as her key only let her in through the gym entrance. Putting the car in gear again, she crawled along the side of the building and then turned right, along the front of the hotel. The car rocked in the wind, which felt much stronger around this exposed side of the building. To her left, on the other side of the drive, was a wide terrace for drinks and dining when the weather was fine. It was empty now, all the chairs and tables and parasols stored away, the swimming pool drained.

She halted, switched off the engine, and without giving herself time to dwell on it, picked up her torch and got out, taking a deep breath. The wind batted her hair around her face and tugged at her clothes. Music travelled from somewhere below. Rag'n'Bone Man, she recognized wistfully. Roger loved Rag'n'Bone Man, ever since they'd seen him live in London a year or so back.

She played the beam across the balconies of each of the guest rooms along the two-storey facade, checking for a broken or open window or patio door, then across the panoramic curved glass wall of the dining room, and finally into the darkness at the end of the building, just in case someone was lurking there. *Although why would any intruder in their right mind be hanging around after setting off the alarm*, she thought, trying to comfort herself. But, of course, the alarm was silent – they might not necessarily have noticed they'd set it off.

So, it was possible that if there was an intruder, and not a cat that had slipped past the maintenance workers earlier, or a spider's web across a sensor, or rodents chewing through a wire, that the intruder might still be in the building. But there was nothing of any real value to take, other than the almost-new gym equipment – and that would be heavy work. The hotel was tired, its refresh only just starting. All the televisions were several years old; there was no cash on the premises, no valuable art. Also, there was no vehicle that she could see. A burglar wasn't going to be able to carry much away from here by hand. And, despite outbreaks of drunken violence on weekends in some of

St Helier's bars and pubs, the island still, mercifully, had a low crime rate.

No, she convinced herself – almost – that if there was a genuine intruder it was more likely to be youngsters pranking about than a burglar after serious loot.

She got back into the car and drove round to the rear of the building again. Ignoring the delineated parking bays, she pulled up as close as she could get to the gym door and jumped out, clutching her torch and the keys. Her first duty would be to check the master alarm box for the hotel, which was located in the corridor between the gym and the kitchen. Hopefully, that would give her the zone where the alert had been triggered. Then would follow the task she did not look forward to, walking along the dark, cold corridors to the zone and checking all the rooms within it.

Payback time for the generous deal the hotel owner had given her. Although at the moment, having to deal with this, it didn't feel *quite* so generous any more.

A few years back, she'd done a kick-boxing course and really enjoyed it. But when the time came – if it ever came – would she actually be able to use her now rusty skills? Maybe.

As she unlocked the glass door to the gym, she reminded herself of the kick-boxing basics, and suddenly felt a lot more positive. She was still plenty supple enough to deliver a KO delivery to someone's chin. So long as she kept her presence of mind in a confrontation.

She entered the freezing-cold room and switched on some of the lights, glancing round at the silent equipment and the motionless egg timers. One overhead neon light flickered with a buzzing sound. Just as a precaution, totally unnecessary, she knew, she locked the door behind her and removed the key, then glanced up at the offending tube. It often did this and then settled down – she decided to leave it. Then she walked across the gym and stopped by the rack of kettlebells, hesitating. *Why not?* She picked up a relatively light one, happier now she had a weapon, and entered the corridor to the kitchens, almost immediately finding the light switch with her torch beam.

She walked along the worn carpet, which smelled old and musty; the walls on either side needed a lick of paint. She could almost hear her heartbeat in the silence, and could feel it fluttering like a trapped bird inside her chest. Her eyes shot in every direction, darting at shadows, gripping the kettlebell tightly in her right hand and the torch in her left, until she reached the alarm cupboard. Setting the weight down on the floor, she opened the door and stared at the large panel. A small red light was flashing, showing her the problem area.

INTRUDER ALERT ZONE F

That zone covered ten rooms at the far end of the first floor of the building as well as the dining room.

She entered the code and the light stopped. It was replaced by a message on the panel display.

SYSTEM RESET?

She did not want to reset the system until she had checked the zone, otherwise if there was a fault, she could risk it recurring and being called out again in another hour's time. She'd see if she could spot anything wrong and, if not, she'd have to call the emergency engineer. Either way, it was going to be a while before she could go home. Although tonight, she didn't mind. With the constant shadow of worry stalking her, she knew she would just lie in bed awake, counting down the hours until she could go back to the hospital. To Roger's bedside.

On top of that she had the new worry about the colposcopy tomorrow.

God, she thought, just when life was going so well it always seemed to find a way to trip you up and dump on you. Yep, well, this time it wasn't going to win. Roger was going to pull through, he'd be fine. And Kath was not going to find any damned cancer.

She stood in silence, listening, staring down the length of the corridor. It was lit dimly by weak bulbs in tasselled pink lamps arranged in pairs, in sconces all the way along. Good that the place was having a major makeover – it was long overdue. As it was, it would be a pretty dismal place for anyone to come for a holiday. Roger had joked, just a few days ago, that they should spend the first night after their wedding here.

Over my dead body, she'd retorted.

How was he now – was he still asleep, she wondered? Perhaps having a better night than last? Or was he awake and lonely, listening to the racket of monitor alarms? She put down the kettlebell and tugged her phone out of her pocket, to make sure she hadn't set it by mistake to silent, in case the hospital called. It wasn't and, to her relief, there was nothing showing on the display.

Have a good night, my darling. Please start getting stronger tomorrow.

She replaced the phone, picked up the kettlebell and carried on, passing closed door after closed door, stopping every few yards to check behind her, her earlier surge of confidence rapidly deserting her.

To her left, she passed by the closed doors to rooms until she reached room 45.

This place felt so damned eerie.

Putting the kettlebell down again, she unlocked the door, then hesitated. She heard a distinct creak, like someone stepping on a floorboard, on the other side of the door.

She stood, listening. She could feel the hairs rising on the nape of her neck.

Nothing.

She waited for several minutes, listening intently. But heard no further sound. All the same, she was tempted just to lock the door again and move on. But she had a job to do and the hotel creaked constantly. She picked up the weight again, ready to swing it at anything that moved, braced herself, then pushed the door hard with her foot, flashing her torch beam around the room as it swung open.

It was empty. She found the master light switch and pressed it.

The ceiling light, a larger version of the pink lampshades in the corridor, came on, along with two matching bedside lamps.

She stared at the wardrobe doors.

Was someone standing inside?

She shuddered, keeping a wary eye on the doors for any movement, and pushed open the en-suite bathroom door. All was normal.

There was no sign of a break-in here.

Then she heard a sound behind her.

The creak of another floorboard.

She spun round, shivers rippling down inside her skin. Stood still. Listening. Listening. Staring at the wardrobe.

Silence.

Brandishing the kettlebell as high as possible, she tiptoed slowly over to the doorway, her heart thrashing. Then, yelling, 'Who's that?' she stepped out into the hall, looking in both directions.

There was nothing there.

She stayed rooted to the spot for several minutes, listening, scared as hell.

Had she imagined it? Could it have been the old building creaking in the wind?

Yes, that's all. She calmed down a little, then cautiously checked each of the other rooms in the zone, which were all identical.

Next, she dutifully entered the cold dining room. All the chairs were upended and placed on top of the tables. To her left, through the windows, she could see the necklace of lights around St Aubin's Bay and the blackness of the sea beyond. She crossed the drearily carpeted room, pushed open the fire door at the far end and reached the start of another long corridor. She checked it out with her torch before stepping into it and switching on the wall lights.

After a short distance she passed a lift and reached a junction, with arrows and room numbers, pointing to the right, left, straight on and upwards.

Then froze as, ahead, she heard the sound of a door closing.

Prickles ran up her spine.

Shit, shit, shit.

Had she imagined this, too?

She stood still. Listening.

She heard the sound again.

Just the wind?

Then a loud, sharp *ping* made her jump in shock. She almost cried out, her heart hammering, her eyes hunting in every direction.

Before she realized.

Stupid!

It was an alert for an incoming email.

She looked at her phone. It was from eBay.

You won with a £125 bid plus £7.75 postage! The next step is to pay. VintageStuff(570) can't post the item until you pay for it, so please don't delay. Once you've paid we'll tell VintageStuff(570) to post your item.

Roger's flying jacket, she realized, her spirits rising. Yay! This was a good sign. All was going to be fine! Truly it was, she thought, closing the door and heading back towards the alarm cupboard.

SYSTEM RESET was still flashing red.

She read the emergency number of the engineer off the panel and dialled it. After a few rings it was answered by a friendly male voice. She felt a lot better having human contact, and explained the situation.

He told her what to press to reset the system, and not to worry if it happened again. He would make a note in the log and someone would contact her in the morning to come over and check the sensors. She followed his instructions and the light changed to green. She thanked him, closed the lid of the box, then made her way back along the corridor, past the kitchens, to the gym.

But as she entered, something felt wrong.

She stopped in her tracks, suddenly afraid again.

Stared around at the machines.

There was no sign of anyone. Nothing moved. But something very definitely felt wrong. What?

She carried the kettlebell over to the rack and placed it back alongside the others. Then, as she turned around, something caught her attention. Something moving.

Green sand was trickling down through the neck of two of the three egg timers.

59

Wednesday 16 January

Frozen in terror, Georgie stared at the egg timers. The top of one-minute timer was empty. The three-minute one was nearly empty. The five-minute one was approximately half full.

Someone had been in here. Less than five minutes ago.

Where were they now?

She stared wildly around. She had locked the outside door when she came in. The door to the office was shut. As was the door to the changing room.

Was someone behind one of them? Or out in the darkness beyond the windows?

She grabbed the kettlebell again, holding it up, and with her free hand, shaking wildly, she thumbed 999 on her phone.

'Emergency, which service please?'

'Police. I have an intruder,' she said loudly in a trembling voice, loudly enough for anyone to hear.

Seconds later she heard a female voice.

'Police, what is your emergency, caller?'

Blinking away tears, she said, terrified, 'I'm in the gym of the Bel Royal Hotel. There's an intruder in here. Please come quickly. Please.'

'Bel Royal Hotel?'

'Yes.'

'Are you in a safe place?'

'No.'

'I'm dispatching a unit to you right away. What's your name?'

'Georgina – Maclean.'

'I'll stay on the line, Georgina.'

'Thank you.' She began sobbing.

'There'll be a car with you in under three minutes.'

'I'm pregnant and frightened,' she sobbed. Staring wildly around. Did the office door just move?

'Is there a safe place you can go to, Georgina?'

'No – not really, no.'

'They're on their way. I'm showing under two minutes.'

Her eyes darted to the changing-room door. The office door. The corridor behind her. She gripped the kettlebell so tightly her fist hurt. The operator spoke to her, but she couldn't absorb any of the words through the haze of fear. The minutes felt like hours. She'd been mad to come here alone, worn out by her anxiety about Roger, not thinking straight.

Then the faint sound of a siren. Growing rapidly louder. Nearer. Please God.

'I can hear them,' Georgie said loudly for the benefit of whoever might be behind one of the doors. 'I can hear the siren. Please tell them to stop at the rear entrance by the gym.'

'They're in the hotel driveway now, Georgina. Are you OK?'

'Yes, thank you, yes.'

Strobing blue light skittered across the windowpanes. An instant later she saw the glare of headlights and heard the roar of an engine.

Relief flooding through her, she ran to the door, key in hand, to unlock it. But as she inserted the key she realized it was, impossibly, already unlocked.

60

Wednesday 16 January

As Marcus came back into the house from his run, Claire was still awake, still reading, the television still on. Her bare, slender legs still on top of the duvet, stretched out invitingly from beneath her dressing gown.

Now, after all, he was feeling horny as hell. Wired! Rampant!

'Good run?'

'Great,' he said, kissing her. 'Terrific! My best time yet!'

My best run ever. Oh yes, oh yes.

So exciting. Georgie – like putty in his hands. *I love you, Georgie!*

'You must be hungry – your meal's still in the oven. Might be a bit dried out.'

He hovered over her. 'I'm hungry for you.'

'Are you indeed?' she responded, playfully.

'I'll just go and shower.'

She reached out and put her arms around his midriff. 'Come closer, I like you when you're all sweaty.'

He grinned. 'You animal!'

'You used to call me that, remember?'

And he did remember. Back in those distant days. Those pre-baby days. But for now, temporarily at least, that was forgotten. He stared at those long legs; at her large breasts loose inside the top of that gown.

This evening's antics had fired him up like nothing, ever, before.

He needed sex.

She was already untying and then pulling down his tracksuit bottoms. Then his underpants, pulling him closer and taking him in her mouth. He fantasized about the touch being Georgie's mouth. He pictured the curve of her lips. Imagining what they would feel like, their soft, sensuous grip.

After a short while Claire released him. 'Maybe take your shoes off, Mr Big!'

He sat on the edge of the bed and untied his shoelaces, almost crazed with desire, kicked his trainers off, unzipped his tracksuit top and then peeled off his T-shirt and tossed it onto the carpet.

Then he began to untie and slip off her dressing gown, whilst she gripped him hard.

All the time he was thinking about Georgie.

Staring at Claire and thinking of Georgie's face.

This was what it was going to be like with Georgie. Only times ten. Times a hundred. Times—

Claire was naked now and he was on top of her. She was holding him, guiding him into her.

Georgie. Holding his hardness. Pulling him in. Whispering.

Oh my God, Marcus, this is incredible!

But it was Claire's face.

Suddenly, to his dismay, he felt his hardness going. Turning flaccid.

No.

He looked down at Claire's breasts. At her thighs, her legs that had so turned him on.

Trying desperately to arouse himself again.

An image from childhood wormed through him. A memory that shamed him. When he'd been a small boy – he couldn't remember how old, exactly, maybe seven or eight – he was in the bath and his mother had come in, drunk, and started flicking the bathwater and staring at his penis. Then she flicked that, too, laughing. 'A little prawn,' she said. 'A tiny, silly little prawn. Like father, like son. Oh dear,' she had sighed. 'You're never going to satisfy a woman with a tiddly little prawn like that. Poor you. Poor Marcus.'

He shrank even more. And slipped out of Claire.

Finally, he rolled over onto his side. Claire worked on him with her hands, then her mouth again. To no avail. She stopped. 'Maybe you're low on sugar, darling? When did you last eat?'

He didn't reply for a moment. He was thinking of Georgie's face. Of her body. 'I had a sandwich at lunchtime.'

'It's late. You need food.' She held up his limp penis. '*He* needs fuel!'

No, he thought. *He doesn't need fuel, he needs Georgie Maclean.*

'You're going to have a hypo if you don't eat something.'

She was right. He was feeling jittery and he was perspiring. Maybe if he ate something, he'd be OK. Be able to perform.

Lamely, he went to the bathroom and tested his sugars. 2.4. Seriously low. He hurried downstairs to the kitchen and removed the dried-up casserole from the oven, and the potato. He poured himself a glass of wine from the bottle in the fridge, then, seated naked at the breakfast bar, he began to eat. Upstairs, he heard Cormac crying. After a short while the crying stopped.

He started feeling a little better, the threat of the hypo receding. It was replaced by an ache in his groin and in his balls. He knew the cause – the frustrated attempt to have sex just now. Claire was right, he had needed the fuel. Another ten minutes or so and he'd be ready to go again. Close Claire out of his mind and just think about Georgie, about how sexy she was.

It didn't work.

He finished his meal and the wine, went up to his den, sank down on the sofa and thought about her. Imagining what it would be like to slip off her clothes and hold her naked in his arms. He kept on picturing touching her and her touching him, until he was rock hard.

He slipped into the loo and closed the door. Then sat on the seat and masturbated.

After he had climaxed, he remained seated for some while, before going back into their bedroom.

To his relief, Claire was asleep.

61

Wednesday 16 January

It was close to midnight when Georgie arrived home, exhausted and wondering what on earth had just happened. There had been no message from the hospital, just a text from Lucy, saying she'd been out and asking if everything was OK. Georgie had been too tired to say anything more than it was all fine and she was going to sleep now. Her nerves were shredded, but hopefully no news from the hospital was a good sign. She wanted so much to tell Roger about what she'd just been through, about the police, how scary it had been, and just to hold him close. If he hadn't been in hospital, she knew for sure he wouldn't have let her go to the hotel on her own. She'd been stupid to think it would be all right.

Together with the two police officers who had attended, she had checked every door and just about every cupboard in the entire hotel. Now, as she let herself into the flat, she needed to sleep, but her brain was racing.

The trickling grains of green-dyed sand were still freaking her.

'Some youngsters messing about,' one of the officers had suggested. And that's what she wanted to believe, and it was an easy answer to everything. But the gym door had been locked. All the external doors of the hotel had also been locked. And all the windows had been shut.

'You know what kids are like,' the other officer had said. 'They get up to mischief. This is such a huge place, they might have found some way in that we don't even know about – or at least can't see in darkness.'

Georgie had nodded agreement. There was no sign of theft or vandalism anywhere. Kids had to be the most likely explanation. And yet, something didn't sit easy with her about that. Why would they have gone to all the trouble of breaking in, just to reset egg timers in the gym? They'd have to have been around still when she arrived, so how come she never saw anyone, and how come the door was unlocked and not broken into? Where had they got in?

Unless, as she had fretted before, it was herself, unconsciously. Her baby brain. Eggs? Timers? Pregnancy was about eggs and timing, wasn't it, at one level?

Am I going nuts from the strain?

From the look one of the police officers had given her, they clearly thought so.

She closed the outer front door behind her, almost too tired to climb the two flights of stairs to the flat, her brain too wired to let her sleep when she got there, she knew. She could do with a drink, a whisky, or even a brandy – that would normally have done the trick. But now she didn't know what to take. Anything to help knock her out and sleep, she needed to be rested and strong in the morning. Was paracetamol safe to take? She googled *paracetamol while pregnant*, then remembered the pills Marcus had given her.

She had never liked taking medication, always worried about side-effects, and was even more wary of anything she took now that might harm her baby. But she took comfort in the knowledge that Valentine wouldn't have given her anything that wasn't one hundred per cent safe as he knew she was pregnant.

Entering the flat, she slung her coat on a sofa, kicked off her boots, removed the vial from her handbag, unscrewed the cap and swallowed one of the tiny white pills with a glass of water from the filter jug in the fridge.

Twenty minutes later, leaving her clothes strewn on the antique chaise longue, and on the floor beside it, she fell into bed and into a fitful sleep. A sleep disrupted by wildly disturbing dreams, in each of which Marcus Valentine was creepily present, his smiling face close up and personal to her, assuring her all was fine. She woke for a few minutes at 3 a.m., certain for a moment there was someone in the room. Roger? Had he discharged himself from hospital, she wondered wildly? She snapped on the light.

The room was empty.

She woke briefly again at 4.20 a.m. Finally, at 7.10 a.m., she swung her legs out of the bed and took a swig of water from her glass.

With a really bad feeling about Roger.

Then she sat up, rigid. Staring around, groggy and tired. Trying to remember. Where were her clothes? They were nowhere to be seen.

Puzzled, she walked over to the closet. Her jeans, T-shirt and jumper were all in there, neatly on hangers.

She frowned. Was her memory playing tricks? She never bothered to put her clothes away at night, always just laying them on the chaise longue.

Naked, she hurried out into the living room, certain that she'd kicked off her boots and slung her coat on a sofa. But they weren't there either. Her coat was hanging on a hook inside the front door, along with her and Roger's hiking puffas.

Where were her boots?

She went back into the bedroom and across to the row of closet doors, opening the one containing her shoe racks. Her boots were in there, neatly together, where she normally kept them. On the rack above them were her three pairs of trainers. She always just shoved them in, haphazardly. But now they were all neatly lined up – and what was even stranger, the laces of each trainer were neatly folded and tucked inside the shoe.

Had the sleeping pill Marcus had given her buzzed her memory? Or was it the stress she was under making her forget?

Or . . . ?

Oh sure, girl, some Good Samaritan came in during the night and tidied everything away for you. Obviously. Just like the Tooth Fairy.

She went into the bathroom, stepped into the shower and turned it on. As the jets of water struck her, she was still puzzled, trying to cast her mind back.

Shit, she thought. *I'm a mess.*

62

Robert Resmes arrived on his bike at the phone repair shop shortly after 8.25 a.m., wanting to ensure he was first through the door when it opened and didn't get stuck in a queue. The sign said its opening hours were 8.30 a.m. to 6 p.m. He padlocked the bike to a railing and for the next ten minutes he stood on the pavement in the narrow street, freezing cold and hungry – he'd not had any breakfast.

Finally, just when he was beginning to wonder if it was going to open at all today, a young man about his own age, with wide-rimmed glasses and lopsided hair, appeared inside the shop, flipped the CLOSED sign to OPEN and gave him an apologetic nod before slipping behind the counter.

Resmes entered and handed the phone he'd found in Marcus Valentine's drawer across to him, giving an explanation that his girlfriend had bought it on Gumtree and it had arrived without a code, then stood waiting while the young techie peered at it, before saying, 'Shouldn't be a problem – you wanna wait?'

'Sure, if it's going to be quick, yes.'

On wall-mounted shelves all around were used phones, chargers, covers and an array of other accessories. Through an open door into a back room, the medical student could see an older man with an eyepiece, holding a tiny screwdriver in one hand, working intently on the innards of a dismembered phone.

The young techie disappeared into the back room. Resmes waited, thinking back with a big smile to last night with Tilly Roberts.

What a night! Truly! They'd chatted so easily over their meal and a sublime bottle of red wine, the beautiful nurse scarcely taking her eyes from his. She had seemed genuinely disappointed when he'd said goodbye to her, turning down her invitation to come up to her place for a coffee with the truthful excuse that he had an early start. And besides, he didn't want her to think he was the kind of guy who wanted to jump into bed with a girl on their first date. He really wasn't.

Especially not with Tilly Roberts. She was very special and already deeply under his skin. His mind buzzed with memories of her lovely face, her scent, her laughter, the cute, delicate way she held her wine glass by the stem with her slender finger and thumb.

'Let's do it again,' she'd said without any prompting. 'Soon.'

'Tomorrow?'

She'd leaned forward and given him a long, lingering kiss on the lips. 'Tomorrow wouldn't be quite soon enough!' she'd said, adding that she had a day off and was going to go to the market and would love to cook them a meal.

Resmes had barely slept; he lay in bed much of the night, thinking about her. What a lady. Back in Romania a friend at medical school had once described another girl he had gone out with – and whom he had been sweet on – as a *keeper*. Unfortunately, she had dumped him. But that's what Tilly was, he could feel it in his bones. A keeper.

It was going to be a struggle to concentrate on his work today. He was already willing the hours away until evening.

'All done!' said a voice, snapping him out of his reverie. It was a few minutes past 9 a.m.

The young man stood in front of him, handing him the phone and a slip of paper on which was written the code. 'Easy,' he said. 'A tenner will be fine.'

Robert Resmes paid the money and thanked him, then unlocked his bike and pedalled, in light drizzle, towards the hospital, five minutes away. He stopped outside a cafe, hesitating, overcome with curiosity about the contents of the phone, and decided he had time. And he was ravenous.

He went in, ordered an omelette and coffee, then sat down with the phone, punched in the code and firstly noticed there were hardly any apps loaded. Immediately he went to the texts to see what the one he had partially read on the screen had said in full.

Super sexy new pussy pics. Hope you enjoy!

He opened Photos. There was one album only. This was labelled 'Favourites'. He tapped on it.

A vast number of photographs of a red-headed woman appeared. He immediately recognized her as Georgina Maclean. Why on earth was she on Marcus's phone?

He began to scroll through them. In several she was running along Victoria Avenue promenade, with the date showing December of last year. Then all dressed up at a dinner party. He recognized several of the group of people around the table, including Marcus, Kath Clow and other colleagues from the hospital.

Next was a screenshot of a laid-out running kit from an Instagram feed. Screenshots of maps with routes marked and running times. More photos of Georgie taking part in what appeared to be a parkrun. Then her running in January around St Aubin's Bay. More running photos. Dozens more.

As he scrolled on through them, he came to a series of photos that really disturbed him. Georgina and the man he recognized instantly as Roger Richardson sitting snuggled up together on a sofa in the living room of what he presumed was their flat. The lights were on. Night-time. The sequence showed them chatting intimately. Kissing.

Resmes was so engrossed he failed to notice the arrival of his coffee, and his omelette and toast.

Was Marcus Valentine spying on the couple from outside their home, he wondered? What other explanation could there be?

Jesus.

He was sickened looking at them.

Sickened by the realization that the highly esteemed consultant surgeon had some kind of obsessive streak. That this was a man who, up until a couple of days ago, he had deeply respected.

Resmes continued looking through the album and was shocked again. He saw several pictures of the woman he recognized as Marcus Valentine's wife. Close-ups of her naked body whilst she was clearly asleep. Then followed close-up after close-up of different women's pubis areas. They were interspersed with occasional pictures of naked breasts and stomachs. And some extreme close-ups of vaginas.

Some had a hospital background and were evidently taken during medical examinations.

Many were taken in the hospital, here in Jersey.

These weren't case-study records, it was porn. Medical porn.

Valentine clearly had a very sick and disturbed mind. Sadly, Resmes knew his initial gut concern on seeing the text message had been right.

He dug his fork into his almost stone-cold omelette and ate a mouthful. Then he drank some coffee. Thinking. And the more he thought, the less he liked the conclusion he was leaning towards.

The tear in Roger Richardson's bowel he was certain he had seen. Followed by Valentine's dismissal of the suggestion. His scornful riposte that it had been scar tissue.

Really? *Scar tissue?*

Resmes might be a student, in his early years in the medical profession, but he was pretty confident he could tell the difference between scar tissue and a cut – or tear.

Was it possible – was it remotely possible – that Mr Valentine had deliberately ignored the tear in Roger Richardson's bowel?

Because he had a motive? A secret thing for Georgina Maclean? Let her fiancé die and she would be his prize?

Unthinkable.

Was it?

The Romanian ate a few more mouthfuls of his breakfast, his appetite gone, gulped down some more cold coffee, left some cash on the table to cover his bill and a tip, grabbed his bike and pedalled furiously towards the hospital.

To his relief, the cardboard he had wedged in Marcus Valentine's door was still in place. He let himself in, pocketing the piece of cardboard, then replaced the phone in the filing cabinet, exactly where he had found it. Still very concerned and trying to make sense of what he had found.

Staring at the door every few moments, hoping Mr Valentine did not come through it.

He'd been a small boy in the first years following the end of the monstrous rule of Ceauşescu, and his parents had talked often throughout his childhood about what living under his regime had been like. And Robert had vowed never, ever in his life to be cowed by anyone dictating to him. He was still smarting from Valentine's fury at him yesterday, for daring to question him. And now the images he had seen were making him question the consultant's integrity. It was a wild thought, and one that as a mere student he really had no business asking, but he asked himself, nonetheless. *Was there a link between Marcus Valentine's apparent obsession with Georgina Maclean and his ignoring the tear in her fiancé's bowel?*

After wrestling with his conscience for some minutes, aware that what he did next could have a serious impact on his future career, he made his decision. He had to follow his conscience. He hurriedly opened the bottom left-hand drawer of the desk. Just as he did so, he heard a knock on the door.

He froze.

Another knock.

Jesus.

Then silence.

Shaking, he rummaged through the papers and put the keys back at the bottom of the drawer. Holding his breath, he waited. Several minutes passed until he felt the coast was clear.

63

Thursday 17 January

Kath Clow sat in her office, checking through her notes for the day ahead. She was well aware that Georgie was booked in for a 2.30 p.m. colposcopy. And she hoped so much, for Georgie's sake, it would show everything to be OK. But she had already decided she would get a second opinion from Marcus to double-check it for her, whatever the result. She had many good reasons for trusting his judgement.

When her son was younger, he'd had a lot of abdominal pain, and after multiple investigations and appointments with paediatricians, it was Marcus who saw this was a Meckel's diverticulum. And soon after she had joined this department, she learned he had saved her predecessor from a potential medical negligence case that could have ended his career.

With Marcus's expertise in the field of oncology, he'd spotted an anomaly in a colposcopy. An early sign of an aggressive stage-2 tumour that her predecessor had very nearly dismissed as old scar tissue from a biopsy. Ever since, she'd made up her mind to defer to Marcus's judgement on anything she was uncertain about, as did all her colleagues in this department. And aside from his professional expertise, she valued and trusted him as a friend.

There was a knock on the door.

'Come in!' she called, fully expecting her registrar with yet another query.

Instead she saw a nervous-looking, dark-haired man in a blue suit, shirt and tie, sporting a light beard.

'Excuse me, Dr Clow,' he said, by way of introduction, 'I'm your new student – I—'

'Robert Resmes?' she queried.

'Yes.'

'I was expecting you tomorrow for your prep meeting – you're starting Monday with me, I believe?'

'Well, no, yes – tomorrow we have one hour – and yes, that's right. Monday. I'm really looking forward to it – you see, I think obstetrics is what I want to do, because it means dealing with happy, excited people!'

She frowned. 'Well, mostly, Robert. But you also have to deal with heartbreak, too, at times.'

He nodded. 'I understand that.' Then he hesitated. 'Thing is, I wanted to come and talk to you because I have a – I don't know how to put it, exactly – I have a concern. It is a difficult situation – I – people say you are a nice lady, and I thought – maybe – I could ask you?'

She smiled at the nervous young man. 'Ask me what?'

'You know the aeroplane crash on Monday?'

'Of course. Terrible.'

'I was with Mr Valentine, in theatre, when he removed the spleen of one of the people involved – one of the pilots. Roger Richardson – I believe he is the fiancé of one of your patients?'

'Yes. I know of his splenectomy.'

'Well, the thing is—' He scratched the back of his head, nervously, aware he was perspiring under her friendly but inquisitive gaze. 'The thing – I saw something that I don't think Mr Valentine noticed.'

'Oh?'

'I'm sure I saw a tear in Mr Richardson's bowel – a very tiny one – that Mr Valentine had not seen.'

'Did you tell him?' she asked.

'I tried. But he didn't take it well. He insisted it was old scar tissue.'

She continued to stare at him, good-naturedly. 'What is making you question his opinion, Robert?'

He hesitated. Was he making a complete fool of himself? 'Well, it's because Mr Richardson is not recovering at all well. I understood he should be out of bed and walking about before now. But he is not.'

'This is your third year as a medical student, right, Robert?'

He nodded.

'I think it's great that you are being so observant, I'm impressed. You clearly have the makings of a fine doctor, whatever discipline you choose to specialize in. But it's still very early days in your studies. What you're going to discover as you learn more is that one seemingly healthy person can be up on their feet twenty-four hours after a major operation, such as a splenectomy. Another can take much longer. Everyone is different.' She shrugged. 'It would be great to have a magic wand and see every patient respond the same way, but that's not what happens.'

He gave a reluctant nod. Before he could say anything, she went on.

'I really think, Robert, that you ought to accept Mr Valentine's opinion. He is extremely experienced, a very fine consultant. If it's of any comfort to you, if I had any problems at all, he would be the first person I'd go to.'

She was being defensive, he thought. Protecting her colleague? Would she feel the same, he wondered, if he were to show her the photographs on Mr Valentine's phone?

But then at some point he would have to explain how he had come by it. That he had broken into the consultant's filing cabinet and taken it to a shop to have it unlocked. He was really struggling with this dilemma. He had hoped Kath Clow might be an ally, but he saw danger signals.

'Please don't tell him I came to you, I don't want him upset with me,' he pleaded. 'I just wanted to do the right thing.'

She smiled, warmly. 'I won't tell him, I promise!' She put a finger to her lips. 'Secret squirrel!'

He reciprocated the sign.

'And, Robert,' she said, as he turned to leave. 'Don't let this deflect you in the future. Always have the courage to do what you believe is the right thing.'

'Thank you, I will.'

He made his way to join Mr Valentine. He looked forward to working with Kath next week, but he was feeling trapped between a rock and a hard place.

64

Georgie arrived in the Relatives' Waiting Room of the Intensive Care Unit shortly before 11 a.m., still feeling groggy and unable to shake off the leaden tiredness she'd felt since waking this morning. As she sat down on a hard chair, she closed her eyes, still confused about how she could have tidied the flat without remembering. She wondered just how strong the sleeping pills that Marcus had given her were, or whether she'd taken one far too late at night and the effects were still working on her.

She dozed off, to be woken with a start a short while later by Kiera Dale's voice.

'How are you today, Georgie?'

Blinking awake, she stared around, momentarily confused by her surroundings, until she saw the nurse standing in front of her. 'Sorry,' she said. I—'

'You look tired,' Kiera said in a kindly voice. 'Are you able to sleep at night OK?'

Georgie nodded. 'Thanks, yes. I—' She was about to tell her that Mr Valentine had given her some tablets, but then wondered if that might get him into trouble. 'I guess not that well at the moment. I worry constantly.' She glanced at her watch. 11.20 a.m. 'How is Roger? Has he improved overnight?'

The nurse hesitated, before giving her a smile that was not matched by her expression, nor her body language. 'Well, he's stable, but to be honest with you, he's still not making as much progress as we would have hoped by now. But as we all know, some

247

patients do take much longer to recover from major surgery than others.'

'Roger's a fit man,' she replied, lamely. 'Surely he ought to be getting better by now?'

'He has a very strong heart,' the nurse said in reply. 'That's definitely helping him. We're monitoring him closely.'

Georgie followed the nurse, stopping, as she did, for a squirt of the hand sanitizer at the entrance to the ward. As she entered the ICU, she was shocked at the sight of Roger. He was back on a ventilator, asleep, his skin looking mottled, and his heart rate was very definitely down from yesterday. He had compression stockings on his legs and Flowtron boots.

What was going on? she wondered, in bewildered terror. Yesterday he'd been looking fine when she'd left the ward. But today he looked very much worse. Stepping away, out of earshot of her fiancé and talking quietly, she told the nurse her concerns. This time, instead of allaying her fears, Kiera concurred.

'It's possible he's picked up an infection,' she said. 'We're giving him a course of antibiotics to try to knock it out.'

'I don't like his heart rate or his blood pressure,' Georgie said. 'Both are worse than yesterday – than last night when I left him.'

The nurse gave her the kind of reassuring smile she hated. 'Hopefully he'll respond to the antibiotics in time.'

'Really?' Georgie rounded on her. 'How much time? In time for what? He seemed to be doing OK last night when I left him – what the hell is going on? Are you really going to tell me this is normal? There must be some complications going on, surely?'

'We're doing all we can for him, Georgie,' the nurse replied. 'Yes, it's not an ideal situation – we would have hoped he would be up and about by now, but as I told you earlier, all patients respond differently. But if he doesn't pick up in the next few hours, the doctors will have to see if there is something else going on.'

'Something else? Like what?'

'I don't really feel it's my place to speculate – we'll wait for the next ward round. It could be as simple as Roger not reacting well to one of the medications.'

'I'm so worried.'

'I know, and I do understand what you must be going through. Please don't worry. I'm sure in a few days he'll be back home and well on the road to recovery.' She glanced at her watch. 'I'm afraid I've got to go to a meeting, I'll be back in a short while to see how he's getting on.' She pointed at the nursing station. 'The nurse, just over there, will be in charge of him in the meantime. Speak to her if you have any more concerns.'

Georgie saw a short, dark-haired nurse standing in front of the counter. She smiled at her and the nurse smiled back.

As Kiera left, Georgie kissed Roger's cheek. It was clammy. Then she held his free hand. It was limp and clammy, also. She leaned over and whispered into his ear, 'Hi, darling, I'm here with you. I love you. Love you so much. You're going to be OK, you'll be fine. We'll get through this together. Just be strong. Little Bump needs you to be better quickly!'

She felt a faint squeeze back.

For the next hour and a half, she maintained her vigil while Roger slept on. All the time she watched the monitors like a hawk, willing the figures to start improving. He seemed stable, at least from the digital readouts. Hopefully, the antibiotics were working.

At 1.30 p.m. Georgie's stomach was rumbling, reminding her she'd not eaten a thing all day so far. Although she had no appetite, she was aware she needed fuel so she left Roger, went downstairs and bought herself a tuna sandwich and a bottle of Coke for the caffeine and sugar hit from the cafe in the entrance lobby. Then, in need of fresh air, she carried them outside, into the biting wind and stinging rain. It refreshed her but was too cold to stay out there. She returned to the hospital, sat on a thin bench inside the entrance and bit into her sandwich.

As soon as she had finished, she hurried back up to the ICU and resumed her vigil on the chair at Roger's bedside. He was still sound asleep, out of it. Just as she leaned across to kiss him, she was aware, out of the corner of her eye, of two figures entering the ward. Marcus Valentine and his student, Robin – no, *Robert* – Resmes. They were accompanied by Kiera Dale and two other medics she did not recognize.

Valentine beamed smartly down as he approached.

'Hello, Georgie, how is my patient doing?' he asked.

'Not that great actually,' Georgie said, before the nurse could respond. 'Is there anything you can do for him, please? He just doesn't seem to be improving.'

Oh sure, Marcus Valentine thought. *What would you like me to do? Save his life so you can live with him in marital bliss?*

In your dreams, lady.

He gave her a reassuring smile. 'Don't you worry, you just relax. He's bound to have a few ups and downs following the accident and such major surgery. He's doing fine, I'm quite happy.' He made a show of studying all the monitor displays. 'All is good, pretty much what I'd be expecting to see.'

He turned on his heels and, followed by his entourage, headed towards the exit.

His words echoed in Georgie's head: *Don't you worry, you just relax.*

Easy for you to say, she thought.

65

Thursday 17 January

As he left the Intensive Care Unit, Valentine was in a troubled mood. And the Romanian medical student was the source of this.

I just wanted to mention something, Mr Valentine. I did not think it was appropriate at the time – in theatre – during the operation. But it looked to me that there might have been a tiny tear in Mr Richardson's bowel.

Fortunately, he was losing him next week. But the young man worried him. How long before he told someone else what he had seen? Once Richardson started to go seriously downhill, which would be happening soon, and Resmes told another member of the team what he suspected, one of the other general surgeons would probably open him up again. They'd find that perforation, repair it and, almost certainly, Richardson would recover.

And almost certainly an inquiry would follow. With Resmes sticking to his claim that he had told Marcus what he'd seen, and he'd ignored it, there was a real threat to his own career. He could be suspended. God forbid, he could be struck off.

Needing time to think, he told Resmes he had to catch up on some paperwork in his office and to go and take his lunch break. The next thing in his diary that would be of medical interest to him, he told the student, would be a colposcopy examination of a patient with advanced cervical cancer, at 3 p.m. He would meet him then.

Unlocking his office door, he went in and sat at his desk. He was about to log on to his computer when something caught his interest. Something out of place. He glanced down and saw that

251

the bottom left drawer of his desk wasn't completely closed. There was a tiny gap.

He always closed it tightly.

Had someone been in there? Why? Who?

Annoyed, he opened it fully, then began to sift through the folders of old documents he kept in there until he reached the bottom, where he kept the keys to the two filing cabinets in the room.

Instantly, another warning bell rang in his head.

The keys were sprawled messily apart. He would never leave them like that.

Who the hell had been in here?

He unlocked the filing cabinet and rummaged, urgently, through the green file folders hanging inside. He pulled out the one with the large bulge and his hackles rose.

As a precaution he always placed the phone with the display side facing away, towards the rear of the cabinet. Now it was facing towards the front. He picked it up. Fuck! It wasn't on mute.

No question. Someone had been in here and removed it. How had he been so careless?

His mind went back to last night. Remembering now the strange phone call he had received from Resmes.

Oh, I'm sorry, Mr Valentine, sorry to disturb you. I – I just wanted to check what time and where I should meet you tomorrow?

For fuck's sake, had the little creep gone into his office after he'd left? Was he spying on him? And, even more worrying, had he seen the contents of his phone?

There was one sure way to find out. *You think you're so fucking smart, do you, Robert Resmes? Great powers of observation, eh? Well, Mr Interfering Fucking Foreigner, how come you failed to spot this?*

On a corner shelf, on the far side of the office, sandwiched between two cacti plants, lay a medical directory. No one entering his office would give it a second glance. But if they picked it up, they might think it was a little light – and they'd be right. Valentine had hollowed out the pages and inserted a video camera, which had a wide-angle view of almost the entire office.

He tapped the CleverCam app on his regular phone to bring up the images. The camera was programmed to take a photograph any time there was movement in the room. The first image he saw was himself, entering the office just a couple of minutes ago. He scrolled back to early evening last night and saw an image of Robert Resmes entering the room. The next showed him halfway across it. Then looking around as if startled by something. Going to the filing cabinet. Tugging the drawer. Then walking to his desk. Sitting at it. Then returning to the filing cabinet. Removing the phone.

Examining the phone.

Then pocketing it. Closing the filing cabinet. Returning to the desk and apparently replacing the key.

The time then jumped to 9.44 a.m. today. Resmes re-entering. Removing, presumably, the key from his desk. Opening the filing cabinet. Replacing the phone. Replacing the key. Leaving.

Valentine fought to contain his rage at the sheer nerve of the man. How dare he? Then, trying to calm down, he thought hard, wondering what the Romanian had been doing with the phone in the interim. Trying to unlock the password, almost certainly.

Had he succeeded?

He had to assume so. Thinking anything else would be too much of a risk.

He was going to have to act fast.

He started by deleting the incriminating contents of the phone, both the duplicated running pictures from his personal phone and everything else.

66

Thursday 17 January

At 2.15 p.m., Georgie Maclean reluctantly left the ICU, where Roger was still asleep, and followed the signs along the hospital corridor to the Maternity ward. She passed a wheelchair, a waste bin with a hazard-warning symbol and a strip across it saying, 'No yellow bags', a yellow cone warning of a slippery floor, and saw the sign she had been looking for.

COLPOSCOPY. CONSULTING ROOM 5

She knocked on the door then entered a small waiting room, with a row of lockers on one side and a curtained-off dressing room on the other. A young Australian-sounding nurse handed her a blue gown and a locker key, asked her to remove all her clothing and put the gown on, and departed, saying she would be back in a few minutes.

Georgie did as she was instructed then sat, barefoot, and waited. The nurse returned and ushered her through into a small room cluttered with technical apparatus, including a monitor and the binocular microscope Georgie remembered from her previous examination, with an elaborate white-and-blue examination chair, with padded leg supports, occupying centre stage. Another nurse in the room helped Georgie position herself in the chair, placing each of her legs on the pads, then reclined her.

Lying back, with her legs almost in the air, she felt helpless and vulnerable, as well as full of her nagging worry about what Kath might find. Another time she might have made an attempt at a joke, but she was too preoccupied with her fears for Roger and her baby.

A few moments later the obstetrician entered, in blue scrubs and gloves.

'Hello, Georgie!' she said, brightly as ever. 'How are you, my love?'

'OK, thanks.'

'And how's dear Roger doing?'

'Not good. I'm very worried about him.'

'He had pretty major surgery,' she said. 'A splenectomy can really take quite a while to recover from.'

'I know, but the ICU team can't understand why he's not showing any improvement in his condition – he actually seems to be going downhill since yesterday.' She gave a helpless shrug. 'He's on antibiotics and currently stable, but I can see they're concerned. I don't know, I just get the feeling something is not right.'

'Georgie, I know from experience that a lot of patients have heightened fears while pregnant. Roger is in the best possible place where he is. Try not to worry too much, he's going to be fine, really.'

Georgie gave her another thin smile. 'Yes. God, I hope you're right.'

'OK, let's take a look at you and see how everything is. I'm pretty confident those small spots of blood you saw are nothing to worry about, but let's be sure, eh? I'm going to take a biopsy, just to eliminate any possibility of anything nasty.'

Kath gelled the tip of the speculum and then, peering into the microscope binoculars, entered it slowly into Georgie, pushing it further and deeper in over the next few minutes. 'As I thought, it's looking pink and healthy, Georgie. There are a few changes, which are probably due to your pregnancy. I'm not seeing anything to worry me at all. But I'm going to take a biopsy just for belt and braces.'

Fifteen minutes later, removing the speculum, the obstetrician placed the tissue sample in a small plastic vial and screwed back the lid. She wrote an instruction to the pathology lab on the label and stuck that on.

This vial, along with all the others in this afternoon's colposcopy clinic, would be taken down to the path labs for analysis straight after the clinic was finished.

'It all looks pretty good to me,' Kath said to Georgie by way of reassurance. 'But let's wait for the biopsy result so we can be one hundred per cent, eh?'

'But you really think it's fine?'

'Yes, I do, I've honestly not seen anything to give me any concern.'

Released from the chair, Georgie retrieved her clothes from the locker and changed back into them. As she walked out into the corridor, intending to return to Roger's bedside, she saw Marcus Valentine, trailed by his student, heading towards her. Both were in scrubs.

'Hello, Georgie!' Marcus greeted her. 'How did your procedure go?' He made this sound like she was a schoolgirl up for a prize.

'I was teacher's pet.'

He frowned, missing the irony of her retort, then said, uneasily, 'Ah.'

'Dr Clow was concerned because I had a little bleeding, but she thinks it's all fine – though she doesn't want me running at the moment.'

'Good to hear – bleeding at your stage of pregnancy should always be investigated, but it's usually nothing to be too worried about.'

'I'm much more worried about Roger, Marcus,' she responded.

'I told you earlier, don't be – he's my friend and I'm looking after him.' He gave her a smile, one which was not mirrored by his student. Robert Resmes had a concerned expression on his face. As if he shared the same doubts that Georgie had.

As the pair went in through the Colposcopy Unit door, she headed on back towards the ICU. Wondering as she walked.

Wondering about the look on Resmes's face.

Then she heard footsteps gaining rapidly on her and turned, to see Valentine hurrying after her. 'Oh, Georgie,' he said, as he caught her up. 'You mentioned that you have an open gym session on Thursday evenings, was it, specifically for running training? Are you having one tonight, by chance, or is everything on hold?'

'Yes, I'm going to have to. I can't let my clients down.'

'Would it be OK if I came along? I think you said 6.30 p.m.?'

'That would be lovely.'

67

At 3 p.m., in the colposcopy room Kath Clow had just vacated, Valentine began the examination of the first of three patients who would take him through to the end of this afternoon's clinic. She was a sixteen-weeks-pregnant Polish woman of just thirty-two, Kasia Mackiewicz, presenting with cancer of the cervix.

As he peered through the scope, the magnified image was displayed on the monitor for the benefit of the nurses and his student, and so he kept his commentary to the very minimum, not wanting to worry the woman. But what he saw was not good news. The cancer was metastasizing. A whole cluster of polyps, like baby cauliflower, with heavy bleeding around them. The cervix was an unhealthy grey colour. He was almost certainly going to have to operate on her as soon as possible – which would mean terminating the pregnancy first.

He took tissue samples for the path lab and, at the end of the examination, as she was getting up from the chair looking worried as hell, he tried to reassure her, deciding it would be better to break the news to her later in a one-on-one consultation, rather than here.

As she left the room, he placed the samples in a plastic vial, screwed on the cap, wrote his instructions to the pathologist on a label and stuck it on the side of the vial. Then he checked his list to read the notes on his next patient.

An hour later, shortly after 4 p.m., when he had completed the third colposcopy, finishing the clinic in the unit for this afternoon, he scooped up all four plastic pots, including Georgina Maclean's, telling the nurses that he had to go and talk to the pathologist on a matter and that he'd drop the tissue samples in for them, to save them a journey.

Walking with Robert Resmes back out into the corridor, shoving the vials into his pocket, he closed the door behind him and turned to the student. 'So, Robert. I hope you've found this past month to be instructive?'

Resmes stared at him.

Valentine could read so much in his eyes and in his body language. And he did not like anything that he saw. The young man was not going to keep his mouth shut, that was blindingly clear. And eventually someone would listen to him and believe him.

'You want to have a chat, don't you, Robert?' he said, all friendly now.

'I think we should.'

'There are things you need to understand if you're going to become a successful doctor. I recognize in you a real talent – you are way brighter than the average student I get. You're smart and you are going to go far, and I can help you – I *want* to help you.' He made a show of looking around, then lowered his voice. 'Walls have ears. This building is not a good place to talk.' He gave Resmes a conspiratorial wink. 'Understand what I'm saying?'

Resmes stared back at him levelly, giving no indication whether he understood or not.

'Do you know the Bel Royal Hotel, Robert?'

The Romanian shook his head.

'It's a couple of miles from here – overlooking St Aubin's Bay. Put it in your satnav.'

'I have a bicycle,' he replied. 'I don't possess a car – or satnav.'

'On your phone? You have a phone. Google maps.'

'OK.'

'8.30 tonight.'

Resmes looked hesitant. 'I have a date tonight. She's cooking for me.'

Valentine smiled. 'Oh? Good for you! Anyone I know?'

'Perhaps.'

'You're a dark horse, eh?'

Resmes frowned. 'Dark horse?'

'Good for you! It won't take long – and in my experience, keeping them waiting just makes them hotter for you!'

Resmes gave Valentine a reluctant nod.

'Excellent!' He gave the student a patronizing pat on the shoulder. 'Right, I've now got some admin to deal with, so we're done. Feel free to do whatever you want, and I'll see you at the front entrance of the Bel Royal at 8.30 p.m. All good?'

'I guess.'

As he walked away, Robert Resmes knew what he should do, but after Kath Clow's reaction, he realized there could be fatal consequences for his career if he tried to report Mr Valentine to someone in the hospital. And he was also curious about what the consultant was going to tell him later – that would have a bearing on what he did next.

68

As Marcus left his student, instead of taking the elevator down to the pathology lab floor, he made straight for his office, entered and closed and locked the door. Then he sat at his desk and laid out the four vials in front of him.

He picked up the one labelled, in Kath Clow's handwriting, GEORGINA MACLEAN, and being very careful not to tear it, peeled off the label and stuck it on the edge of his desk. Next, he did the same with the one containing tissue scrapings from his first patient of this afternoon's clinic, Kasia Mackiewicz. Then he swapped them over, smoothing down each, meticulously. When he had finished, he held each of them up, in turn, admiring his handiwork.

Next, he dialled Kath Clow's mobile phone. She answered after a couple of rings.

'Yes, hello, Marcus?'

'Are you busy at the moment, Kath? I just wanted to chat about the handover of my student, Robert Resmes – he's starting with you Monday.'

'I am – just dealing with an emergency – a patient going into labour.'

'No problemo! Call me when you're free – nothing urgent.'

'Will do!'

As he ended the call he was smiling. Good. That meant she wasn't in her office and would not be for a while. The gods were smiling. Everything was aligning very nicely indeed!

Using Clow's password, he logged on to her computer and did a search for Georgina Maclean's notes.

Good girl!

She had updated them at 3.07 p.m. today. Straight after Georgie's colposcopy.

He read through what she had written, carefully. A bit of preamble before she got to the essence.

Patient had reported minor spotting of blood in her urine. Colposcopy examination carried out at 2.30 p.m. today revealed no abnormalities; tissue scrapings taken as precaution for pathology examination.

After several minutes' consideration, Valentine made a minor adjustment to her notes. All he had to do was delete a few words. Kath Clow's notes now read:

Patient had reported minor spotting of blood in her urine. Colposcopy examination carried out at 2.30 p.m. today. Tissue scrapings taken for pathology examination.

He knew he was getting in deeper, but now he felt he had no choice. In any case, if Kath Clow's workload was as rammed as his and everyone else's here in the hospital, she'd never notice these changes.

He logged out and, feeling in a very good mood – a very good mood indeed – went down to the basement and along to the pathology lab, where he casually handed in the samples.

At some point soon he'd have to deal with Kasia Mackiewicz, who had a serious cancer – but all in good time.

And there it was again. Rearing its ticking head . . .

Timing!

69

Thursday 17 January

Roger remained unresponsive throughout the afternoon, but at least, to Georgie's slight relief, his duty nurse said he was stable. The doctors seemed reasonably satisfied after their ward round, although they didn't tell her much, other than to confirm that there had been no worsening of his condition. He would continue to be closely monitored throughout the night. Roger's parents were hugely grateful for Georgie giving them regular updates.

She talked to Roger constantly. It was a one-way conversation, but she hoped he could hear her. On the websites she'd looked up it said that comatose and semi-comatose patients could hear everything, even if they did not respond.

Finally, approaching 5.30 p.m., she stood up, telling him she would be back later. Although reluctant to leave him, she had six clients booked in for her running training session this evening – seven including Marcus Valentine. She would be back at the hospital by 8.30 p.m., latest.

Kissing him on his cheek, for which she got no reaction, Georgie told him she would be back. 'Be strong, my darling!' she urged.

She drove home, changed into her gym kit and headed, as fast as she dared, towards the Bel Royal Hotel.

Shortly before 6.10 p.m., she pulled up in pitch darkness at the rear of the hotel, climbed out of her car into bitterly cold, gusting wind, fumbled her key in the lock and let herself into the gym. Thankfully, she had twenty minutes before her clients were due. Time to do a warm-up and set up tonight's programme. Snapping on the lights and setting the temperature to 22 degrees, Georgie picked out some music, starting off with one of her current favourites, Passenger's 'Simple Song'. It began booming out through the overhead speakers. She walked around, moving to the music. It lifted her mood, a little, and despite wanting to be back at Roger's bedside, she found herself relishing the brief change of scenery and the normality of doing what she loved.

Suddenly she had the intense feeling she was being watched.

She stopped, looking around, and jumped, startled. Barely visible, Edouardo was standing in the darkness of the corridor, motionless, staring at her.

'Shit, Edouardo, you gave me a fright. Why haven't you got the lights on?'

'Fuse blown. I fix.'

'No clown suit tonight?'

'Not my funny night,' he said. 'You sure you not change your mind and run with me this weekend?'

'Quite sure, thank you! But have a good one.'

'Make sure you lock up. I . . . I think your client here.' As he walked away, Edouardo stopped. 'You should try ultrarun. I know you good runner, I know your times.'

'One day maybe,' Georgie said and waved him off, as through the windows she saw the flare of headlights. More lights followed. The door opened and Marcus entered, in a flashy tracksuit and brand-new trainers.

'I love your music!' he said to her, approvingly. 'Love it, I really, really love it. Great choice!'

She increased the volume, put him on a treadmill to warm up, deliberately set the speed to a level she hoped he would find uncomfortable and left him to it, as one of her regulars, followed by another, arrived.

By 7.30 p.m. all of her clients except for Valentine had left. He lingered behind, sweating profusely and looking drained.

'Thank you, Georgie,' he said. 'That was a good workout. How much do I owe you?'

She shook her head. 'Tonight was a freebie, treat it as a thank you for all you've done for Roger. If you decide you'd like to come again, we'll work something out.'

'Oh, I will come again, for sure. That was brilliant!'

'Good,' she said, impatient for him to go.

He put one hand on the door then turned back as if he wanted to say something. Instead he smiled and blew her a kiss. She blew him a half-hearted one back and then, to her relief, he left. Concerned to get back to Roger as quickly as possible, she decided to skip her usual inspection. Tomorrow she would do a thorough one, to make up for it.

Outside she heard the roar of an engine. Through the window she saw Valentine in his Porsche, window lowered. He waved at her then drove on. The Porsche reminded her of her narrow escape last month. That idiot. Instinctively, she put her arms protectively around her midriff, hugging herself. 'You OK in there, Bump? Like it in the gym? You're going to be the fittest Bump ever – and the most loved!'

As Marcus's tail lights disappeared, she switched off the music, the heating and the lights, locked the door and hurried out to her car.

As she got to the exit ramp, she looked in her rear-view mirror and saw Edouardo, again standing still, watching her.

She was tempted to stop, reverse back and ask him what he was doing. But she drove on, deciding the less engagement she had with the strange man, the better.

70

Resmes phoned his date, Tilly, very apologetically, saying he wouldn't be with her until close to 9.30 p.m., explaining that an emergency had come up. Happily, she was totally understanding. 'Just get here when you can,' she said. 'But don't be too long, because I'm really quite looking forward to seeing you!'

'And me you!'

And he was. It had been a long time since he had looked forward to anything quite so much. God, she was lovely! After Mr Valentine had released him early, this afternoon, he'd gone into town and bought a large box of chocolates from Artisan du Chocolat. He had them carefully packed into his rucksack strapped to his back, over his yellow reflective vest.

As he pedalled against the strong headwind, up the hill towards the dark silhouette of the Bel Royal Hotel, following the directions on the map on his phone, he was deep in thought. Clearly Mr Valentine was disturbed, suspecting that he'd been rumbled, and wanted to talk confidentially, possibly to persuade him not to expose him. This was the way things worked in powerful professional circles, he realized, confidential conversations and cover-up.

He'd become acutely aware, in the relatively short time that he'd been in the medical world, that doctors looked after their own. He'd already had evidence of that when he'd attempted to explain his concerns to Kath Clow, and she had been – albeit pleasantly – dismissive of them. It had left him well aware that he would be stonewalled by anyone else in the hospital he tried to tell.

Perhaps Mr Valentine was worried about his reputation if it got out that he'd missed something crucial in the operation? That seemed the most likely explanation. When they met, maybe they would discuss a way for Roger Richardson to be taken back into theatre and the tear in his bowel discovered without any blame falling on Mr Valentine for having missed it.

If his career was ever to progress, he needed good reports from all the consultants he spent time with. Hopefully, he and Kath Clow could work out a deal. Something that would leave Valentine looking good to his colleagues – and in return, some high praise back for himself. Now was not the time for things to go wrong with his medical career, especially not with the hope of something good sparking with that lovely nurse, Tilly.

Buoyed by that idea, he pedalled even harder up the incline. As he drew closer, he was surprised that he couldn't see any lights on. Perhaps there were few occupants at this time of year? Or a power cut?

Finally, in the bright beam of his cycle lamp, the hotel sign appeared to his left. He swung in between two stone pillars and struggled up a twisting driveway that was even steeper than the hill he had just navigated. After several minutes, perspiring heavily, he crested the summit and saw, in his weak bicycle lamp beam, the dark, silent rear of the hotel below him, with an empty car park. A series of arrows indicated the driveway around the building to the front reception area. He pedalled on, the wind behind him now, pushing him at speed down the incline.

As he swung around to the front of the hotel, with the lights of St Aubin down to his left, all he could see to his right was black windows. The hotel appeared to be in total darkness. He braked to a halt outside the front entrance and dismounted. Frowning.

Was he in the wrong place?

He checked on his phone the name of the venue that Mr Valentine had given him.

Bel Royal Hotel.

This was the Bel Royal Hotel.

Then, right behind him, he heard a footstep. A second later, as he started to turn, he heard a voice.

'Hello there.'

The blow to his head sent him crashing to the ground, his bicycle clattering beside him. There was a tinkle of breaking glass and the front lamp went out.

71

Friday 18 January

Inside the curtains drawn around Roger Richardson's bed, on their morning ward round, stood James Swale, the duty ICU consultant, his registrar, an anaesthetist, along with Kiera Dale and Marcus Valentine. They were all studying the battery of monitors around him with apparent concern.

Richardson's skin was even more mottled, his breathing fainter than yesterday afternoon. His arterial blood gas reading was down significantly, as was his heart rate. His pulse was racing.

'Something's not right,' James Swale said quietly. 'You operated on him on Monday, early afternoon, Marcus?'

'Yes. A pretty straightforward splenectomy.'

'Could he have picked up an infection?' Kiera Dale ventured.

'Yes,' Valentine said, firmly. 'That's by far the most likely explanation.' He nodded at each of the others in turn, making sure to catch their eyes. 'I would suggest another course of antibiotics for the next forty-eight hours and see if that has an effect. Otherwise we'll need to open him up and see if we can spot anything going on.'

Swale, a reedy-thin and tall man, pondered for some moments before nodding assent, bowing to the senior consultant's experience.

'I think that's a good call, Marcus.'

One floor below, Kath Clow sat at her desk, uncharacteristically irritated. She had blocked out an hour to run through her work routine with Robert Resmes, who was going to be spending the

269

next month with her, starting Monday. But, annoyingly, the medical student hadn't shown up for his prep meeting. Was he not bothering with her because she'd not taken his concerns about Marcus Valentine more seriously, she wondered? Well, this was a small hospital, offering a wide range of services. It was vital that everyone got on, trusted their colleagues, and that there was joined-up thinking. In the many years she'd been here, Kath had not been given any reason to doubt the ability of any of her colleagues. All of them shared the same views as herself – to do the very best that they could.

She glanced at her screen, checking her commitments for today. A colposcopy clinic at 12 p.m. The weekly conference call with the Oncology department of Sheffield Hospital at 2 p.m., to discuss the cancer treatment programme of a number of patients. After that she was free to go home, but of course she wouldn't. She had several patients in the Maternity ward, on the verge of giving birth.

She would hang around as long as possible but would have to leave by 7 p.m. as her husband was taking her out to dinner tonight, for a belated anniversary celebration at one of the island's swankiest hotels, Longueville Manor, and she had been looking forward to it for weeks. She'd peeped at the dinner menu online and had already decided what she was going to have to eat.

The ping of an incoming email took her out of her thoughts, and she glanced at her inbox. At the top was a message from the senior pathologist, Nigel Kirkham. It said:

Kath, please call me on this number when you get this.

She dialled and Kirkham answered almost instantly.

'Kath, thanks for calling.'

'Sure, what's up?'

He sounded hesitant. 'Well, I've got the biopsy results on your patient, Georgina Maclean.'

'That was quick! I wasn't expecting them until Monday.'

'I'm going away for the weekend – got a family wedding in England – so I thought I'd better clear my workload. These results aren't good, so I thought you ought to know right away.'

'Not good?' she said, surprised and dismayed.

It was his turn to sound surprised. 'Not at all good, Kath, this looks like advanced squamous cell cancer of the cervix.'

'Are you absolutely sure, Nigel?'

'I'm afraid so.'

'Shit. I saw her, she was bleeding a little, but I never thought there was advanced cancer. Her colposcopy looked clear to me.'

There was a moment of silence before he responded. 'It did?' He sounded surprised. 'It's not what the biopsy is showing me.'

'How advanced?'

'Possibly stage-2B.'

Stage-2B meant the cancer was in both the cervix and lymph vessels and had extended to the pelvic side walls. This would require urgent surgery, followed by radiation and chemotherapy. Which would mean termination of the pregnancy. Oh jeez, poor Georgie.

'I'm sorry if I'm sounding surprised. This lady presented with stage-1 pre-cancer a year ago. I was pretty sure she was clear now. I'll make the call. I know her as a friend, and this is going to come as an awful shock.'

Fortunately for Kath's sanity, most of the time doing her job she delivered good news, and delivered happy, healthy babies, putting a smile on everyone's faces. There was nothing more rewarding in the world than doing just that. But with it went the downside. Some days she had to be the bearer of bad news. She knew just how much this baby Georgie was carrying meant to her, after all her years of trying. She and Bob had been overjoyed when she had finally become pregnant with their son, Charlie, after many emotionally draining rounds of IVF. Now there was a real danger she was going to have to break her friend's heart.

She picked up her phone and dialled Georgie's number with a sense of dread.

72

Friday 18 January

As was starting to seem like her new morning routine, Georgie perched on a chair in the Relatives' Waiting Room, waiting for the morning ward round to be completed. She was relieved to be alone in the room, not in any mood to have to chat to someone. Her mind was all over the place and her stomach was fluttering – despite having done an early-morning walk which usually, at least, energized and calmed her. But not today.

She gazed around, staring at the leaflets – over the past few days she'd already read every word of them. She checked her phone, scanning her emails – so many she hadn't replied to while her life was on hold. She looked at her to-do list. A private client was booked in for this evening. She debated whether to cancel him but decided to keep the booking. The timing fitted in reasonably well with the afternoon ward round and she'd already cancelled him once this week, on Monday. He was an impatient guy, a fund manager who was full of himself and not her favourite client, but nonetheless, she didn't want to risk losing him and having him bad-mouth her for blowing him out again. She needed her clients now more than ever.

She began checking her diary for the following weeks ahead and saw the skiing trip to Val d'Isère in France they'd planned for mid-February. Roger had been so much looking forward to it, although with her being well into her second trimester at that time, she'd been advised that the risk of a fall causing a miscarriage was too great. She'd be limiting her activities to finding a hotel spa and gym she could use. But could Roger possibly be well enough by then, less than a month away, to ski?

Would he even be alive?

That thought struck like a massive wave of icy water surging through her.

Shit. Shit. Shit. Oh God, please Roger—

Her phone was ringing. She grabbed it and saw a landline number she didn't recognize. 'Hello?' she answered, and could hear the tremor in her own, edgy voice.

'Hello, Georgie.'

It was Kath, but sounding less vivacious and more subdued than usual.

'Hi,' she said.

'You sound very low. How's Roger today?'

'I'm just waiting to go and see him – after the ward round. Yes, I guess – I'm feeling more and more scared – I'm so worried about him. I know he's in the best hands, but – I guess I was a bit stupid – I sat in bed last night googling the mortality rates of people after splenectomies – 3.2 per cent get infections following the operation and 1.4 per cent of those die.'

'Georgie!' Kath admonished, good-naturedly. 'Googling stuff like that is just about the worst thing you can do to yourself! And anyhow, 1.4 is a tiny percentage.'

'But what if Roger is in that 1.4 per cent?'

'You see, that's what googling stats doesn't tell you. The people at that end of the spectrum are almost certainly elderly and frail. We both know your Roger is a pretty fit person, isn't he?'

'Yes.'

'So, stop worrying – the more positive you are, the more you'll transmit that positivity to Roger. OK?'

Georgie smiled, thinly. 'Thanks.'

Clow suddenly sounded more serious. 'Georgie, the reason I'm calling you is I've had the results from the biopsy I took yesterday and there's something not quite right. I want to get an MRI scan of your cervix to see what's going on. From—'

'Not quite right?' Georgie interrupted. The room seemed to have darkened, suddenly, and it felt as if all the warmth had been sucked out with the light. 'What – what do you mean?'

'Honestly, from my assessment, Georgie, I don't have any real worries at all, but I'd like to try to book you in as soon as possible, just so we can eliminate the Pathology department concerns. Is there any time that wouldn't work for you? I don't know how busy they are – if they can't fit you in today, would tomorrow be possible?'

'Yes, that's fine. I'm clear all day today and tomorrow – but what do you mean that something's not right?'

'I really don't want you to worry. What I saw during your colposcopy appeared normal.'

'But you took tissue for a biopsy, and now the path lab is telling you otherwise. They won't have made a mistake, would they?'

'What I think he's almost certainly seen is some of that precancerous tissue that you had removed eighteen months ago. There may be some residual scar tissue, too small for even the colposcopy to pick up, containing a few cells which have shown up in the biopsy. If that's the case, it's a five-minute job to remove them. I know how much this baby means to you, Georgie. Trust me, as your friend first, and obstetrician second, I just want to make sure everything is one hundred per cent, which I'm confident it is. My assistant will be in touch with a time for the scan. OK?'

'Kath, promise it's OK?' Georgie said, lamely.

Before ending the call, Kath tried to reassure her. 'Listen, Georgie, I'm on it, I'm looking after you.'

Georgie stood, too unsettled to remain seated, and paced around the little room. Wondering. What was all that about? What was her friend not telling her? What was so urgent that the MRI scan needed to be done immediately, even tomorrow, on a Saturday, rather than waiting for next week?

There's something not quite right.

Something more than Kath was telling her.

Behind her, she heard the sound of the door opening and the voice of Kiera Dale.

'Hi, Georgie, good morning!'

Georgie turned and mustered a smile.

'How are you today?'

'I've had better mornings. How is Roger?'

'Well, the assessment team have just been with him. The good news is there's been no deterioration in his condition overnight.'

'Does that mean he's responding to the antibiotics?' she said, hopefully.

Kiera nodded but her expression was less positive than Georgie would have liked. 'Yes. But I'm afraid there are concerns at the levels of his readings and his bloods – they are indicative of sepsis.'

Georgie felt a swirl of terror at the word. 'Sepsis? Blood poisoning? That's fatal, isn't it?'

'It can be if not treated in time, yes, but very rarely in an ICU environment. The medical team is going to make a treatment plan and timescale for Roger right away.'

'Timescale?'

She nodded. 'If Roger doesn't start responding they will have to operate and see if they can find something going on.'

'Like what?'

'Most likely an infection around the area of the splenectomy.'

Georgie thought for a moment. 'If you suspect that, why don't you operate right away and have a look?'

'Anaesthetics – and surgery – take a big toll on patients, Georgie. They're worried at the moment whether Roger's strong enough to cope with anaesthetics.'

Georgie stared at the nurse, the full realization of what she had just been told sinking in slowly. 'What you're saying is you're worried Roger isn't strong enough to survive surgery, right?'

Evasively, she said, 'Hopefully he'll respond to the drugs and surgery won't be necessary.'

Too upset to speak any more, Georgie followed her into the ICU, after the ward round had been completed, and sat beside Roger, placing her phone, switched to silent, on his bedside table. Roger was asleep but she kissed him and took his hand, trying to be positive as Kath had advised, chatting to him about her class last night, and how Marcus Valentine had come along – and was very unfit.

Then she lapsed into silence.

When, she wondered, would this nightmare ever end?

And how?

Something not quite right.

Biopsy.

Cancer?

Her phone vibrated. It was Kath Clow's assistant asking if she could come to the hospital tomorrow at midday for an MRI scan.

Georgie replied that she could and thanked her. The moment she ended the call, she googled cancer of the cervix. Half an hour later, after reading everything she could find, she wished she hadn't.

73

Friday 18 January

By five o'clock, Georgie, sick with worry about Roger and with fear from what she'd found on the internet about cervical cancer, was feeling badly in need of a break. The medical team had just arrived for the late-afternoon ward round and she decided to use the time she would be excluded from Roger's bedside to carry out the check of the hotel that she'd skipped last night. Anything to give her a few moments away from dwelling on her thoughts.

Leaving the Patriotic Street car park she drove slap-bang into the Friday evening rush hour. With one ear she listened to the news on Radio Jersey, but she barely absorbed any of it. So far Roger had failed to respond to the antibiotics. At least, small mercy, he had remained stable throughout the day – maybe that was a positive.

Less positive were the words of Kath, still ringing in her ears.

I've had the results from the biopsy I took yesterday and there's something not quite right.

What was *not right*?

So *not right* that she needed an urgent MRI scan?

Wouldn't that be dangerous for her baby?

The baby that Roger might never live to see?

Forget that line of thought. Think positively. Roger is going to be fine. You are going to be fine. Bump is going to be fine!

She turned away from the news, none of which was fine, to a music channel. As if in some kind of synchronicity, 'Everything is Fine' from the band All Time Low was playing.

She hummed along quietly to it. Usually, when it ended, she shouted out, 'Yayyyyyyyyyy!'

But not today.

Ordinarily the drive from the hospital to the hotel took ten minutes. But tonight, it was closer to twenty. It was 5.45 p.m. when she pulled up in front of the gym entrance. The entire hotel was in darkness, and hopefully Edouardo would have left for the day. Holding the keys in her hand, she unlocked the gym door, switched on the lights, then locked it from the inside, shooting a nervous glance at the three static egg timers on the wall. At that moment a text pinged from her client cancelling, apologetically.

She cursed momentarily, but actually it would enable her to do her checks and get back to the hospital more quickly. She sent him a polite acknowledgement, then, leaving the gym by the doorway through to the corridor, she pressed the light switch. To her relief, the lights came on – Edouardo must have repaired the fuse, she thought, gratefully. She switched on more lights as she made her way past the kitchens and then dutifully began her security sweep.

It was strange, she thought. Normally, walking down the long, dark corridors scared her, but tonight she was fine, confident that no spectral lady was about to climb out of a bathtub or that no intruder was about to bash her over the head. She had bigger, far more real, worries on her mind.

Finally, after a sweep of the bar and the restaurant, reassured that she could report back to Tom Vautier that all was in order, she headed back along the corridor towards the gym, reaching the one area she had not yet checked today – the kitchens. As she stopped outside the door, she heard a faint electrical hum.

She pushed open the door and entered, switching on the lights and looking around at the range of cookers, the multiple sinks and work surfaces. The hum was louder now. It was coming from the far end of the room where there was a large steel door. A red light glowed beside it.

She stood still for some moments, thinking. Vaguely recalling the tour of inspection that Tom Vautier had given her back in September. This was the entrance to the deep-freeze room, where Tom had told her they hung beef, sheep and pig carcasses as well as storing fish and shellfish and some vegetables.

But why hadn't she noticed the hum before? Or the red light?

She tried to rationalize it. The freezer couldn't have switched itself on, so either someone had been in here since her last inspection and turned it on, or else she had missed it.

She would call Vautier and ask him, she decided, pulling up his number from her Contacts list. She dialled and got the overseas tone.

'Hi, Georgie!' he answered after just a couple of rings.

'I'm sorry to bother you, Tom,' she said. 'Just a very quick question about the hotel.'

'Sure, what's on your mind, Georgie?'

'The deep-freeze room. I've not noticed it before, but the power is on – I just wanted to check if you keep it running all winter?'

'The power's on?'

'Yes. I'm sorry but I only just noticed. I mean – I don't want to bother you unnecessarily – just in case you weren't aware. Of course, you've probably got frozen stuff in there.'

'No, Georgie, I haven't. It gobbles up a lot of power. We make sure everything in there is used up or thrown away before the end of each season. Are you saying it's been running since the end of September?'

She thought hard for a moment before answering, not wanting to sound stupid for missing it. 'I don't think so. I've not noticed it before, until just now – I'm sure I would have if it had been on earlier.'

There was a brief silence. 'I just don't know how it could have happened. There's nothing in there, Georgie – at least, there shouldn't be. My suppliers don't start deliveries until a couple of weeks before we open for the season. There's a master switch – a big red one – to the right of the door. Just push it up, please – but

I guess you'd better first check there isn't any meat or anything that could go off in there. I really don't think there is.'

'I'll do it right away.'

'Thanks! Everything else OK?'

'All looks fine, I've just done my checks.'

'Brilliant! Kill that freezer. I'm really grateful to you for spotting it – my electricity bills are sky high as it is.'

'No problem. Are you skiing at the moment?'

'Yes, fantastic snow. Two degrees today and sunny. How's Jersey?'

'Eleven degrees and blowing a hooley!'

'Don't worry, kiddo, it'll be summer in six months! How's that Edouardo, still dressing up in that clown outfit? He scares the pants off me when he gets that on!'

'Tell me about it! He's fine. It's his day off but I'll update him about the freezer tomorrow.'

Ending the call, Georgie strode over towards the deep-freeze door, which was the size of the entrance to a bank vault, and before switching off the power, just to check there wasn't anything in there, turned the handle and tried to pull the door open.

Even heavier than it looked, it took a firm yank to budge, swinging open slowly and releasing a blast of cold air that enveloped her. She stared into the semi-darkness at racks of empty wooden-slatted shelving, then found the light switch and turned that on.

It was a substantial size, extending back further than she had realized, with recesses towards the rear to the right and left. Shivering from the cold, she investigated further, walking past a row of butcher's hooks along a tiled wall, with a drain gulley beneath, until she reached the far wall. The recess to her right was in darkness and she used the beam of her phone to peer in. A rack of marble shelves.

She turned the beam to the other recess. And instantly saw the shape on the floor, in the middle of it. Her first instinct was to rush forward. But she only managed a few steps before the beam of light struck his face.

74

Robert Resmes was lying on his back, motionless, his face blue, eyes open as if focused on something on the ceiling. But there was no flicker of the lids; no twitch or shimmy of his facial muscles; no sign of his chest rising and falling; no sound of breathing. There were crystals of ice in his hair.

Vapour rose from Georgie's mouth. For an instant, she stood still, shaking, her vision blurred with panic and fear. Then she rushed over to him calling, 'Robert! Robert!' She knelt and touched his face. It was as hard as stone. He was like something she had once seen at Madame Tussauds waxworks. Like a dummy. Not a real person.

She felt his wrist. It was equally hard – there was no pulse. She drew back and felt like she was about to pass out.

There was a sound behind her. Like the shuffle of a foot. She spun. 'Who's there?' she called out. 'Who's there?'

She listened.

The only noise was the thudding of her heart.

She stabbed out 999 on her phone. Her heart sounded like a boxer pummelling seven bells out of a punchbag. There was a roaring noise in her ears, as if she was standing on a platform with a tube train entering.

The phone did not ring. She peered at it and could immediately see the reason why – there was no signal in here. *Shit.*

She was going to have to step out. To where she'd heard the sound of someone moving. Was there someone waiting, out of sight, ready to strike her? The person who had done this to Resmes?

As loudly as she could, making out she was talking into the phone, she said, 'Police, please. I need an ambulance and the police.' Then a moment later, still loudly, Georgie said, 'Hello, police, I'm in the Bel Royal Hotel, St Lawrence, I've found a body in the deep-freeze room of the kitchen.' Holding the phone in front of her, ready to use it as a weapon, she stepped back into the kitchen, and then, her eyes darting wildly left and right, out into the corridor.

No sign of anyone.

She stood, listening. The roaring in her ears persisted; she was shaking, eyes still darting, fixing on shadows, checking for movement. Her phone had a signal again. She pressed the button and almost instantly the call activated.

'Emergency, which service do you need?' said a calm female voice.

'Ambulance and the police. Please.'

She held her breath. Was that a shadow moving at the end of the corridor, where it kinked right?

'May I have your name and location, please, caller?'

Georgie blurted it out to her, her voice hushed now. Fearful. 'I've just found a man in the freezer of the Bel Royal Hotel. He's dead, I know he's dead.'

'Does he have a pulse, Georgie? Is he breathing?'

'No – no – I – I checked. Nothing I could find. I'm sure he's dead.'

'An ambulance is on its way to you, Georgie, and a police car. They'll both be with you in less than ten minutes.'

'Thank you.' Her voice came out as a squeak. She shot another petrified glance behind her. Did a shadow move in the corridor?

'I'm staying on the line with you, Georgie, until they arrive.'

'Please,' she gasped.

'Are you safe?'

'I – don't know. I – I'm not sure.'

'Can you wait outside to guide the ambulance and police to where you've found this person?'

She hesitated. Did she dare move from here? 'OK.'

Taking a deep breath, she walked along the corridor and towards the foyer of the hotel, stopping every few moments to listen. Then finally reached it. The silent reception desk. The pigeonholes for the guests' mail on the wall behind. A stack of American Express leaflets, and another stack of Jersey tourist maps. The revolving door was locked in position. So was the side, wheelchair access door, next to it. She knew the keys were in a drawer beside the printer in the back office. She grabbed them, ran back, unlocked the door, pushed it open and burst out into the night air.

'I'm outside,' she said to the call handler. Below, she could see the lights of vehicles travelling around St Aubin's Bay. Faintly, in the distance, was the wail of a siren. And a second siren, fainter. Both growing louder.

Nearer.

'I can see their positions, Georgie,' the call handler said, re-assuring her. 'They are now less than five minutes from you.'

'Oh God, thank you.'

'There's no one with you?'

She turned again, looking behind her. All around her in the darkness. 'I – I think I'm on my own.'

Moments later, a siren even nearer now, Georgie saw a flicker of bright lights. Then blue streaks. Headlights appeared around the front of the building. Shards of blue showered the darkness. Seconds later, as she stood in the middle of the driveway, waving her hands wildly, an ambulance pulled up in front of her and two paramedics jumped out.

'The ambulance is here now,' Georgie said.

'The police are just a couple of minutes behind. Are you OK if I end the call now?'

'Fine, yes, fine, thank you. Thank you.'

Numbly, she led the paramedics inside, along the labyrinth of corridors through the kitchen and into the deep-freeze room. Then she hurried back out just as the police car pulled up and guided the two officers in.

They were visibly shocked as they saw the body.

'How did he get locked in here?' asked one of the officers, a young woman PC, reaching up and silencing a crackly voice on her radio. She didn't direct the question at anyone in particular. 'And how long has he been here?'

'I don't know, but it's really weird – we had a break-in on Wednesday night, two of your officers attended but we couldn't find anything and assumed it was just kids playing about.'

'Do you work here?' asked the male officer.

'I run some gym classes and I'm keeping an eye on the place in the winter, along with the caretaker, who is on his day off. But I know who this person is – Robert Resmes. I saw him yesterday afternoon,' Georgie said in a faltering voice.

'Here?' the officer asked.

'No, at the hospital – he's a medical student at Jersey General Hospital. I saw him yesterday – he was with the consultant obstetrician, Marcus Valentine.'

'What time did you see him?' she quizzed.

'It was about 3 p.m.'

'Did you see him after then?'

Georgie thought for a moment. Thought about the strange expression on his face. Almost, she wondered now, as if he wanted to say something to her. 'No, I didn't,' she answered. Unable to take her eyes off Resmes.

'Do you also work at the hospital?' the other officer asked.

'No – my fiancé's there after an accident. He was badly injured in that crash at the airport. I – was visiting him.'

Her mind was spinning.

How? How on earth – what on earth – had happened? How could this young man possibly have ended up dead in this hotel freezer?

And why? Was Edouardo involved in any way?

Over the course of the next hour, Georgie felt increasingly help-less. She called Tom Vautier to tell him what had happened, promising to update him when she knew more. He was horrified, disbelieving, but rang off after saying he'd book a flight back right away. Crime-scene tape was placed over the hotel's front entrance, and she had to stand outside it as a posse of police vehicles began arriving. One contained the Duty Inspector, who spoke to her briefly, asking her not to leave and telling her she was a significant witness and that someone would come and talk to her to take a brief statement.

Next to arrive was a woman called Vicky, who was introduced to Georgie as the Scientific Services Manager. She was followed shortly after by two Crime Scene Investigators.

Approaching midnight, dog-tired and almost numb with cold, Georgie had a chat with one of the original officers who had attended and was now acting as scene guard. She told him she was pregnant and asked if it would be OK for her to go to her car. Sympathetic and frankly freezing himself, he told her absolutely, yes.

Gratefully, she told him where she would be, then hurried back to the rear of the hotel, climbed into her Golf, started the engine and, after a couple of minutes, turned the heater to full blast. Ten minutes later she was finally beginning to feel as if she was thawing out.

At a few minutes to 1 a.m. a young man in a suit approached, who introduced himself as Detective Constable Langdale. He sat in the car with her, asking her a number of questions and tapping in her answers painfully slowly on an electronic pad. When he was done, he gave her his card and asked her to call him in the morning so he could arrange for her to come into the station to make a more detailed statement. Then he suggested she go home and try to get some sleep.

She didn't take much persuading.

75

Saturday 19 January

Kath Clow woke early, as she did most mornings, and slipped out of bed as quietly as she could, so as not to wake her husband. She'd slept badly, her mind troubled by one persistent, nagging thought – worrying her like a dog worrying a bone. The biopsy report on dear Georgie Maclean.

How could she have missed the results that the biopsy had shown? The pathologist was a meticulous man – could he have made a mistake? She doubted it. But she was meticulous, too. Mistakes did happen.

The house was quiet. Charlie was no doubt still asleep and would be until breakfast in a couple of hours' time, before which she'd spend ten minutes trying to shake him awake. She shrugged on her dressing gown, thinking about the day ahead. Bob was taking Charlie to rugby today, and she'd agreed to take him to practice tomorrow, so her husband could go and play golf. Although she had the weekend off, she intended going into the hospital for a couple of hours, later on, to catch up on a mounting backlog of paperwork.

Kath made her way downstairs in the semi-darkness, almost tripping over the cat, which liked to curl up and sleep on the bottom step, and went into the kitchen, closing the door behind her. The cat, Pogo – named because when she was a kitten she jumped rather than walked around the house – followed her in, meowing.

Kath opened a tin of fishy cat food and Pogo eagerly started to eat before she'd even finished scooping the contents into the bowl.

Then she switched on the radio, to catch up on the local weather and news whilst she made herself a macchiato. The forecast for today and tomorrow was fine, thank goodness – she was due to take part in a round-the-island cycle race next weekend, and had planned to get in a couple of long rides for practice.

Through the window, dawn was breaking on a fine morning, as the forecast had predicted. She would go for an early-morning training ride, she decided, unpeeling a banana and taking a bite for some energy as the coffee machine gurgled and spat. Pips on the radio signalled the 7 a.m. Radio Jersey news.

The first item was the discovery of the body of a man in a hotel on the island, the Bel Royal. His name was being withheld until relatives had been informed, the announcer said. Then came a statement from a Detective Superintendent Stewart Raven.

'We are treating this death as suspicious,' he said with fitting gravitas. 'My Major Crime Team have commenced an investigation and a postmortem will be carried out this morning. I have no further information at this time, but we will be giving an update later in the day.'

Random murders were, fortunately, rare on this island. This was big news for Jersey. Perhaps it had been a fight between a couple of employees, Kath speculated. The news moved to another item, a controversial planning issue on an area of land designated as a nature reserve. It was then followed by a mention that Jersey States Police had arrested a suspect in connection with the collision between two aircraft at the airport on Monday.

Good, she thought. *God, that had caused such a terrible tragedy. And it was probably some idiot flying the drone who'd had no idea of the consequences.*

She finished the banana, drank her coffee and went upstairs to put on her winter cycling kit. Five minutes later, exhilarated by the cold morning air, she rode out of her driveway, clipping into the pedals, and enjoyed the ride down the steep, twisting hill towards Bouley Bay, with the glorious view of the sea beyond. Although as she pedalled, she noticed an unfamiliar clicking sound in some gears. After a brief plateau at the bottom, she prepared for the steep climb up the far side.

All the time thinking and worrying about her friend.

How can I put Georgie through such shit when she's already in a terrible place, worrying about her fiancé?

If the diagnosis was correct – and the MRI scan would show later whether it was for certain – the only sensible option would be termination. Had the foetus been more advanced, it might have been possible to save it, but not at this early stage. How could she break that news to Georgie?

Standing up on the pedals and working hard, the chain suddenly slipped on the cogs and she almost came off. She was going to have to get the bike looked at before tomorrow, she realized, then her thoughts immediately returned to Georgie, as she finally crested the hill.

As she rode along a stretch of flat, rural road, her heart was heavy. Normally, she tried not to get emotionally invested in her patients. But Georgie was her friend, so it was different. She tried to remain professional, but she really sympathized with her for all the years she had been trying for a baby, and especially because of all the years that she and Bob had been through the same thing. The frustration, the disappointments, the gradual erosion of hope. And the moment of indescribable joy she had felt when the pregnancy test finally showed positive.

Kath had seen that very same joy in Georgie's face, the realization that her dream had at last come true. Followed by the terrible accident and poor Roger in such a bad way. An emotional trauma like that was enough to cause some people to miscarry, but fortunately, so far, that had not happened. It would be too cruel if after all Georgie had been through she would now have to have a termination.

She had to delve further, she owed it to Georgie. Abruptly changing her route, Kath made a sharp left turn onto a narrow lane and pedalled in the direction of St Helier, and the hospital.

Twenty minutes later, shortly before 8 a.m., as she rode past the front entrance – the clicking sound even more pronounced now – Kath saw a police car parked outside. She turned down towards the Gwyneth Huelin wing, where she always padlocked her bike in the covered rack. A police presence in the hospital on a Saturday morning wasn't an unusual occurrence – they were often there, interviewing victims of a drunken Friday-night brawl in one of the town's bars.

As she walked in through the entrance to the wing, she was greeted politely by a uniformed female police officer who was standing like a sentry, accompanied by a man in a suit, a detective she presumed, who stood a short distance behind her.

'May I ask your business here?' the female officer asked.

'I work here – in Obstetrics – although I realize it doesn't look like it,' she said with a smile, noticing the officer take in her cycling outfit.

'Would you mind having a word with my colleague?' the officer asked, pointing behind her.

'What about?' she asked, politely.

'He'll explain, he's looking for background information,' she said, immediately distracted by a young woman entering the building.

Kath walked over to the man in the suit. 'I was asked to come and talk to you,' she said.

He introduced himself as Detective Sergeant Peter Shirreffs.

'You work here?' Shirreffs asked.

'I do, I'm an obstetrician.'

'Have you ever met a gentleman by the name of Robert Resmes?' he asked.

'Robert Resmes? Yes, he's a medical student who's been with the department shadowing various consultants. Why?'

'Would you mind going to the admin office by the ICU unit? My colleagues there would like to talk to everyone who knew him.'

She stared at him for some moments. '*Knew* him?'

But even before the last word had escaped her lips, the penny was dropping.

Robert Resmes.

The news item she had heard earlier about the discovery of the body of a man in the Bel Royal Hotel. Was that what this was all about?

'Please tell me, has something happened to Robert?'

The officer was poker-faced. 'If you go up to the admin office, I'm sure they will explain everything to you.'

She left, hurried up the two flights of stairs to the ICU floor and along the corridors to the admin office. The early-morning sunshine felt as if it had been blotted out by a dark cloud.

76

Saturday 19 January

After a restless, troubled night, in which he was woken at 3 a.m. by a registrar in the Maternity ward, worried about a patient, Marcus Valentine had finally drifted back into sleep as dawn was breaking. Almost immediately, it seemed, he was woken by the twins crawling across the duvet, tugging at it, tugging at his ears, tugging at Claire's hair and yelling.

And yelling.

Unable to stop himself, he yelled back, 'Be quiet, for fuck's sake, be quiet!'

'Marcus!' chided Claire, now awake, too.

He rounded on her. 'What the hell is your problem?'

'You,' she said, simply. 'What's got into you? They're just being kids.'

'I'm working my arse off at the moment, and I'm on call all weekend – I have to put up with them using me as a play mat? I'm tired, I need some sleep.'

'They're your children, Marcus,' she said. 'Just as much as mine. When you raise your voice and swear, you scare them, and anyhow, I'm also working my arse off, in case you haven't noticed.'

Rhys and Amelia were staring at him, open-mouthed. They'd never been shouted at like that before. But it had an immediate effect on them. They shut up.

'Hey, guys!' Marcus said. He sat up, threw the top of the duvet over their heads, then began tickling them both through the cover.

It was only a few moments before the twins were giggling and writhing again. He tickled them harder and they responded by wriggling and laughing even more. Just then, on his bedside table, the 8 a.m. local news came on the clock radio.

The first item was the discovery of the body of a man in the Bel Royal Hotel.

He sat up, rigid. The twins were still giggling, but Marcus tuned them out, listening intently.

'What's the matter?' Claire asked.

He waved with his hand for her to be quiet, listening to the voice of Detective Superintendent Raven. Then the news switched to a planning dispute.

'Marcus?' Claire asked. 'Are you all right? You look pale.'

Through the baby monitor, Cormac could be heard crying.

'What is it?' she insisted. 'What's the matter?'

'Nothing.'

'Are you doing the parkrun today?'

'No, I'm on call, I have to go in.'

Marcus climbed out of bed, went through to the bathroom and shut the door behind him, needing to think. He sat down on the closed toilet seat without lifting the lid. Trembling. Heard the scolding voice of his mother, as if she was shouting with a megaphone pressed to his ear: 'You are an embarrassment, Marcus, a failure. You're such a failure. Can you do *anything* right?'

That body should have remained undetected in that freezer for months. How had he been found so soon? Georgie had specifically told him the kitchens were all shut down and they didn't regularly check them.

There was something that concerned him deeply: who might Resmes have talked to?

He was thinking back to Thursday. When he'd asked the young student doctor to meet him at the Bel Royal Hotel.

His reply. *I have a date tonight. She's cooking for me.*

What had Resmes told his date? What excuse had he given her

for being late? Had he told her where he was going? Had he mentioned his name to her?

But he was fine, he'd covered his tracks. He'd been at Georgie Maclean's gym session. And after that, he'd returned to the hospital, with a coat covering his gym wear, and made sure several people had seen him, chatting briefly to a number of them. Perfectly natural he would be there late, as he was on call. If questioned, he would simply say he'd asked Robert Resmes to come to his office for a debrief before he moved on to Kath Clow. But Resmes had never showed up.

He relaxed a little. After his session with Georgie on Thursday night, when he'd returned to the vicinity of the hotel to meet Resmes, he'd worn a swimming cap with a bobble hat over it, his scuba wetsuit beneath his coat. Latex gloves. No exposed flesh. No DNA at the scene. He was confident about that. At least he'd had the benefit of forensic awareness from Claire's obsession with the *CSI* series over the past years. The police would be trying to figure out the cause of death; who had caused it; a motive.

Searching for prints and DNA.

They weren't going to find either from him. And even if they did, because he and Resmes had been in regular contact, it wouldn't be of any evidential value.

That was a comfort.

So, OK, they had a body. Big deal. Hopefully, there was plenty to keep the police occupied with that one, with no obvious motive. And nothing to connect him.

What was of much more importance was Georgie. Her welfare and her future. He stepped into the shower and turned it on. Standing under the hard jets, he was again worrying about Resmes being found so soon. His plans needed urgent tweaking.

His plans hadn't included being watched by someone from the car park.

77

She stood outside the door in the weak throw of light from the corridor's wall lamps, staring at the number, 237. She held the key in her hand. Hesitating. Every time. Tonight, there was a preternatural feel. Expectancy in the ether. She unlocked it and stepped in, even more nervous than usual. The room felt icy, like entering a walk-in freezer. She could see her breath.

Slowly, having to make a real effort to move her legs, as if she was walking through waist-high water, she made her way over to the en-suite door and opened it.

Panic gripped her throat tight. She tried to scream, but nothing came out. Staring, bug-eyed in terror, she tried again and again to scream, to shout for help. Only silence. She tried to step back, to turn and run, but her feet would not move.

Robert Resmes, naked, his hair wet, his skin covered in green blotches, rose out of the bathtub, hauling himself up on the grab rails, putting his feet over the side. She tried to back away again, but her legs still would not move.

He came towards her, his hands outstretched, an imploring look on his face. Stumbling towards her, putting his blotched arms around her, pulling her towards him, pressing his face close to hers, whispering something she could not hear.

Beep-beep-beep . . . Beep-beep-beep . . .

Georgie woke with a start, still afraid. Daylight. She was in bed. Sunlight streamed through a crack in the curtains.

Beep-beep-beep . . . Beep-beep-beep . . .

The alarm clock. Georgie reached out an arm and hit the button. Silence. She lay, sodden with perspiration and shaking. God, the dream had been so vivid, so real. Slowly, the events of last night came flooding back to her.

Robert Resmes lying on the floor in the recess of the deep-freeze room.

The police.

Questions churned in her brain. What had happened? How on earth had Robert got in there? And why? Had he fallen or had someone put him there? Who, why? She couldn't take much more of this, it couldn't be good for her or her baby.

She glanced at the clock. 8.31 a.m.

Saturday. It was Saturday morning. *Shit.* She had planned to walk the parkrun today but now it was too late to get to the start line in time for 9 a.m. Too late and she was too tired. Too wired. She hadn't gone to bed until after 2 a.m., which was why she'd set the alarm for much later than usual.

How was Roger? There'd been no phone call from the hospital, which was a relief. That had to be good news at least. She hoped. Hoped so much that when she went in to see him today the ward nurse or a doctor or someone would give her good news about him. That they'd say he was improving, the antibiotics were working.

And at midday she was having her MRI scan. The thought scared her. Despite Kath's constant reassurance, she knew there must be something worrying her, for her to have requested the scan. And so urgently.

She got out of bed and a sudden shiver rippled through her. *Someone walking over your grave*, her mother used to say, when she was younger. She never understood what her mother meant, exactly, but the words always made her shudder; she shuddered now, entering the bathroom.

She splashed some cold water on her face, then brushed her teeth, dutifully doing the full two-minute cycle, glancing at her tired face and wondering whether going for a walk might make her feel better. She still had plenty of time before the morning ward round finished and she could go in and see Roger. She dressed in her kit, sat on the bed and phoned the hospital. She was informed there'd been no change in his condition overnight. Ending the call, she went through into the living room.

As she entered, she noticed the business card on the coffee table. Blue, white and gold with the Jersey States Police shield. She remembered putting it there last night when she'd come in, to remind her that she had to call the officer today to make an appointment at the police station to give a statement. She thought for a moment. The officer had stayed on after she'd left and had quite possibly been there all night. He was likely to be asleep now. She could go this afternoon, after the scan. Besides, last night she had pretty much told him everything she knew, and simply could not explain what the medical student was doing in the hotel or how he came to end up in the freezer.

She took a couple of swigs from an energy smoothie she'd made herself and always kept in the fridge, pulled on her pink cap, then went out into the cold, bright early morning and walked briskly, warming up, down to Victoria Avenue. Kath had told her not to run but that walking was fine.

Making a left, she walked along the pavement to the crossing, then waited for the traffic lights to change. Even after they went red, she hesitated for a moment, checking that all the vehicles had stopped. Then she crossed, walking down between a hedge and the side of the Old Station Cafe to the promenade, and turned left, striding along the curve of the bay, towards St Helier. The tide was far out and several people were down on the beach and the mudflats, their dogs running free.

As she walked, her dream – nightmare – came back to her.

Robert Resmes rising out of the bath. Putting his arms around her. Whispering.

All her life she'd had vivid dreams. Strange dreams. Many of them deeply disturbing. There had been a time, back when she'd been married to her former husband, Mike Chandler, after they'd been trying for some years for a baby, when she'd gone to therapy, on the recommendation of a fertility specialist they'd consulted. He'd suggested that her anxiety was perhaps preventing her from conceiving.

The psychiatrist he'd referred her to, Dr Stafford-Jones, a bright, sympathetic man she had trusted, was an advocate of Freudian dream analysis. Dreams, he had told her, were the result of the brain trying to deal with unresolved issues that presented to the subconscious – and were usually masked in symbolism. If she could interpret the message of a dream, to establish what was bothering her subconscious, the issue would go away.

So, what was the message of last night's dream? What unresolved issue was bothering her subconscious?

On the surface that seemed pretty clear. Robert Resmes was dead. He had been with Marcus Valentine. Valentine had operated on Roger. Roger was not recovering, to everyone's concern. Had Marcus Valentine been the right person to do this operation? Did he have any past history of making errors, or of negligence?

Was it that simple? Was the dream telling her to check on him? She tried to think back to the expression on Resmes's face as he stumbled towards her. Was that dream meaningful in some way – or just a nightmare after what had happened at the hotel?

She thought back to Dr Stafford-Jones. *Unresolved issues. Bothering her subconscious.*

Was her subconscious warning her there was something sinister going on?

In what way?

Suddenly, she remembered the strange thing Valentine had said to her at his dinner party. When he'd asked her if she'd ever hated anyone enough to kill them. And had then confessed that he had hated his mother.

What was that about?

She realized that she knew almost nothing about him, that she had simply accepted he was a trusted consultant, and made a mental note to check him out a bit more.

There was one way she might do that – and she wondered why she'd not thought to do it before.

Cutting short her planned route, she turned and headed for home as fast as she could.

78

Saturday 19 January

As Kath Clow entered the admin office, she saw that a smartly dressed man and woman were seated in there. The man was in his forties, short and clean-shaven, with close-cropped hair, wearing a dark suit and shiny black shoes. He had the physique of a runner, Kath thought, always able to recognize a fellow athlete. The woman, in her thirties, had shoulder-length brown hair and was dressed in a navy two-piece. She appeared less fit than her colleague but wore a more welcoming expression. They looked like detectives. As if in confirmation, the man held out a police warrant card.

'I was asked by the officers down in the entrance to come up here,' Kath said.

They both stood up.

'You are?' the man asked.

'Kath Clow – I'm one of the obstetricians here.'

'Thank you for coming to see us,' he said in a dour, neutral voice. 'I'm Detective Sergeant Sturton and my colleague is Detective Constable Campbell. We'd just like to ask you a few questions, if that's all right?'

'Fine – but I can't really spare you very long.'

'No problem,' DC Campbell said. She had a trace of a Scottish accent. 'Have a seat. We won't keep you for more than a few minutes.'

Kath sat down opposite them. DS Sturton wrote down Kath's name and address and phone numbers.

'Kath,' he said. 'OK to call you that?'

'Fine.' She smiled.

'OK, Kath, can you tell us if you know a student who has been on assignment here from his medical school in Romania, Robert Resmes?'

'Indeed, yes. He's due to start with me on Monday.'

'Start with you?' DC Campbell asked. 'How exactly?'

'We have a programme, like most hospitals, of taking in medical students. They spend time shadowing consultants across different disciplines. Why are you asking?'

'I'm afraid he has been found dead, but we can't say anything more at this stage.'

'Dead?'

Even though she had been anticipating this from her conversation with the officer down in the foyer, the words hit her like a punch in the stomach. 'Dead? Robert Resmes?'

Both detectives nodded. 'I'm afraid so,' Detective Sergeant Sturton confirmed, grimly.

'But – how – I mean – I saw him on – on Thursday. What – what's happened?'

'I'm afraid we can't give you any more details at this stage. You saw him on Thursday? Can you tell us about that?' Sturton asked.

Kath's brain was racing. Thinking back to the news item this morning on the radio. 'Is this anything to do with what I heard on the news about a body found in the Bel Royal Hotel?'

She could see, instantly, from their body language that it was.

'As I said, Kath, I can't tell you any more at this stage,' Sturton repeated. 'How well did you know Robert Resmes?'

'Not well. I met him a couple of times when he was assigned to the senior consultant gynae-oncologist here and he was due to join me on Monday.'

'Did you form any opinion of him?'

She shrugged. 'Not really – other than that he seemed very enthusiastic and bright. A nice young man, highly ambitious I'd say. How terribly sad this is.'

'You saw him on Thursday,' DC Campbell said. 'What was the reason?'

The obstetrician hesitated. Thinking back to Thursday, when the young Romanian had come into her office. And she'd sent him packing with a flea in his ear. 'He just popped in to introduce himself,' she replied, not wanting to open a can of worms.

'Do you mind if I ask you a very blunt question, Kath?' Sturton asked.

'Not at all.'

'Did Robert Resmes make any enemies here?'

'Enemies? What do you mean?'

'Perhaps a love rival? We don't know enough about his background at this stage, Kath, but the circumstances of his death make us think he might have upset someone.'

'I honestly didn't know him well enough, or anything about his background. What I have heard is that he had several run-ins with the registrar Barnaby Cardigan and Marcus Valentine had had to step in more than once, but whether that is connected or not I don't know.'

'No worries,' DC Campbell said.

There was a brief silence, broken by DS Sturton.

'Kath, if there's anything that comes to mind over the next day or two, please give me a call.' He handed her a card, on which a number was crossed out and another written in ballpoint. 'This is my mobile, call me any time, day or night.'

The obstetrician zipped it into her rucksack. 'I will,' she said. 'Of course.'

They all stood. The two detectives thanked her for her time, and she left.

79

Saturday 19 January

Georgie sat on a sofa with her laptop and googled the name 'Marcus Valentine'. A whole list of Marcus Valentines appeared, mostly across America, one in Trinidad and Tobago and a few in the UK. One was a dental intern, another a logistics specialist, another a stacker at Walmart and another a mortgage banking analyst.

She narrowed the search by typing 'Marcus Valentine obstetrician'.

Instantly a row of images appeared, three of them bearing his face, then two other complete strangers. Below was a link. She clicked on it.

Marcus Valentine, FRCOG, *consultant gynae-oncologist. Jersey, Channel Islands.* There was a single photograph of Marcus Valentine, suited and looking serious.

Below was a long list of further links. They told her little she didn't already know, other than that he'd cycled from London to Paris some years ago, in aid of Mind, the mental health charity, and had recently set up a Jersey charity which had raised almost £5 million of a £10 million target to establish a local research institution. He was formerly married to a woman called Elaine and the marriage had ended the decade before.

She scrolled on down the links. A testimonial from a patient; controversy over a new site for the hospital, which he had been outspoken on. A piece on Macmillan cancer care.

The search on him was pretty much exhausted. Most of the links here were for other Marcus Valentines.

She carried on to the bottom of page four, but there were no further links to him. She went back to his fundraising page for the London-to-Paris cycle and clicked through.

Hi and thanks for visiting my fundraising page. I'm cycling to raise money for Mind because I must be mental for once marrying my now soon-to-be-ex-wife Elaine, and let's not talk about my mother. (Only joking!) Hope you can help me raise lots of money, then I might come begging for more when the ex rinses me in the divorce!

That's obscene, Georgie thought. To publicly write that, and to belittle the work of the charity by doing so, was incredibly crass.

Then she wondered. Marcus's former wife was Elaine.

She typed 'Elaine Valentine' into Facebook. There were two in the north of England and one 'Elaine Gower-was-Valentine' in Surrey. The profile picture of this one really stood out – she was staring at a woman who bore some similarity to Claire, if fifteen or so years older. There was nothing in her entry to link her to Marcus, but she was the closest geographically, so she decided to take a punt and see if it was actually his ex. She sent her a private message, hoping she would accept and read it.

Hi, I'm hoping I've got the right person, I'm sorry for this random message as you don't know me, but it's really important. Are you the lady who was once married to the consultant Marcus Valentine?

To her surprise, a reply came back almost instantly.

Yes, I am. Sadly.

George read the reply. *Sadly*. What was that about? Before she could respond, another message came through.

Are you in trouble?

Georgie sent back:

I'm not sure, but I'm very worried about something. Is it possible to have a phone call? I just want to ask you a few things, offline.

Elaine agreed and asked Georgie for her number. A couple of

minutes later Georgie answered the phone to a guarded, cultured voice.

'I really appreciate your calling,' Georgie said.

'I don't know if I can help you, but I'll try.'

'Thanks. It may sound odd, but I really need to know something about your ex-husband.'

'Are you in a relationship with him, Georgina?' the woman asked, warily.

'He's not my partner – I know him through friends – but there's a few very weird things happening, and I just need to know if he's trustworthy or not.'

'Trustworthy?'

Georgie could hear the surprise in her voice. 'Yes.'

'I wouldn't trust Marcus an inch.'

'Can you tell me more? I mean, why not? Please, you have to tell me, I'm so worried.'

There was a long silence. 'Look, I can hear how distressed you are, and I wouldn't normally say this to a complete stranger. But let's just say he has a real dark side. Something closed off no one can reach. There was something very strange that happened when he was a child that he would never speak about.'

'What do you mean? What kind of strange?'

'Well, there was talk in his family that when he and his sister were young he'd somehow put her down an abandoned well and kept her there overnight – apparently, he'd said it was to punish his mother when she was late yet again collecting them from school. His parents were frantic, thinking she'd been abducted.'

'Bloody hell!' Georgie thought for a moment. Back to that dark conversation she'd had with Marcus at the dinner party. Was that what he had been referring to?

'I'm afraid Marcus is a very complex and disturbed character,' Elaine went on. 'Outwardly, he's got all the charm, but in my experience he's a control freak and a sociopath and I'm not just saying that because he's my ex. I feel lucky I got out.'

'How did that manifest in your marriage – if I can ask – the control?' The conversation was feeling easier now.

'Well, we were fine at first: he was charming and great fun to be with, we were on a real high. Then his behaviour started getting more and more frightening – he was a complete narcissist. He'd fly off in rages. I stayed with him for a while, hoping he'd stop, that he'd change. But then I knew I just had to leave – I had a brief affair with a work colleague, which didn't last long. Marcus found out and I was actually scared that if I stayed, something very bad would happen.' She hesitated, then went on again. 'I'd been pregnant in the very early days and lost the baby, and now I look back I'm pretty sure he did something without telling me, because he wasn't ready to start a family. He had a very clear idea of when he wanted children in his life, and it wasn't then.'

'You mean he caused you to lose the baby without you being aware what he was doing?'

'Well, who knows.'

'I'm so sorry.'

'Don't be, I now have two very healthy, lovely children, and I'm happily in a relationship.'

'In what way was he a control freak?'

'He's completely obsessed by time.'

Georgie thought back again to the evening of the dinner party, how he'd continually checked his watch. 'I got the impression he had some issue about it.'

'That would be an understatement! He had a very weird upbringing; his mother was a raving alcoholic and he practically cared for her towards the end. She'd been a failed actress, then she made a living giving piano lessons and had an obsession with turning him into a concert pianist. He told me she'd whack him on the knuckles if he missed a note, and scream "Timing, timing, timing!" I mean, the woman was nuts, and his dad was no better. It left him really fucked up.'

'Listen, I don't know him at all well, but I've sensed there's something odd about him.'

'You can say that for sure. He's also obsessively tidy. He couldn't bear to have a thing out of place in the house. He'd organize my clothes in colour order so I could never find anything, and my cookbooks in order of date of publication – I mean, how weird is that?'

Georgie paused. 'Can I ask you, did he ever tuck the laces into your shoes?'

'Oh God, all the time. It was so infuriating!'

Georgie fell silent for a moment. Her skin crawled. Thinking back two days ago. Thursday, when she'd woken after taking the sleeping pill that Valentine had given her. Everything in her room had been tidied away, immaculately. The laces of her three pairs of trainers were all folded and tucked neatly inside the shoes.

Had Valentine come into the flat whilst she was unconscious and done this? But why on earth would he? That just did not make sense.

But nor did it make any sense that she had done it herself.

After she had thanked the woman and suggested they might meet when she was next over in England, she ended the call and sat still for a long while, engulfed in turmoil.

Then she called Lucy.

80

Saturday 19 January

The hospital was buzzing with rumours about Resmes. En route to her office, several staff members stopped Kath Clow to ask if she had heard the terrible news. Everyone was shocked. The young, always smiling medical student had been popular.

Then Kath bumped into Marcus Valentine's registrar, Barnaby Cardigan. He told her, in a conspiratorial whisper, it might have been a Romanian mafia hit – perhaps, he postulated, Resmes had been involved with a drug cartel's attempts to gain a foothold in Jersey?

Kath pooh-poohed that instantly and angrily. How dare he bad-mouth Resmes just because they hadn't seen eye-to-eye, she demanded? Then she asked him if Marcus was in yet. He told her he hadn't seen him but was expecting him shortly. 'Shall I get him to call you, Kath?'

'Please.'

Reaching the sanctuary of her office, she sat at her desk, feeling a sense of both shock and sadness. It didn't feel real and yet it was, horribly, sadly real. Robert Resmes. Dead. In a hotel deep freezer.

Enemies?

Who could the diligent student have upset so much, in his brief time here in Jersey, that they would kill him? Cardigan and he clearly hadn't got on, but it couldn't have got that bad, surely? She knew little about Romania, other than its reputation for human and organ trafficking. No doubt there were major drug dealers, too. Was it possible Barnaby could be right? Might Resmes have been a sleeper, however these things worked? Gone and crossed the wrong people? Attempting to muscle in on someone else's patch here?

No, absolutely not, none of this fitted with how sincere Resmes appeared – to her at least – to have been. There had to be another explanation, and perhaps a far simpler and less dramatic one, and she didn't want to go down the unfounded stereotype route.

She remembered from her own time as a student just how tough it was being a young medic. The endlessly long days and nights, your shifts getting extended then extended again until you'd been on your feet for eighteen hours straight and you were like a zombie, hardly knowing what you were doing even though the lives of some of your patients were dependent on you getting their meds right. Oftentimes you didn't even know or care whether it was day or night. You were terrified of making a mistake. Terrified of failure. Two of the students who had started in the same year as herself had cracked and taken their own lives.

Had Robert?

Surely not – and besides, the pressure here in this hospital was a lot less than in the health service on the mainland. And would a student doctor really have put himself through the slow horror of freezing to death, when he would have known plenty of ways to do it quicker and more effectively? And had access to the drugs to do it.

She switched her focus, with some reluctance, to the more pressing issue of Georgie Maclean, who was booked in for an MRI scan in just two hours' time.

The more she thought about it, the more concerned she was by the pathologist's report. How could she have missed Georgie's advanced cancer? How? It just wasn't possible for her to have made a mistake of this magnitude.

She logged on and pulled up the colposcopy images, and sat, staring at each of them in turn. There was no sign of cancer and certainly not the aggressive stage-2 the pathology report stated.

She just had to hope, for Georgie's sake, that the MRI scan might give a different result.

But if not?

She stared again at the images, one by one. Something was niggling at her mind and she had to know for sure, one way or the other, before putting Georgie through the scan. There was no evidence that an MRI was harmful to a foetus, but all the same, Kath hated for any patient to take an unnecessary risk, however small it was.

She left her office and walked briskly along the corridor and down the stairs to the ground floor, then along to the Radiology department. The ever-helpful Diana was on reception there, which she was glad about, although a bit surprised she was working at the weekend.

'Hi, Kath!' Diana greeted her.

'Is Andy B-C here today, by chance?' she asked.

'No, he's off until Monday.'

'Bugger,' Kath said. Andy Borthwick-Clarke was the senior radiologist. 'Who's on?'

'Ana Gomes. Do you want to talk to her?'

The young registrar radiologist was a trainee, having completed two years in a British teaching hospital, and had been with the unit for just a few months. Although still a trainee, the team of consultant radiologists at this hospital considered her competent enough to analyse and report on scans. On the past occasions when she had done scans for Kath, the obstetrician had been impressed with the young woman's diligence.

'I'd like a quick word.'

'Go ahead, her next patient's not due for ten minutes.'

Kath thanked her and walked through into the department. A lot of money had been spent on the Radiology department recently and it had a calm, hi-tech feel, like a NASA sub-station, Kath always thought when she came here. There was a bank of monitors above a worktop that covered over half of the room, and an assortment of electronic apparatus.

On the far wall was a large window looking onto the doughnut-shaped MRI scanner itself. The room was manned by a radiographer and the assistant. The six consultant radiologists and the recently appointed junior registrar, Ana Gomes, shared a small network of offices to the side.

Ana, curvy, dark-haired, around five foot, with heavy but flawless make-up, was seated in the smallest of the offices, tapping a keypad and staring intently at the screen. She looked up as Kath entered. She always appeared nervous. 'Oh, hello, Dr Clow.'

'Hi, Ana, how are you?'

'Yes, OK, thank you. We are getting a puppy today – this evening my husband and I are picking it up.'

'Really? What kind?'

'A Jack Russell. We're calling him Oliver.'

'Nice dogs! Be careful at the sand dunes – one went missing there last year for several days – dug himself down into a rabbit warren and couldn't get out.'

The registrar gave a worried frown. 'That happened?'

'Check it out in the *JEP* online.'

'I will, thank you.' She hesitated. 'Is there something I can do for you?'

'Actually, yes – you're doing an MRI scan on a patient of mine at midday.'

'Midday?' Gomes glanced at her screen and tapped her keypad. 'Georgina Maclean?'

'Yes. I'm very concerned about this lady. I'm not officially working today so I'm going to be leaving soon. Would you call me as soon as you've done the scan? I need to know the results. She's a friend of mine.'

'Of course.'

Kath thanked her, gave her the number then returned, quickly, to her office. She sat down at her desk, found Nigel Kirkham's private mobile number in her Contacts and dialled it.

When he answered, she said, 'I'm sorry to bother you at the weekend.'

'Not a problem, Kath, it's good to be interrupted. I'm in Wiltshire, trying to assemble a flat-pack hen coop for my son and his betrothed.'

The image made her smile. 'You're a handyman? I didn't know!'

'A wedding present for his bride – he wants it to be a surprise for her. He wants them to start their married life off being more self-sufficient. I gave my bride a diamond necklace, he's given his hens! So, what can I do for you?'

'When are they getting married?'

'In about two hours' time!'

'Right, I won't keep you. A quick one – you carried out a biopsy on tissue I sent you on Thursday afternoon, following my colposcopy examination of a patient, Georgina Maclean, and you rang me yesterday, concerned about the histology results.'

'Yes, not good at all, I'm afraid.'

Trying to be as tactful as possible, Kath asked, 'Is there any possibility, any at all, that a mistake could have occurred, Nigel – that it was the biopsy of a different patient?'

She sensed an immediate change of tone in his voice, to defensive. 'Absolutely none, Kath. To be honest, I'm a little bit surprised you're even asking. We've worked together a long time, surely you know me better?' Then he said, 'Ouch!'

'Are you OK?'

'I've just got a sodding splinter! Look, no chance at all, Kath. Six Sigma. That's the discipline I've strived to achieve in here and which we adhere to.'

'Six Sigma? What's that?'

'In a nutshell, it's a standard of quality control so tight that any company who achieves that standard wouldn't need a returns or complaints department. Not wanting to sound arrogant, Kath, but we simply don't make mistakes. We've eliminated any possibility of carry-over in our histology pathology.'

'Carry-over' was a problem that occasionally occurred in path labs, when traces of previous tissue remained after the equipment wasn't sterilized thoroughly enough.

She realized she may have offended him with the question. 'Listen, Nigel, I'm not trying to question your procedures but I'm trying to get my head around the results, which just don't chime with my findings. I'm not questioning your methodology. I'm having my patient do an MRI scan today, which will clarify things more. I'm just wondering if there could have been a mistake on the labelling, somehow. Who actually brought the jar containing the tissue sample to you?'

'Marcus Valentine,' he said. 'Anything else, Kath? I've got to go and get my glad rags on.'

'Marcus?'

'Yes, he brought a whole bunch of tissue scrapings down from Colposcopy.'

'Thanks, Nigel. Enjoy the wedding.'

He ended the call.

It wasn't normal for a consultant in the colposcopy unit to take samples down to the pathology labs, although Kath had done it herself in the past, just to help out.

Her phone rang. Answering, she heard Valentine's voice. 'Hello, Kath, you were looking for me?'

'Yes, good, thanks for coming back to me, Marcus,' she said. 'Just a quick thing – you were doing some colposcopies on Thursday afternoon, weren't you?'

'Thursday?' He was silent for an instant. 'Yes, yes of course, Thursday afternoon. We bumped into each other in the corridor.'

'Yes. I did a couple before you – and I understand you kindly took all the afternoon tissue samples down to Nigel Kirkham for biopsy.'

'On Thursday?' He sounded like he was trying to recollect. 'Ah yes, of course, I had to go down there anyway, so I took them.'

'You remember by any chance seeing the labels on all the vials?'

'The labels?'

'There weren't any of the vials where the labels had come off, I don't suppose?'

'Not that I noticed, no.' There was a pause. 'No, absolutely not. Why, is there a – a problem?' he fished.

'Yes, I have something of an anomaly. What I saw in my colpos- copy examination of Georgie Maclean just doesn't tally with the biopsy report from Nigel Kirkham.'

'But surely this is the reason we have biopsies done – to check something we can't necessarily see with our naked eye? They tell us what's really going on.'

'Normally, I'd agree with you. But I don't know, it's just not making any sense to me. I suppose I'll know for sure after the scan.'

'I really hope she's OK, she's got enough on her plate, poor thing,' he said.

'I know. Are you around over the weekend, in case I want to discuss the scan result with you – as a friend?'

'I'll be at home most of the weekend, but if you need me, I'd be more than happy to come in and go through the result with you, Kath. Just call me any time, as soon as you've got it – no problem at all, that's what I'm here for.'

'I might do that,' she said. 'I'd appreciate your opinion.'

'Of course. And with all her worries about Roger, we really do owe it to her to be extra diligent.'

'We do.'

'By the way, what time is the scan booked for?'

'Midday,' she said. 'I've told them it's urgent and they've fitted it in.'

'You've done exactly the right thing,' he purred.

81

Saturday 19 January

Georgie left the Patriotic Street car park shortly after 11 a.m. and crossed to the other side of the road, into the bright winter sunshine. But she barely noticed it as she walked quickly along towards the hospital entrance. She felt only a deep darkness inside her, which darkened further as she saw the two police cars parked outside.

She hurried up the ramp and went in through the automatic door. A uniformed police officer stood just inside and smiled at her politely.

'May I ask your business here, madam?' she said.

'Yes, I'm coming to visit my fiancé who's in Intensive Care and then I'm having an MRI scan.'

'OK, thank you.'

As Georgie climbed the stairs, her phone pinged with a text. It was from her friend, Lucy, confirming their quick lunch at 1.30. She confirmed back, looking forward to seeing her and having some company. She walked on to the Relatives' Room and was surprised to see a man and woman seated in there. She smiled and sat down some distance from them.

Before any of them spoke, the door opened and Kiera Dale looked in. 'Ah, great, Georgie, you're here. Follow me.'

She left the room and as they reached the ICU entrance, she took a squirt from the hand sanitizer and rubbed her hands together. 'How is Roger this morning?' she asked, anxiously, seeing nothing in the senior nurse's face to give her any comfort.

'He's had a stable night. But still no sign of him responding to the antibiotics. The doctors are changing his meds to put him on stronger ones, and we'll see if that makes any improvement.' She gave her a smile. 'Hopefully, it will.'

Georgie sat with Roger for the next forty minutes, trying to chat, trying to sound cheerful, telling him about a text she'd had from her cousin, Chloe, that she and her husband sent all their love and that they were expecting their second child. She said nothing about the horror of last night. Occasionally, Roger opened his eyes and looked at her for some seconds before closing them again. Each time, hope rose inside her. At least he seemed to be showing he was aware of her, which was an improvement on yesterday, wasn't it?

At 11.45, trying to make it sound as positive as she could, she said, 'Darling, I've just got to pop down to Radiology. Kath wants me to have an MRI scan, to make sure all is well with me and the Bump. Then I'm having a bite of lunch with Lucy. I'll be back as soon as I can.'

She didn't add that she had to go to the police station after lunch to give a statement.

Kissing him on the forehead, she said, 'I love you so much, be strong,' then turned away, a giant lump in her throat, and walked, tearfully, out of the ward and towards the stairs.

At the bottom she followed the signs, taking her down a long incline. Her nerves were jangling. What were they going to find in the scan? And she was scared of the machine. She'd been in an MRI scanner before, a few years ago, and remembered vividly the feeling of claustrophobia and the din of the machine.

She stopped in front of twin granite arches, reading the signs. Through the left one were elevator doors, with a magenta floor-standing sign in front warning, VISITORS: DO NOT VISIT THE HOSPITAL IF YOU HAVE EXPERIENCED ANY DIARRHOEA AND VOMITING OVER THE PAST THREE DAYS, TO HELP PREVENT THE SPREAD OF NOROVIRUS.

Beneath, on the same sign, was a translation in a Slavic language and below that in Portuguese.

Through the right arch, beneath a sign which read GRANITE BLOCK – ENDOSCOPY AND BARTLETT, RADIOLOGY (X-RAY), were double doors.

They opened automatically as she approached. Passing through, she went down a long corridor and entered a very modern, softly coloured waiting room bearing silver lettering on one wall, WELCOME TO LIGHTHOUSE MRI, an array of chairs, a two-seater sofa, a smart, loaded magazine rack and a wall-mounted television showing a cookery programme.

A young, plump, smiley woman appeared through a door, clutching a bunch of forms. 'Hello, Georgina Maclean?' she said in what sounded to Georgie to be a Mediterranean accent.

'Yes.'

'OK, good. I'm the registrar. I just need to go through some paperwork with you and then we'll get you ready for the scan. Do you have any music you would like played?'

'Music?'

'We can put on whatever music you would like when you're in the scanner.'

'Oh, OK.' She tried to think. Music. Van Morrison? No, that might upset her too much. Who did she find soothing? Alec Benjamin? 'Do you have any Alec Benjamin?' she asked.

'Yes, no problem, we can fulfil most requests!' the woman said, brightly.

They both sat down. Georgie was handed a two-page form and a pen, and began to fill it in, while the woman asked her a series of questions about her health and whether she had any metal implants in her body. It was only when she got to the section marked 'Next of Kin' that she wobbled.

She wrote, 'Roger Richardson.' And nearly added, *Please God.*

'Are you claustrophobic, Georgina?'

'I am, very.'

'Would you like any sedation?'

She shook her head. 'I'll be fine, thank you.' *Somehow*, she thought.

When she had finished, the young woman fetched a dressing gown and slippers, and led her to a changing cubicle with brightly coloured curtains.

'Please make sure you remove anything metal from your body, including your ring,' she asked.

'Sure.'

As Georgie entered the tiny space and heard the curtains behind her close, her fear deepened.

82

Saturday 19 January

Marcus Valentine entered the quiet calm of the Radiology room. A young female assistant was tapping a keypad, staring at a monitor. The radiographer, a young, dark-haired man, was switching focus between the person who he could see currently inside the MRI scanner and the images that were coming up on the monitors. At 12.20 p.m. the scan was well underway.

'Hi,' he said.

Both glanced fleetingly around at him.

'I just popped in to see Ana Gomes – Kath Clow asked me to discuss Georgie Maclean's scan results with her.'

'Ana is monitoring the scanner now, Mr Valentine,' the radiographer said. 'She'll be done in about twenty minutes.'

'Great, thank you, I'll wait. Don't let me disturb you.'

They both returned to their tasks. He stood, keeping quiet, not wanting to break their concentration. What they were doing was important.

And the woman inside the scanner was important to him.

She was his future.

Georgie was in the room that was lit by a soft haze of sky-blue light, the white machine almost ethereal in the middle of it. He could just make out her head. He knew what she would be experiencing in there. The curved inner wall of the machine inches from her face. The intermittent metallic drumming. Having to remain absolutely still. He asked the assistant if Miss Maclean had chosen any music to be played.

'Here. Take a look,' the assistant replied.

Alec Benjamin, 'If We Have Each Other'. *Interesting choice*, Marcus thought, then skipped it on a few tracks . . . Alec Benjamin, 'If I Killed Someone For You'. Much more appropriate with its lyrics about changing for someone you love. Well, maybe not really *changing*, but more *enriching*, he felt. She would thank him for it someday soon.

He watched the images appearing on the screens, changing by the second, all in black and white. Changing too fast for him to be able to assess them. That did not matter. The one thing that mattered was the junior registrar. Today, all the gods were aligned. None of the six consultant radiologists were on duty. Instead, they had left Ana Gomes to interrogate the scans. That was lucky, but in a short while he'd truly know if luck was on his side or not. All he could do was wait.

And think.

And dream.

He pictured what the scanner was seeing through her clothing. Her naked body. So vulnerable. She needed protecting. Why wasn't her fiancé protecting her?

Two floors above, Roger Richardson was slowly, steadily, day-by-day, drifting away as sepsis increased its grip. And hopefully his luck would hold, and the doctors didn't decide to open him up. Really, there wasn't any need.

Finally, the radiographer turned to him. 'All done, Mr Valentine. Ana is in the second office on the left, I've just sent the images through to her.'

Thanking her, he slipped through the door into the office suite, gave a courteous knock on the door and entered.

Ana Gomes was seated at her desk in the tiny room, with four monitors in front of her.

'Hi, Ana,' he said.

She turned, then smiled in recognition – and respect. 'Hello, Mr Valentine, can I help you with something?'

'These are the scan results for Georgie Maclean?'

'Yes, just through.'

'Kath Clow's off today. She's very concerned about this patient and asked if I'd give her an assessment after the scan had come through.'

'Of course, thank you, I'd value your opinion.'

'It would be my pleasure, Ana. How are you getting on here?'

'I like it, everyone is so friendly and helpful, much more than in the previous hospital I was in, in England.'

'Good!' he said. 'So maybe you'll consider staying here in Jersey?'

'I would love to. My husband has a job he loves with the Indigo Medical Practice and we're just about to get a dog. So, I'm really hoping!'

Valentine beamed. 'I'm sure I can help you, Ana. All my colleagues have been very impressed with your work – and your attitude, which is so important. We run a tight team here, and we rely on mutual respect. If you'll allow me to be your mentor, I'll do all I can to ensure you have a future with us, in this department.'

Ana's eyes widened. 'Really? That's incredibly kind of you.'

He shook his head. 'No, it's not about kindness, it's about recognizing real talent. We have a high standard in this hospital. I think, from all I hear about you, that you have what it takes, Ana.'

'Thank you,' she said, looking delighted. 'Thank you so much. I will work as hard as I possibly can to justify yours and the hospital's faith in me.'

'I know you will. I can see that in you.' He smiled again.

'You are very kind.'

'I just want the best for this hospital, which I love.'

'Thank you. I'll always do my best.'

'I believe you will. So, may I take a look at the scan images?'

'Of course, sir.'

On one monitor, the split screen showed four different black-and-white images of Georgie Maclean's endometrium. On the next was a full screen of her cervix. It showed her placenta covering much of the cervix.

His luck was in. He could scarcely hold back his excitement. This was truly a gift!

He peered closer. Top right on each image was ACC. NO. 91870499. Below was AGE 41Y, and below that SEX: FEMALE, and each was labelled A, B, L, R.

The one that interested him was B on the third screen. He leaned in, looking at it closely. Covering much of the cervix was a large sac that, blown-up, looked a little like a hunched rodent.

'So, Ana, tell me, what is your assessment of this scan?'

Observing what he was looking at, the registrar said, 'It looks to me like Placenta Previa – low-lying and encroaching. Would you agree?'

'No.' He shook his head. 'I agree it looks like the placenta is low-lying and encroaching – but that's a mistake I once made in my early days, with catastrophic results for the patient. I still have guilt about it almost twenty years later.'

'Really?' She turned to face him, shocked.

He nodded, looking very sad. 'She died from cervical cancer just months later. I'm afraid it's easily done when you haven't got experience. And it's an understandable mistake. It's very understandable to miss what is really going on.' He pointed. 'You see that area of white?'

She looked back at the screen, to where he was indicating, and nodded.

'That's *high signal* in the region of the cervix. This lady's colposcopy showed a stage-2 cancer, which was supported by the histology.'

'Oh my God,' Ana Gomes said, sounding shocked. 'I would have missed this.'

'Honestly, don't feel bad. As I said, it's a very easy mistake to make. I'd be happy to help you write your report.'

Ana turned back towards him, bright-eyed with gratitude. 'Would you really? Thank you so much.'

'There's something I tell all my students, one of the first things they are going to learn when they start, which is that medicine is a very inexact science.'

'I think I've just had my first lesson in that.'

'I think you have, Ana.' He smiled.

83

Saturday 19 January

'Ex-wives – or ex-husbands – can be very bitter people, George,' Lucy said. 'I think you have to take anything that woman said to you with a pinch of salt.'

She and Lucy were seated in the bar of the Yacht Club, over-looking the port of St Helier. It was 2.15 and with the sky heavily overcast it already felt that the day was drawing to a close. Lucy, with hair that managed to look both wild and tamed at the same time, was elegant as ever, wearing a quilted Barbour over a roll-neck, jeans and leather boots. She was the kind of person Georgie aspired to be herself – calm and seemingly always able to cope with anything, someone who loved her work and study but didn't let it totally dominate her life.

Lucy sipped her glass of wine, which Georgie looked at envi-ously, her own lime and soda on the table, untouched, like her tuna salad.

'So the radiology people wouldn't give you any information at all?'

Georgie shook her head. 'They said the report would go to my obstetrician and she'd be in touch with me. Luckily, my obstetrician is a friend, so at least I feel I'm in good hands there. She's the one who does all those triathlons.'

'Kath Clow, right?'

'Yes.'

'She's lovely – she delivered both my sister's children, we really liked her.'

Georgie nodded glumly. 'I know she cares. But . . .' Her voice tailed off.

'But?'

'I don't know. I just have a really bad feeling. I mean, if she wasn't worried, why would she have rushed me in for a scan on a Saturday?'

'I wouldn't read too much into it. She's highly conscientious.'

'I asked if they routinely saw patients on a Saturday, Luce. She said Saturdays were mostly for catching up on stuff, but they did scans where consultants were concerned and wanted results quickly. I wish I hadn't bloody asked.' Georgie lowered her head, her eyes moistening, voice cracking. 'God, what have I done to deserve all this?'

Her friend reached across the table and stroked her arm. 'You poor love, you really are going through it. Just think, when it's all over, we'll go and celebrate.'

'A month ago, I felt so happy. When that pregnancy test showed positive, honestly, it was one of the greatest moments of my life. Ever since, everything's turned to crap.' She felt Lucy's hand on her arm. Closed her eyes so her friend couldn't see her tears, then looked away, sighing. 'I just don't know what the hell is happening – or how much more I can take.'

Lucy was silent for some while. Then she said, 'You've had a big shock, finding that body in the freezer, and that just a few days after poor Roger's accident. I think you're probably actually suffering from shock. Roger will be fine, believe me, he will.'

Back with her eyes closed, Georgie said, 'I wish I could believe you.'

'Georgie, I had a friend who went through a similar situation after a motorbike accident. She was over a month in the ICU before she started to improve. She's right as rain now and back on her bike.'

Georgie nodded.

'You're not exactly having the best day of your life today, are you? Seeing Roger in Intensive Care; having an MRI scan, which can be a frightening experience, then going from here to give a statement at the police station? I'd come with you, but I've got to pick up my sister's Harry from a party, I promised her.'

Georgie gave a wan smile. 'Yep, not exactly the *best* day ever.'

And one which had the potential to get a whole lot worse, she thought, gloomily.

84

Saturday 19 January

Still in her cycling kit at 2.40 p.m., Kath sat on a sofa in the bike shop, leafing through a cycling magazine. The problem with her bike was worse than Chris, the mechanic, had first thought. He was in the back with the entire chain and gear mechanism in bits. He'd explained something about alignment, tension and the derailleur and she'd let him get on with it. His original estimate of half an hour to fix it had increased, when he'd seen the extent of the problem, to an hour, then an hour and a half. It was now nearing two hours since she'd come in.

Glancing at her watch, she felt slight panic – the day was running out on her. She had a big food shop to do, and then she and Bob had planned to grab an early bite out before going to a symphony concert at the Opera House. She stood up and walked to the rear of the shop, to see how Chris was getting on, and to her relief she saw the bike was all back together. He had it mounted on a roller, testing the pedals and going smoothly up and down through the gears.

Her phone rang. She answered and heard the voice of the young radiologist.

'Hi, Ana,' she said. 'Hold on a sec!'

She walked back to the sofa and perched on an arm. 'I'll have to talk quietly, I'm in a busy shop.'

'I'm calling you as you asked for my report on Georgina Maclean.'

'Yes, thank you.' She waited expectantly.

'It doesn't look good for the lady,' Ana said.

'I was kind of expecting that.'

'Very fortunately Mr Valentine came in to help me interrogate the images.'

'OK, great,' Kath said. Good of him, she thought, he must have been having a quiet day in the hospital. And she was very comforted to know that this inexperienced radiologist had someone so experienced on hand, helping her – it saved her the need to get one of the consultants to double-check the results on Monday. 'Yes, so tell me, Ana?'

When Kath ended the call, the bike was ready and waiting. She paid the bill, then wheeled the bike out onto the pavement, stopped and strapped on her helmet. The light was already beginning to fail and a cold breeze was blowing. It felt as if it was blowing right through her. She had to deliver bad news in her job, and although it was never easy for her, she was normally at arm's length from her patients, and whilst being sympathetic, she was able to be dispassionate. But it was different with Georgie, she was her mate. She was dreading having to tell her – this was something no amount of medical training could prepare her for.

She used the twenty-minute cycle ride home to collect her thoughts, plan what she was going to say to Georgie and how she was going to say it.

85

Saturday 19 January

Georgie had to sit in the police station waiting area for some while before a young, suited man appeared through a glass door, introducing himself as Detective Constable Price. Apologizing for keeping her waiting, he led her through the doorway and towards a lift.

'Do you know what happened?' she asked.

'I'm afraid not fully at this stage – we're hoping you may be able to help us.'

They emerged into an open-plan area, on the second floor, and he led her past several people at their workstations into a smart conference room, where a middle-aged man with a big bushy beard stood up and shook her hand.

'Detective Inspector John Cunningham,' he said. 'We appreciate you coming, Miss Maclean – can we get you a drink?'

'I'd love some tea, please. No sugar, just some milk.'

The younger man went out and she sat down opposite the DI. He had a tablet in front of him and a recorder. 'I'd like to stress that you are not a suspect in any way, Miss Maclean, we'd just like to ask you some questions about what happened at the Bel Royal Hotel on Thursday night, and we would like to take some elimination fingerprints before you leave.'

'Of course,' she said.

The window looked down over the roundabout in front of the police station, and the entrance to the tunnel on the far side. It was growing dark. A large, white, Ferryspeed lorry with its headlights on was emerging from it, with a line of traffic following.

For a few minutes they chatted, pleasantly, about how long she had been in Jersey and where she lived, and he told her he'd been here ten years – before that he'd been with the police in Norfolk.

Then DC Price returned with a tray of teas, sat down beside his colleague and they began.

'Are you OK if we record this interview, Miss Maclean?' the DI asked.

'Yes, fine – please call me Georgie.'

The interview was a laboriously slow process, as she recounted all that had happened from the time she'd arrived at the hotel until she'd found Robert Resmes's body. She was stopped intermittently by one or the other officer, asking for clarification on points.

What they repeatedly came back to was how Resmes might have got into the hotel and whether it had anything to do with the events a couple of days ago. So far, the Crime Scene Investigators had been unable to establish a point of entry. All the windows were secure, all external doors locked. Georgie was unable to explain it either. She told them how she always locked the external door to the gym when she did her inspection round of the building. But she mentioned that Edouardo also had a key and she wasn't entirely sure where he was at the time because it was his day off. She suggested that if they hadn't already, they might want to speak to him.

Suddenly her phone rang. Apologetically, she removed it from her bag, and saw on the display it was Kath.

'Do answer it if you need to,' DI Cunningham said.

She desperately wanted to. It had to be news about the scan, but that wasn't going to be a thirty-second conversation. Silencing it, but totally distracted, she put the phone back in her bag. 'It's fine, thank you, I'll call her back later.'

What was the news? Her mind, momentarily, was all over the place. *Was it bad or good?*

'Georgie,' the DI said, 'can you think of anything that's happened at the hotel – or your gym – that's struck you as unusual, either on Thursday night or before then? Anything you might have seen?'

She frowned, concentrating again. 'Well, apart from that weird incident the day before, obviously, no. I—' Then she remembered. Could it possibly have any bearing on this or any connection? 'For a while now I've had a feeling that someone has been creeping around the hotel whilst I've been there. It's a pretty difficult place to make totally secure, it's got very old window latches. Anyone who wanted to break in could get in fairly easily.'

'Did you actually see anyone?' the DC asked.

She again told them about the egg timers. And how she'd agreed with the police officers who had attended that it was probably kids who must have got into the building, somehow.

'Seems an odd thing to do,' Cunningham said.

'I don't know. If you wanted to spook someone out, I'd say it was a pretty effective way – it sure spooked me!'

'But you never saw the kids, or whoever, and no one else saw the egg timers?'

'No, I was there alone. But I guess the locals would know a lot of the hotels are closed for the winter, and as I said, it wouldn't have been difficult to break in.'

'Is there anyone else working at the hotel in the daytime?'

'Just the caretaker, Edouardo.'

'And he's never there in the evenings?'

'He comes and goes at odd hours sometimes. He works as a children's entertainer, as a clown, and occasionally in a cabaret act in town – he stores his costume and props in his room there.'

'A clown?' Cunningham said.

She nodded.

He frowned. 'Dunno what it is, but there's something about clowns I find very creepy.'

'And me,' she said. 'But Edouardo's all right.'

'OK, we have his full name and contact details and we will have a word with him.' He made a note to explore it later. 'It may be significant. There was no phone on or near Resmes when he was found, yet he had his wallet on him with over £100 in it. It opens up the possibility it was someone mugging him for his phone, but it doesn't make much sense to take his phone and not his wallet. We need to speak to this caretaker as a priority.'

'And it still doesn't explain what Resmes was doing in the hotel, does it?'

He shook his head. 'You had no personal relationship with him?'

'No, I didn't know him very well, only through my visits to the hospital. Do you know anything about what happened – why he died? He wasn't locked in that freezer – there was an internal door – so presumably he either passed out or was incapacitated.'

The detectives shot each other a glance. 'You'll appreciate, Georgie, we cannot say too much at this stage. We'll know more after the postmortem, but we have to wait for his body to fully defrost, and for a Home Office Pathologist to arrive from the UK.' Cunningham leaned forward across the table. 'In confidence, Robert Resmes was apparently meant to meet the consultant he'd been under, earlier in the evening at the hospital, and never showed up.'

'Marcus Valentine?'

'Yes, I believe that was his name.'

Marcus had some serious issues, but that was for another day.

'Resmes was then going on to see his girlfriend – she'd had a day off and was cooking a meal for him.'

'Girlfriend?' Georgie said.

'A nurse at the hospital. She's on the floor, utterly distraught, hasn't a clue what could have happened. The last time anyone saw him was in one of the Maternity wards at around 7.30 p.m. on Thursday. His pass card has been retrieved – he had it on him – and the High Tech Crime Unit will be able to get the last time it was used off it, which should give us an accurate time for when he left the hospital.' He shrugged. 'It's a real mystery but we are now very keen to speak to this caretaker.'

When they had finally finished, the DI asked Georgie to let him know if she thought of anything else, however trivial, over the next few days, then thanked her for her help.

'I don't think I've been much help, really,' she said. 'I'm just so sad for him. And his girlfriend – and his family back in Romania. Maybe Edouardo will throw some light on it all.'

'We'll get to the bottom of it,' the DI said. 'We normally do.'

'But not always, right?' She smiled.

He smiled back. 'This is a small island community where, thankfully, incidents of this nature are a very rare event. I'm confident we will find out what has happened, it's still very early on in our investigation.'

'I hope so.'

As soon as she was back out in the dark, cold street, just after 5 p.m., in her coat and gloves, she pulled out her phone and listened to her voicemail. There was just one message, from Kath Clow.

'Hi, Georgie, it's Kath. Call me back when you've a moment.'

Her normal cheerful voice was tinged with a trace of hesitation, which instantly alarmed Georgie. She stopped and dialled. And got Kath's voicemail. Leaving a message that she was returning her call, she walked rapidly down towards the town centre and the hospital.

She entered the pedestrian precinct of King's Street, teeming as always with people, and hurried on, past January sales signs in almost all the windows, clutching her phone in her hand, willing the obstetrician to call back.

A couple of minutes later, to her relief, the display lit up and she heard the ring tone.

'Hi, Kath,' she answered, instantly.

The woman, normally so bright, sounded subdued. 'Georgie, look, I've just had the results of the MRI scan.'

'That was quick,' Georgie said.

'Yes, well, the thing is that when I did the colposcopy, I didn't see anything abnormal. But the histology showed the possibility of something not right. Now I've got the scan result which has also indicated something I'm not happy with. I'd like to see you first thing Monday. I know it's over a day away, but we can't do anything until then, so take tomorrow to relax as much as you can, then we'll tackle it all when you come in to see me and we are both fresh.'

Georgie stepped into a shop doorway, in a daze. 'Oh my God, Kath, what is it? What are you trying to tell me?' she asked.

'I may need you to make a decision,' Clow said.

'What do you mean?' Georgie asked, bewildered. 'What kind of decision?'

'Let's go through it all on Monday.'

'Please tell me, Kath, tell me the truth. What – what has the scan shown?'

'Georgie, I don't want to worry you. I want you to know it would be much better to talk about this face to face.'

'You don't want to worry me? Let me tell you as your friend, I'm fucking worried. OK?'

'Hey, listen, don't be worried, there are plenty of options. You're going to be fine, trust me. We just have to make some decisions.'

'Trust you? What kind of decisions?'

Kath sounded more serious and firmer than ever before. 'Ten o'clock Monday, come and see me at the hospital. We'll discuss it all then.'

'Why can't we discuss it now, Kath?'

'Because I need some more information before we do. Please, my love, try to relax – as I said, there are plenty of options.'

'Is one of the options that I'm a healthy mother-to-be, and that the MRI scan showed everything was OK, and that by Monday the man I love will be up and about and dancing around the ICU?'

There was a long silence.

86

Monday 21 January

At 6.05 a.m. on Monday morning, despite feeling exhausted, Georgie decided to give up on any attempt at sleep and hauled herself up in bed. Thinking. Gathering her thoughts.

A week, today, since Roger's accident.

He should have been alongside her, lying in the large bed, but instead, there was just a void.

A Roger-sized void.

He was still in Intensive Care. No improvement on yesterday, instead a further decline. Slight, she had been assured. But still a decline.

Was he dying? Was sepsis, so common in hospitals, steadily poisoning all his internal organs?

She'd been in the grip of fear every second since her phone conversation with Kath on Saturday, after leaving the police station. All day on Sunday she'd sat with Roger, worried sick about him, and worried sick about herself. What on earth was Kath keeping from her?

Trying to make sense of that conversation. Thinking it through, as much as she could remember, word by word.

Only a few hours now until she saw her. Found out. *Oh God, please let everything be OK.* She closed her eyes, exhausted but wired. She opened them again and glanced at the calendar on her phone, checking what else she had for the week ahead, and saw she had an appointment with her hairdresser at 11 a.m. How long would she be with Kath Clow? How would she be feeling after she'd

334

seen Kath? Why was she even having a haircut when she, her baby and her fiancé were all going to die anyhow?

Gathering herself together, she made a mental note to call as soon as the salon was open to push back her hair appointment, and if that was not possible, to reschedule. Then she got out of bed, put on her kit and let herself out into the darkness.

The cold air on her face felt good and she wished so much she could run rather than walk. After a gentle warm-up stroll, turning left along the promenade towards the lights of St Helier, she started power walking. She kept going, keeping up the pace. And as she did so she began to feel better. So much better. She was feeling good.

Sod you all, I'm going to be fine! Bump's going to be fine! Roger's going to be fine! We'll cross each bridge as it comes.

87

Monday 21 January

Marcus Valentine was feeling fine, oh yes, so good! He stroked the heads of his little twins who had climbed into bed with them, as they always did around 6 a.m., usually waking him.

But today, they hadn't woken him. He'd been awake for a long time.

Claire was still sound asleep.

He stroked them again, fondly, but detached. In his vision of his life post-Claire, he would get to choose the times when he saw his children, and it certainly would not be at 6 a.m. every morning. Early morning would be his and Georgie's time in bed together. With their insatiable appetite for each other, they would keep their passion alive and never let it go the way his and Claire's had.

They were destined for each other.

It was all working out so brilliantly.

He got up feeling in a great mood, and even better still after a long shower. He dressed and went downstairs, adjusted the time on one of his precious clocks and sat down.

On his phone he opened RunMaster and saw that Georgie Maclean had been out already, impressively early. Her time wasn't so impressive though. Barely above walking pace. He could beat that, beat it easily!

That's what being pregnant does to you, young lady.

But don't worry. In a couple of days, it'll all be taken care of. You won't be running for a while. Really don't worry, you'll get over it and be back to form come the spring. And you'll have a spring in your step! A whole new life beckoning. Roger will be long gone, and all those dumb hormones telling you that you need to reproduce, they'll be gone, too. Up in smoke. That's where your foetus will be in a couple of days, in the hospital incinerator, rising up that tall chimney stack out the back of the building.

I will have set you free!

88

Monday 21 January

On the dot of 10 a.m., Georgie knocked nervously on Kath Clow's office door.

'Come in!'

As she entered, instead of being in her usual scrubs, her friend was sitting at her desk dressed in a smart suit. And instead of her usual warm smile, there was a much more forced one on her face. Kath got up and hugged her hard, then pointed her to a chair. 'Georgie, come in, come in, my love. You must be feeling dreadful, absolute shite.'

'Pretty shite, actually, yep, Kath. That's about the right word for it.'

The consultant nodded, sympathetically. 'What have you heard about Roger, any signs of improvement?'

'No – they've changed his meds again.'

Kath looked down at her desk, shuffled some papers around, then peered at her screen for a moment.

'OK, look, let's not beat about the bush. I'm really sorry, but when I did your last colposcopy it didn't appear to me that there was anything wrong. But the lab report has shown that the biopsies I took on Thursday are cancerous, and the MRI scan has confirmed it. It's not good news, Georgie. We have to deal with it, and we will.'

Numbly, Georgie replied after a long moment. 'Yes, of course. I mean – how bad is it?'

Kath relaxed a little and sounded more positive now. 'It's stage-2 adenocarcinoma of the cervix, which means it is serious, but can, hopefully, be stopped in its tracks if you agree to the treatment. It's an aggressive cancer, which means that every day matters, so it's important to start the treatment as quickly as possible.'

Georgie stared back at her. 'What treatment, exactly?'

'Well, this is the hard part. I've spoken to Mr Valentine, and I've talked to the Royal Marsden, which is the leading cancer hospital in the UK. You need chemo-radiation over six weeks and I'm afraid this can't be done while you're pregnant, because of the damage it could do to your baby.'

There was a long silence as Georgie's mind went into free-fall.

When she finally spoke, her whole body was trembling. 'What are you saying, Kath? That I have to wait for my baby to be born before I start any treatment?'

'Honestly? If you want my opinion, and it is Mr Valentine's view, also, you don't have the luxury of that time without very seriously risking your life. He feels that if you wait for the baby to go to term – and this is backed up by the Royal Marsden – your cancer will almost certainly progress. If we act now, with luck, we could prevent that from happening. I'm recommending termination, I'm afraid, Georgie.'

'Termination? No, oh God, no. Please – there must be an alternative, surely?'

It felt as if all the air had been sucked out of the room. As if she was in some kind of decompression chamber. Her ears popped. She bowed her head, staring at the floor, gripped with fear and totally lost. God, all the years of trying. Now she had a healthy baby growing inside her.

'How – how would you – what – will happen to my baby?'

'You need a hysterotomy, which means going in through the abdomen to remove your foetus. When that's healed, I'd organize for you to go to the Royal Marsden for chemo-radiation.'

'Hysterectomy? Removing my uterus?'

Clow shook her head. 'No, Georgie, it's a *hysterotomy* – the same cut into the uterus we would perform for a caesarean.'

'What – what happens to my baby?'

'I've been through this before, with other patients, my love. Some have opted for a funeral with a priest attending.'

'What?' she screamed. 'Funeral? My baby has to die? This is going to kill it? No. Fucking. Way. Kath. No. *No. No!*'

Kath held back from telling Georgie that one of her patients had had a cast made of her baby's feet, and another a tattoo from her baby's cremated ashes. And another had had the cremated tissue put in a glass pendant. Everyone coped with grief in a different way. Georgie needed time to absorb this terrible shock, with everything falling apart around her now. Kath's heart ached for her friend.

Georgie held a stoic, numb silence. Before exploding into tears. 'I can't lose it, I can't, I just can't go through with this. I can't lose my baby.'

89

Monday 21 January

After several minutes, once Georgie had collected herself a little, Kath pulled up a chair next to her and held out a box of tissues.

'I know it's terrible news, Georgie, I can't begin to say how awful I feel to tell you this.'

Georgie looked at her with wide, staring, bloodshot eyes. She took a tissue, then crushed and held it in her hand. 'I'm dying, aren't I? My baby is dying, Roger is dying and now I'm dying.'

'No, Georgie, you are not dying. The treatment for this type of cancer, if caught early enough, gives a very good prognosis and we are early enough if we don't delay. OK?'

She nodded, blankly. 'What a mess – it's all a fucking nightmare.'

Kath put an arm on her shoulder, facing her. 'Georgie, the ICU team are going to get Roger straightened out and back on his feet, I'm sure of it. But we do need to terminate your baby, and I know how tough that is for you.'

Georgie placed a hand on her brow, scraping back her hair, and the other on her midriff. 'I don't even know if it's a boy or girl.'

'Do you remember I sent you an envelope?' she said gently. 'It's in there, if you want to know.'

Tears rolled down her face. 'I don't know, Kath. How can I decide this shit? My life is a total wreck. Part of me is thinking, do I have any moral right to kill it just so I *might* live?'

Kath pulled out another tissue and dabbed away more of Georgie's tears.

'Don't torture yourself. Just think it through. If you went to term

341

without any treatment, you'd be creating a very serious risk that the baby would lose its mother in infancy – how would you feel about that? Who would take care of it?'

Georgie sat in miserable silence, her thoughts all tangled, desperately wishing she could talk to Roger about this. They'd work this through together.

'When would you do it?' she said, in a voice barely above a whisper.

'I'd like to get you into theatre tomorrow.'

'After I've done all the chemo and radiation treatment, if all's good, would there be a chance I could conceive again?' Georgie asked.

Clow gave her a sad smile. 'I'm afraid not. There'll be too much radiation and chemo damage.'

Georgie said, 'I've read about people who have to undergo cancer treatment having things like eggs, ovaries, frozen. Is that a possibility?'

Kath shook her head. 'To do that I'd have to put you through a programme of hyperstimulation, which takes time – and it would accelerate the progress of the cancer. It's also very possible there are cancerous cells in your ovaries – we can't risk preserving those and passing it on.'

'Great,' she said bitterly. 'It's just fucked up, isn't it? I feel like I'm the filling in a triple-shit sandwich.'

Clow gave a sympathetic smile. 'Not a bad analogy.'

Georgie lapsed into her thoughts. Then she said, 'So tomorrow – that's when you want to do it?'

'Yes. I've already spoken to the Marsden and booked you in for next Monday.'

'Next Monday? You've already booked me in? What about Roger? I want him to be a part of this decision.'

'Hopefully, he'll be a lot better by next week. But whatever his condition, I think he would be very upset to think he'd caused any delay in your treatment starting. Time really is critical.'

'How long after this op – abortion – will I be on my feet again?'

'After the procedure you'll be in hospital overnight and it will take you a few days to recover, but you should be able to fly on Monday morning. The States of Jersey will cover your travel and hospital costs, so there won't be anything to pay.'

'Sod the money,' she said.

'It's not going to be cheap and I don't want you having to worry about the costs.'

'Very thoughtful,' Georgie said, more bitterly than she had intended.

'I've also spoken to Mr Valentine. He's not scheduled to be operating tomorrow – he has a day at his private consulting rooms – but he's very kindly agreed to move something around and fit you in at 2 p.m.'

'What?' She sat bolt upright. 'Marcus Valentine? You mean he's going to be doing it?'

'Yes, Georgie. I want you to have our top gynae-oncologist.'

She shook her head wildly, and shouted out, 'No!' The vehemence in her voice startled Kath.

'You'd be in the best possible hands.'

'You think so, Kath? I'm not convinced. He makes me feel uncomfortable. There has to be an alternative. Please.'

The obstetrician looked at her. 'If this was me in your situation, it's Mr Valentine I would ask for, Georgie.'

She shook her head. 'Couldn't you do it? Surely you can do it?'

'If that's what you really want?'

'It is.'

Clow pulled her appointments diary up on her screen and studied it for some moments. 'Well, OK, there's a meeting I can duck out of.'

'Thank you.'

She could see the relief on Georgie's face. It was Georgie's decision and if she felt more comfortable with her doing it then so be it.

But why, the obstetrician wondered, was Georgie so against Valentine? She couldn't even begin to know the emotional turmoil that must be going on inside her mind. Was it that she'd just prefer a female surgeon? If it gave her some crumb of comfort, then why not do it herself, she supposed.

All the same, she would have been a lot happier if Marcus Valentine had been doing it. He was much more experienced than she was, and more able to assess what else might be going on inside Georgie.

'OK,' she said. 'Please can you check in with the Gynaecology ward before 11 a.m. tomorrow. Don't eat anything after 8 a.m., and no fluids after 11 a.m. All clear on that?'

'Clear, thank you, Kath,' Georgie said, quietly.

90

As soon as Georgie had left, Kath Clow dialled Marcus Valentine's internal number. He answered on the first ring.

'It's Kath. Do you have five minutes?'

He hesitated. 'I'm due at a meeting – but yes, five minutes max. In your office?'

'In my office.'

'I'll be right there.'

He entered a brief while later, dressed in a dark suit. 'What's up?'

She ushered him to the chair Georgie had just vacated and sat opposite, looking intently at him. 'A couple of things. The first is I'm so terribly sad about Robert Resmes.'

'Me too,' he replied. 'I'm just devastated. Such a terrible waste. He was such a lovely, bright guy, with a big future ahead of him. I told him he had all the makings of a truly great doctor.'

His body language gave her nothing but genuine sadness.

'I didn't have the chance to know him as well as you did,' she said. 'But I had that impression, too – so did all the staff here.'

'They did.'

'Look, there's something I didn't want to tell you, Marcus, because I didn't want him to get into trouble for seeming disloyal to you.'

'Oh? What do you mean, Kath?' He smiled. 'Sounds rather cryptic.'

'Well, it doesn't matter now he's dead, poor man. Robert Resmes came to see me on Thursday and said he'd been assisting when you'd removed Roger Richardson's spleen.'

'Correct, he was.' He frowned. 'Came to see you?'

She hesitated. 'Look, this is difficult for me to say, but he told me he was sure that he had seen a tear in Roger Richardson's bowel, which you hadn't spotted.'

She saw the sudden fury in his face. 'Oh, for God's sake, Kath! He said the same thing to me. It was scar tissue from a previous exploratory op – probably years back. Utterly ridiculous! But I suppose an easy mistake for a student to make.'

'That's what I told him.'

'Good.'

'The other thing is that Georgie Maclean would rather I performed her termination.'

For an instant his face seemed to tighten, then relax again. 'Really? Yes, fine, if that would make her feel better – poor thing – I don't have a problem. I've frankly got a damned busy day over at Bon Sante.'

'Good, thank you, Marcus. Are you OK if I use the theatre time you've booked in for it?'

'Oh, absolutely, you might as well.'

'You're a star!'

He smiled. 'It's a pretty poor prognosis she has.'

'It is.'

'If I can give you one small piece of advice, Kath. I can see you care about this delightful lady. Don't let it get to you, OK?'

She nodded. 'Thank you.'

'We're a team, Kath. Any time, you know that.'

91

Monday 21 January

Marcus Valentine left Kath Clow's office and hurried down to the meeting of the hospital's oncology team. For the next hour he barely listened, contributing almost nothing. His mind was totally focused on tomorrow and on what he had just heard from the obstetrician.

It was too much of a risk to let the woman carry out the termination, in case of what she saw – or rather, didn't see. And he hadn't liked the way she was looking at him. Was it suspicion he'd seen in her expression?

So that little shit, Resmes, had shot his mouth off to her, and to who else?

He needed to resolve this mess, fast, to follow through the chain of events that he'd carefully planned.

While various PowerPoint images appeared on the screen in front of his assembled colleagues, he was preoccupied making mental notes. Slowly a revised plan was taking shape, haphazardly at first but steadily crystallizing into something that might work.

Would work.

Had to work.

Sometimes you had to be bold, make the biggest leaps to achieve the greatest victories.

He remembered Kath telling him, a while back, that her son – his godson – was being bullied at school. And that she was worried because Charlie had kept hinting that he was planning to take revenge on his tormentors, but refused to elaborate to her.

That had possibilities. He just needed to do a little detective work.

As soon as the meeting was over, he was due at his private consulting rooms. He asked his registrar to head on over and to tell his assistant to apologize to the private patients he had booked in and say that he would be there as soon as possible. Then he hurried up to his office. He was trying to remember the name of Charlie's school. He momentarily berated himself for not showing more of an interest over the years.

Seated at his desk, he logged on and clicked onto Kath Clow's Facebook page.

He began trawling through her posts. A recent photograph of her husband amid a flock of sheep at their house in the Lake District. A post of her in running gear, breaking the tape at a 10K event. Then one of her in cycling kit, standing next to her fair-haired son. Behind them were road bikes propped against a bridge wall, with a canal running through a pretty town in the background.

My boy Charlie and me on a bike ride around glorious Annecy last summer!

Marcus smiled. Why hadn't he thought of it? His godson was bound to have online profiles of his own.

He did.

It took only a couple of minutes to find him on Instagram, where he was a prolific poster.

The most recent post was of the boy, in rugby kit, lying horizontal in mud on a playing field. The caption read:

Scoring my third try of the game for GdL! Grève de Lecq School v Grouville Academy Under 10s.

Grève de Lecq School. He googled it.

The school had an active Facebook page. He trawled through the other links. Saw photographs of all the teachers with their mini bios beneath. Then a list of recent sporting achievements. There was a team photograph headed 'Under 10s Rugby Squad'.

Charlie sat surrounded by the team, holding the rugby ball.

He'd always been generous to his godson, giving him a lavish christening present, as well as generous birthday and Christmas gifts every year without fail. He'd not seen as much of him in recent years as perhaps he should have, and had he done so that might have been useful now, but hey-ho, onwards all the same.

Now, Charlie, now it's payback time. Your chance to do your godfather a little favour!

92

Monday 21 January

Seated at her kitchen table in silence, Georgie refilled her glass yet again. It didn't matter any more. She'd drunk the tiny drop of white that had been in the bottle in the fridge, and in the absence of anything else was now making inroads on a red. It was a bottle Roger had been saving for a special occasion. Well, hell, this was a special occasion. It was a special need.

She took a photograph of the label, making a mental note to try to replace it. She'd search online for an identical bottle tomorrow – hoping it wasn't going to be too crazily expensive.

'Cheers, my darling, here's to your recovery. Soon. Please!' She raised her glass.

Jesus.

There had been plenty of shit days in her life but, boy, this one topped the lot. This one was the doozy of doozies. She put the bottle down harder than she'd meant and it wobbled, nearly toppling over – she just grabbed it in time. Then stared at it, struggling to focus on the label: *Château Lafite, 1989.*

Must be past its sell-by date, she thought with a grin. What was the story with old wine, she wondered? When did someone realize it tasted better long past the date when any other product would have been binned? Thirty-year-old vintage tuna? How long could you keep cheese? Until it walked out of the kitchen?

I'm getting a little wasted. Probably shouldn't be drinking, having an anaesthetic in the morning, she knew, but she was beyond caring. *I'm a dead woman walking.*

I FOLLOW YOU

It was 11 p.m. Earlier, she'd done what she always did when she was upset, she'd put on her kit and run. And run. On her route she'd gone up to the Bel Royal Hotel, but there was still a police scene guard outside, and no one was allowed in. So, she'd carried on. Almost eight miles. But it hadn't made her feel any better. She'd moped around the house, unable to settle, then called Lucy, needing a friendly voice. They spoke on the phone for over an hour, mostly about Georgie, what she had to do. Lucy offered to come over and cook for her, but Georgie refused, needing time to herself. Lucy tried to cheer her friend up by telling her about some of her latest online and speed-dating exploits.

Despite them all being disasters, Lucy remained positive. There was someone out there for her, she only had to find him. *Just like you and Roger found each other*, she'd added.

When they ended the call, Georgie felt in a better place. But then, stupidly she knew, she googled cervical cancer again – undoing all the good of the last hour's conversation – and spent nearly two hours looking at images, reading forums, checking out alternative treatments. Then the dismissive reports of experts.

Sod experts.

Roger always had a healthy scepticism of experts. He had something he always trotted out whenever an expert was pontificating on television or in the papers about some matter of high importance. *On the day the world ends*, Roger would say, *the last sound anyone will hear will be the voice of an expert explaining why it could not happen.*

Then she'd started hitting the wine, thinking, what did it matter? Remembering the past warnings from Kath and the midwife when her pregnancy had been confirmed, that alcohol might harm her unborn baby. Oh yes, sure. She laughed silently, bitterly. Probably wouldn't harm it as much as an abortion, eh?

She reached out for her glass, then peered at it suspiciously, struggling to focus. It was empty.

Didn't I just fill it?

Reaching out for the bottle, this time she did knock it over. But nothing poured out. Just a few drops.

Shit.

She tried to stand, but didn't feel too confident about it, swaying and having to grab the table to steady herself. She sat back down, much harder than she had intended. Then she stared down, for the hundredth time tonight, at the printout of Kath Clow's scan of the tiny creature inside her, barely three centimetres long, that she and Roger had been given just before Christmas, a month ago. God, they'd been so happy then.

How big are you now? she wondered, tears rolling down her face.

Next to it sat the still-unopened envelope from Kath, containing the information on the baby's sex. Should she open it now?

And just feel even worse?

She ripped the envelope in half. Then in half again. Then tore all the bits of the envelope and the sheet of paper inside into smaller and smaller pieces. She scooped them up and dumped them in the bin, and sat back down again.

She'd hoped having a drink might numb some of the misery she was feeling, but it hadn't. It had made her feel even worse.

'I'm sorry,' she whispered. 'I'm so, so sorry.'

Her eyes felt leaden; her head gave up its struggle with gravity and sank down to the surface of the table. She rested her cheek on the hard, warm wood and in seconds was asleep.

For a brief while after she woke up, she stared around, confused. The clock was showing 2.55.

What?

Someone was poking a blowtorch around inside her head and she had a raging thirst. After downing two paracetamols with a glass of water she staggered, still unsteady, into the bedroom, pulled off her clothes, just remembered in time to set the alarm and crashed out again.

93

Tuesday 22 January

At 10.15 a.m., not sure if she should be driving after all she had drunk last night, Georgie cruised slowly along the lower level of the multistorey that was reserved for hospital patients and visitors, looking for a parking space. Before leaving home, she'd postponed her clients' appointments. She felt terrible, on the verge of throwing up at any moment. The blowtorch was still searing the insides of her head. Her hands were shaking. She had a bitter chill under her skin.

She was pregnant. Carrying her baby. Their baby. Hers and Roger's.

An expectant mother.

Her dream for years.

In a few hours she would no longer be an expectant mother.

From his mother's womb, untimely ripped.

The words popped into her head. Macduff? From *Macbeth*? She'd never been a big Shakespeare fan, but Macbeth was one play that had always fascinated her. Something about Lady Macbeth herself. So damned evil.

She wished now that she'd asked Lucy to come with her, but pride had stopped her. She'd thought she could deal with this. But as she reversed into a narrow slot, then switched the engine off, she was really struggling.

She patted her stomach. Wanting to give Bump some reassurance. But all she felt was guilt.

Her baby was in there. What did you say to a baby you were

about to abort? The baby she was going to kill so that she might have a chance of living – however good or meagre that chance was?

When she returned to her car, there would be nothing.

Already, she felt empty. Hollowed out.

Would Roger forgive her?

God, Roger, we need you so much.

Would she ever be able to forgive herself? To live with this?

She sat for some moments. A Billy Joel song was playing faintly in the background, on Radio Jersey.

For the longest time . . .

Roger loved Billy Joel. He wanted his music at their wedding. She loved him, too. Normally.

But not now. She turned the ignition off and the music died. She took the printout of the scan from her handbag and just sat staring at it, crying again. Finally, reluctantly, she replaced it and closed her bag.

As she climbed out of the car, paid for the parking on her app, then carried her overnight bag with slow, heavy steps towards the hospital, it felt that everything she loved had died.

94

Tuesday 22 January

With only a short amount of time to spare, Georgie went up to the ICU, to find out how Roger had been overnight, and was pleased that the duty critical care manager was Kiera Dale. Popping her head around the ward door, Kiera asked her to wait in the Relatives' Room and told her she'd be with her in a moment.

Five minutes later she came in, looking rushed. 'Sorry, we've got a couple of crises simultaneously. You're earlier than usual!'

'I'm going to be tied up all day – I just wanted to see how Roger's doing. Any change?'

To her dismay, the nurse was able to offer little to dispel her deepening despondency. 'Stable,' she said, nodding and slightly distant. 'Stable, which is good.'

'Stable?' Whenever Georgie had talked to her last week, the nurse had always looked and sounded positive. But her body language worried Georgie now. 'Stable and improving or stable and—?'

'Roger's still not improving – yet – but it's early days with his new meds.'

'Are there any positive signs at all, Kiera, or is he getting worse?'

Her pause gave Georgie the answer before she even spoke. 'He's still not progressing as we would hope,' she said, finally. 'Believe me, Georgie, I so want to be able to give you good news – the whole team does – and I'm sure that will be very soon now.'

Georgie locked eyes with her for an instant, before the nurse looked away, uncomfortable. 'You're sure?'

'I have to get back into the ward. But yes, I am sure. So, what are your plans for the day, anything interesting?'

'No,' she said, unable to hide the bitterness in her voice. 'Not exactly. I'm having an abortion.'

'What?' The nurse looked at her, truly shocked. 'An abortion?'

She nodded, wanly.

'Oh God, poor you, what's happened?'

'I have stage-2 cervical cancer, a particularly aggressive tumour, apparently.'

'When was that diagnosed? How long have you known?'

'Since yesterday.'

'Diagnosed yesterday? Oh no, Georgie, I'm so, so sorry. Did you have any inkling? Symptoms?'

'I had some stage-1 pre-cancerous tissue about eighteen months ago. That was removed and Kath Clow was pretty sure I was clear. It seems not. She wants me to start chemo-radiation at the Royal Marsden next week.' She folded her arms, protectively, across her midriff, then shrugged. 'I don't have much option about my baby.'

Kiera was shaking her head in disbelief. 'You poor thing. You have Roger in here and now this?'

'Yep, well, at least I'll be getting plenty of hospital loyalty card points,' she joked, thinly.

The nurse grimaced. 'I'm really sorry for you. Look – if there's anything – anything at all I can do, please tell me.'

'Maybe you could find a magic wand and wave it and make Roger and me both back to how we were.'

'I wish I could.' She glanced down at her watch. 'I'll have to go – if Roger comes round, I presume you don't want me to say anything to him?'

Georgie shook her head. 'Thank you,' she whispered.

After the nurse had left, Georgie had a few minutes before she was due to report at the ward. She sat down on a chair, thinking again as she had done a thousand times. Why wasn't Roger improving? He was a fit man and from all she knew about his past, he'd always been healthy. Sepsis was a word she'd never heard of until a few years ago, and now it seemed to be constantly in the news. But if his blood was being poisoned by something, how come all these damned experts weren't able to figure it out?

She glanced at her watch. It was time.

She stood up, sick with nerves, and clasped her hands around her stomach again. Whispering, she said, 'I'm sorry, I'm truly sorry.'

As she made her way to Gynaecology, feeling like a condemned prisoner, her pace became slower the nearer she approached. She was almost shuffling as she reached the entrance to the section and approached the reception desk. A woman in large glasses and a brisk, friendly manner greeted her. 'Hello, can I help you?'

Georgie struggled to get any words out, as if her voice was refusing to work. Finally, barely above a whisper, she croaked out her name.

The clerk checked down a list, frowned for an instant then looked up, smiling. 'Georgina Maclean?'

She nodded.

'OK, I need you to fill in this medical history form.' She pointed at a couple of chairs. 'If you take a seat, a nurse will be along to take you into your room – you are in 216. Then Dr Clow will come and see you in a while and have a chat with you about what's going to happen and get you to sign a consent form.'

Georgie thanked her, took the form and a pen, went over and sat down, then stared at the words on it. They were blurred in her shaking hands and she couldn't read them. She was cold, so cold.

'Georgina Maclean?' A warm Irish accent.

She looked up bleakly and saw a short, grey-haired woman in her early fifties standing in front of her. Her name badge read LAURA O'KEEFE, STAFF NURSE.

'Yes.'

'I'll be looking after you until you go into theatre, and I'll be in the recovery room when you come round.' She smiled and a tiny amount of the edge came off Georgie's nerves.

'Thank you.'

'I'll take you to your room – you can fill the forms in there and afterwards get changed.'

They walked a short distance along a corridor, then the nurse opened a door and Georgie followed her in.

'I'm afraid I can't get you anything at all now to eat or drink, but you can make up for it after.'

'Perhaps a large whisky?'

'Only one?'

Georgie managed a weak smile.

95

Ten minutes later, Georgie sat alone on the edge of the hospital bed in the small, bland room. There was a clock on the wall, showing 11.15 a.m., a television on an extender arm, an array of equipment and different-shaped electrical sockets, and a single hard chair, on which she had put her overnight holdall. To her left was a door to an en-suite bathroom, and to her right a window giving a view of an ugly cluster of buildings and the hospital's incinerator chimney stack. There was a cold draught and, in keeping with her mood, the sky was clouding over.

She concentrated on the forms, ticking questions about her medical history and filling in some details where requested. Nurse O'Keefe reappeared just as she finished, with a gown and slippers. She took her blood pressure and temperature, and put a band on her wrist. Dr Clow would be along soon, she told Georgie, and the anaesthetist would be coming in as well to offer her a pre-med to relax her. The nurse asked her to go into the bathroom to change and she would wait to settle her in the bed.

A few minutes later, changed into the flimsy gown, Georgie lay on the bed and Nurse O'Keefe cranked it until she was lying semi-recumbent. Would she like anything to read, she asked – any magazines? Georgie thanked her and shook her head. 'I just can't believe this is happening,' she said.

The nurse put a hand on her shoulder and smiled, sympathetically. 'You're in the best hands here. We all understand and we're looking after you.'

She thanked her again, softly.

The nurse picked up the forms, glanced through them and left, saying she would pop back in a little while. She closed the door.

Georgie was alone. Alone with her thoughts. So weird that she and Roger were both in this building. Maybe one day they would laugh about it. Maybe. She doubted it. At this moment, she could not see herself ever laughing again.

Her phone made a sharp *ting* and she saw there was a Whats-App message from Lucy.

Hey my lovely, hope it's all going OK. Thinking of you and sending love and hugs and thoughts. Call me later when you can. In a nightmare of a queue in town, oh I love the post office. xxxxxx

She smiled, then tried to compose a reply. But she couldn't get her brain enough into gear to come up with anything witty. Instead she just replied:

In a room with a lovely view – of the hospital incinerator chimney. Would rather be in your queue! xxx

She opened the Podcasts app on her phone, but there was nothing in her library she was in any mood to listen to. Half an hour passed. An hour. No Kath Clow, no anaesthetist, no Nurse O'Keefe. Had they forgotten about her, she wondered? She had never, in all her life, felt so alone. And scared.

Her nerves were as tight as violin strings. Taking the scanned image from her bag again, she laid it in front of her. Clasping her hands around her stomach, she whispered, 'I'm sorry, Bump. I'm so, so sorry. I'll spend the rest of my life wondering about you and what you would have done with your life. I know you'd have been a good person. Your father and I would have loved you, we'd have been the best parents ever.'

A short while later there was a knock on the door and an energetic, purposeful-looking man in scrubs, whose face reminded Georgie of the actor Ralph Fiennes, came in, holding a paper cup in his hand. He looked hesitant. 'Hello, Georgina Maclean, yes?'

'Yes.'

'I'm Tony Le Moignan, your anaesthetist. How are you feeling?' He sounded as if he really did care how she was feeling.

'Pretty shit, actually. Nervous as hell. I've signed up to kill my baby to save myself. I keep thinking how selfish this is.'

'Understandably. Poor you – not a great thing to have to go through.'

'Nope.'

'I've read through your notes and see you have no other medical problems or allergies, is that correct?'

'Yes.'

'I'm going to anaesthetize you and look after you during your surgery today. You're not on any other medications and you don't smoke, nothing to eat or drink today?'

She shook her head.

'Would you like something that will help relax you? It's a very mild sedative – OK?'

'OK, I guess,' she said forlornly. 'Sure.'

He wrote on her medication chart to have a sedative immediately.

'If you hold out your hand.'

Georgie complied and he tipped a tiny pill into her cupped palm. 'Just swallow this.'

Putting it in her mouth, she picked up the cup, which contained a small amount of water, and downed it as he watched.

'All done?'

She nodded.

'Good! I'll see you again in a little while.'

'Thank you,' she said.

Then she was alone again.

An hour later, at ten past two, she was feeling drowsy and much calmer – and her hangover had gone. She barely heard the knock on the door. Then Kath Clow, in a smart two-piece, was standing in front of her, all smiles.

'How're you doing, Georgie?'

'All right, I guess.' She was glad to see her.

'I'm just off to gown up. They'll be taking you through into the anaesthetics room in a short while. You're still OK to go through with this?'

'Do I have any choice?'

'It's for the best, it really is.'

'Yup.'

'I'll come and see you again in the recovery room in a while and let you know how it's all gone.'

Georgie held out a hand and the obstetrician took it, squeezing gently.

'You're a brave person.'

She shook her head. 'If I was really brave, I'd tell you to go to hell and tough it out.'

Clow smiled. 'No. What you are doing is brave. Trust me.'

96

At a quarter to three, Georgie was woken from a muzzy haze by two people coming into the room, Nurse O'Keefe and a lean man in his thirties in blue pyjamas.

She looked at them, drowsily.

'All set, Georgie?' the nurse said.

'Rock and roll.'

She felt nicely woozy as she was lifted out of the bed and onto a trolley of some kind. The ceiling above her began to move. She saw a door frame, felt the vibration of motion. Travelling along a corridor, a row of chairs slid past, a noticeboard, a hand sanitizer fixed to a wall, a caged trolley, then a yellow lift sign.

It was all quite pleasant, really. Quite jolly.

They were going up in a lift. Or was it down?

Steel doors opened and they were trundling again. Into a room filled with apparatus. Tubes, wires, monitors. The motion stopped. She saw a face peering down at her. A familiar face. Ralph Fiennes.

'Hello, Georgina,' he said. 'How are you feeling? Relaxed?'

'A bit smashed!'

He smiled.

She felt something on her wrist. Saw another face, a woman in scrubs she'd not seen before, who was looking serious, too serious. Georgie wanted to tell her to chill. Relax. Take a pill. Take one like she had!

'I'm going to send you to sleep, Georgie,' Ralph Fiennes said. 'When you wake up, it will all be over and you'll be fine!'

'I'll be fine.'

She felt something in her left hand; it stung a bit. Her arm felt as if it was filling with fluid. An oxygen mask was placed over her nose and mouth.

Then, seconds before she fell asleep, she saw another face. It sucked all the light from the room. Leaning down over her, smiling.

'Hello, Georgie,' Marcus Valentine said. 'I just popped in to reassure you, you're in the best possible hands.'

97

Tuesday 22 January

As Kath Clow, followed by a new registrar, an immensely courteous medic, Neil Wakeling, entered the Anaesthetics room, Marcus Valentine, also in scrubs, emerged.

She looked at him in surprise. 'Hello, Marcus – I thought you weren't operating today?'

'I wasn't, Kath, but I had an emergency.'

'OK, right.'

'You're doing the termination on Georgina Maclean?'

'I am, yes.'

'So sad, terrible. Unbelievable, really – talk about a jinxed couple.'

'How's her other half doing?'

He shook his head, with a sad expression. 'Not good, really not good at all. As you well know, sometimes, when sepsis gets its grip, it doesn't matter what we do. But the whole team's trying its hardest to pull Roger round – and I'm on it.'

Clow and her registrar walked through into the operating theatre. Tony Le Moignan, the anaesthetist, in his scrubs and bright-red shoes, along with two nurses and an operating department practitioner, were standing by Georgie Maclean, who was unconscious and swathed up to her neck in green cloth, brightly lit by the overhead theatre lights.

They went across to the scrub recess and in turn washed and dried their hands, then held them out for gloving-up, before walking over to the table.

Kath Clow still had a feeling of deep unease that would not go away. She was about to terminate Georgie Maclean's baby, and knew the emotional devastation to the woman it would cause. But all the medical evidence pointed to this being the right decision, Georgie's only option.

'Neil,' she said, 'we need to catheterize her. I'd like you to do it, but also do a vaginal examination with your fingers. I want you to tell me what you think – if you can feel any traces of the cancer.'

'Yes, of course.'

Kath stood whilst Neil, studious, carried out his examination. When he had finished, he turned to her and she could see the surprise in his eyes above his mask. He shook his head.

'I'm sorry, Dr Clow, but it seems to me she has a perfectly normal cervix. It's really odd because it's showing on the MRI scan report, but I can't feel anything that might be cancer.'

'No?'

'I can't feel anything abnormal at all.'

She stepped forward. 'I'll take a look myself.'

At that moment a scrub nurse called her name. She turned.

'Dr Clow, someone needs to speak to you urgently.'

Wakeling pointed and she turned and recognized one of the hospital receptionists, Madge, standing in the doorway.

She hurried over.

'Dr Clow, I'm so sorry to disturb you, but I've just had a phone call from your son's school.'

'What?'

'There's been an incident. The school said they need to see you or your husband immediately, otherwise they're going to be obliged to call the police.'

'What incident? I – I mean – what did they say?'

'That's all. It sounded really quite serious.'

'Is Charlie all right, Madge, did they say? Is he hurt?'

'It didn't sound as if he was hurt, Dr Clow. But they need you or your husband there very urgently. They didn't say much, just that they'd explain it all once either of you got there.'

Kath's mind was in free-fall. An *incident*? What kind of incident? She thought, terrified, about all the school shootings that had happened around the world – that kind of incident? Or something totally different?

They wanted to see her or Bob immediately or else they would call the police. Christ, what had Charlie done? Had he got into a fight? Unlikely, that just wasn't him. A weapon? What? What the hell had happened? Police?

'My husband's in England, up in the Lake District at our farm there,' she said, feeling hollowed out. *God. Please let him be OK.* 'Thank you, I'll be there as quickly as I can.'

She tried to think clearly. She had to get over to the school. But Georgie was all prepped for the hysterotomy. And now Neil Wakeling was telling her that he felt her cervix seemed normal.

Wakeling was standing right behind her. She turned to him. 'Neil, I'm going to have to go – you're capable of carrying out the procedure yourself.'

'Well, yes, I could.' He sounded hesitant.

She was desperate to run down to the car park and get over to the other side of the island to Charlie's school. But she had to be sure about Georgie, she owed her more than just duty of care. 'No, wait, actually, I want you to hold off, Neil, until we've had another opinion from a consultant, before doing anything. I'm really not happy.'

Her deputy on-call colleague this week was Maria Dowell and she was solid. Was she in the building? 'Neil, call Maria and see if she could come into theatre. If she has any doubts at all – absolutely any doubt – you don't go ahead, and we'll do more tests on Georgie. Understood?'

'Absolutely, Dr Clow.'

Then she remembered. 'Oh – on second thoughts – Marcus Valentine is probably still here. He might be changing – see if you can get him.'

98

Kath changed hurriedly back into her two-piece, fleetingly checked her face and hair in the mirror, then ran along the corridor, down the stairs and into the hospital's staff car park. She climbed into her battered Subaru workhorse, anxiety gnawing her insides, drove to the end of the street and waited impatiently for someone to let her out or for the lights to change.

A Jersey Post van flashed its lights, slowing politely for her, and she turned right, accelerating hard down past the Opera House to the lights at the junction with Victoria Avenue. As soon as they changed, she headed west along the avenue, oblivious to the view of the bay, to her left, that she normally loved.

Charlie. What's happened? What on earth has happened? What could have happened?

He was such a good boy, hardworking and passionate about his sport. What kind of trouble could he possibly be in? Something so serious they were threatening to involve the police. Was it those bullies? Oh God. Had he done something stupid to get at them?

On top of that she was deeply worried about Georgie. Hopefully, by now, Neil would have found Marcus Valentine and got him into the theatre for his opinion.

Vehicles were slowing in front of her. There was trouble ahead. The traffic backing up. Blue lights in her mirror. A fire engine raced past, then an ambulance and a police motorbike, all with sirens wailing. Cars and vans were trying to move out of their way, some driving up onto the pavement to create a path as the emergency vehicles somehow squeezed through. Then the gap closed up.

And everything stopped.

Gridlock.

Kath sat, desperate for it to start moving, desperate for any sign it might start moving. She switched on Radio Jersey to see if there was any information about what was happening and heard the voice of Cathy Le Feuvre interviewing what sounded like a gardening expert.

She looked around for any possible escape, but she already knew that was pointless. She was trapped on a dual carriageway with a hard divide making it impossible to do a U-turn. The first junction was several hundred yards ahead, and at this rate she had no idea when she would reach it. Ten minutes? An hour?

Oh God, oh God, oh God.

Pulling her phone from her handbag, she stuck it in the hands-free cradle and tried to call Charlie but got no answer. Next, she called the school to speak to someone there – see if she could get the headmaster. She found the number and dialled.

After a few rings it was answered by an efficient-sounding female voice. 'Grève de Lecq School.'

'Oh – yes – hello. This is Dr Clow, I had an urgent phone message about my son, Charlie, who is a pupil with you. Charlie Clow.'

'Dr Clow? Who would you like to speak to?'

'I had a message that there'd been some kind of an incident at the school and I needed to get there right away. I'm on my way but I'm stuck in traffic – I think there's an accident ahead. I just need to let someone know I'm on my way and I'll be there as soon as I can.'

The woman sounded puzzled. 'I'm sorry, did you say an *incident*?'

'That was the message, yes.'

'I'm not aware of any incident here, Dr Clow. When did you get this message?'

'About ten, fifteen minutes ago.'

'Your son is Charlie?'

'Yes, Charlie Clow, in Grade Four.'

'Can you hold the line?'

'Sure, yes.'

Kath frowned. What did the woman mean, she wasn't aware of any incident?

Several minutes passed. Another emergency vehicle was battling through the long line of traffic that had built up behind her. Still nothing moved in front of her. The phone was silent and she was just starting to wonder whether she'd been cut off when the woman came back on.

'I'm really sorry, Dr Clow, this is a mystery. Your son is out in the school grounds playing rugby. I've spoken to several people, including just now the headmaster – and no one knows anything about an *incident*. Everything is fine here. Are you sure you're not mistaken?'

Kath stared at the phone, bewildered. 'I'm not – not mistaken. No. I – there was a message left at the hospital switchboard for me to go to the school urgently. That my son was involved in some incident and you were going to call the police otherwise.'

'I'm afraid this sounds like it might be some kind of wind-up. Everything is fine here, I can assure you.'

The siren behind her was coming closer. Still nothing moved ahead. 'I – I don't understand.'

'You don't know who might have left this message?'

'No, I got called out of an operating theatre by a switchboard operator.'

'There must be some mistake.'

'There – there must be,' Kath said. 'I'm sorry to have troubled you.'

'Do call back if you find out anything – but I can assure you, everything is fine here.'

Kath thanked her and ended the call. Then sat in silence. What was going on?

She called up the main hospital number and rang it. When the operator answered, she asked to speak to Madge.

'This is Madge.'

'Hi, Madge, it's Dr Clow. The call you took earlier from my son's school, saying there was an incident – would you be able to tell me where that call came from – what number?'

'Yes, with our rather fancy new equipment, I might be able to – so long as it wasn't from a withheld number. Would you like me to have a look for you?'

'Very urgently.'

'Is everything all right?'

'No, it's not, not in any way all right.'

'Give me a couple of minutes and I'll call you back. I have your number on my screen.' She read Kath's mobile number back to her, to be sure.

'That's it.'

'I'll be as quick as I can!'

Kath sat. Vehicles in front of her were crawling forward. The car directly in front moved over on the pavement and she followed. An ambulance, siren wailing, squeezed past, almost taking off her wing mirror but she barely noticed.

Who could have made the call? Why?

Her phone rang and she answered instantly.

'It's Madge. Rather odd this – the call was made from the internal phone extension in Mr Valentine's office.'

'Mr Valentine? Our Mr Valentine? Mr Valentine's office?'

'Yes, that's right.'

'You're certain?'

'Oh yes, absolutely certain.'

'Thank you.'

Kath ended the call. Had Marcus Valentine really made that call? Why on earth?

Then a lead weight dropped through her.

She was thinking hard, fast. Remembering Marcus's strange

reaction yesterday when she'd told him that Georgie wanted her, not him, to do the hysterotomy. The flash of anger in his face. What was that about?

Something else didn't make sense either, she realized. Why had he been in the hospital today, gowned up, when he'd told her he was going to be in his private Bon Sante consulting rooms all day?

Fear threaded through her. The sense that something was very wrong. She thought about the uneasy phone call she'd had on Saturday with the pathologist, Nigel Kirkham, who was in England to attend his son's wedding.

I'm not questioning your methodology, Nigel. I'm having my patient do an MRI scan today, which will clarify things more. I'm just wondering if there could have been a mistake on the labelling, somehow. Who actually brought the jar containing the tissue sample to you?

And his answer.

Marcus Valentine.

Marcus had carried the tissue samples from her colposcopy examination of Georgie down to the lab, along with a bunch of others, in their little vials. It was pretty unusual for a consultant to run a menial errand like that. So why had he? To tamper with them?

That must be it.

Her thoughts became even darker as she went back again in her mind to Saturday morning, when she'd spoken to Marcus on the phone.

I'll be at home most of the weekend, but if you need me, I'd be more than happy to come in and go through the result with you, Kath. Just call me any time, as soon as you've got it – no problem at all, that's what I'm here for.

But Marcus hadn't been at home. He had been with the young radiologist, Ana Gomes, helping her interpret Georgie's scan images. Except, she'd not asked Marcus to do that, she'd only asked him if he might be able to help her if needed.

Why had he gone in?

She felt a rush of blood to her head.

Then she thought about poor Robert Resmes. Telling her his concerns that Marcus had missed a tear in Roger Richardson's bowel.

And now Resmes was dead.

She and Valentine had had a drink after work one evening about six months or so ago. More than one drink, in fact. Marcus had got quite smashed. He'd confessed to her then that his marriage was becoming rocky. And he'd surprised her, for a man who'd made his career in obstetrics, with a sudden bitter rant about children. He'd told her how he'd used a line from a writer – she couldn't remember who – to console a twenty-four-year-old woman whose cancerous womb he'd had to remove.

That great enemy of promise: the pram in the hallway.

She'd always been dismissive of any rumours about Marcus's behaviour because she'd seen just how good a consultant he was. He was godfather to her son. A good and generous friend. This just could not be. But why was Georgie so adamant she didn't want him performing an operation on her?

How could it be even remotely possible that Marcus Valentine had an agenda of his own? Had she been blind to it? Why would he have made that phone call about Charlie? There was only one possible reason.

To get her out of the operating theatre. How dare he use her son – his godson – as a decoy.

A deeply disturbing thought occurred to her. She'd asked Neil to get Marcus's opinion.

Jesus.

Frantically, she hit the number for the hospital switchboard, which she had dialled earlier. Madge answered.

'It's Dr Clow again,' she said.

'Yes, how can I help you?'

'Madge, this is really, really urgent. Operating Theatre Five. Life and death. Get security up there now. Tell them to stop any attempted procedure on the patient in there, Georgina Maclean. This is really urgent. Can you do that?'

She sounded hesitant. 'Well – yes – I suppose.'

'Please believe me, Madge, this is a real emergency. I don't care what they have to do, but they have to stop anything from happening until I get there, they have to stop Georgina Maclean's abortion from proceeding. Get them to speak to my registrar, Dr Wakeling. OK? Operating Theatre Five. I'm on my way now, but it's going to take me time. Tell him he has to stop the operation, there's been a misdiagnosis. You've got to help me, please – this is really critical.'

Grabbing her phone from the cradle, Kath turned off the engine, leaving the keys behind, jumped out of her car, oblivious to the strange look from a man in a Mercedes behind her, and began to run. She weaved through the stationary vehicles, darted across the far side of the carriageway, right across the path of a lorry, and onto the safety of the pavement in front of the Grand Hotel, then up the side street beside it, breaking into a full-on sprint, stopping as one of her court shoes came off.

Jamming it back on her foot, she sprinted again, dodging around a couple pushing a baby in a buggy. Holding her phone out in front of her, she found the Favourites on her contacts list, then a name, Alberto Pinto, and held the phone to her ear as she ran. The hospital's in-house geek, who had recently installed her new computer, answered almost immediately.

'Kath, hello, how are you?' he said in his broken English accent.

'Listen, Alberto, this is an emergency. Could you do something for me urgently?' she gasped, breathlessly. 'You have my password?'

'Yes.'

'If you log on to my computer – would you be able to tell me if anyone else has been logging into it?'

'Yes, sure.'

'I need to know really urgently.'

'I've one job to finish, I could do it first thing tomorrow.'

'No!' She raised her voice. 'No, tomorrow's no good, I need you to do it now, this second – it could save someone's life, Alberto. How quickly could you do it?' She tripped on a paving stone and stumbled. The phone flew from her hands and tumbled into the road.

Shit.

She knelt and grabbed it. To her relief the glass was intact. 'Sorry, Alberto, I missed what you said.'

'Five minutes. It'll take me seconds to have a look once I'm there. I'll be there in five minutes.'

'Five's too long, you've got three.'

Disconnecting, she stabbed out 999.

99

Marcus Valentine had just changed back into his suit when Neil Wakeling hurried, apologetically, into the changing room. He explained to Valentine that, despite all the affirmative tests, Dr Clow had asked him to carry out a last-minute internal examination on Georgina Maclean, prior to commencing the hysterotomy. He had carried this out and could find no traces of cancer at all. But she had asked him to see if Mr Valentine, with his specialist oncology experience, would mind coming to theatre to give his opinion on whether the lady had cancer of the cervix or not.

Ten minutes later, gowned, scrubbed and gloved, Valentine strode across the theatre floor and carried out his internal examination of the unconscious Georgina Maclean. He gave a slow, precise commentary as he did so, mostly for the benefit of the registrar but also for the rest of the operating theatre team.

'I'm feeling a number of lumps, almost like, as were present on the scans, baby cauliflowers. No question at all, absolutely none, this lady is presenting advanced cancer of the cervix. Stage-2. I have no hesitation in saying she needs immediate chemo-radiation treatment, which means the hysterotomy must proceed.' He looked at the registrar. 'I don't know how you could have missed this, young man. Do you understand how dangerous to this lady's life a misdiagnosis could have been? The best chance for survival is always an early diagnosis, you would do well to remember that for your future career.'

Looking suitably chastised, Neil Wakeling said, 'Thank you, Mr Valentine. I am very indebted to you.'

Valentine shook his head. 'It's not you who's indebted, it is this lady here. Take this as a lesson. With your assessment there could have been a very different outcome. Do you understand?'

'Thank you again.'

Valentine looked down, lovingly, at Georgie's face, before he turned to the anaesthetist. 'OK, since I'm here, I'll step in and perform the hysterotomy myself.' He looked at the registrar. 'No offence.'

'Oh no, sir, not at all, I would be very grateful to observe you – and assist in any way.'

'Good. Right, Neil, I need music – Van Morrison. I never operate without music. Let's start with "Queen of the Slipstream".'

As Wakeling hurried off to comply, and with no other eyes on him, Marcus Valentine looked down at Georgie's face and stroked it. Even with an oxygen mask across her nose and mouth she looked serene. So incredibly beautiful.

Not long now, my love. You'll be free of that pilot appendage to your life and that thing inside you. You may not know it at this moment, but one day soon you will be so grateful to me, the surgeon who saved you from the baby that was going to kill you! Because in the process, thanks to his immense skills, he was able to excise the cancer cells, as well. And now, boom boom, they're all gone. No need for horrible weeks of chemo-radiation any more. You'll have your life back.

Just how grateful to me will you be?

He heard music start to play. Van Morrison. Yes! He thought about the words, staring down at her face.

You're my queen of the slipstream . . .

Valentine reached over to the instrument table and picked up a scalpel. He held it with a flourish. And for a brief moment, silently to himself, sang along to the lyrics.

All attention was now on him. He was the king, the master of his universe. Oh yes!

He turned to a nurse, asking her to swab Georgie's belly,

watching while she applied a brush with the brown antiseptic liquid across the exposed flesh. One day soon he would be kissing that skin. Kissing her bare tummy all over. Kissing her little scar, so fine, no one would notice it. That was another of his skills, his delicate touch.

When the nurse had finished, Valentine announced, theatrically as always, 'Knife to skin!'

He pressed the razor-sharp blade to Georgie's abdomen and slowly, crunching it through the skin and the muscle tissue beneath, sliced down her abdomen, the blade chased by a ribbon of blood. Just as he reached the end of the incision, he was startled by the sound of the theatre doors crashing open. He looked up.

Kath Clow stood there in her day clothes, perspiring heavily, accompanied by a security guard.

'Stop! Marcus! Stop!' she yelled. She saw Neil Wakeling looking at her in astonishment, and the eyes of all the rest of the team frozen on her.

'Have you gone mad, Kath? Get out of here.' Addressing his team, imperiously, Valentine commanded, 'I will not have this – get that woman out of here at once. This is a sterile environment, she is contaminating my theatre and putting my patient at serious risk!'

'I don't think so, Marcus.' She walked across towards him, followed by a security guard, and then a second who came running in, panting. 'Put that scalpel down!' she demanded.

'Guards, I am the senior consultant in this theatre – I'm ordering you to get that woman out of here now, she's gone mad! She has no right and no authority in this procedure, do you understand me? I'm ordering you to remove her this instant.'

The guards looked uncertainly at Valentine, then Clow, then Valentine.

'Disobey me and I'll have you both fired on the spot for contaminating this theatre!' His voice rose to a bellow.

Kath Clow put out a hand to stop the guards. 'There's only one thing contaminating this theatre, Marcus. Would you like to explain to everyone why you made a phone call to the switchboard, half an hour ago, pretending to be a teacher at my son's school, saying there was an emergency? Can you explain to everyone in here why you wanted me out of this theatre? Was it so you could abort the perfectly healthy foetus of a perfectly healthy woman, pretending she has cancer? Just how sick are you?'

There was a moment of complete silence. He took a step towards her, placing the scalpel down on the tray, as two scrub nurses staunched the bleeding, eyes wide in disbelief, but clinical professionalism on autopilot.

In a flash, all smiles, he turned on the charm. 'Kath, this is ridiculous, come on. This operation has to proceed to save this woman's life. I don't know what's going on, there's clearly someone very mischievous at work here.'

'There is, Marcus,' she said calmly, holding her ground. 'And it's you. You've logged on to my computer nine times in the past week, without my knowledge, and you've tampered with this patient's records. That's a criminal offence. But I've also a suspicion you've committed a much bigger offence, even, than this.'

'Kath!' He was still feigning complete innocence, continuing the charm offensive. 'Kath, come on, we're colleagues and good friends – has someone been poisoning you against me? What on earth are you implying?'

'Poisoning me? You mean, like the way you're poisoning Roger Richardson? Now get out of this theatre.' She took a threatening step towards him.

As she did so, Marcus grabbed the scalpel back off the tray and held it out, brandishing it like a dagger. 'Get back, you mad woman, and get the hell out of my theatre. This is an outrage. I'll have you bloody struck off for this.' He glared at the guards. 'Get this woman the fuck out NOW! This operation to save my patient's life is continuing. Do you hear me? Remove her immediately.' He took another step towards Kath, nodding at the guards. 'Do you know who I am? I'm Marcus Valentine and I'm the senior doctor in this room. Do what I say immediately or I'll have you both fired. I call the shots in my theatre and this operation is continuing.'

The two guards hesitated.

'Don't listen to him,' Kath Clow urged. 'This man's a monster.'

Waving the scalpel, threatening, staring wildly in every direction, Valentine stepped back and commanded the scrub nurses to apply clamps. 'I'm in charge here,' he shouted, his voice close to hysterical. 'This operation is continuing.' He looked at the hesitant nurses. 'CLAMPS!'

Kath took a step towards him and he lunged at her with the scalpel. 'Get away, I'm warning you.'

She took a reluctant step back. 'Marcus! Stop this. Please! Stop this!' Then she raised her voice to a shout. 'Everyone, listen, this patient does not have cancer!'

Valentine turned to the two scrub nurses who were standing, paralysed by confusion. 'Clamps, do what I say, CLAMPS! This operation is continuing!'

As they began to clamp the cut skin back, a new voice called out from the doorway. 'Marcus, stop immediately! This operation has to cease!'

It was the hospital director, Anthony Maitland.

'Don't listen to her, she's out of her mind!' Marcus shouted back. He leaned over Georgie's abdomen and Kath could see he was about to plunge the scalpel in.

She launched herself at him, oblivious to any danger from his blade, striking him head-first in the ribs, unbalancing him and sending him, arms flailing, crashing to the hard floor, the scalpel skittering away out of his hand. An instant later the two security guards were on top of him, pinning him down.

'You idiots!' he gasped. 'Don't you know what you're doing?'

Kath stood over him. 'Yes, Marcus, we do. We know exactly what we're doing. Just in time, eh?'

100

Sunday 8 March

Spring had come early to Jersey this year – although on this glorious March morning it felt more like a summer's day on the island. For the past week the temperature had hovered around 19 degrees Celsius and yesterday's front-page splash in the *Jersey Evening Post* had screamed about global warming.

But the happy couple pushing their baby daughter, in her smart pram, along the Victoria Avenue promenade weren't worried about that, or anything much today. They were just enjoying the moment, as was Kathy Lucy Richardson. Eyes wide open, reaching out a tiny hand, she was spinning one of the brightly coloured plastic discs in front of her.

And Georgie was enjoying finally having closure.

There had been a different headline in the *Jersey Evening Post* two months ago.

TOP ISLAND CONSULTANT GUILTY OF MURDER

Followed by another just two weeks ago, after Marcus Valentine's second trial.

ISLAND OBSTETRICIAN SENTENCED TO 36 YEARS

Georgie and Roger had been called as prosecution witnesses, and on all the other days had been in the public gallery for both of Marcus Valentine's trials. They had felt a deep need for closure on the man who had so very nearly destroyed their lives. She had been surprised, when the first jury came back with their guilty verdict on the murder of Robert Resmes, that she hadn't felt much emotion. It was the verdict in the second trial, of the attempted attack on her and their unborn baby, that really hit her, making her sob loudly and uncontrollably in the public gallery while Roger squeezed her hand. It was the realization of just how close Valentine had come. If it hadn't been for the quick thinking and incredible bravery of Kath Clow, this little miracle in the pram, who had brought so much light and joy into their lives, would have died in the operating theatre on that day in January, last year.

Claire Valentine had been in court every day, too, also sitting up in the packed public gallery, accompanied by someone who looked like she might be her sister. She'd acknowledged Georgie and Roger on the first day with a bleak smile and seemed about to say something but then didn't. With every day of the trial she had looked increasingly hurt, upset and more pale, frequently closing her eyes and shaking her head. In disbelief? Shock? Or numb acceptance that the man she had married was a monster?

She had looked particularly bleak when a witness statement from Marcus Valentine's former wife, Elaine, had been read out, stating how he had bullied her and that she had always believed, when she had fallen pregnant, much to his anger, that he had given her something to cause her to miscarry.

At one point, Claire had been called by the defence to give a character reference for her husband. She stood in the witness box and the statement she made, to everyone's astonishment, was as damning as the worst of any of the evidence. 'I know you are expecting me as the dutiful wife to say good things about my husband. That he is a loving father, a brilliant and caring surgeon, and a generous benefactor to local charities. But I can't. I can't. Yes, for a long time I've had my doubts, but he is the father of my children. Our relationship was becoming troubled, but it's only when I have sat here in this court, listening to everything that has been said about Marcus, that I realize how badly he has needed help, for so many years. I'm so sorry for all those people he has hurt—' Then she broke down in tears.

The judge had ordered a recess for fifteen minutes.

The man in the dock was a far cry from the assured charmer Georgie had sat next to at his and Claire's dinner party less than eighteen months ago. He looked broken and had aged twenty years. The same prosecutor in both trials had been brilliant. Brutal. And justified. At no time did she feel remotely sorry for Valentine. Not even after learning about his horrific upbringing, which his defence barrister had detailed over two full days in the first trial, and had repeated in the second.

The judge had adjourned sentencing, awaiting the outcome at the end of the second trial, and then pending psychiatric reports. Finally, that sentence had been delivered this past Friday morning.

Valentine would never again be a danger to any patient. He had been struck off the medical register immediately following the first verdict. Georgie had sat in the public gallery, watching the judge address him on Friday. In a voice laden with contempt and barely restrained anger, he had passed sentence:

'Marcus Valentine, please stand. You have been found guilty of murder at trial, and of attempted murder and of grave and criminal assaults. As you know, the sentence for murder is life, and under our law we have to set a mandatory minimum period for you to serve. The murder was aggravated by the fact that you did so to avoid the consequences of your previous actions. Were you being sentenced for that offence alone, a mandatory minimum period of twenty-seven years would, the Court feels, be appropriate.

'But the count of murder does not stand alone. You have also been found guilty of these additional crimes. You attempted to destroy an unborn baby and you committed a grave and criminal assault on the baby's father by your deliberate neglect. Usually grave and criminal assaults attract a far lower sentence than we are going to hand down today. But in the court's experience, this is the most

serious case we have ever encountered. You abused the trust not only
of a patient, but of the health service and your colleagues, for purely
selfish ends. The consequences, had you not been thwarted, are almost
too awful to contemplate. It was the most evil of plans.

'*We have heard from your defence counsel about your childhood,*
in which you were undoubtedly deprived of the love and affection
that is the duty of care all parents owe to their offspring. There are
many people who endure childhoods that are wanting in affection.
Or indeed who are bullied in many different ways by their parents.
But that does not give them an excuse to go out into the community
as adults and commit crimes. Especially none as wicked as yours.
When you entered the medical profession, you would have taken an
oath to do no harm. In your warped obsession with Georgina
Maclean, you utterly flouted this oath, you threw it to the wind.

'*The Court's view is that these assaults should add significantly*
to the minimum period you are to serve, to reflect the horror that
right-thinking people must feel when hearing of your crimes. You
will serve a further term of nine years in prison, consecutively.
Therefore a total of thirty-six years.'

For a while they walked in silence, wrapped in their thoughts, Roger
pushing the pram and Georgie lending a trailing hand. Out of kindness – and perhaps a little curiosity – she'd called Claire after the
initial verdict. It had gone to voicemail and, not knowing what to
say, she hadn't left a message. She'd tried again on Saturday, after
the sentencing, but again it went to voicemail. And again, she'd left
no message. What could she say that would mean anything to the
poor woman?

Roger said he'd heard, from another medical client, that Claire
Valentine was leaving the island, taking the children to the mainland, because they'd never escape the shadow of their father, here.

It was a good decision, Georgie thought. But, despite all she
felt about Marcus Valentine, she couldn't help feeling something

for the woman who had been so sweet to her at that dinner party, and who had extended the hand of friendship.

They were passing the busy patio of the Old Station Cafe, every table occupied by people enjoying their al fresco drinks or brunch. Some with young children. Conversation and laughter. Normal life. Something she had for so long craved.

They'd married in beautiful St Brelade's Church last summer, officiated by Mark Bond, a vicar they adored, a former rocker who wore an earring and welcomed their choice of a Van Morrison song for their wedding march.

Georgie would never forget just how close she had come to losing Roger. His life had been saved by a brilliant surgeon, who had opened him up shortly after Valentine's arrest and had confirmed the tear in his bowel. And she would never, ever forget seeing Marcus Valentine's face over her in those moments before she fell unconscious from the anaesthetic.

There had been times during the first trial when Valentine's defence counsel had put up such convincing explanations and arguments that she really did think the jury might acquit him. It was the evidence of Edouardo that had been a major turning point for the prosecution. He had seen Valentine's Porsche parked a short distance from the Bel Royal Hotel at the very time Valentine had claimed he was waiting at the hospital for Resmes. And dear Edouardo, despite all Valentine's barrister's ferocious cross-examination and some difficulty in getting his point across, in a language that wasn't his mother tongue, had stood his ground. He had said, clearly and loudly, that he had been returning his clown outfit to his office in the Bel Royal when he had seen Valentine emerge, run to the car and drive off at speed. That evidence was corroborated by the police interrogation of the car's navigation and tracker systems, which put the Porsche there at exactly this time.

Georgie wondered for a long time if the drone triggering the accident that nearly killed Roger had also been of Marcus Valentine's doing, but just a few months ago a mother had walked into St Helier police station and confessed it had been her eleven-year-old son who had been flying the drone – and he'd been too traumatized to own up after hearing the extent of the accident he had caused. No doubt something that would haunt the poor boy's conscience for the rest of his life.

They'd named Kathy as a salute to Kath Clow. And Kath sure deserved that tribute. She had delivered both their healthy, bonny baby and the news that Georgie was completely clear of any signs of cancer. If they wanted a bigger family – and looked sharp about it, she said – well, hey, why not?

A brother or sister for Kathy? Georgie could scarcely believe that was a possibility. But . . . she had just missed a period.

On the far side of the cafe, Roger suddenly stopped and kissed her. 'Penny for your thoughts,' he said.

She shook her head. 'No amount of money can buy what I'm feeling.' She kissed him. 'It's strange we've stopped just here.'

'Why?'

She pointed at the traffic lights. 'Remember I told you about that idiot in a Porsche who almost ran me down?'

'Yeah.'

She pointed. 'It was right here.' She stood for a moment, reliving that instant. 'Kathy's a miracle baby in so many ways. How she came along when I'd all but given up hope of ever having a child. How I could have lost her then on that crossing. She and I were saved by a split second. And when I was in the operating theatre I was just minutes, if that, from Valentine killing her – and he would have succeeded if Kath Clow hadn't rushed in.' She hugged Roger, hard. 'And I was so close to losing you, from that vile man's attempt to kill you, too.'

Roger hugged her back. 'And if I'd turned up to that party just five minutes later, which you were on the verge of leaving, you and I might never even have met. Timing, right?'

Georgie looked at him, content and smiling. 'Timing. Yes. Timing is everything.'

ACKNOWLEDGEMENTS

The notion of an author toiling away in a garret in blissful solitude is a romantic one, but for me not an entirely accurate one! I write alone, and I'm seldom happier than when I'm at my laptop, hammering out the first draft of a new novel, but I'm very conscious my books would never happen without an enormous amount of help and input from so many other people.

One question we novelists get asked repeatedly, more than any other, is: *Where do you get your ideas from?* Well, my answer for this book is very simple. My wife, Lara, is a keen runner, who has competed in thirteen marathons. She had the spark of an idea about three years ago, while using a running app that plots your route, distances, times and all kinds of other data. Part of the fun of the app is to compare your times against other runners – as a runner myself, I know they are a competitive lot. But one day, she acknowledged a stranger who was running the same route as her, around local Sussex country lanes and footpaths. A short while after she got home, she discovered he had started to follow her on the app. That in itself didn't initially bother her, but then she realized that, by looking at her start and finish point, this stranger could easily work out where she lived. And patterns in her routes, timing and locations could open up a wealth of information that, in the wrong hands, could be dangerous.

From the moment Lara told me this, the idea for this book took root. I debated whether to write it as part of the Roy Grace series, but I felt I could write a more claustrophobic story just keeping the

ACKNOWLEDGEMENTS

focus entirely on the principal characters themselves. But, as with most of my novels, I had a huge amount of research ahead of me, both in understanding the world of my medics in the story and learning more about the island of Jersey, our new home, and I felt totally overwhelmed by the enthusiasm and the level of help I received from so many people in Jersey, and in particular from the General Hospital and the States of Jersey Police.

One person I have to thank above all others is Dr Kathleen Gillies FRCOG, a consultant gynae-oncologist. Her enthusiasm for the story and her tireless patience in helping me get the key medical aspects correct extended to getting eager support from so many people at the hospital. I can't now imagine how I could have written this book without her help. Dr Adrian Noon, MB ChB FIMC RCSEd, has also been quite wonderfully kind and helpful, too. And of course I owe a very big thank you to Robert Sainsbury MSC RN, Group Managing Director for Health and Community Services, for his kind sanction.

But I guess before any of the above I have to thank Kevin Lemasney, who opened so many doors for me in Jersey, and Dr James Mair, MBBS MRCGP, who kindly contacted me, as a fan, soon after we arrived on this island, offering any help I might need. He put me in touch with Matthew Stephenson MBBS MSc FRCS, who in turn introduced me to Dr Gillies.

The people from Jersey General Hospital I want to particularly thank, in addition, are Dr Sarah Butler BSc MB ChB, Dr Andrew Borthwick-Clarke MBBS FRCS, Samantha North BSc, Dr Nick Payne, Dr Robert Resmes, and Dr Alan Thompson BM FRCA FFICM.

I also owe a massive thank you to Julian Blazeby, Director General of Justice and Home Affairs for the Government of Jersey, as well as Deputy Chief Officer James Wileman, Detective Superintendent Stewart Gull QPM and Sergeant Callum O'Connor of States of Jersey Police. Also Mike Canas, Claire Forbes, Rupert Maddox, Richard Pedley, Dr Graham Ramsden and Tom Vautier.

Thanks also to Graham Bartlett, James Hodge, Martin and

ACKNOWLEDGEMENTS

Jane Diplock, Anna-Lisa Hancock, Helen Shenston and Linda Buckley.

I'm blessed with wonderful agents: in the UK, Isobel Dixon, Julian Friedmann, Conrad Williams, Louisa Minghella, Sian Ellis-Martin, James Pusey, Hana Murrell, Daisy Way, Lizzy Attree, Samuel Hodder, Tia Armstrong and all the team of Blake Friedmann; and in the US, Mitch Hoffman of Aaron M. Priest. And my wonderful publicists, Preena Gadher, Caitlin Allen and Emily Souders at Riot Communications. And a very special thank you to Geoff Duffield, my long-term friend and mentor, and to the brilliant Susan Opie.

And I have so many to thank at my UK publisher, Pan Macmillan. The litany of names has to start with the main man, and my friend, MD Anthony Forbes Watson, and of course my superstar editor, Wayne Brookes, and the whole stellar team: Sarah Arratoon, Jonathan Atkins, Lara Borlenghi, Emily Bromfield, Stuart Dwyer, Claire Evans, Samantha Fletcher, Elle Gibbons, Richard Green, Emma Hetherington, Daniel Jenkins, Rebecca Kellaway, Neil Lang, Rebecca Lloyd, Sara Lloyd, James Long, James Luscombe, Holly Martin, Jo Mower, Rory O'Brien, Sarah Parry-Jones, Guy Raphael, Simon Rhodes, Alex Saunders, Holly Sheldrake, Jade Tolley, Jeremy Trevathan, Toby Watson, Karen Whitlock, Charlotte Williams and Leanne Williams.

I'm blessed with a wonderful team around me that we call *Team James.* First and foremost, after Lara, is my very good friend David Gaylor, who has a brilliantly creative mind as well as being ruthlessly analytic and a very trusted critic, and who is the one standing over me, cracking the whip on every book, demanding to know how many pages I've written each week! Susan Ansell, who is my long-term and much trusted 'unofficial' editor; Dani Brown, who does a terrific job as our social media manager; Sarah Middle, who tries to rein in our spending on animals and keep us solvent; Chris Webb and Chris Diplock, who keep our computers and all our tech going; Martin Walsh and Erin Brown, who curate our video content; and

ACKNOWLEDGEMENTS

we are delighted to welcome on board our fabulous new PA in Jersey, Kate Blazeby.

And, as ever, a big thank you to our ever-growing menagerie of pets: our dogs Oscar, Spooky and Wally; our Burmese cats Woo and Willy; our ducks Mickey Magic, Clarissa, Locky, Maija and a dozen more; our pygmy goats Bouscaut and Margaux, Ted and Norman; our emus, Wolfie and Spike; and our alpacas Alpacino, Fortescue, Jean-Luc, Boris and Keith. In a world that sometimes seems a little crazy and scary, none of these beautiful creatures has a care beyond ensuring they get their food and their treats. Bones, carrots, blueberries, grapes, popcorn, ginger biscuits, sweetcorn and peas. Would that life should be so simple for us all!

My final word is to thank all of you, my readers. I always love to hear from you – your letters, emails, blog posts, tweets, Facebook, Instagram and YouTube comments are wonderful to receive.

contact@peterjames.com
www.peterjames.com
You Tube peterjamesPJTV
peterjames.roygrace
@peterjamesuk
@peterjamesuk
@peterjamesukpets
@mickeymagicandfriends

COMING 2021

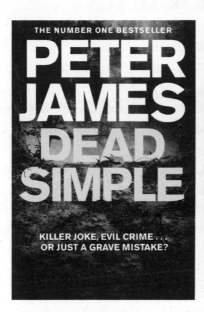 

Peter James's first two books in the Detective Superintendent
Roy Grace series, *Dead Simple* and *Looking Good Dead*,
have been commissioned by ITV. They are being adapted for
television by screenwriter Russell Lewis and will star
John Simm as Roy Grace.

FIND THEM DEAD

By Peter James

After his secondment to London's Met Police ends, Roy Grace is back in Sussex and right in the middle of a murder case.

Five years after the car crash that killed her husband and son, Meg Magellan feels she has her life back together. When she receives a summons for jury service, she feels this will help distract her from constantly worrying about her daughter, Laura, who is travelling overseas. But when she is selected for the trial of a major Brighton drugs overlord, everything changes.

Gradually, Grace's investigation draws him into the sinister sphere of influence of the man on trial, a man prepared to order the death of anyone to enable him to walk free.

Arriving home late one night, Meg finds a photograph lying on her kitchen table of Laura, in Ecuador. Then the phone rings. The caller tells her that if she ever wants to see Laura alive again, all she has to do is make sure the jury says just two words . . . Not guilty.

THE SECRET OF COLD HILL

By Peter James

Cold Hill House has been razed to the ground by fire, replaced with a development of ultra-modern homes. Gone with the flames are the violent memories of the house's history, and a new era has begun.

Although much of Cold Hill Park is still a construction site, the first two families move in to their new houses. For Jason and Emily Danes, this is their forever home, and for Maurice and Claudette Penze-Weedell, it's the perfect place to live out retirement. Despite the ever-present rumble of cement mixers and diggers, Cold Hill Park appears to be the ideal place to live. But looks are deceptive and it's only a matter of days before both couples start to feel they are not alone in their new homes.

There is one thing that never appears in the estate agent brochures: nobody has ever survived beyond forty in Cold Hill House and no one has ever truly left . . .

'James is a compelling storyteller and he ratchets up the tension in increments, so that his readers will be suitably terrified. By the time you want to scream "Look behind you!", it's already too late'

Daily Mail

THEY WATCH... THEY CHOOSE... THEY KILL

ROY GRACE IS BACK ON STAGE!
IN
PETER JAMES
LOOKING GOOD
DEAD

UK TOUR 2021
Book now at PeterJames.com